BEAUTIFUL EXILES

ALSO BY MEG WAITE CLAYTON

The Race for Paris

The Wednesday Daughters

The Four Ms. Bradwells

The Wednesday Sisters

The Language of Light

BEAUTIFUL EXILES

MEG WAITE CLAYTON

This is a work of fiction. Names, characters, organizations, places, events, and incidents are either products of the author's imagination or are used fictitiously.

Published by Lake Union Publishing, Seattle

www.apub.com

ISBN-13: 9781503900837 (hardcover)
ISBN-10: 1503900835 (hardcover)
ISBN-13: 9781503949270 (paperback)
ISBN-10: 1503949273 (paperback)

Cover design by Shasti O'Leary Soudant

Printed in the United States of America

First edition

For Dad,
who inspires me, always

For Chris,
my favorite Hemingway fan

and

For Mac, this is our book,
but then they all are, yours and mine

Catscradle Cottage, Wales

1994

We start with the oldest—letters mostly. My son reads Matie's words to me ("Martha, dearest") and mine to her, thin blue airmail homing birds of love. He reads from my exchanges with editors and with H. G. Wells and Eleanor Roosevelt (me at my ghastliest, even if she never would say so), correspondence I doom for the most part to large brown envelopes bound for the archives in Boston. This little writing cottage has become too much for me and my fading eyesight, however fierce an old lady I might be, so my son is helping me clear it out, reading every letter for a paragraph or two, and often to its end, before I decide its fate. When he extracts a crinkly airmail sheet and reads, "'Dear Mookie,'" though, I take it from him and set it to the fire in the grate, and watch the page blister blue and red until it falls to ash. I don't need to see the ink to know the signature: "Your comrade, E.," in the early days, or later, "With love, your Bug" or "your Bongie." Bongie—one of several nicknames we called each other interchangeably. But I was never really his Bongie, even if I meant to be, or wanted to be, or tried. I was only ever Martha Ellis Gellhorn, even after I became Mrs. Ernest Hemingway.

PART I

Key West, Florida

December 1936

It was a bright stinking mess of a time, the winter I met Ernest. Dad had been dead a year that Christmas, my twenty-eighth, and while Matie was bearing it, the blue of her eyes was faded and the gray in her blond hair suddenly overwhelmed. She hadn't wanted to spend the holiday in St. Louis without Dad, of course she hadn't, but we were going mad with boredom in Miami. So we set off in the car toward a little seaside town whose name on a tour bus captured our imaginations. Key West. My brother drove, with Matie beside him and me buffeted in the open-window back seat, as we crossed the long stretch of bridges to the end of the earth: a place that was delightfully decadent and decaying, with folks content to do nothing but fish for sea turtles and crack coconuts, to gossip and sweat on the worn porches of charmingly colorful white-frame houses, and on beaches fishy with the sweetness of *The Odyssey*, *Moby-Dick*, the little mermaid who can't bring herself to slay the prince to save herself.

"Surely we can't pass by a place called Sloppy Joe's without a peek inside, can we?" Matie asked. Already, we'd climbed the lighthouse for the view and picnicked on the beach, brushed the sand from our toes, piled our sweaty selves back into the car to look for a place where I could wash the wind-tangles from my hair in a cooling bath. But I was never one to deny my mother anything, any more than she denied me. Dad, he'd been the denying one.

Did we see Hemingway first, or did he see us? People do turn to the light of a door opening in a dark bar, and our pupils were shocked by the contrast from brutal sun and hard road to dim light and soft wood, melted-ice-dampened floors and bottles of Campari, whiskey, rum. A huge bartender welcomed us from behind a long curved bar, while at one end of the place, patrons returned their attention to a rowdy pool game, with money on the rails to make it real. Another man nearly as large as the bartender rose with effort from a chaos of papers on the bar. Grubby white T-shirt. Dingy white shorts held up by, of all things, a length of rope. He made a surprising racket in the few steps it took to reach us, to add his voice to the bartender's welcome.

"Ernest Hemingway," he said.

A slow bead of sweat trickled down my spine to settle into the fabric of my black sundress, already damp from all the time pressed to the car seat and no better for the time on the hot sand. Matie touched a hand briefly to my shoulder, a reminder to stand up straight and never mind my gawky tallness, as I tried to square the rope belt and the shoeless feet with this man's asymmetric widow's peak that was, indeed, Ernest Hemingway's. I knew that hairline, and the sad, seductive eyes too; I'd awoken every morning at Bryn Mawr to those eyes staring down at me from a photo tacked to my dorm room wall.

"I'm Edna Gellhorn, and this is my son Alfred," Matie said to Ernest Hemingway. "And this is Martha."

Just "Martha," not "my daughter, Martha." You can see how that might have left Hemingway taking my brother and me to be newlyweds fresh off a yacht, but I was lost in thinking, *Ernest damn Hemingway*, who ought to be out catching an impossibly huge marlin off the coast of Cuba, or shooting some heartbreakingly wild creature in Kenya, or writing from Paris where, in the years I'd lived there, I'd forever hoped to catch a glimpse of him the way any writer hopes for a glimpse of her literary hero. He and F. Scott Fitzgerald, whose photo I might have hung in place of Hemingway's if only his looks were as grand as his writing.

"Nothing ever happens to the brave"—I'd used Hemingway's words as the epigraph for my already-wanting-to-be-forgotten first novel, *What Mad Pursuit*. Words spoken by his Great War ambulance-driver protagonist in *A Farewell to Arms*, to which the nurse he had fallen in love with responds simply that they, too, die.

My brother told Hemingway we were here on vacation for the weather, and Matie said St. Louis was unbearable this time of year. I dug frantically through the wordy bit of my brain for something more worthy, but already Ernest Hemingway had turned away from us, to the bartender.

"Skinner," he said in a conspiratorial tone that rang of true friendship, companions in size, perhaps, "how about some Papa Dobles for these friends of mine from St. Louis?"

These friends of mine. He'd known that would charm us, and I saw that he knew it, and still I was charmed. Charmed and relieved that we hadn't already lost his attention. Sure, this Hemingway looked more Matie's generation than mine, but something in his clumsiness was outsized and dear, like watching a *Balaenoptera musculus*—a great blue whale—emerge from the sea.

As Skinner squeezed four perfect grapefruit and eight clean limes one by one into a rusty blender and topped them with a frightening amount of rum and a maraschino drizzle, Hemingway said, "I knew St. Louis in my youth. All the women in the world worth knowing come from St. Louis." Both his wives had gone to school there, he said, tossing off the fact of abandoning his first young love for a richer, more sophisticated second with discomfiting ease. "And my friends Bill and Katy Smith," he said. "A fine city, St. Louis." Then he too talked about the weather, but in a Hemingway sort of way, telling a grand and gory tale of a hurricane that destroyed half the buildings in the Keys and swept away hundreds of veterans living in rehabilitation camps.

The rumble of the blender cut through the story before he could blame President Roosevelt for the deaths of those veterans and, in the process, get Matie's dander up. In the pause, I noticed a sawed-off pool cue on the wall behind the bar.

"Skinner and his pool cue, oh! But don't they belong in Havana?" I asked, remembering something in a newish men's magazine that my brother had pointed out to me, one of a series of "letters" that Hemingway sent from exotic places—this particular one describing a bartender who kept a pool cue handy for banging heads when fights broke out.

"Havana?" Hemingway said.

"You were fishing in Cuba," I said. "'A Havana letter'? In *Esquire*?"

"I was fishing in Cuba while poor Skinner was back here in Key West, working his magic with the booze."

Skinner swished drinks into glasses and handed them around. It was hard to see a man as big as he was ever needing that pool cue. It was hard to rehang that pool cue here in Key West, when it was so set in a dive bar in Havana in my mind.

Hemingway gathered his papers and journals and mail and moved them aside in a jumbled pile he set on the far barstool. "Sit before you decide you don't want to disturb me or some bunk like that," he insisted, pulling out a barstool for Matie, then one for me. He lowered himself onto a seat that didn't quite contain him, his dark gaze still focused on my mother, but I imagined myself at the edge of his vision, I imagined him wrapping a story around Matie and my brother and me, dedicating us to a page and a book and the immortality of his prose.

As my brother cleared the chair overrun with Hemingway's work for himself, Hemingway raised his glass to Matie and me and said, "Welcome to my little corner of hell."

He focused on Matie as he took a sip—not his first drink of the afternoon, or even his second. (Custer, taking a last stand in paint above the bar, surely frowned.)

Matie said, as easily as if Ernest Hemingway were anybody, "My son is just finishing medical school, and my daughter—surely you've heard of her new book, *The Trouble I've Seen*?"

"Mother," I said.

Ernest turned to me, so close beside me that I could almost hear the thought swirling in his expression: Matie's *daughter*. I lit a cigarette before he could offer to do so, or fail to offer. Daughter was a disappointment to him somehow, or writer was, or both.

"*The Trouble I've Seen*—sure, I've heard of that, haven't I? About the Depression?" he said, not recalling exactly, but grabbing from the title and something like memory. "Tell me so I'll know a bit about it, Miss Martha Gellhorn, daughter of the lovely Edna."

Hemingway smiled at Matie as Skinner placed a glass ashtray in front of me.

"It's not my book, really," I said quietly, the only way I could speak about the stories I'd collected trudging around the Hoovervilles—tumbledown shacks and tents surrounded by scum-covered water, open sewage ditches, flies and mosquitos and rats and miserably scrawny cats and dogs and goats, even more miserably scrawny sick people. There was nothing to do but try to give those people what little I had without offending their dignity, and write out the rage of it.

"It's a novel, but the stories are real, sure enough," I told Hemingway. I'd written it as fiction to protect these people who were so ashamed, always blaming themselves. "A little girl digging through slop and filth in hopes of finding a handcart wheel. A mother making a feast of canned salmon for her daughter. A—"

I stubbed the half-smoked cigarette out in the clean ashtray, trying to avoid making an utter sobbing fool of myself in front of Ernest Hemingway. *A baby,* I meant to say, but I never could get that word up through my cottony throat. That baby, just four months old, was paralyzed with syphilis, but the doctors refused to give her shots for want of twenty-five lousy cents. I'd emptied my pockets at that hospital for that tiny, dying infant with her big, hopeful name: Abigail June.

Hemingway said, "It's a thing, to write about something that sticks to your insides like that, isn't it? It's the only way any of us should ever write, with a sharp shard lodged between our tickers and our spines."

My brother said, "One reviewer likened Marty to Dostoyevsky, Dickens, and Victor Hugo—all of them—and her photo was on the cover of the *Saturday Review of Litera—*"

"I've read all your books, Mr. Hemingway," I interrupted, quite sure that if I were Ernest Hemingway, I would run but fast from this crazy family who imagined their writer-daughter deserved mention to him. "*A Farewell to Arms*, that one was something." The ambulance driver better delivered than the nurse, but still a moving story. "After I read it, I quit everything and grabbed my typewriter and set off for France."

Ernest said, "That's a fine thought, my work encouraging girls to drop out of school."

My brother said, "Marty didn't need encouragement. She'd already dropped out. Don't let her fool you, sir."

"Sir?" Ernest turned to me and said, "If you call me 'sir,' Marty, I'll have to ring up the good new King George and demand my Grand Cross star." He laughed then. He laughed, and he threw back the rest of his Papa Doble, and he raised his empty glass to Skinner.

"College would just have prepared me for some scratchy bore of a desk without so much as a window view," I said. I'd been rotten at the world of clothes and lipstick colors, dates with Ivy League boys, gossip and secrets kept for the sake of seeming to be someone better than the other girls. I left college to write—and maybe I didn't always write, and maybe when I did, my first novel was all college-girl sex and nonsense

(Dad's verdict all along), but my second was better; it was the best I could write.

"A fine, good girl like yourself, you'll be working on a new book?" Ernest asked.

"I'm not for anything if I'm not writing, Mr. Hemingway."

"Ernest," he said.

"Ernest," I repeated, thinking that, in the end, the writing was the only thing that saved me, that kept me from being sucked down into the sludge pit of darkness and doubt. Wondering if any small bit of Ernest Hemingway might be the same way, if a writer as successful as he was ever questioned his words, his worth, the cost of what it took to pour all of yourself into a book that people might just abandon, half-read, on a chair in a bus station, even with a whole long journey to pass.

I found myself telling him about my writing then, because he really did seem to want me to. After I'd finished *The Trouble I've Seen*, I'd pitched a hundred million ideas to *Time* and the *New Yorker* and anyone else with a printing press, hoping to write pieces about what was going on in Europe. For years already, Hitler had limited the number of Jews who could attend university or practice medicine or law or appear on stage, but in September of 1935 he'd stepped it up a horrid notch with the Nuremberg Race Laws. All my pitches were for nothing, though. No one cared. So I scraped together passage to Paris (where everyone was glum for having to make their own beds at the fancy hotels), and on to Stuttgart and Munich. The hateful Nazi thugs there left me so furious, though, that I'd come home to write it out in a new novel, a German pacifist thing.

"After I finish the novel, I mean to go to Spain to cover their civil war," I said.

We had a good long chat then about Spain, the front line for stopping the rot of Fascism.

"Blood as deep as a man's palm, that's what they're saying," I said. "And the whole damned world looks the other way."

Hemingway said, "I've paid passage for two volunteers going to fight with the International Brigades, and I mean to send fifteen hundred dollars"—as much as most people made in a year—"for the Republicans to buy ambulances."

I said, "Money is just money, though. The thing is to tell the truth about it, and you can't tell a truth you haven't seen."

Matie said, "You'll excuse my poor parenting, Ernest. My daughter's passions will override her manners."

But he was already laughing. "Well, Daughter, I have in mind to go to Spain myself after I finish *my* new novel, so perhaps you'll let me use some of my money to buy you a Papa Doble in Madrid?"

I said, "We'll have to bring Skinner along."

"We'd need a terrifically big suitcase for that."

"A trunk."

"A fine big trunk," he said, and we all laughed, and he signaled for Skinner to bring me another Papa Doble. Matie's and my brother's glasses were still full.

I pulled out another cigarette, and he took the lighter from me, saying, "War is one of the hardest things to write truly; it's a great advantage for a writer to experience it directly."

He flicked the lighter and put the flame to my cigarette, sending a surprising little shiver through me as he steadied my hand with his touch. Ernest damn Hemingway.

He said, "But of course the bastards who haven't seen war are always jealous and try to make it—and you—seem unimportant."

I inhaled strongly on the cigarette, hiding behind the smoke of my inexperience. I'd seen plenty of the threat of war in Europe, but I had yet to see war itself.

"Spain, yes, that's the place when the book is done," he said. "I have a nice house here and a fine family. Still, the quiet gets to a man when a book is done."

"Will you tell us about your new book, Mr. Hemingway?" I asked.

"Ernest," he said.

"Ernest," I repeated, and I lifted my fresh Papa Doble to my lips with my free hand, steadying myself to the crazy notion of being on a first-name basis with Ernest Hemingway.

He began telling us about the draft of the story that would become his third novel, *To Have and Have Not*—a story of a man who, in an effort to keep his family out of the have-nots, finds himself running rum and other contraband from Cuba to Key West. It was something, to hear him talk about his new lump of literary clay, to realize that even Ernest Hemingway wasn't Ernest Hemingway in the early drafts. I was sure that if I listened hard enough, I could understand how he did it, how he hammered on the nail of every word until it was driven straight and true into the wood of a story, and how I might do it as well, or nearly so.

He was deep into the telling when a well-dressed man appeared in the bar's doorway, calling out, "Ernest, old friend, here you are!"

Ernest stood and introduced his friend. "Thompson here owns the local hardware store, and he fishes with me," he said. "Thompson, this is Edna Gellhorn. Her son Alfred. And her daughter, Marty, the writer. *The Trouble I've Seen*? Mrs. Roosevelt has been touting it, you know."

"Yes, yes," Thompson said. "But Pauline has a splendid crayfish dinner waiting."

Ernest offered his friend a seat and a drink, both of which he declined.

"The Gellhorns are from St. Louis," Ernest said. "Edna's husband was a doctor there." He was already charmed by Matie. He liked that she was a doctor's wife like his own mother and yet nothing like his own mother, open in the way a woman ought to be rather than dictatorial.

Thompson acknowledged us. He hoped we found Key West suitable, which my brother assured him we did.

"But Ernest, everyone is waiting dinner," Thompson repeated.

"That's fine, that's fine," Ernest said. "You all go ahead."

"Pauline sent me to fetch you," Thompson insisted.

Matie said, "We ought not keep you from your dinner guests, Ernest."

"You go ahead, Thompson," Earnest repeated. "Tell Pauline I'll have something to eat here, she needn't worry that I'll starve. Tell her I'll catch up with you all later, for drinks at Peña's." Leaving the man to report to Pauline that her husband was too busy having drinks to attend his own dinner party. And Thompson would barely mention Matie and my brother. He would focus on the leggy blond in the black sundress, as if that said even one true thing about me.

Key West, Florida

December 1936

As a girl, I was tall for my age, and gawky, and half Jewish when being part anything other than pure and white and Protestant as the damned Easter lily was held against you. There were other things to hold against me too. My mother was fair-haired and charming, a woman who might have had any beau but chose an intelligent and accomplished doctor—one who was entirely too Prussian and bald and unconventional to please St. Louis society. Matie had no love of St. Louis society, though. She preferred a man who would never bore her, and Dad was that. She preferred a man who would believe her his equal in every way when men just didn't, who would gather liberal minds of all races to his dining table and the devil be damned if a white man wasn't supposed to invite a black one through the front door. We were scandalous progressives, we Gellhorns. In the early years before suffrage, the years when I started school, mothers would warn their daughters against me and my dangerous radical suffragette mother, who'd been their perfectly respectable friend until she began taking her young daughter to suffrage rallies she organized herself, for heaven's sake.

I was cursed as well to be sent into the boy-girl world of fortnightly ballroom dancing classes at my tallest and gawkiest. Not that I didn't get taller; of course I did. But that was the height of my relative height, when I'd grown and the boys I was to dance with hadn't, so their eyes stared right at my budding breasts. They were boys, too, who imagined themselves boys still, with none of the madness for love that already consumed us girls.

My best friend was as plump and uncontrollably redheaded and freckled as I was tall and talkative and quick to laugh at my own jokes. Her parents, like mine, made her attend the ballroom dancing classes, our mothers and fathers imagining us fox-trotting gracefully with respectful boys when the truth of it was that forty-some girls were made to stand at the edge of a sweat-stinking gymnasium while a dozen pimply-faced boys chose among us. We stood so hopefully at first. But boy after boy passed us by to choose some other pimply-faced girl with the good fortune to be more appropriate somehow than we would imagine ourselves even years later, when the boys' heights and their appetites for love had caught up with ours.

After those first humiliations—waltzing hand in hand with the unchosen girls—and with our parents refusing to relent, we began to hang back as our classmates flooded the gymnasium, and to duck the ordeal by hiding in the coatroom. We spent whole evenings in the wet-wool stink of abandoned coats, whispering about the gawky boys and the prettier girls as if we really didn't want those boys to be holding our own sweaty hands, or massacring our toes, or stealing kisses from us while the dance instructor schooled some other poor pair about the lilt and tilt of the waltz.

There was no one I loved more than my mother, no one of whom I was prouder, but I don't suppose anything hardens a heart faster than being an eight-year-old given wide berth by the other girls in the lunchroom. I don't suppose any amount of blond hair and blue eyes makes up for hiding in a coatroom when a girl is thirteen and just beginning to form her opinion of herself, not even after she can see how young and disinterested those boys were, how much they would rather have spent their Saturday evenings reading comic books or torturing frogs.

And so, even when I looked my very best and I could occasionally enter a room with my long legs and my blond hair and my blue eyes and feel men looking, it was someone else they were admiring, some imposter who never had hidden from the fortnightly boys or the lunchroom girls. I always knew that one moment of a closer look would reveal the ugly truth: my weak chin and my hooked nose, my nonexistent eyebrows, my hair that generally took its own frizzy path through humidity and fell flat as the stinking farmland around St. Louis most of the rest of the time. I never thought myself attractive until I grew old and could look back at photos and see that I had been, but no longer was.

Key West seemed to me the best place I'd found in America—a haven where I might make progress on my novel. There was the sea to swim in, and a young Swedish fellow I'd met swimming, a bum to be sure but one who was a lark, who swam with me in the afternoons and danced with me at night. So when my brother headed back to St. Louis with Matie, his break from medical school over, I took a room at the Colonial Hotel on Duval Street for another week or two, to write.

The day they left, Ernest invited me to a dinner party at his and Pauline's stone wedding cake of a mansion on Whitehead Street. I ought to arrive in the late afternoon, he said, and he'd show me the gardens, and we could chat about writing without boring the others. He was known for his generosity to other writers, and if there's a novelist in this world who couldn't use a little generosity in her life, I don't think I want to know her. And he was wonderful about the writing.

He'd recently bought a fishing boat, he told me as we sat together on a bench in the shadow of the carriage house in which he wrote, a white cat in his lap, and he used the fishing to talk about how he wrote.

"Whether it's the beads of water on the line as it tightens like a hanging rope, or the drops thrown by the thrashing fish—that's what you need to know. Remember the noises, the light, the exact action that made you excited or angry or scared. Then write down the details so the reader feels your exact feeling."

My exact feeling in that moment was revulsion mixed with pity and something else I couldn't name as I registered the white cat's six toes. The something else had to do with Ernest and his affection for the cat, as if he were responsible for the deformity, or saw it as his own. I looked away, to the top of the Key West lighthouse visible above the palm and banana and mahogany trees, to the peacocks and the funny flamingos blandly roaming in the earthy undertone of sea air. I knew what he was saying, and yet I didn't know it. I wanted to say, *But look how well I write, will you? You don't have to tell me how to write.* I wanted to chide him for what he did in "Cross Country Snow," humiliating my ex-beau Bertrand de Jouvenel, a French journalist Ernest had known in Paris, who could talk in nine-syllable words. Ernest was no good with big words himself, so maybe he *couldn't* deliver Bertrand as a talker. But I only reached out and touched the cat's odd little paw. I knew if I kept Ernest talking—even about things I already knew—he would come to things I didn't know, or things like the fish talk that I knew without really knowing, that I might do more cleverly with the knowledge right where I could see it as I wrote.

"Don't forget the weather in your books," he said. "The weather is damned important."

"The weather is hot and muggy," I said, wiping my hair—still damp from my afternoon swim with The Swede—back from my forehead.

"Muggy? Only if you're unhappy, Marty, and how can you be unhappy spending your afternoons swimming and your nights dancing? A dancer like you ought to find this 'sultry.'"

"Am I spending my nights dancing?" I said lightly, wondering how much he could know about The Swede.

"Key West gives up its secrets more easily than you imagine."

I laughed, and I said, "Perhaps the word I'm searching for, then, is 'steamy,' Ernest. Setting the stage for some marvelous crime of passion?"

"Love is a fine subject for a writer, as is murder," Ernest said. "But make it love and murder set in wartime. A day at war offers more action and emotion than a whole life at peace."

By the end of the week, Ernest had dubbed me "Mermaid" for forever arriving for our late-afternoon chats with my hair wet from a swim, and he'd given me his Cuban rumrunner novel manuscript to read—a task nearly as provoking to me as I imagined war would be.

"A modern *War and Peace*, that's what it will be when I've finished the thing," he said. The editor and cofounder of *Esquire* had suggested he make the novel from two of his short stories. "Key West and Cuba," Ernest said. "Rich and poor. Smuggling and corruption and sex. That's the thing to put me back where I belong." His braggadocio hiding something; when a man brags like that, most often the person he's trying to convince is himself, and, sure, *The Sun Also Rises* was a terrific book and *A Farewell to Arms* perhaps even better, but what had he written since 1929? Three books that hadn't been much liked by the critics, that had sold better than my first novel, but not by much.

The truth was that while Ernest's prose made me swoon, I sometimes balked at his stories; his women were so often such infuriating little prigs. There was trash in this new novel too—the kind of self-aggrandizing poop that ruined his 1933 story collection, *Winner Take Nothing*, and plenty of it. His writer-friend John Dos Passos was disguised as an alcoholic womanizer, and F. Scott Fitzgerald—who'd taken Ernest under his wing when Scott was already terrifically famous and Ernest was no one at all—was treated even worse. What ought to have been a tidy rope of story threads was fraying out in all directions too. Still, the way Ernest used words—spare and flowing, poetic—that was there, and hard to shake off. Your writing was a different thing after you read Hemingway, even if you didn't want it to be. His dialogue in this new book left me in crazy awe, and I told him that, I praised that.

He said, "The damned critics want me to be a cheerleader for the Reds, but that's just one little horseshit corner of the world Dos Passos can have."

"How do you mean to end the book?" I asked.

"My hero will get his guts shot out in a bank robbery, but I'm still groping for the old miracle to end it."

"The 'old miracle'?"

"You can't end a book with anything less than a miracle, Stooge."

Stooge? And yet he'd said it with such affection, as if it were an honor.

"And just whose straight man do you think I am, Hemingway?" I asked.

"Well, that fellow who moons around you at the beach seems to think you're his stooge, doesn't he?" he said, repeating the nickname I didn't suppose was worse than "Mermaid," and I did give my own friends and family nicknames that weren't always flattering: "The Swede," of course; and my favorite teacher from Bryn Mawr was "Teachie"; and my old Paris love, Bertrand de Jouvenel, was "Smuf."

"I'm pretty sure I'm the comic and The Swede is the straight man, Ernesto," I said.

He laughed and he said, "A writer has to take a lot of punishment to be funny, I hope you know that."

Me, I'd had punishment enough to write funny all day and night.

"I'm close to nailing this book," he said. "I've got to go to Havana again, though. I can sort it out in Havana."

He asked to see pages of mine, which was intimidating but also really something, to have Ernest Hemingway taking my work seriously. It made me take it more seriously myself. It made me look as closely as I could, and I saw that it was all just a think-book, everyone moping about town without one single interesting thing occurring, not even a cat with six toes. So I chucked every damned word of the rotten stink. It killed me to do it, but I chucked it and I started new, mulling it all while I swam and while I talked with Ernest.

Nights, I danced with The Swede, and lay alone in bed with the humid air softening my lungs and my skin and my despair, invoking my gods—who all look like typewriters—to give me strength to write a book as alive as five minutes ago. I woke with the sun hot on my whole long body and the writing sloshing in the mush of my brain. The story I meant to write was lovely and dire, and I knew it would be a fine book if only I could do it the way it ought to be done.

Key West, Florida

January 1937

We were a tableful at dinner one night: the Thompsons and me, and Pauline and Ernest and their two sons, eight-year-old Patrick with Ernest's serious face and the nickname of "Mouse," and bright-eyed five-year-old Gigi (pronounced like "piggy"), who was really Gregory. They were such nice boys that I thought I might even have children myself someday if I knew they would turn out as well. Ernest had another son too—"Bumby," who lived with Ernest's ex-wife, Hadley, who had been dear friends with Pauline. People like to put that on Pauline; they like to point out the irony of a devout Catholic stealing a husband without jeopardizing her relationship with her unforgiving God, the way rich girls often do. But Pauline wasn't the one who'd done the leaving.

The evening started well enough over cocktails in the front room, not Papa Dobles, but whiskey for Ernest and a Cuba Libre for me, because it's such an easy thing to ask for, just rum and cola and lime, and I didn't want to put Ernest to any trouble. After he started making Pauline's drink—an extravagant cocktail for which Ernest opened a whole new bottle of champagne—I did wish I'd asked for something more elegant, but I didn't want to look an absolute fool for not knowing what I liked to drink. So I sipped my Cuba Libre and listened to Pauline, who wore her hair cropped short as a boy's and no more makeup than I did. She was smart and quick-witted in a cutting sort of way that left us laughing together at the funny people on the island, and feeling a bit guilty for laughing at someone else's expense.

After cocktails, we moved across the hall to the narrow dining room with its pale-yellow walls and white-painted trim, all those arched doorways that would bring in sunlight if it weren't winter and dark. Pauline, as we settled into studded-leather chairs at the heavy wooden table, described the changes she and Ernest were going to make to the gardens.

"We want to replace the wood with stone and put in a swimming pool where Ernest's boxing ring is now. The first saltwater pool on—"

"*You* want to do it all, Pauline," Ernest interrupted. "*You* want to drag in diggers and pavers to assure I'll have no peace in which to write for a good long spell. You ought to be a happy wife for your happy husband, Fife. You ought to leave me to my work."

Thompson said soothingly, "Pauline tells me the room you're building for the kudu heads you bagged in Africa is going to be something."

"A man could waste a whole lifetime choosing stone and cabinetry," Ernest said. "A man could waste a whole life here in Key West when he ought to be doing something about the real world."

"Darling," Pauline said.

"Spain is the place a writer needs to be now. I've got to get to Spain."

Perhaps he meant to vex Pauline by wading through all that blood at the dinner table. I wondered sometimes if he didn't include me in these dinners to vex her too. He sat me to his right, and he would lean toward me and speak in a low voice that Pauline, at the table's far end—with the Thompsons closing rank on either side—had to strain to hear.

Pauline said to me, "He's already arranged ambulances and paid two men to fight in Spain—don't you think he's doing enough, Martha?"

Looking to enlist me in keeping Ernest in Key West.

I did want to be agreeable. I liked Pauline fiercely, and she'd opened their home to me, included me almost as family. But I never have been terribly good at saying what wants to be said if I don't think it's right.

Ernest said, "You can't woo Stooge here to your side, Pauline. She's already lectured a few thousand snobs at Rockefeller Center on the need for writers to 'dramatize, advertise, and sell democracy' to their readers lest we end up like the Nazis."

Pauline tilted her tiny face up to the chandeliers she'd brought from Paris as if to a crucifix in an ancient church with wooden pews and padded kneelers, white lace draped over her head. Ernest softened as the seconds clicked by without her chiding him again about Spain.

Thompson said, "The Republicans aren't any saints, old man."

"Sure the Republicans aren't saints," Ernest agreed, the Republicans in Spain being the ones any reasonable person would be rooting for. Five years after the Spanish shrugged off the tyranny of king and Church to elect their own government, Francisco Franco and his Fascist forces marched in to attack the new Spanish Republic, and now the good Republicans were all in against him in a civil war. "They shoot priests and bishops, I grant you that," he said. "But why does the Church stand with the oppressors?"

"The Church isn't in politics," Pauline protested.

"Everyone is in the politics of Spain, Pauline," I said. "In Stuttgart this summer, the Nazi papers went on and on about the 'bloodthirsty rabble' attacking 'the forces of decency and order,' calling the properly elected Spanish government 'red swine dogs.' And the Nazi papers have one solid value: whatever they're against, you can be for."

"If the choice is between exploited working people and absentee landlords, my sympathies are with the people, with the Republicans," Ernest said.

"Even if you do shoot pigeons with the landlords and drink their booze," Pauline said.

Ernest laughed mightily at himself, and said, "Even if I do, Fife. Even if I do."

Pauline said to me, "Really, *Stooge*, don't you think Ernest is doing enough for Spain?" The nickname offered with something that wanted to be humor and warmth but came out as distaste. Already I understood that Ernest reserved his most offensive nicknames for those he liked best: one childhood friend was "Barge" and her poor sister "Pudge" or "Useless," and his sisters were "Nunbones," "Masween," and "Ted," and even his publisher, Charles Scribner, was "Scribbles," although Ernest made me promise that if I ever met Charles Scribner I wouldn't call him Scribbles to his face.

"Pauline," I said, "the Fascists herded eighteen hundred Republican prisoners of war into a Badajoz bullring and opened fire with machine guns. If that repugnant madman Hitler really sends two divisions to support them, we'll have all of Europe in war, you can bet on it."

Pauline said, "But surely the world would be better served by Ernest writing his novels."

Ernest said, "A man could get a hundred stories in Spain."

"Your editor is standing by to read the Cuban rumrunner manuscript," Pauline insisted.

"There's no hurry, there'll be war enough to last a good while," he conceded. "And it's cold as a corpse in Madrid right now." He laughed again, a signal that we were all meant to laugh with him, and I did laugh. I laughed even as I wondered why the thoughtful soul I knew from the garden—the fellow who talked about how important it was to have time to fail, who lamented that there was so little time to do anything with war looming in Europe—disappeared with the predinner cocktails.

Pauline, with a disingenuous smile, said, "Do what you want, Ernest. You always do."

Leaving me wondering if the rumor The Swede had told me was true, that Ernest was having an affair with the twenty-two-year-old wife of a wealthy American living in Cuba. Ernest, according to The Swede, drove his mistress's sports car in games of chicken, with her refusing to say "slow down" even when Ernest drove the car off the road. Pauline was a smart girl, though. She'd been a journalist before she married Ernest. She'd written for *Vogue*. She would see what there was to see unless she chose not to. Pauline was a smart girl who was choosing not to see so many things: how close we were to war, how much we needed to live the sun and the laughter and the love as terribly fast as we could before it was all gone.

"As soon as I finish the novel, then, sure, Spain is the place to be," Ernest said. "Until then, I'll keep sending the damned money."

"That's swell, Ernest," Pauline said, her hardening mouth turning her pretty face ferociously ratlike. "Do go put your life at risk for a bunch of cranky Spaniards while Patrick and Gigi and I die of worry. And Hadley and Bumby too."

Ernest stood, bumping his chair back loudly and muttering under his breath, "Oh, muck this whole treacherous muck-faced mucking existence." He tousled Patrick's hair, saying, "You never worry, do you, Mousie, even if Gigi does." He tousled Gregory's hair too, then walked out through the arched doorway, headed, I supposed, back to Sloppy Joe's and his drinking friends.

I'd just finished reading the last pages of Ernest's Cuban rumrunner novel—a typescript with corrections in his rounded handwriting—and I was sitting beside him on the garden bench, telling him how swell it was, when he leaned toward my dipped face and kissed my forehead, just a brush of lips on skin.

"You're a good daughter," he said.

I felt his gaze on me, his eyes a soft brown where Dad's had been an unyielding blue, his voice low and unaccented and warm where Dad's had been Germanic and strident and as unforgiving as the stone Pauline wanted to lay throughout this lovely yard.

"I'm not a very good daughter," I said lightly, adding a spunk I didn't feel.

"You're a fine daughter, Stooge," he said seriously, as if he could see inside me, as if he knew more about me from reading my pages than I meant him to know.

"I never do the things I'm meant to."

He leaned forward and scooped up a passing cat. "That's someone else's idea of you. The thing is to be a true person. The thing is to tell it true like you see it."

"I'm good at true, Ernestino, but true only gets me called 'selfish scum.'"

"Selfish scum?"

My father's charge, along with an insistence that if I wanted to write I ought to do it now instead of, as he scolded, "capitalizing on your yellow hair." And so I had written, four months holed up in New Hartford doing nothing else, and even Dad hadn't been able to put down that second book of mine, *The Trouble I've Seen*.

"Not by anyone whose opinion matters, Daughter," Ernest said.

He pushed the disfigured cat from his lap, and he lifted my chin to meet his gaze as I was still thinking about Dad, thinking he hadn't lived even for me to get back to St. Louis to say how sorry I was for the slime I used for a brain and for being twenty-seven already and having produced only two stinking books.

We both turned then to the sound of something shifting on the path across the garden. The cook stood by the kitchen door with a dish towel in her hand. The fact of her startled me, but Ernest seemed not the least surprised, and paid her no attention.

"You're a good daughter and you must stop worrying about your book so much," he said. "You've got it all dark in your head. Just write it, Daughter. Just sit down and write."

Key West, Florida

January 1937

On sunny Saturday afternoons when I was a girl, Matie and I used to climb on the clanging, swaying streetcar, hauling picnics of sandwiches and eggs, fruit and lemonade, and her volume of Robert Browning poetry, headed for the lake at Creve Coeur. Creve Coeur—"broken heart"—is named, or so the story goes, for some poor brokenhearted fool of a girl, or for the shape of the lake itself, if you like that better. Legends are all about what people think they like to hear, and nothing about the truth.

For me, Creve Coeur wasn't at all about broken hearts, but rather about found ones. My mother's heart, when we were home, was so often distracted by all the problems of the world that needed fixing, but it was all for me alone those afternoons we settled beneath a willow tree by the waterfall and peeled our eggs. The tree limbs drooped comfortably around us in our secret little world, and the lighthearted *plip plip plip* of the waterfall splashing over the layered rock made background music for the poems Matie would read, "Soliloquy of the Spanish Cloister"—*Gr-r-r—there go, my heart's abhorrence!*—because the sounds of the words always made us giggle. "Will you write me a 'scrofulous French novel / On grey paper with blunt type!'" she liked to ask me, and I always answered that I would write her a horridly scrofulous one, and

I'd "double down its pages at the woeful sixteenth print," too, surely I would.

"What is 'scrofulous'?" I once asked.

"Well, sweetie, scrofula is a disease, a tuberculosis of the lymph nodes in the neck. And scrofulous means . . . well, I suppose it means diseased, but here the poet means morally diseased."

"Full of bad words?"

"I suppose so."

I said, "But it oughtn't to mean that!"

Matie laughed, and she asked, "What ought 'scrofulous' to mean, Martha?"

"It ought to mean marvelous. It ought to mean magnificent with an undertone of delightful, and a pinch of silly!"

Matie laughed again, and she said, "Scrofulous, Gellhorn style: magnificent with an undertone of delightful."

"And a pinch of silly."

"And a pinch of silly," she agreed.

There was never any hurry to those afternoons. There was blue sky and just-right sun and Matie listening to me like I was all there was, letting me have words mean whatever I thought they should. In the spring, there was the sweet scent of lilies of the valley, and violets blooming as heart shaped as the lake. I always wanted to pick them, to make love bouquets for Matie, but she insisted I leave them be.

"They're to be seen, not owned, like every beautiful thing in this world, including you."

To her, I was beautiful, and I was to Ernest too. *Legs up to your shoulders in that sleek little black dress*—that was his first impression of me back in Key West, I learned years later. *Heels that emphasized your height when most girls would slump. Blond hair and high cheekbones and a sensuous mouth in a schoolgirl face. Yes, you knew how men were.*

But I didn't know how men were. Does any woman?

That winter in Key West, I was still all queer and scrambled about my looks and my body and sex. I'd gotten it twisted up in a tangle of morals and fear and Matie's little phrases—"how like animals"—which I'm sure were meant to keep me a good girl but had the opposite effect. The one real love I'd had by then, Bertrand de Jouvenel, hadn't helped. Bertrand was as twisted up about it as I was, as sure you would be too if your stepmother seduced you when you were a shy, bookish sixteen, even if you didn't remain her "little leopard" for five years, even if your stepmother wasn't Colette, who would write about it so the whole world gasped. I was twenty-one when I met Bertrand, which seemed so old to have done nothing at all with my life, and he was twenty-seven and married, but in the French way—living apart from his much older wife, who had taken another lover—and I fell for him in that giddy schoolgirl way that is all adrenaline and hormones without an ounce of sense. Bertrand made me laugh; I suppose he was the first man who really did, and if there is anything better than a man who makes you laugh, I don't know what it is. By the time my first novel was published in 1934, the press had me made out as some fascinating Madame de Jouvenel, and Bertrand and I did think of ourselves as married, even if his wife refused to give up the social standing that came with being a de Jouvenel, even if in the end I would get what a gal gets for wanting everyone to call her lover her husband, for imagining the fact that his wife took another man long before he took me was the same as her meaning to give him a divorce.

Your affair with that cuckolded runt, Dad called that first love of mine. Dad was dead a year by the time I danced with The Swede in Key West, but I carried his disapproval in my head like a tumor. If I led a man on, if I swam with him and danced with him and kissed him, well, I ought to be thinking of my reputation and be a better girl than that. And if I was a bad girl and did what bad girls did, then a man could expect more, and if a bad girl didn't hand over the goods, then she was a tease. If a girl wasn't a virgin, then who was she to be playing coy? I was forever feeling I owed men what they wanted, and I suppose some part of me was thinking that if I just found the right man, it wouldn't be disgusting painful self-loathing. Real pain. Physical pain. And so I did my usual bit with The Swede, paying off my debt for the evenings of dancing and laughter and companionship.

I woke as I always did, knowing that I didn't feel the way I ought to feel to wake up in a man's bed. I woke regretting the lovemaking, regretting everything that hurt and everything that didn't. Regretting ever having swum with The Swede, and danced with him, and kissed him and let him hold me, and climbed into his bed. Needing to flee from the shame of who I was and who I wasn't, to be the leaver rather than the left.

When a family friend offered me a lift as far as Miami, I packed my bags and made my goodbyes to Pauline and Ernest and the boys. And, when I arrived home in St. Louis, I wrote Pauline about how fine her children were, and her husband, too, and herself. I wrote how good she was not to mind having me as a fixture in her home. I wrote that I was producing a dozen pages a day, intent on finishing the book so I could be free to set off somewhere again. I sent her pictures of Bertrand too, even though there wasn't any point in mentioning my old love except to save Pauline the worry that I might be a threat to her marriage. By then, Ernest had begun calling me from a trip to see his publisher in New York, I supposed because he could talk to me about Spain when he couldn't talk to her about it, and he could talk to me about the writing without offending the gang he oughtn't offend in New York. He complained in those calls that the editor at *Esquire*, which was going to serialize his new novel, was asking foolish questions—although to be honest the questions, when it came down to it, were the kinds of things I'd wondered, like whether there weren't too many real people being caricatured in his fictional ones.

"He can sit his sorry ass down and wait until June, I've got to get to Spain," Ernest said. "That's what I told Max Perkins too."

"You didn't really," I said into the plain black phone receiver, keeping my voice low lest Matie hear. Max Perkins was his editor at Scribner, an old-fashioned, polite sort who wore vests under his suit jackets, and funny plaid ties done in proper Windsor knots, and was so politely spoken that even men like Ernest would hesitate to say "ass" in his presence.

"I did," Ernest insisted. "I told Perkins that if he wasn't happy about it, to hell with him."

Ernest went from Max's office at Scribner straight to see the general manager at NANA, the North American Newspaper Alliance, which provided syndicated pieces for some fifty major newspapers. He signed a contract for $1,000 a story from Spain and $500 for shorter pieces, a dollar a word when the best journalists in Spain were paid something much closer to nothing.

Still, he was cranky about *Esquire*, and he was cranky about Max Perkins, and he was cranky about his sister-in-law, who had an apartment in New York and was on Pauline's side about him going to Spain. He was all torn up, too, from visiting the son of some dear friends who was dying at a sanitarium in the Adirondacks. Tuberculosis, which the poor kid had been battling for seven years, and the friends' older son had died two years earlier, from meningitis. Ernest was an odd bird, but very generous, and I did love those calls. I loved hearing him all churned up about Spain and about the writing just when the St. Louis horror was setting in for me, when I was beginning to feel I was the only one who gave a fig about anything other than wearing the right kind of perfectly appropriate dress for the right kind of boringly respectable man.

Ernest gave a story I'd written—a thing titled "Exile"—to his editor. The publisher, Charles Scribner, wrote himself to say he'd like to run it in his magazine if only I would make it shorter. I tried not to be bothered about his treating my writing as a thing cut and made to order: I'll have the jacket shoulder a bit more snug, please, the slacks up a quarter inch; I'll have mine medium rare with a bottle of 1929 Bordeaux. I can hack a journalism piece all to bits, and that's fine, but fiction is another thing. I'd already let the words age in the barrel. It was time to pour them out and drink.

"Ah, but Scribbles is worth listening to, Stooge," Ernest said. "It's not just the magazine space he's thinking about."

My crankiness was just the boredom and the fear of being stuck in the St. Louis Wednesday Club or left behind at the gymnasium's edge—boredom I tried to dampen by working with the Red Cross, helping flood victims in south Missouri. I exchanged letters with Bertrand, who was in still in Paris and, like me, considering going to Spain to cover the war. And of course I did shorten the story just like Mr. Scribner wanted. It wasn't a book, after all; it was only a magazine story meant to be read on a train.

I wrote my novel too, finally. I holed myself up on the third floor like a *hermitus maximus* and barely looked out the window to McPherson Avenue, much less to the ghastly coal-smoke haze of St. Louis. I wrote the way I always wrote back then, getting each chapter right before moving on. I wanted to write a hell of a book, to choose the words properly and string them together just so, to move people the way Ernest's writing moved me. But I was chewing cement, and Mrs. Roosevelt, when I wrote her about it, suggested I'd gotten the jitters and lost the flow in my obsession for the perfect words. I took her advice to save the revising for later, and I wrote like a slave, ten new pages a day no matter my mood or my temperature or the state of my winter constitution. I wrote with one ear to the war humming louder in Spain. Yet for all of Hemingway's urging me to let him arrange for me to get to Madrid, there was something daunting about him, something that left me squawky about being under obligation to him or dependent on his patronage.

I finished the novel draft and sent it to *Time* magazine journalist Allen Grover; we'd been a bit more than friends for five minutes some years before but had settled into being the best of pals, and starkly honest with each other in the way that every writer needs.

Grover pronounced my novel a credible political tract but not much of a story.

I abandoned the damned thing, and I wrote to Bertrand to wait for me in Paris if he could, that we might travel together from Paris. And I wrote Hemingway that I would see him in New York on my way to Spain.

New York, New York

February 1937

There was plenty of trouble to find with Ernest in New York, but it was Hemingway's brand of trouble, all dashing and vulgar and alcohol fueled. There was always a gang, and we were always going or coming, rushing about in the evening and recovering in the day to rush out again to the Stork Club or to "21." The "21" Club—what a name for a place and never mind that I was twenty-eight and Ernest thirty-seven and we weren't any older than anyone else. It was just the address, a brownstone at 21 East Fifty-First Street that had been a speakeasy, with a wrought-iron fence and a doorman and a tiny jockey statue you wouldn't know announced a club unless you were in the know. We shunned the wood-paneled bar and the dining room hung with model ships and cars and planes for a private room where Ernest and his pals spent long nights plotting a film they meant to change the future of Spain. *The Spanish Earth* was to be directed by Joris Ivens, a vodka-drinking Dutchman with the kind of rough dark-hair-blue-eyes-cleft-chin looks that bring respect for a man, while a good-looking woman cannot possibly be sharp or witty—or if she is, then she must be up to something that will do a man harm.

"Stooge is going to Spain too," Ernest told them, "as soon as her papers are in order."

"We're co-conspirators, Ernestino and I. I've brought my false beard and dark glasses," I joked, trying to win them over with my favorite orange dress and a good old-fashioned laugh at myself. "We're both going to say nothing and look strong."

But I couldn't just go to Spain without a travel visa on account of the nonintervention pact banning civilian travel to the country, and Ernest, whose papers were already in order and only waiting for him to decide to go, was providing me none of the help he'd offered in all those phone calls when I was back home. He would talk without ever taking a breath (except to drink his whiskey) about how the Republicans had pulled back together and counterattacked at Jarama, and how Fascism was the only kind of government that couldn't produce good writing, and how we needed to set aside our own happiness and do our bit. Despite all his talk, though, he began to seem like a man who wanted to be going to Spain with no desire actually to arrive at the war.

I begged an editor I knew at *Collier's* to play along with some bunk I made up about being a special correspondent for them, to give me an excuse to get my travel papers. Just after he agreed, Ernest finally set sail for Paris, taking along Sidney Franklin—a sandy-haired bullfighter from Flatbush he met while writing *The Sun Also Rises*, who didn't even know which side of the war they meant to cover. Me, I dug up a commission from *Vogue* to write fluff about "Beauty Problems of the Middle-Aged Woman" to earn my own passage to Paris. To write the piece, I had to try a new treatment that peeled away the skin on my face, to expose fresh layers underneath. I was a ghastly sight when I sailed, in a cabin with an exploding radiator, a telephone that worked occasionally, and an elevator and a service bell that never did. But I'd have done a fan dance in Times Square or sung *Aida* in Madison Square Garden to earn passage to cover the Spanish war.

They say hindsight is twenty-twenty, but it isn't; it's as fogged by the goggles we swim through life wearing as anything is. Nostalgia goggles, or goggles of regret? See the difference? My life, looking back on it, seems a series of running toward excitement, covering Hitler's early violence, the Spanish Civil War, World War II, Korea, Vietnam, the civil wars in Central America, and, when I was eighty-one, the US invasion of Panama, which folks like to remark upon, but really there is so little upside to acting your age as an old woman that it would have been more remarkable had I stayed home. In the view through my own goggles, though, it's less clear what direction I'm running, and I have as company a ghost in an ugly traveling hat.

I was barely twenty when I first began running. Already, I'd failed my first exams at Bryn Mawr, only to pass them with high marks on a second try; I'm not sure which enraged Dad more. Before I could pass or fail the next exams, I landed in the school infirmary, too lousy with dullness to get out of bed. After recuperating in St. Louis, I went to New York for a job marking galleys—misspellings, punctuation, on a good day a split infinitive. I managed to get a piece I'd written about Rudy Vallée published, I suppose for the plain reason that nobody older than I was could explain the attraction of Vallée's wavy hair and wavy voice. On the strength of that piece and one other, I landed a job as a journalist in Albany, reporting on crime and divorce—improbably never the divorce of the city editor whose drunken advances I forever parried. Weary of the task (which always seemed to be mine to deal with), I returned home again to Dad's haranguing me to return to school. At the reappearance of the St. Louis blues, Matie lent me train fare to New York, where I could sleep on my brother's couch until I pulled together passage to Paris. Running *to* Paris, not *from* anything, I would have told you; I meant to take whatever job I could find there, and live cheaply, as you could back then, and write.

I certainly didn't imagine I was running from Dad's fierce disapproval, clear as that is now through any of the goggles I might wear. But at the St. Louis train station, as I was saying goodbye to Dad, I began sobbing. He was a man who stood proudly for independent women when others shamed them, but somehow I'd become a daughter of whom he was ashamed.

It never was a thing Dad could tolerate, a woman sobbing, especially when that woman was his own daughter and she in a public place, with people who might know who we were turning to look. He demanded I get ahold of myself, which of course made it impossible.

When I went to kiss him goodbye on the platform, he leaned away from me, with all those people watching. I was left to wipe my eyes and blow my nose and pretend interest in my hat—an embarrassingly homely thing I could no longer imagine I'd ever admired.

In the first minutes of that steamy chug toward my new life, I lowered the window and chucked the damned hat out toward the muddy Mississippi drifting below us. Goodbye, hat. Goodbye, St. Louis. Goodbye, Matie, I'm off to write scrofulous French novels on grey paper with blunt type. Goodbye, Dad, and all the disappointing, flunking-out failure daughterness, the lunchroom rejection, the wet-wool stink of the coatroom as, in the gymnasium, others waltzed.

The lousy hat didn't even make it to the river. It landed on the westbound tracks, to be crushed by a returning train, or dragged all the way back to St. Louis.

It was on that trip to Paris that I met Bertrand de Jouvenel, who, despite everything, I was looking forward to seeing again. Because of the delay in my travel papers, though, by the time I finally arrived in Paris, he'd given up on me and gone ahead to Spain. He was reporting for *Paris-Soir* with the gang at the Imatz in Hendaye, journalists from the *Chicago Tribune*, the *New York Herald Tribune*, and London's *Daily Mail*. "Rabbit, you'll think I'm off my head marching with the troops," he wrote to me. And, sure, Josephine Baker was singing at the Folies-Bergère and Maurice Chevalier at the Casino, but Paris was so wet that the Seine threatened its banks, and everyone was surly or outraged or stunned by one thing or another: deficits and government incompetence, worker protests, even books.

Hemingway too had already set off for Spain by the time I arrived in France, and my efforts to find another journalist with whom to travel came to naught. There was nothing to do in the shadow of the Eiffel Tower except wait for the French government to do with issuing my papers to Spain what they did so well with helping Spain and confronting Hitler and everything else, which was to delay and delay and delay.

Paris, France

March 1937

I spoke no Spanish and had only fifty dollars in my pocket, but I studied my maps and pulled on sturdy gray flannel trousers and a sweater and windbreaker, stuffed my bar of soap and spare clothes into my knapsack, loaded a duffel with canned goods, and caught a train south from Paris. I rode second class, changing trains once before the Spanish border. When the sun rose or I rose or we both did, it was to a world of trees blooming pink and white. An hour later, the snow was falling in flakes as huge as those blooms had been.

I disembarked at Puigcerdá; the French and Spanish trains ran on different-sized tracks, so I had to walk across the border. I stood alone on the platform, watching the French train reverse and disappear, the field around me as white as my face might have been if not for the cold making it red. I'd been to almost-war, to pending-war, to this-place-is-about-to-explode, but I hadn't actually been in the midst of shells falling and people shooting guns at each other, popping each other dead.

The cold was a blessing as I heaved my backpack and duffel and tromped over the snow-covered border to the Spanish side. The cold left me sure I would freeze to death before I ever got a chance to be killed.

A customs officer examined the nonintervention papers finally granted me by the French administratoramuses with their scratchy pens and their scratchy personalities. He stamped my passport, and I climbed onto the train to Barcelona, an old pile of junk with no heat and no comfort beyond the fact that the snow was falling on the outside of the windows and the windowpanes stopped the wind, more or less. The train was rowdy with recruits on their way to join the Republicans, boys dressed in whatever they could find in an army where the soldiers fed and clothed themselves. I was glad to see them, though, glad to see the Republicans might have what it took to turn back the Fascists at Madrid. They'd been abandoned by every government in the world to survive on their own sweat and blood while Hitler and Mussolini provided weapons and aid to Franco's murdering Fascists. They were good boys too—boys who gave me bits of their garlic sausages and their bread that must have been made from chalk, who quieted at each stop when a senior soldier poked his head into our carriage, only to return to rowdiness as the train set off again.

Barcelona, when I arrived, was all swarms of soldiers and rifles and political posters plastered along the Ramblas, and red streamers everywhere. It was cold cold cold, and there wasn't one bit of coal in the whole city, and no butter, even at the hotels. Everything about it pleased me. Life's damned funny that way, isn't it? The hotels were jammed full of young Brits and Americans meaning to get themselves killed if only they could get to the front, but the Ministry of Foreign Propaganda found me a room. I was so exhausted that I slept through the bombing that night without even a dream.

I poked around Barcelona for two days before hitching a ride to Valencia, where the woman in charge of the government press bureau found me a ride on to Madrid. "With Ted Allan, a young pup who's been recruited from the International Brigades," she said, the Brigades being the foreigners fighting with the Republicans against the Fascists.

"Ted is here to work on a film about the surgeon who established one of the first mobile blood-transfusion units for the front."

"Mr. Allan," I said on our introduction, the scummy rub of the long time on the road falling away with his smile.

"Ted," he said.

"You don't seem like a Ted," I said. "You seem like a Mr. Allan. Or perhaps just Allan."

He laughed easily, although he'd spent months with the International Brigades already and had plenty of reasons not to laugh.

"You'll be a witch, will you?" he said. "My given name was Alan. Alan Herman."

"So you traded two first names for a different two first names?" I said, flipping my hair in a way Dad would have found shameful. My yellow hair.

"I like change," Ted Allan said.

I allowed myself a long look at him, wondering what really lay beneath this nice boy from Montreal wanting to be a Spanish hero. He was young and smart and gypsy-eyed, intense and playful all at once, and full of himself in that way I never can resist. In addition to the blood-transfusion film he was working on, he wrote for a Canadian paper, and he broadcast on Madrid radio.

He said, "What makes a pretty gal like you want to live covered in the dust of warring Spaniards?"

"I'm from St. Louis," I said.

He laughed again.

"And I like to live," I said, reminded suddenly of Bertrand, thinking this Ted Allan, too, was the kind who could stick in your guts for a while if things went bad.

A car pulled up to fetch us, a Citroën with a Spanish driver and Ernest's bullfighter friend Sidney Franklin in the passenger seat. Also two typewriters; a half-dozen enormous hams; coffee enough to send you to Jupiter; a crate of oranges, lemons, and limes; and some fifty jars of marmalade. Butter too. Trust Hemingway to find butter when there was none to be found, or to send Sidney Franklin to do it for him.

"Martha," Sidney said in his New Jersey bark. Just my name, but he managed to deliver in it all the disapproval I'd felt in New York.

"Well, this is sure to be some ride," I said, "with Sidney Franklin who is really Sidney Frumpkin from Flatbush, and Ted Allan who is really Alan Herman from Montreal."

I cut a glance at Ted, wanting him to laugh and yet not. If you made the wrong kind of fun of Sidney, you put yourself in danger of him knocking your lights out. Sidney wasn't big, but he was a bullfighter, and a good one. It said something about Ernest Hemingway that Sidney Franklin who was Sidney Frumpkin would be his errand boy in Spain.

Sidney pulled a handkerchief from his pocket and blew his nose.

"You stay put, Sidney," Ted said. "Marty and I will manage in the back."

We tied my duffel to the front fender, and Ted and I wedged ourselves and our other gear into the overstuffed back seat, far from the car's shabby heater. We made the best of it, though, snuggling together for warmth as we traveled through the coastal mountains to the high, pale hills and fields of La Mancha.

Ted briefed me on the details of the fighting he'd seen. He'd recently taken a film crew to the Jarama front at Morata.

"I'd hoped to find some of my International Brigade mates," he said, his mirth evaporating, "but twenty of them—chaps who crossed the Atlantic with me—died in the ruined olive groves at the heights of Pingarrón."

"Suicide Hill," I said.

There is nothing to gain in dwelling, though, so he just laid out the details: how the Fascist rebels had begun an offensive three weeks earlier, meant to encircle and capture Madrid before winter's end. It took them only two days to overrun Brihuega, a walled city fifty miles northeast. Ted had nearly been killed on the twelfth when bullets shattered the windows of a station wagon taking blood supplies to the front. But a change in the weather had allowed the Republicans to send bomber support to the troops and turn back the assault.

"Eight months into this war before the good guys finally get one decent victory," I said.

"If anyone wasn't yet convinced that Mussolini has a dog in this fight," Ted said, "I'd like them to explain the Lancia trucks and Fiat tractors left behind in that retreat, and the bags of mail with Italian addresses. That little Italian Fascist is respecting the Non-Intervention Agreement as surely as Hitler is respecting Jews."

As Ted and I talked and laughed—sure we found things to laugh about, as you do whenever you're in a tough spot if you want to survive—Sidney fumed in the relative cold of the heated front seat, all the while blowing his nose and turning to give us scolding looks.

It all began to seem less of a lark the closer we got to Madrid, as more and more the road was crowded with trucks and soldiers. When we were stopped at a barricade to produce our papers, something rumbled in the distance although the sky was clear.

"Guns?" I asked.

"Guns," Ted said.

Farther down the road, Madrid rose up at the horizon, framed by great clouds of smoke and dust from exploding shells.

The streets of Madrid, when we reached them, were a maze of bomb craters and dug-up-paving-stone roadblocks, yellow trams scurrying about, camouflaged trucks and cars full of soldiers, and slogans plastered everywhere: *"EVACUAD. Confiad vuestra familia a la REPUBLICA"* and *"¡¡MADRES !! Proteger vuestros hijos."*

"Evacuate. Protect your families. Help us to victory," Ted translated for me.

Franco had vowed to destroy the city rather than cede it, and he'd spent much of the fall firebombing it section by section with the help of German planes.

We carried on, inhaling the dust of the day's shelling and the improbable smell from the coffee roasters' carts as we passed rubble-filled courtyards, apartments from which outside walls had been stripped by bombs so that the bedrooms and dining rooms and kitchens were visible, and children gathering firewood from the ruins. When we passed a circle of brick in front of the city hall, Ted explained that it had been built to protect the fountain of Cibeles.

"The great mother goddess, riding a chariot pulled by lions," Sidney elaborated dismissively. "Anyone who knows anything about Madrid knows it's the city's most important symbol."

I decided by the time we arrived at the Hotel Florida—a terrific marble thing, ten stories of opulence across the Plaza de Callao from a sandbagged cinema offering Lionel Barrymore in *David Copperfield* and shops still showing, behind windows latticed with protective tape, furs and French perfume—that I didn't like Sidney any better than he liked me.

I did like Ted immensely. As we unloaded the car, he asked when he might see me.

I answered, "And this such a glamorous place for romance?"

Ted laughed, a sound that seemed to fend off the enormous dark of the city, the cold, the dread, and even Sidney Franklin's disapproving glare.

"In a few hours?" Ted asked. "I've got to go to the blood-transfusion unit, but I'll have reason to hurry now."

The Hotel Florida, Madrid, Spain

March 1937

A lone concierge minded his stamp collection at the Hotel Florida reception desk, behind a "Take One" box offering a single tired brochure for a hotel in Cuba. Six months of regular shelling from the batteries on Garabitas hill had relieved the hotel of some of its top stones, and the glass atrium above the circling floors was covered with soot, leaving the place feeling abandoned and downright despairing. Still, Hemingway stayed there, and Herb Matthews of the *New York Times*, Sefton Delmer of the *Daily Press*.

"I can give you biggest, most beautiful room at front with view of *castillo*—seventh century, *castillo* is—for one dollar," the concierge offered. "But Señor Hemingway, he say you must have best room, so I give you at back. It is more cost and view is alleyway, but more safe. The shells, they come from this direction," he said, nodding toward the front.

The considered wisdom was that unless the Fascists changed their gun positions more dramatically than they likely would, the buildings across the street would block the angle of any shot. Yes, we were awfully close to the front, close enough that the military used the newly built Telefónica skyscraper down the block as a lookout to watch the movement of Franco's troops. But that was the good news for a journalist.

We'd find everyone at the Gran Vía restaurant, the concierge said. "It is run by government so you will not expect much." He suggested if we hurried we'd get there before the next shelling. He took my duffel and led the way to my room. "Third floor, no lift, because not enough electricity."

In my room, I unpacked my most prized possession—a new cake of soap—and put it to my nose to inhale the warm honey smell, the jammy, powdery intimacy. I washed the grit of the road from my face, then dried the soap and tucked it into my coat pocket, and I headed off with Sidney Franklin who was really Sidney Frumpkin to join the other journalists in Madrid, while Ted Allan who was really Alan Herman did whatever he was obliged to do.

Sidney hurried me along the side of the street least likely to take a shell. In a few relatively quiet minutes, we reached a cacophony of clattering silverware and voices rising up from the storage basement that was the Gran Vía. I was glad of the safety of guards demanding our press credentials and, with the threat of shelling, would have paid extra for the restaurant's added protection of being underground.

Inside, at a long, dingy wooden table in a long, dingy room, journalists and soldiers, police and prostitutes—"whores de combat," Hemingway called them when he was in his cups—crowded on plank benches. The place stank of greasy cooked meat (mule or donkey or horse) and the blue haze of cigarette smoke. I didn't need to light a cigarette; I could just inhale.

Hemingway was his usual outsized self, dirtier than ever in a torn shirt, filthy trousers, and a beret, his voice booming out some memory of the day's shelling that left you imagining he might have barehanded one of those incoming shells and tossed it back. I stood watching him, wondering how a man who was such a pig in his personal habits could be so elegant with words. He wasn't precisely sober, I didn't think.

When he noticed me, he adjusted his round wire rims as if not quite sure of what he saw, and he stood and grinned, his expression warm and welcoming. He was a big lug, but a lovable one.

I went to him and pulled off his beret. "Manners, Hemingway!"

"I knew you'd get here, Daughter!" he said, putting a hand on my head like I really was his daughter and he the proud father to claim such a resourceful girl.

"Did you!" I replied, as gleeful now to be in Madrid as I ever had been to be anywhere.

"I knew you'd get here, Daughter," he repeated, "because I fixed it so you could."

I smiled the way a girl learns to smile to mask irritation, resisting the urge to fling his filthy beret back in his face. The ride from Valencia may or may not have had a Hemingway finger in it, but the whole lousy journey from St. Louis to Valencia was on my own damned sweat.

"Did *you* fix it for me to get here, Ernestino?" I said. "That's awfully funny, because I sure as hell wasn't sure I'd get here myself."

To the others, who were all watching as I handed his hat back to him and planted a daughterly kiss on his filthy, scruffy cheek, I said, "Which part of this Nesto-arranged adventure do you suppose I enjoyed most? Bludgeoning *Collier's* into giving me a letter back in New York? The dreary days I spent begging every functionary in Paris to let me come along to Spain? Of course that was all before I had the pleasure of hiking my sad rumpus over the border in the lousy cold—trying like hell not to get shot—for the luxury of five hundred hours on an unheated train. And to think I might have taken the night train to Toulouse and flown in from there like Ernesto did, and missed all the fun."

The men laughed, and if the whores didn't, it was because they spoke no English, or weren't very smart, or both. What kind of woman stays in a war zone just to sell herself?

To the assembled table, Ernest said, "This is Marty Gellhorn, if you don't know her. A hell of a lot of trouble she is, but everything here is trouble, and most of it doesn't come with legs like hers."

Ernest asked an American airman sitting beside him to slide down one to make room for me, and I sat as Ernest directed, and he slid me his glass of whiskey and called for another for himself and some dinner for me.

"Sidney," he said to Sidney Franklin, "why don't you tell Stooge here how *you* got into Spain?"

"The part where I had to remove all my identification and look in the square in Toulouse for men dressed a certain way and giving a signal that I surreptitiously followed to a bus I wasn't supposed to be on?" Sidney turned to me, and in his face I saw how he must have looked when facing a bull, all that pugnacious fury under the thinnest layer of charm. "We were guided by flashlight signals through a field, in danger of being shot by border guards the whole time."

"No, the river bit," Ernest said.

"Oh, the fun stuff," Sidney said. Then to me, "Eighty feet wide, that river was, in the middle of winter, and chin deep and sometimes deeper, which maybe you could swim, but you couldn't swim and hold your bundle of clothes over your head at the same time."

He pulled out his handkerchief and blew his nose again, still suffering from the dangerous border crossing he had made just to be Ernest's errand boy.

Ernest, as satisfied as if he'd made Sidney's journey himself, said to everyone, "As long as there's a war, you always think perhaps you'll be killed—so you have nothing to worry about. We're not dead, so we must write."

I took a sip of the sharp booze, wishing it were a nice fresh orangeade but glad to be talking about the writing, or listening about the writing, as the waiters served wine and whiskey and sold contraband cigarettes for fifteen pesetas a pack, lest the smoke of the room grow thin.

"Living is much harder than dying, and damned if writing isn't harder than living," Ernest said as he drained half of his fresh whiskey. Yes, he was drunk. They were all drunk. They were all drinking nearly as much as he was, and addressing him as "Pop," and talking about Guadalajara thirty miles northeast of Madrid, where the Nationalists held their position against Italian tanks. And all the while the whores stroked the correspondents' shoulders and their cheeks. Ernest didn't have a whore; I thought I might write Pauline to tell her so, then thought I shouldn't. I hadn't imagined whores dining with journalists until I'd opened the door, and I didn't suppose Pauline would enjoy imagining it any more than I enjoyed the company.

A waiter brought me a bit of stinking fish—truly stinking, not just "stinking" in the way I like to say so many things stink. The little pile of mess with it might have been chickpeas. I was hungry, but not that hungry. I was hungry to begin seeing what was here too, but there would be nothing until the morning except bad booze and bad food and whores and Hemingway the myth instead of Hemingway the man. I tolerated the whole scene as long as I could before making excuses and pulling a few coins from my knapsack.

"No, Daughter," Ernest said, touching my hand that held the money.

I looked at him, wondering which Hemingway this gesture came from—but perhaps the man and the myth weren't as separate as I'd thought them back in Key West. I hoisted my backpack and said, "Thank you, Ernestino," and kissed him on the forehead, and headed back to the hotel, where I climbed the stairs to my room and took my soap from my pocket, and turned on the tap.

The Hotel Florida, Madrid, Spain

March 1937

I washed up again in cold water. (The hot water ran no more often than the elevator did, but the Florida was the only place in Madrid that had even occasional hot water.) I brushed my hair. I put my things away so the room looked decent, no panties hung to dry from the doorknob, although I was in sorry need of cleaner clothes. When Ted Allan knocked on the door, I called, "Who is it?" as if I might be expecting any number of visitors.

When I opened the door, he took me in his arms and kissed me, his lips closed at first, and then soft and warm and devastating. Yes, he was definitely the kind who would stick to your guts, but this was Spain, and I was the one who would be doing the leaving, and I've always liked men best in foreign places, where I'm not Dr. Gellhorn's horrid daughter, where people don't judge or, if they do, I don't care, the St. Louis rules don't apply.

Ted Allan and I talked, and we kissed, and we talked some more.

"We could get some dinner. Would you like some dinner, Marty?" he asked.

"A nice dinner with two dozen drunken journalists and their whores," I said.

I zipped open my food bag. We chose a tin of green beans and one of tuna, and we ate together with our fingers, feeding each other.

He said, "God, I love a woman with an appetite."

With the tins empty, the last tastes licked from our fingers, we sat side by side with our backs to the pillows, our legs stretched out on the bed so the warmth of his thigh was long against mine as we shared a chocolate bar.

"Most Spanish hotels need a key to lock the door," he whispered.

I kissed the chocolate off his lips and smiled. "No key."

He took my head in his hands, his fingers on my hair and on my ears. My brain thought no, my brain thought this was a fellow who could stick to your guts if you weren't careful, but I was never much for careful. I would rather be dead than careful, that's the thing.

I kissed him again, and tucked a finger in the gap between the buttons on his shirt, to a muscled chest without much hair.

Someone knocked at the door.

Even as I moved to a more respectable position, calling that it was open, Ernest burst in like he owned the whole damned war-zone hotel, saying, "Stooge, you should—"

His big brown eyes looked vulnerable, betrayed, as he took in the empty food tins, the chocolate bar wrapper, Ted and I together on the bed.

"Ernestino," I said, touching a hand to my lips as if the gesture might hide the crushed red rather than draw attention, thinking if Ted was a man who would stick to your guts if things went bad, Ernest would rip them out and leave them on the street to be trampled. I wasn't his girl, though, I was just his daughter, his protégée, and he had a wife and two boys in Key West, another wife he'd left behind with another son, and random mistresses scattered about. I wasn't his girl, and I didn't want to be. I wanted to learn from him, to talk writing with him, to feel inspired and accomplished. I wanted him to say again how swell my words were, and help me make them as good as they could be. Not like his, exactly, but the best I could make them.

"Ernest, this is Ted Allan," I said, rising, and Ted stood too. "He's—"

"Sorry to find you just as you're leaving, kid," Ernest interrupted.

"Oh!" Ted said. And then nothing. The poor fellow really was only a kid—a good-looking one with some confidence, and I might have fallen bad for him if he'd stood up to Ernest. But he was just a gypsy-eyed kid, and you couldn't fault him for wilting in Hemingway's wide shadow.

I said, "I'll catch up with you later, Ted."

"Okay. Yeah, sure," Ted Allan said, and he lit out of there like a teenager caught necking in the back seat of a car. He left only the maw of the open doorway, and me thinking that was my trouble, that I couldn't love without admiration, and wondering if I'd be happier if I could.

In the middle of that first night, I woke to the sound of a subway train screaming at my window and the end of the world in my throat. With the boom boom boom of the first shells landing, I bolted—only to find my room locked from the outside. No amount of frantic rattling of the doorknob did any damned good.

In the quiet thud-groan of another round releasing from the distant guns, the walls were alive with the scraping scattering of rats running for their lives. The maids called to each other somewhere down the hall, like little birds flying away. I pounded on the door and shouted for help, pounded and shouted, pounded and shouted as the boom boom boom continued, the terrifying whiz of shells ever closer. I felt ridiculous, panicked. I couldn't bear to be seen this way, but I had to be seen, I had to get out.

Again the scream of the shells. Higher-pitched and sharper. Faster. Nearer. The building trembled as if it might collapse in a smash of stone on stone. Again the pounding and the frantic sound of my own voice as a distant thud started the terror again.

This time the whirring whistle was surely-crashing-into-my-window close. My brain filled with the granite thunder of shells hitting across the street and at the corner and in front of the hotel, never mind all that crud about the angle protecting us.

The windowpane juddering. The tinkle of glass breaking somewhere, crystal on stone. My windows were closed, but still the shattered-stone dust rose around me. It stuck in my lousy lungs as I screamed, "Help me, oh, please help!"

I nearly broke my fists on the hard wood of the door.

Finally an eerie silence settled for a longer moment, followed by the pop of animated voices.

"Hello!" I called out. "Is anyone there? I'm locked in!"

A voice I'd never heard in my life, a man's voice from the other side of my door, said, "Hold tight. I'll get the key."

I stood staring at the door, the little sign assuring me I could have my clothes pressed immediately, and warning there would be an additional 10 percent charge for meals delivered to my room. The edge of my hand was red, and the sign no better for my flailing.

I fumbled for a cigarette and lit it, inhaling deeply despite the dust. A few moments later, I exhaled relief at the merciful metallic tink of someone keying my door.

I coughed my thanks out into the hallway, to the banister and the lobby three floors below, where people were gathered in a dusty gaggle. I stumbled downstairs to hear the concierge, unharmed in his dusty concierge uniform, say, "It is regrettable, of course," as if a collar had been sloppily pressed. "Most regrettable that they break the schedule today. But I do assure you, yes, that it was far worse last week."

"The schedule?" I said.

"Before breakfast is the shelling, and before and after the midday and evening meals. Usually there is no more after that."

We stood together in the lobby, the war dust already settling on the wicker furniture. Was it over? Beyond the hotel entrance, people stood at the doorways of buildings on the square, poised but hesitant.

"In any case, we each will die only once," the concierge said.

He turned his attention to the maids jabbering excitedly. He hurried up the stairs, and I followed, to see a jagged opening in the wall of a guest room in which the furniture was now kindling. A twisted iron bed frame sat preposterously upright, some new and dreadful art.

A guest complained that his bathroom had been ruined by a shell fragment, his toiletries gone. It would have been laughable, how intent he was on the tragedy of his toothbrush and shaving things, if one didn't understand how close to his person they'd been. I pushed back a rush of wanting to return to my own bathroom, to see my bar of soap safely where I had, in my panic, left it behind.

Instead, I found Ernest playing poker in a back room, smoking and dirty and drunk.

"Hemingway, someone locked me in my room," I said.

He looked up from his cards. Someone whistled, and I realized I was still in my nightclothes. I wrapped my arms around myself, but didn't turn from Ernest's gaze, his expression much as it had been when he'd walked in on Ted Allan and me, vulnerable and betrayed and a little sheepish.

"Daughter," he said, "this hotel is full of pimps and drunks. I didn't want any of the men here to bother you. I didn't want you to be taken for a whore."

The word stung like my father's hand on my cheek, like "capitalizing on your yellow hair." But I wasn't Ted Allan who was really Alan Herman. I wouldn't wither, and I wouldn't have Hemingway think I would.

"A whore, Ernesto?" I said as lightly as I could manage. "You screwball. I don't wear enough makeup to be mistaken for a cigarette girl."

The Hotel Florida, Madrid, Spain

MARCH 1937

I followed the delicious odor of fried ham and eggs the next morning to find the gang from the poker table and then some crowded into Ernest's rooms. Herb Matthews of the *New York Times* arrived just as I did, wearing peasant trousers that accentuated his long limbs and espadrilles on impossibly long, thin feet. He had shy, deep-set eyes behind horn-rimmed glasses, a generous chin, and a barrage of questions for me.

"Did I sleep well?" I repeated, thinking his face belonged above a starched white collar in a starched white office.

"Oh, that," he said. "I suppose I ought to ask whether you're the variety of gal who packs her suitcase after such an enticing night, or one who takes a good old-fashioned shelling as a warm welcome."

"I didn't bring a suitcase. I brought a duffel bag full of canned goods with a change of clothes." And a bar of soap, but I didn't advertise that.

Herb laughed warmly. "A duffel full of canned goods? Come sit by me and be my friend."

He tendered a tin of sausages to Sidney, who, with a disapproving look at me, tucked it into a tall wardrobe already overloaded with ham and coffee and marmalade.

"Ernie's typewriter, Sid's kitchen," Herb whispered as Sidney returned to a pan over the gas stove on the dresser. "Sidney does Hemingway's typing and cooking, and bunks here as well. Ernest will spot anyone anything, but old Sid isn't wild about folks showing up without something to contribute. That's what that look was about."

Ernest, still in the filthy trousers and torn shirt he'd worn the prior night, held forth from a settee, educating a Swedish gal who wore men's clothes (which I rather liked) on the situation in Guadalajara. He slid over to make room for me, and introduced me to the assembled gang, including two other writers: a strong-jawed German novelist named Gustav Regler, who was fighting with the International Brigades, and a General Lucasz, who was better known as the Hungarian short story writer Máté Zalka.

I said, "Imagine that: someone here going by a name other than his own." But all of us in Spain were trying to be something other than what we'd been born.

A maid brought me breakfast while Ernest said, "Job number one that I've got to do today is take Stooge to the Telefónica."

"The Telefónica is where just about everything in Madrid is managed, Marty," Herb Matthews explained. "These luxury accommodations. The occasional fuel voucher."

"Safe-conduct passes," Ernest said.

Herb said, "Which have nothing to do with safety or our conduct, for what it's worth."

After I'd gobbled a bit of breakfast, Ernest shepherded me to the door, stopping to tell Sidney we were headed to the government offices to get me those safe-conduct papers.

"Sidney, do you think I might have a tin of that marmalade so I won't have to get up for breakfast?" I asked.

Ernest laughed. "Don't do it, Stooge. Don't dangle the red cape in front of old Sidney. He always beats the bull."

"Are you calling me a bull, Ernest?"

"Bullheaded," Ernest said. "Not the long, lovely rest of you. But the head, yes."

The Telefónica was nearly as busy as Ernest's hotel room, with journalists begging for fuel vouchers, collecting mail, and sharing gossip. Ernest introduced me to a skeletal man with slick dark hair, darting black eyes, and an improbably sensuous mouth who, as Madrid's foreign press chief, vetted anything any journalist wrote before it could be transmitted out of Madrid.

"And this is Ilsa Kulcsar," Ernest said. "Ilsa left Austria on false papers years ago, and she speaks eight languages, and she keeps this guy straight on what the press should be allowed to print, never mind that he's the boss." Ilsa shared a bed with her boss too; neither one's spouse was with them in Spain.

To Ilsa and me, Ernest said, "I expect you two beautiful troublemakers will get along splendidly." He put a friendly arm around my shoulders. "This is Marty Gellhorn. Be nice to her. She writes for *Collier's*, that's a million readers." As if it were as true as the fiction he wrote.

A few minutes later I had my safe-conduct papers.

Ernest and I left the hotel with Herb and "our ruddy English bishop," Sefton Delmer—a big, balding fellow in round black glasses of the type I imagined when I imagined myself disguised in a funny mustache.

"Del has a great wine cellar in his room, compliments of the Spanish king," Ernest said. "But he got it from an anarchist bartender friend rather than from looting the royal cellars himself. Don't let him tell you otherwise."

Del was a fine reporter too. He'd just gotten the cover of *Time*.

Ernest opened the passenger door for me on a car flying the Stars and Stripes and the Union Jack, his chest threatening the buttons of his coat, from which he drew out a canvas hunter's cap. He'd picked up some weight or some pride or both since leaving New York. I climbed in the front while Herb and Del took the back. Ernest took the wheel and we set off.

Elsewhere, journalists were heading off on foot or catching the tram out toward the university to the north and walking to the front from there, few graced with Ernest's car and full tank of gas. I wrapped a green chiffon scarf around my head and neck as we left the shoe-shine boys and the market lines, the crowded downtown streets. Past the barricades, we bumped along on increasingly badly rutted roads, the repair crews that smoothed new asphalt into the damaged downtown having given up among the bombed-out roads farther out. In a few minutes, we arrived at a park on the southwest side of Madrid, Casa de Campo, where, in the distance, men in slacks and white shirts stood behind a stone wall and sandbags, rifles poised. Beyond the wall, trees were just beginning to show the tiny green promise of spring. I felt terrified, inhaling air that smelled of blooming explosives, listening to the birdsong of firing guns.

Herb and Del set off for the soldiers at the front, while Ernest stayed back to help me get the lay of the land.

"The first thing you ought to know, Stooge, is how to take cover," he said, and he gave me a useful little lecture on what to do if the shooting got too close. "It won't from here, though," he said, and he launched into an explanation of the Republicans' strategy for holding the line against the Fascists, how long the stalemate had lasted, and why. We moved closer but not too close, hanging back in an area where men were eating or resting, one reading a book as if there weren't men shooting just yards away.

"Everyone says the 'pop' or the 'rattle' of gunfire," Ernest said, "but that's not it, is it? There isn't one sound. The machine gun has its sound and the rifle has another. *Rong cararong rong rong*—that's a machine gun."

"Like church bells," I said, wanting to laugh but not yet comfortable enough with war to laugh in its presence—although that would come soon enough. Laughter is the only real way to express how glad you are to be alive when you know too much of death.

"And the rifles, Ernest?" I said.

"Racrong carong carong."

"I don't know, Nesto. It makes it sound romantic, all those round sounds. Melodic. It's more brutal than that."

"Racrong carong carong," he repeated. "That's the true sound of it. The sound. It *is* round. It *is* melodic."

He made a note in his notebook, satisfied.

There, standing at the edge of the war, I watched Hemingway, and I listened, and I tried to imagine what it would be like to have my brothers living in holes in the earth dug around St. Louis, shooting across the fields at the boys from Illinois. I didn't speak a word of Spanish, and I had no idea what these soldiers were calling to each other over the gunfire, but that's the way they seemed to me: just like the boys I knew at home, regular boys who liked to tinker with car engines and smoke cigarettes and kiss girls.

When I lit a cigarette, the soldiers eyed it so hungrily that I opened the pack and handed out what I had left. I'd be sorry later, but right then I wished I'd brought more. I wished I had a better memory, that I would be able to remember every line of every face of every soldier, every touch of finger to finger. I tried to fix in my mind the exact tone of the voices saying *"gracias,"* the tilt of their heads and the slant of their shoulder blades as they curved against the wind to let the tobacco catch the flame, the indent of cheeks at the first inhale, and whether they exhaled through their noses or mouths, whether they blew rings of smoke and how high the rings went into the air before they became nothing at all. And when the pack was empty and the men still watched me, I took my own half-smoked cigarette and handed it to a tall, good-looking fellow with eyes as deep set as Dad's had been.

"Take it."

His buddies jostled him, jabbering words I couldn't begin to understand, and laughing.

"Si le gusta su pelo," Ernest said to them, *"espere a ver sus piernas."* And he too laughed.

Much later, when the sun was low and the gunfire quieting, I asked Ernest what he'd said to them.

He opened the car door for me, then kissed my forehead the way I sometimes kissed his. "Daughter, I'm afraid you're going to cause a stir every time those poor shits see you. It's not often they set eyes on a girl with yellow hair and legs like yours. There's a war on, you know."

The Hotel Florida, Madrid, Spain

April 1937

Josie Herbst arrived in Madrid a couple days after I did, entering the Hotel Florida lobby with exploded-shell dust powdering her curly hair. She hadn't set down her gigantic suitcase and folding typewriter before Ernest—looking dapper in a swanky uniform and shiny boots that morning, having managed to source a change of clothes after all—spotted her and scooped her up into a big lugging hug.

"Josie, I'll never forgive you for letting that sixty-pound kingfish off your line!" he said.

"And here I am in a war zone with that old fish looking me straight in the eye," Josie answered, the nasal tone of Iowa in her voice despite the years of Berkeley, Berlin, and Paris.

They'd been friends since she'd worked at H. L. Mencken's *Smart Set*, where she was publishing short stories while Ernest was being rejected and Spain was a place you went to eat pipas and cheer the bulls. They caught up as old friends often do, skipping the stone of shared moments over the pond of friendship.

"Max is disgusted with us all, you know, and it has nothing to do with that fish," Josie said, meaning Max Perkins at Scribner. "'What's gotten into the lot of you?'—that's what he asked me. 'Hemingway. Dos Passos. Gellhorn.'" She nodded in recognition to me, although we'd not met before. "'Everyone rushing off like fools to have Spanish bombs dropped on them.' That's what Max thinks of us all being here." She brushed the dust from her hair as she continued. "Is that shelling supposed to convince anyone of anything? I half expect raindrops and a good old-fashioned Iowa thunderstorm, don't you?"

"Josie here wrote a fine series for the *New York Post* about Nazi Germany," Ernest said.

"'Behind the Swastika,'" I said. "You told a helluva truth about that pig Hitler, if only someone would listen."

Josie had reported from Germany in the early 1920s before marrying John Hermann, and found her way back there after he left her. I liked that she wrote the ugly truth about Hitler even though no one wanted to hear it. I liked that work might be a fine solution to a husband who left. But she frowned at me even on that first introduction, and seemed forever to be frowning in my direction that spring. Mornings, while I was still in my bed—too early even to be thinking of my marmalade—she would ignore Ernest's imploring that Sidney had a very fine omelet just for her and instead settle in the first-floor lobby, with nothing more than tea and a bit of stale bread, to chat with the soldiers on leave. She did the responsible thing always, sometimes with Dos Passos, who could be as maddeningly virtuous as Josie when he wasn't carrying on about the disappearance of his left-wing activist friend José Robles, who was presumed to be awaiting trial not by the Fascists but by his own duly elected government. Josie couldn't very well leave her visitors just for a bit of marmalade when the boys might be dead before the end of the day, she said. She always said "marmalade," too, judging my reclusive mornings more harshly even than she judged Ernest's breakfast parties. I wasn't writing; I wasn't steeped enough in

Spain to write the real gen. It was all too much that I didn't know well enough yet to capture in words. But Josie disapproved of a journalist in a war zone who didn't turn in her thousand words by nine o'clock each night.

If Josie didn't much care for me, I did strike up a friendship with Ilsa Kulcsar. Ilsa, who as Ernest had said controlled the whole journalist show from her office at the Telefónica, assigned me a guide and interpreter, the Swedish gal in men's clothes who'd been sitting beside Ernest that first morning. She was exactly the kind of tall, red-gold-headed beauty to make any woman feel dull, even if you were dressed in a silk gown and she in the men's trousers, but she spoke seven languages and knew her way around, and I adored her.

Another I soon counted as a friend was Randolfo Pacciardi, a dashing Italian with a broad, big chest and an imposing nose and eyes that would not let go. Randolfo had come to Spain to lead the Italian faction of the International Brigades fighting with the Republicans, which was called the Garibaldi Brigade. Back home in Italy, he'd been sentenced to five years' imprisonment for having founded an anti-Fascist party, but he escaped first to Austria, then to Switzerland, then to France, and from there brought his battle against Fascism to Spain. Randolfo and I first met at a Brigade party, where he flirted with me, and I had the good sense to flirt back even before learning who he was. There was nothing to it; he was in it for the publicity I could give his troops. But he could give me access to the war, and he was great fun to flirt with too, the way intelligent, intense men with whom you have no future whatsoever can be. He liked to squire me around the quieter parts of "his front" in Madrid on his motorcycle, where I shared cigarettes and stale bread with his troops, and flirted with them even more enthusiastically than I did with Randolfo. But it was only when the front was quiet that he would collect me to show me around.

It was my beautiful Swedish interpreter who got me my first close peek at the front in full battle. She introduced me to the blood-transfusion fellow to whom Ted Allan who was really Alan Herman had been delivering blood that first night, and he, in turn, introduced me to a British biologist who knew of a planned Republican assault at Cerro Garabitas. Ernest, going to observe it with Joris Ivens, was all in a twist about this first real assault, but he hadn't invited me along. So when the British biologist suggested I observe with him from a house on the periphery of the Casa de Campo, I went.

We had a pretty good view, and field glasses to bring it closer: the tanks dashing about; the soldiers running and dropping to the ground when the firing began, and getting up and running again; the big guns flaring and the smaller ones popping, the machine guns alive with Ernest's *rong cararong rong rong*. I couldn't bear to watch, nor could I turn away. If these boys could fight this war, then surely I could focus and remember, and someday find the words that might make others understand what I could not understand myself. How does an eighteen- or twenty- or twenty-four-year-old boy rush ahead with his life held up for target practice, in defense of something as nebulous as the right to govern oneself? Or not even that much, really. Only the right to elect those who will govern.

Hemingway returned the evening of the assault at Cerro Garabitas complaining of having been too far away, but saying still it had been exhilarating. I agreed about the exhilaration. The taste of that battle left me wanting to get closer too.

Ginny Cowles, who would become one of my dearest friends, joined us a few days later, walking Madrid's busted-rubble streets in gold jewelry and spiky heels as if she were Coco Chanel on the Champs-Élysées. She'd made a name for herself in an interview with Mussolini just after the Italian leader invaded Abyssinia, when every accomplished journalist on the Continent was begging for the chance. "I had the opportunity to smile at the minister of propaganda at a party when I was in Rome," she explained. She was the kind of swanky Bostonian who was invited everywhere, and she had the voice and vocabulary to prove it, along with long-lashed eyes in a heart-shaped face. If Dad would have said she was capitalizing on her smooth brown hair, well, she was just doing what we all did, using whatever advantage we had to get to a story that ought to be told.

Most days, Ginny and I went visiting at the nearest front, a good brisk walk in the rain, or I took the tram out to University City with my interpreter or went out with Ernest in his car. Madrid was surrounded on three sides by the Fascists, so almost everywhere you went was a front. I walked to the stone barricade where I showed my papers to a Republican guard in corduroy slacks and a sweater, who allowed me to get close enough to sop up the mud of communication trenches with my shoes and to burn my thigh muscles with crouching. We forever found funny people in the trenches, new faces, something to talk about, someone to write about. But still I didn't write.

Sometimes we visited the makeshift hospital set up in the Ritz Hotel, where stretchers were carried up and down the grand staircase and blood was donated by chandelier light, or the one in the Palace, needles and bandages filling its Empire bookcases while a sign at the concierge desk still offered "Coiffeur on the First Floor." I wondered, watching the nurses, if they bleached their hair and painted their nails the way they did to cheer the dying, or if that was the way they'd always looked, even before the war. Ernest never would go to the hospitals, so Ginny and I alone spoke with handsome soldiers who told us their wounds were of no importance, that they were alive and they would recover to walk with limps or they would see well enough with one eye, and the thing was the cause. Or they wouldn't talk; they would be left with no lips to talk with, from a plane crash or a shell or having been caught in a fire. They would find us to tell us a boy in room 507 had a whole mimosa branch in bloom, had we ever seen anything so beautiful? And we would laugh with delight at the unfathomably bright yellow, and I would inhale the scent of the branch, which was not mimosa but rather acacia, the scent of the soap made from these flowers in the boy's hometown of Marseille, which I took everywhere.

Afterward, Ginny and I often went shopping together, our feeble attempt to shake off the climb up the blood-stained marble steps and the stink of all that pain and all that courage. I ordered shoes from a cobbler. I priced furs I never imagined I would buy. But there was no getting away from the war.

One day, four women were killed in a shop's doorway. Three men sat in the same chairs where, the prior morning, others had been reading the morning papers and drinking coffee when flying shell fragments ended their quiet lives. An old woman and a terrified little boy hurried through the square toward the imagined safety of home one afternoon as a shell crashed into shards of hot, sharp steel that pierced the boy's neck. It happened, and because it could happen to any of us—anytime, anywhere—as long as it didn't happen to us, we lived as best we could. Women with market baskets remained in line, never mind the new round of shelling. Customers might heed a shop owner's suggestion to move back from a window, but they continued slipping on one sandal and then another, as if summer surely would come.

Ginny and I went together to Chicote's in the evenings, picking our way with a flashlight through the rubble to get a little tight with Ernest and Joris Ivens and Herb and Del and Josie and anyone else who would drink with us as we talked about the war and the world and what anyone with any sense was doing in Madrid in the spring of 1937. "Do our typewriters stand a ghost of a chance against machine guns?" we asked each other. "What good are words?" There was fear in the talk, and there was courage. You paid attention. You listened hard and you watched, always, and in the listening and the watching, you lived more fully than you ever had. Josie liked to say that security isn't the heart's true desire, that it's the unknown we long for. Maybe she was right for everyone, or maybe she was right only for a certain kind of person who drank in a bar in Madrid in the middle of a war and was happy to do so with anyone else who showed up to drink.

Ernest was at his braggart worst at Chicote's. It was true that he got to places others didn't because of Joris Ivens's political contacts, but the way he told the stories . . . "I was walking the battlefields with the general, suggesting strategies." "The kid aimed like a boy just learning to piss outside his diaper, so I took the gun and schooled him in how to shoot a Fascist." No one could know anything about the war he didn't already know. No one had maps like his. No one had food or booze or weapons that he didn't have. And when he wasn't telling the stories of his own bravery, he was pulling out his guitar and playing and singing loudly, and not very well.

"Josie," I said one night, loudly enough for Ernest to hear, "don't you think Scrooby here ought to do a piece on the fellas in the hospital?" Scrooby, I'd taken to calling him, like screwball but rounded like the sound of gunfire. I suppose I meant it about the hospital, but I was trying to win Josie over as surely as if I'd brought my little jar of marmalade to the lobby and joined her chat with the soldiers on leave. "Don't you think Ernest writing about the poor boys in the hospital would tell everyone as much as anything about what's happening here?"

Ernest laughed, which perhaps he didn't mean as dismissively as I felt it.

Josie said, "Ernest doesn't do blood transfusions or sawing off limbs."

Ernest laughed again, and he made quite a stink about what they'd filmed that day for *The Spanish Earth*, in case anyone might have forgotten why he and his gang went tootling off in two cars every morning while most correspondents took the trolley or walked.

The conversation turned, as it so often did then, to the number of shells that had fallen and the number of soldiers, packaging the war up in tidy numbers that could be boxed away.

Josie leaned closer to me, saying, "Ernest is no good at returning to what hurts him."

I waited. I've found if you can leave a silence alone, someone else will fill it.

Ernest pulled out his guitar and began to sing in Spanish.

"Scrooby," I said, "you know how much I love your singing, but here in public you're going to make all the whores swoon, you know you are."

It was a little lovable—his veneer of bravado meant to hide the same fear we all felt, the fear only a fool would fail to feel. The doctors hadn't been able to remove all the Great War shrapnel from Ernest's leg, and I supposed it said something about him that he was willing to haul it around this new war in his funny lurching gait. I supposed it made us all feel better about ourselves to see our own brand of fear under the skin of a man as outsized as Ernest.

"Scrooby," I said, "the *rong cararong rong rong* of that guitar is worse than the machine guns and the rifles together, never mind the singing."

"Daughter, this is as fine a song as was ever written."

"That may well be, Scrooby, but it's a bit hard to tell under the thick layer of booze."

Undeterred, he sang on.

"That girl in Milan did hurt him," Josie whispered to me. "What was her name? Maybe it's great for the rest of us because Ernest made a story from that hurt." Catherine in *A Farewell to Arms*, Ernest's novel about a love affair between the nurse and an American who drove an ambulance in Italy in the Great War, as Ernest had. "He was in love with that girl."

"In love with the nurse?" I said. I knew Ernest had spent too much time in a hospital in Milan after being wounded in that war, not as a soldier but delivering cigarettes and chocolate to the Italian troops.

"She gypped him, that's as much as he'll admit to. And nothing hurts like being in love and being jilted when you're nineteen."

Ernest ended one song and began another, saying this one was particularly for me—no doubt something about some woman who never was good to her man.

"The truth is he wanted to marry her," Josie said. "The truth is he was just a kid and she was twenty-six. Agnes. That was her name."

I wondered if the sadness in her eyes was all from her husband leaving her even though they'd had a "free love" marriage, even though she'd tolerated all the other women he slept with when she was his wife, or if Hemingway had broken Josie's heart somewhere along the way.

She said, "The truth is she wrote Ernest a letter saying she was going to marry someone else, and she ought to have told him in person, but his arguing wore her out and, anyway, she was afraid he would do something desperate."

Madrid, Spain

April 1937

Ernest's cranky mood the morning we set off with *The Spanish Earth* film crew toward the Guadarrama front might have been the simple result of a night so cold that the hot water bottles at my feet made no difference, and the morning's high explosive wake-up call. The sunrise view out my window, where a drunk had sung half the night (sometimes accompanied by music blaring from loudspeakers in the Casa de Campo), was of a single man who lay dusty and headless in smashed cement, steam from a broken gas main enveloping him. Downstairs, two workmen in blue smocks helped a woman into the lobby, her arms wrapped tightly across her belly, but the blood still steaming through her fingers. Even on the worst mornings, though, Ernest tended toward chipper. His foul temper was on account of a cable from the North American Newspaper Alliance that I'd gotten a glimpse of while he was holding forth over eggs.

We took provisions to stay out a few days, in case we found some action, and we traveled in two cars, Ernest and I in one, and Joris Ivens and the film crew in the other, the sun warming us as we made our way precariously through gorges and limestone mountains from which anyone might shoot. Ernest talked with soldiers we met in the road along the way, giving them cigarettes and telling them what fine, brave boys they were, asking them to show him how they used their weapons. He would lie in the mud to offer some improvement, not giving a thought to his own comfort. And when they balked at having me in their presence—a woman?—he responded, "Marty here is the bravest woman I've ever met. Sure, she hasn't undergone a true baptism of fire yet. But she's good for it. She's as good for it as any of you."

The countryside between Madrid and the Guadarrama front was so quiet, though, that we stopped our car for lunch on a blanket by a stream while Joris Ivens and his crew carried on to scout filming locations. We ate bread and ham and drank a little wine from a collapsible cup Ernest seemed always to have with him, and he continued to tutor me in the ways of war: hopping up to show me how to do one thing or another, and explaining that if you understood the tactics of war, you would have some idea of what might happen and when and where, and how to cover it without getting yourself killed.

"There's the getting the story and there's the living to tell it," he said, "and the first is no good if you don't have the second."

We lay on the blanket, looking up at the sky.

"You must write, Daughter," he said. "It's the only way we have to serve the *causa*."

"But I'd need something gigantic to write about, Scrooby. What has happened to me that hasn't happened to everyone here?"

"You know Madrid now, even if you don't know the war yet."

"Daily life doesn't make a story."

"Daughter, daily life in Madrid is a different thing from daily life in St. Louis."

If daily life in Madrid was worth reading about, though, he'd already done as much writing of it as anyone wanted to print. The cable he'd received (which I had better sense than to mention) read: "ADVISE HEMINGWAY MAXIMUM ONE WIRE STORY WEEKLY. ONLY WORTHWHILE MATERIAL." He'd wired off too many stories describing the politics and military tactics when, for $500 a pop, NANA wanted the war delivered right into their readers' hearts.

"I suppose I might write about the boys in the hospital," I said, rolling over to face him, wanting to give back some of the attention he was forever giving me. He'd once been a wounded boy in a hospital. He could make readers feel that story. He was so like Bertrand, with such a thick crust of charm and success that no one looked more closely, no one saw the thin fissures through which the real stuff he was made of oozed. He had such a thick crust that must have started when he was that boy falling bad in love with a nurse who loved someone else.

"The thing is to write something truly worthwhile, something they can't possibly reject and don't want to," I said as if to myself. "But I don't know how to write in cablese, Scroob." Cablese, the bare-bones language of cablegrams, every noncritical word pulled from a piece for the sake of cheaper and faster transmission. "I don't know how the spirit of a thing survives being reduced like that," I said. "It's the words that make you feel a thing in your heart. Not just the thing, but the way you tell about it."

As if I were speaking of my own writing. If you came out and said a piece Ernest had written had been the real gen until he boiled it down to cablese, he would give you what for about how wrong you were. You had to say it about yourself and let him loop it around his own neck, until it became something he thought to do himself.

"Then just mail the whole damned thing so nothing gets lost in the cable," he said. He reached up and tucked my hair behind my ear, repeating, "Write the whole thing and send it in, Daughter," the beginning of the loop.

A breeze kicked up, and I shivered, and he said, "You're cold, Daughter," and he pulled me to him. "I'll keep you warm."

I tucked up in the crook of his arm, his body warm alongside me. It was the middle of the afternoon, and it wasn't anything; it was just two friends helping each other, and if Pauline had read that cable criticizing Ernest's writing, she wouldn't have wanted him to have to bear it alone.

The front, when we'd packed up our picnic and carried on, was so quiet that we might have spread our picnic blanket there. With no war to film, we all climbed back into the cars and returned to the Hotel Florida for the night.

Ernest and I set out alone early the next morning toward the Jarama River, where the Fascists were trying to take the road to Valencia. We had lunch in a little nothing of a town—a church, a hall, a café, and a collection of stone homes in disrepair—and headed from there up through rounded hills of olive trees and grapevines to an old farmyard: wet and abandoned hay bales, a few chickens, a bony cat. The farmhouse—a supply station supporting the front but well behind it—was all whitewashed rooms and tidily made cots open to the day. In the kitchen, three International Brigade soldiers in baggy trousers and polished boots sat at a huge white table, peeling scrawny potatoes. They eyed me the way the soldiers in that war forever eyed any decent woman—hungry and confused.

Hemingway yammered with them for a good long bit before asking about going up to the front. He'd have to have a pass, they told him, from their headquarters across the hill. I offered them cigarettes, making sure to connect hand to hand with these men who hadn't had the touch of a woman in weeks or months. Moments later we were on our way to the house that was the headquarters, where my Italian friend Randolfo Pacciardi greeted us.

Randolfo's troops were fighting like hell to hold back a new assault, he told us. If the Fascists cut off the road from Valencia, the Republicans would have no way to supply Madrid. But it was too dangerous for journalists.

"You need the press there," Ernest argued. "You need the stories told so the world will see."

"The Fascists, from their position, can fire on the field you must cross just to get to the dugout and the trenches," Randolfo said.

"Their fire reaches behind the line?" Ernest said.

"You see what I mean. It's fine for you, Pops." He turned to me, fixing me with that gaze that was so hard to turn from. "But Marty, dear, this will not be like our quiet little jaunts around Madrid."

"Don't be an idiot, Randolfo," I said. "If it's as bad as you say, you need Hem and I *both* to go, so one of us will survive to write about it."

"But who would forgive me for losing the war's prettiest correspondent?"

"Really, Randolfo," I said, "Ernest is *not* that pretty."

Randolfo laughed, and Ernest did too, and Randolfo conceded. He arranged for two little stamped cards that served as our passes, and a boy to drive us in an open car with excellent tires.

We set off up a crooked, old donkey road, one widened to allow supplies and ambulances to reach the line but still a rotten road. It petered, finally, into nothing. We had to leave the car behind, to cross the open field on foot.

The view behind us as we walked up the hill was stunning: the fields stretching down to the farmhouse and Randolfo's headquarters, the olive orchards and grapevines, the church spire and the town, and, in the far distance, a man plowing another field. But the sounds ahead were of machine guns and rifles. *Rong cararong rong rong. Racrong carong carong.*

As we crested the hill, the boy dove to the ground, and we did too. Ahead, the field gave way to a chaos of craters and strewn earth, olive trees split open and circled with blackened branches.

The boy set off again, keeping low and moving quickly.

Ernest and I hurried after him, stooping as the *rong cararong rong rong* of machine guns began again, terrifying bullets whizzing around us.

Holy Christ, holy Christ, holy Christ. My thighs burned from crouching so low so long and running at the same time. My heart shredded from the effort and the terror that I wouldn't keep up.

If I were the boy, I'd leave me behind.

Up ahead, the boy flattened to the ground again.

I dove behind him. Ernest was beside me, one hand forcing my head down.

I lay hugging the muddy earth and praying to a god I wasn't sure I'd ever believed in, tensing in readiness at the boy's every twitch. I couldn't think for the fear. I could only run when he ran, and flatten when he did, and try to keep from crying from the pain and exhaustion and fear.

We moved from olive tree to olive tree, bullets rattling the branches and showering leaves down on us.

It seemed forever before we reached a dugout, which opened to a room with a table, a single telephone, and soldiers—Italian and English and American boys who looked at me with such delight that I laughed and laughed, and Ernest did too. We laughed with relief at having made it to their little part of this war.

"My sister would have wet herself before she made it here," one soldier told me, and another said his mother would have fainted—which would have saved her.

Ernest said, "Marty here is the bravest girl I've ever met, braver than I am." And I didn't believe it, not for a minute, but there's a difference between believing a thing a man says and being moved to hear it, and it did move me to hear it. It made me want to prove him right.

The soldiers made us hot coffee and explained their position and that of the Fascists. If they were heroes, someone else would have to tell you so. I offered cigarettes, again making sure to touch, and I admired their guns, and asked about their sweethearts, their mothers, their homes. They told me about Suicide Hill and took me on a guided tour of their trenches: soldiers manning machine guns, and boys lying with rifles aimed in the direction of the boiled ground and burned olive trees. Some of the guns were so ancient it was hard to imagine they would shoot.

We spent the night there, the soldiers insisting I have one of the camp cots in the relative safety of the control room.

"You can't deprive these boys of this rare opportunity to be gallant for the sake of a beautiful woman," Ernest said, "and anyway, nobody will sleep at all if you don't take the cot."

There was firing all through the night, and no chirp of birds in the morning, and as we readied to move on, one boy asked me to stop and see his brother, wounded and in a hospital we would pass on the return to Madrid.

"We're not going back to Madrid, not yet," Ernest answered. "You're not the only boys who need a good, long look at Stooge's legs."

"Of course we'll stop and see him," I said. "Your brother. Tell me his name."

A Village on the Jarama River, Spain

April 1937

Over dinner and drinks at a tavern that night, while another patron played guitar and sang beautifully for his friends, I asked Ernest what it had been like in Italy. "Was it like on that hill with those boys?"

There was shame in the way his gaze slid away from me, to the singer.

"When I heard the Red Cross was taking volunteers to drive ambulances, I resigned my position at the *Kansas City Star* and headed off," he said. "That was where I learned to write, you know, Stooge, at the *Star*. They gave me the best lesson I ever had in writing: short everything—sentences, paragraphs, pieces—and active verbs, and everything immediate and true."

Changing the subject lest I stumble upon a truth I'd already learned: they wouldn't let Ernest in the army on account of his lousy eyes. Why do the bits of ourselves we have no responsibility for so often torture us?

"And then in Italy?" I pressed.

He took a big slug of whiskey. I took a small sip, then a bigger one.

"Italy, that was a long time ago," he said, his gaze again trickling over to the singer and yet fixed in that earlier time. "A munitions factory exploded the day I arrived in Milan," he said, and he described carting out mutilated bodies and bodiless limbs and heads. His voice was dispassionate, almost dull, as if he could subdue the mountains of emotion with the steady plateau of his voice. "Two days later, I was sent to an ambulance unit in Schio, where, a few weeks later, an Austrian mortar shell struck just feet from where I was handing out chocolate and cigarettes."

July 8, 1918.

"There was one of those big noises, and I felt myself coming right out of my body, a handkerchief pulled from a jacket pocket," he said. "I floated above myself and then somehow came back and I wasn't dead anymore, not like I'd been at first, not like the soldier next to me still was."

The guitar player ended his song and began another before the applause could even really begin. Ernest drained his whiskey, then waved two fingers at the waitress, calling for another round.

"Did you pray as a kid, Stooge?" he asked me. "When I was a kid, we knelt down every morning in the first-floor parlor, where Abba Bear—my mother's father—read to us from *Daily Strengths for Daily Needs*."

The waitress set the fresh whiskeys on our table, setting mine beside my half-full glass and clearing Ernest's empty as I absorbed this odd, improbable fact offered up as a diversion or an intimacy, I wasn't sure which.

After she left us, I replied softly, "I never imagined you as someone who prayed."

"When I misbehaved, Papa gave it to me with his razor strop and then made me kneel to ask God's forgiveness," he said, laughing now as if he really did find it funny, never mind the deep hurt in his soft brown eyes.

"Mother liked to dress me up in dresses," he confessed with the same false bravado. But she dressed his sister in boy's clothes sometimes too, he said, and they'd held his sister back a year in the first grade so the two of them could go to school together. "No thought of putting me ahead," he said glibly.

"Every summer, we took the steamer from Chicago across Lake Michigan to Harbor Springs," he said. "There, we caught a train to Petoskey and a dummy train to Bear Lake, then a two-decker steamer around to Windemere Cottage, where I spent summers fishing for perch and pike and bass, and swimming with my sisters."

His gaze on the whiskey now. I watched him watch the whiskey, attention he must have felt, but like an animal who finds himself cornered, he sat perfectly still.

"No giant water bugs in the lake?" I asked finally, trying to answer his tinted humor with my own, recognizing it was my turn to offer up something.

He looked up, as surprised at the turn of conversation I offered as I had been at the twisting path of his. "Water bugs?" he asked.

"Thoroughly disgusting creatures that lurk in the ponds around St. Louis. Big as your hand, I swear. If one bites your toes—and that's what the vile things live for, to take huge chunks out of poor unsuspecting little toes—it's nasty business."

He laughed and he said, "A swimmer like you would let a bug keep you out of a pond?"

"Of course not," I said, laughing too—it felt good to laugh after the night with those boys. "But have you seen the scars on my toes?"

We sipped our whiskeys as the patrons around us sang along with the guitarist, Spanish words that were as rounded as *rong cararong rong rong.*

"I spent winters teasing my sisters incessantly," Ernest said, "giving them nicknames they abhorred."

"None of them so bad as 'Stooge,' I hope," I said.

"You're in a class of your own, Stooge."

I took a sip of my whiskey, which was growing warmer, more satisfying. I thought I ought to stop drinking, but I took another sip.

"I was called 'Rabbit' by an early love," I offered.

I wished I hadn't the moment the confession was out, as he looked at me with great interest, recognizing this as the little crack in my veneer that it was. *Rabbit*, Bertrand had called me, and I'd called him Smuf, and he took me so completely that he left me nothing of my own use. He was leaving his wife the whole time he was loving me, but he never could finish the task. In the end, I'd called him "the Angel of Destruction," although he wasn't the destroyer, really; the destroyer was his wife and my impatience, my bending to my father's will.

Ernest said, "I think 'Stooge' fits you better than 'Rabbit.'"

I slowly spun the whiskey glass with my fingers. He didn't press me the way I pressed him.

I collected myself and I smiled, and I said, "What did your dearest friends call you when you were a kid, Scrooby?"

"Oh no, you don't! Scrooby is bad enough." Laughing again that way he did, that way that allowed the steam of emotion a release that neither of us need admit. A graceful exit.

"I can come up with worse," I said. "Cottonmouth? Now there's a nickname that could bring down a writer."

"A manly, dangerous snake?"

"Little Scribbles," I offered.

"The thing about those 'Little' nicknames, though, Stooge, is that everyone knows they mean 'Big.'"

"*Giant* Water Bug, then."

"*Giant Water Bug?* It's a helluva name, Stooge, but it doesn't exactly roll off the tongue."

"I'll take that under advisement," I said, and I offered up in exchange for what he'd said about his father and the leather strop, which had stuck with me, that I'd had that hard time with my dad. Not that he was the one who called me "selfish scum" for loving Bertrand, but enough that Ernest might draw the conclusion himself.

"Dad died just over a year ago," I said.

"That was the darkness in your mother, in Key West."

The room had grown quiet. The singer's chair was empty, his guitar leaned against the wall.

"My father had the darkness his whole life," Ernest said. "He did himself in with a Smith & Wesson when I was twenty-nine."

He stood and went to the bar before I could say anything, and came back with fresh drinks, sitting again and saying, "You really were brave out there, Stooge."

"Did you have a nickname for the nurse?" I asked gently.

"The nurse?"

"The one in Milan."

For just a second I was afraid he might slap me, but he only shoved his chair back and stood, grinning in a way I saw was meant to put me at ease but didn't. He reached for the guitar and began to strum it and sing too loudly.

The guitar's owner appeared back in the doorway, understandably alarmed.

"Scrooby," I said in a gentle, teasing voice, nodding to the man in the doorway, "perhaps you ought to return that guitar to its rightful owner so we can get some sleep?"

Ernest handed the guitar to its owner as if doing him a favor. "You carry on, son," he said. "This lovely lady needs me elsewhere."

I felt my face flush, but I didn't rise to defend my virtue. It wouldn't do to tell him in front of the entire bar that I meant in our separate rooms, and my virtue was a shabby enough thing in any event. My yellow hair. But as we climbed the stairs, I said, "Thank you, Giant Water Bug, for saving me from having to report back to Pauline that you aren't getting your proper rest," invoking his wife's name to defuse any expectation.

Alone in my own room, I took my soap from my pack and set it at the edge of the tiny sink, and I washed the grit of war from my face and chest and neck, from behind my ears. I shucked off my boots and washed the dirt from my toes, which, despite all the talk about water bugs, were perfectly unscarred. I set my soap out to dry, glad for the lumpy mattress and the pillow and the walls, for the distance from the gunfire, for the booze in my belly, and for the more intimate glimpse of Hemingway.

We were back at the little supply farmhouse, talking to the soldiers the next morning, when we heard the groaning thud of a shell being launched, the flutter of it growing frantic and high-pitched far too quickly, whistling right at us, spinning. We dove into the trenches. We held our breaths, as if the shell were an animal we might hide from if only we remained completely still. I lay with Ernest on top of me, his weight anchoring me as the whine grew so piercingly loud that the sound alone might kill. The thing exploded in such a terrifying boom that it seemed a part of me.

By the time we climbed from the trench and shook off the bomb dust, the charming little farmhouse was a pile of rubble, the air full of the sounds of the boys trapped inside. We moved aside stones to try to save them, Ernest and the soldiers and I did. I was immune to it, I told myself. I'd seen this. I knew this. The twisted iron bed left by the shelling at the hotel. The man who lay dusty and headless amid the steam from the broken gas main and the blood steaming through the fingers of the woman brought into the lobby. The terrified little boy hurrying through the square, holding his grandmother's hand as the hot shrapnel pierced his neck. I didn't suppose I would have survived this time myself if Ernest hadn't taught me the different sounds of the guns, and when and how to fall flat. I recognized that debt even as I hauled off one stone and then the next, trying all the while to blot out the voices calling out for their mothers, crumbling my heart into hard little stones as if it were the farmhouse that had been so charming. Keeping myself to myself, careful not to touch these soldiers I'd been so careful to touch as I handed them cigarettes just days before, lest my crumbling heart landslide all of me into a dusty, useless pile.

A Hospital near the Morata Front, Spain

April 1937

On the way back to Madrid, we passed right by the hospital I'd promised to visit, a tired, old building kitted out with American-bought medical gear. "It's the poor kid's brother, Bug," I said when Ernest balked. "You were wounded. You spent how much time in a hospital half a globe away from home? Think what it would have meant to you to have Ernest Hemingway the Writer with a capital *W* visit you then."

"Bug?" he repeated.

"Giant Water Buggy Bug," I said. "Huge, nasty, ugly beetle-y thing that eats poor unsuspecting children's toes."

"Somehow, I don't think 'Bug' alone conveys that."

"Ah, but *you* know," I said.

He laughed. "All right, then. All right. You always get your way, don't you? Sure, let's stop at your lousy hospital for five minutes so you can keep your promise."

Love bug. The phrase came to me unbidden. But that was just a nasty thing too, stuck together after mating, even in flight.

Inside the hospital, the word that Ernest Hemingway was visiting spread like blood from a head wound. Soon, one of the staff was telling Ernest that a boy called Raven was keen to see him. Ernest allowed us to be taken to an upstairs room where this Raven was revealed as a lump of scratchy wool blanket, a scabbed face, bandaged eyes. The boy had been burned by a grenade, but he didn't mind the pain, he explained in words formed weakly from a lipless mouth. He only wished he could see what his friends were doing in the war.

I tried to call up the bravery Ernest had bestowed on me in the trenches, to will myself not to cry as I listened to the blind boy from Pittsburg who wanted to be a writer, who never again would be a boy any girl would want to kiss.

Ernest, speaking toward the boy without looking at him again any more than I was, told the boy what we'd seen at the front. He described it in detail so the boy could imagine it, laughing at the fuss the soldiers had made over me and only realizing as he laughed that the boy couldn't see me to know whether I was anything to look at.

"I'll bring you a radio the next time we come this way," Ernest promised the boy. "So you can hear all about what your pals are up to."

"Maybe John Dos Passos could bring it," the boy said. "He promised to visit me."

Ernest pursed his lips. He said, "I'll bring Dos to see you when I bring the radio," as if the idea had been his own to bring along a fellow writer the boy might just admire even more than Ernest Hemingway.

"Would you really?" the boy asked.

"I will," Ernest assured him.

"Soon, Ernie?" the boy said.

"Ernest," Ernest said.

"I can call you Ernest?"

"You can call him Bug," I suggested. "All his closest friends do."

"Bug?" the boy said.

Ernest said, "As soon as Dos Passos gets to Madrid, I'll bring him to see you. And I'll bring that radio."

"And Sinclair Lewis too?" the boy said, registering the reluctance in Ernest's voice that Ernest himself refused to acknowledge.

"Sure," Ernest said. "Sinclair Lewis too. I'll get him to bring his Nobel Prize along for you to—" *To see,* he'd almost said. He looked at the boy then for the first time since that awful initial glance, when we'd both seen that the boy couldn't see us look away.

That night, while Ernest and his poker pals were taking each other's money over a round table and a frayed deck of cards back at the Florida in Madrid, or I supposed they were, I rolled a blank sheet of paper into a typewriter I'd borrowed from Ginny. Hemingway thought maybe I could do it, and that was something, that was a whole hell of a lot. But how was it possible to explain this war? All you could say was one thing happened or another, but that doesn't really tell the story of the boy from Pittsburg left without lips, or the brother on the hill who might have had a safe life as a doctor or a dentist, or the boys peeling potatoes on the safer ground of a farmhouse only to be buried in stone. I stared at the blank white paper behind the metal holding bar, trying to recall exactly the sound of that shell coming toward us. Not how Ernest would describe it, but how I would. The thud of it launching. The cough and the whistle. The detail. The senses. The shape and cool smoothness of the telephone on the table in the bunker atop the hill. The guilty press of the cot on my back while soldiers slept on the cold ground. All the things Raven didn't yet know, but would.

I put my still-dirty fingers to the black keys before I could scrape my guts back inside where they belonged, where I liked to pretend they were all nice and tidy and invulnerable when any fool could see them caught in the tangle of my yellow hair. I couldn't write about the time at the front. I wasn't good enough to write that. But I could write about the way the women in Madrid carried on with their shopping. I could write about the silly hospital-benefit play a group of soldiers put on a few days before, a play that couldn't have been more amateur but still we delighted in it. I could write about how, after the curtain was lowered, the hero came out and apologized for forgetting his lines, and how enthusiastically we applauded him. A crowd can be pretty forgiving when an actor has learned his lines in a trench near Garabitas, in the midst of an attack.

I would write the piece, and I would revise it as best I could, and I would mail it to *Collier's*, maybe. I would let Ernest read it, or I wouldn't admit the writing to him, but I would write it and I would send it. *Collier's* would never publish it, but I did have the letter claiming me as their special correspondent, and theirs was the only publication whose address I had.

It felt so good, the sentences connecting toward something that might (with a lot more work) become a story worth reading. It was the only thing that didn't fill me with self-doubt, my writing. Not while I was putting the words down. After it was done, yes, but not while I was writing. The thing was to write my damned heart out, to have a go at doing something that would have made Dad proud.

The Hotel Florida, Madrid, Spain

April 1937

It wasn't late—not yet the 9:00 p.m. wire deadline—but I was asleep in my bed in my relatively safe back room, exhausted from the time at the front and the writing afterward, when Ernest barged in.

"Stooge, read this, will you?" he demanded, thrusting pages at me as I blinked against the sudden light.

"Scrooby," I said, "I think I liked it better when you locked me in all by myself."

"I've been writing like hell since we got back."

Writing like hell.

I sat up, registering the thud of a shell in the distance, its whistle mercifully far away. I took the pages from him. I thought to ask if he meant to watch me while I read, but of course he did, and there was nothing to calling him out about it. Anyway, I could see from the first line that he'd pulled his heart out and carved it into little bits.

It was a long article—too long to squeeze down and send by cable before nine.

"Bring me a whiskey, will you, Bug?" I asked.

By the time he returned with the whiskey, I was crying in the way I had been so careful not to cry in the hospital, in front of the boy. Ernest had delivered the conversation with Raven in all its rawness: the poor kid's vulnerability but also, as movingly or more so, Ernest's own. He wrote the truth of it, the sick relief we all felt on seeing someone like Raven. That boy was the one who'd taken it; we hadn't taken it ourselves.

He handed me the glass and asked if I'd finished. I took a big slug of whiskey, and, as he paced back and forth across my little room, I read on, heart-wrenching words about how that boy would have been honored for his sacrifice in prior wars, and how in this war there were no honors, no medals. The only things soldiers would take away from this Spanish war were their physical scars—blindness or missing limbs, missing lips—if they were lucky enough to survive it.

I finished, and I reread the last sentence aloud, about how changed war was now, and how, from it, you could learn just about as much as you could believe.

"You don't like the ending?" he said. "I thought—"

"I love every word."

He plopped down at the edge of my bed and gathered me in his arms like a toddler who just pleased his mother with a crayon self-portrait.

"I'm going to mail it to those sons of bitches!" he said.

"Of course you are."

"It's a fine piece, isn't it, Stooge?"

"It's a fine piece," I agreed.

He kissed me on the forehead, like he so often did, and I saw that he meant to kiss me in a different way, his eyes in the night as solid as the moon, and the night was cold, and there was nothing at all between us but the bedding, and the gunfire was awfully near, and before I could see whether I wanted him to kiss me or not, he kissed me on the lips. I thought I ought not to kiss him back. There was Pauline to think about, and maybe Pauline wouldn't mind the daughterly affections, but she wouldn't like this. But I thought of the boy too—Raven who had no lips. And already it was done. It was done and I felt it but good, and I wanted to kiss him back, I wanted to sink into the comforting alive touch of skin to skin.

I pulled back, all the selfish-scum admonitions puddling.

I asked, "Aren't you ever afraid, Bug?" Knowing he was even as I said it, from the story he'd written, the words he'd chosen to tell how relieved we all were that Raven wasn't us.

He reached out with his big, dirty hand, but gently, as if I were that crumpled farmhouse at the Morata front that had been so charming.

"You collect the fear, Daughter," he said, "and you pour it into the story."

I dipped my head against the selfish scum and the St. Louis rules and the second kiss I could see he meant to begin. One kiss was an unguarded moment. One kiss could be a mistake. A second kiss would mean something that couldn't be taken back.

"Without the fear, Daughter," he said, "what would we have to write?"

"What would we have to write?" I repeated, wondering how I'd never seen the truth of it until he'd said it. Wondering how he could be such a goofy Scrooby and such a dear, wise old soul at the same time, so warm and so full of the juice, of wanting to do what he could to make the world bearable and doing it so gloriously with his words and with his running across fields of machine-gun fire when he was already Ernest Hemingway.

"I suppose that's part of why I've come to Spain, Mookie," he said, and he put his dirty fingers to my chin, tilting my face to meet his gaze. "To see I haven't lost my nerve for war."

Mookie. Offered as casually as if we were already lovers. He wasn't just the kind of man who could stick in your guts if things went bad, though; he was the kind who could rip them out and leave them on the street for the whole world to trample. And things would go bad. There was always the closer look, and things always went bad for me, and if I had an ounce of sense I would pack my soap in my knapsack and find my own little corner of war, as far away from Ernest Hemingway as I could get.

But I was already falling. Not for Bug, exactly. Not for the whole Ernest Hemingway. I didn't imagine I could ever bear the guitar playing and the bad singing, the drinking, the need to be Ernest Hemingway the hero. And maybe I was just falling the way I always fell, except with Bertrand. Maybe I was falling for his idea of me, for the way I could wrap myself up in his confidence in me. But this one little bit of him that surfaced in this story of Raven, yes. That I already loved.

PART II

The Hotel Florida, Madrid, Spain

April 1937

It wasn't yet dawn, but Ernest, Ginny, and a few others were huddled in Ernest's suite making plans to film at Fuentidueña when the first shell hit the hotel. I woke in Ernest's bed to the smell of cordite and blasted granite dust, the high-pitched screams of women, the lower-pitched but no less frightened calls of men, and Ernest pulling me to my feet.

We all tumbled out of the room into a scene by Dante: Pieces of masonry fell through the skylight. Shattering glass sprinkled the banisters and the floors and the chairs in the lobby. Hot mist and dust. The clamor of guests. Even the staff was in a panic as the boom of guns continued outside.

Journalists crowded out into the atrium, most still in nightclothes, many in the company of the kind of women who would leave with more money than they'd arrived with the night before. A barefooted Dos Passos peered out his door, and Josie, with her nightclothes plastered to her skin, shot out from hers just as Ernest smoothed the dust from my sleep-tousled hair.

"How are you, Josie?" Ernest asked brightly.

She opened her mouth, but no sound emerged. She ducked back into her room and closed her door as if when she opened it again she might be greeted with a different morning altogether.

"Very considerate of the bloody water tank to take the shell for those of us who'll miss its warm water," Del said, eyeing my nightclothes as we folded into the stream of dazed hotel guests flooding the stairs, headed down to the lobby.

At the bottom stair, someone said to me, *"Voudriez-vous un pamplemousse, Mademoiselle?"*

A funny fellow in a blue satin robe handed a grapefruit out to me as if this were exactly why I'd awoken, to share a predawn grapefruit with Antoine de Saint-Exupéry.

He bowed to me, then turned to Ginny and, bowing again, repeated, *"Voudriez-vous un pamplemousse, Mademoiselle?"*

"My first shelling," he said, as if the eating of grapefruit to mark a baptism by shelling were as natural as champagne to mark a new year. He'd brought two cases from Valencia. I supposed the weight of the grapefruit in his hands kept them from trembling.

Another journalist held a coffeepot. It was empty, but one of the hotel staff filled it. A clerk toasted bits of stale bread on a hot plate. The maids began sweeping the glass from the chairs and floor.

Josie reappeared, sinking into her favorite wicker chair, dressed now but still uncharacteristically frazzled.

Ernest poured a full snifter of brandy and set it in her hands. He couldn't just give it to her and leave her to recover her composure, though: he began to lobby her to persuade Dos Passos to stop poking into the disappearance of José Robles. "You need to talk to Dos, Josie," he insisted. "The fool can't go around questioning the motives of the government. He'll end up in prison awaiting trial himself, like Robles certainly is unless he's off with some dame."

Josie took a healthy slug of the brandy. "He's dead."

"Who?" Ernest asked.

"Robles."

"José Robles is dead?"

If José Robles was dead, then his own Republican government had executed him, and they'd done it in secret, without a trial. If José Robles was dead, then the Republican government Ernest had risked his life for had summarily executed a patriot and friend.

"José Robles is dead," Josie repeated.

"Bullshit, Josie! How can you know that?" Ernest demanded.

"Shot," Josie said in a low whisper. "Executed as a spy for the Fascists."

"But he's no more a Fascist spy than we are!"

She drained the brandy and stood and smoothed her dress, and walked away, leaving Ernest trying to piece it together: Why kill Robles? Why entrust the secret that it had been done to Josie Herbst instead of to Ernest Hemingway?

Dos Passos appeared, with shoes on his feet now but still wearing his plaid robe. Ernest, unable to fathom how to break the news to him that his dear friend José Robles had already been executed by the good Spanish government, disappeared just as Dos caught sight of us.

Dos Passos raised one brow toward his balding pate, offering me a chance to deny that I'd spent the night in Hemingway's room, or to explain it as something other than what it was. I looked away lest he learn the truth about José Robles from the pity in my eyes, but looked back as quickly so that he wouldn't misread my compassion as shame. My own little bar of soap was still beside my own sink in my own bathroom, but that was a truth that would tell a lie on a morning already overrun with them.

"Congratulations on *Collier's*," Dos said.

Collier's had just accepted my piece about the bombing of Madrid and the play at the hospital, the actor apologizing for forgetting his lines. They wanted to see more too. Bug thought I should insist they pay me better, but I'd accepted what they'd offered and spent the first of it on the best damned champagne in Madrid. If I were as sensible as I made myself out to be in the piece, I'd have gone to my own bed alone, and early, but I'd drunk far too much champagne instead, and when Ernest told me I was even more beautiful when I was successful, I felt beautiful, and I let him kiss me the way I let him kiss me the night I read his Raven piece. When he touched me, I touched him back, and when he lifted me up, I let myself be carried to bed. I was lousy rotten at sensible.

"They mean to call the piece 'Only the Shells Whine' rather than my title, 'High Explosives for Everyone,'" I told Dos Passos, wanting to say too that they weren't otherwise editing the piece, they were running it just as I mailed it to them, but not wanting to brag.

"*Collier's.* That's big," Dos said. "Well, be careful, Marty. It's dangerous, you know."

He didn't mean the war, or writing for *Collier's*.

"Nothing at war is as clear and simple as in peace," I said, wondering if he was the kind of man who would tell Pauline he'd seen me leaving her husband's room in my nightclothes, or the kind who understood that I was no threat to Hemingway's marriage, that I was the kind who hid in coatrooms, while Pauline, like the Marquise de Jouvenel, would hold a husband simply by refusing to give him up.

Madrid, Spain

May 1937

A few nights before I meant to leave Spain, Randolfo Pacciardi invited me to dinner. It was invigorating to flirt casually over greasy lamb and red wine in tin cups with someone who knew what it was like to be here at the Spanish front. And I badly needed invigorating. The darkness was creeping in at the edges, where thrill ought to take up all the space. The darkness forever came when I could see the end of a thing. I couldn't wait to leave Spain, and I couldn't bear to leave it, and the closer I came to leaving, the stronger both feelings became.

I hesitated when Randolfo suggested a walk out near one of the fronts after dinner. As often as I toured "his front," this time seemed more fraught. But surely I was being unreasonable: timid in my final days here at war, or nervous around a man I did find attractive, or both. But Randolfo was so insistent that it finally seemed easier just to climb into the back of his car with him, his driver and orderly already in the front.

I accepted a tin cup of red wine from the bottle he brought along to keep us warm. Before I'd finished it, the driver pulled the car to a stop.

Randolfo topped off our cups, and he hopped out as his driver opened my door for me.

"Shall we see the front at night once then, before you leave us?"

I'd seen the front at night by then, and he knew I had. He had given Ernest and me the passes and had assigned the boy and the car to take us up to the front, the trip when we met Raven about whom Ernest had written so movingly that I'd fallen hard for him. But every time at the front was its own time.

We set out in the dark, sipping the tinny wine and talking about the war. Randolfo did most of the talking, and I did most of the listening. Men do think a girl is clever and fine if she does nothing more than ask questions and nod at answers, and clever and fine gets a girl who wants to report a war what it's hard to get any other way: access and information. Yes, I was leaving Spain, but I was already planning my return.

We got lost, or we seemed to. The idea that this military leader who buzzed around every bit of the Madrid front on his motorcycle might become lost here seemed improbable even as it happened. I couldn't exactly say that, though. I couldn't call him straight out on his little game any more than I could call out Ernest for his silly pretenses that made him feel clever or brave or lovable. And there was a thrill, too, to being there in the dark near the enemy lines—perhaps even over them—with a man who was doing the dangerous work of trying to save Spain, rather than just reporting the war.

Randolfo moved to kiss me. I thought to tell him about Ernest and me, to tell him we were headed to Paris together, where Ernest was to do a bookstore reading. But Randolfo was, like Ernest, the kind of man who was most attracted to women who belonged to other men, so I said simply, "Randolfo," with a gentle laugh to suggest I understood him to be joking. It's a tricky thing to fend off the advances of a man you want to keep as a friend.

After we'd found our way back to the car, finally, I relaxed. How much trouble could I get into with his driver and aide in the front seat?

Randolfo took my hand and wouldn't let go. I tried to laugh again, but it didn't work this second time.

"Randolfo," I whispered, "I can't be falling in with a fellow who is going to get shot before I return to Spain."

"I promise not to get shot before you come back," he said.

"You'll make that deal with the Fascists, will you? Give them your men, but not your own skin?"

"Don't leave, then. Stay here with me. Stay and enjoy this," he said, and he pulled my hand to the front of his trousers.

I yanked my hand away, horrified and repulsed.

Randolfo leaned close to me and whispered, "So brave about rifle and machine-gun fire, so frightened of sex!"

He laughed so joyfully that I almost couldn't bear to remain quiet, to allow the two men in the front to imagine what they might. But I remembered the soldiers laughing that first day Ernest took me to the park, when I'd given them cigarettes. What a girl is doing and what she is seen to be doing don't always line up, and a girl who protests only draws attention and doubt.

Back at the hotel, I raced up to Ernest's room. I didn't mean to tell him about Randolfo's advances—I admired Pacciardi for all he did for the cause, and it would only set Ernest off to think of another man trying to seduce me—but I wanted to be with him, and to see how the fund-raising broadcast he was doing that evening had gone.

He was just back himself, with no idea that I'd been out.

He gave me some copy to read, a new piece he'd been working on, and he poured us each a whiskey. He lit my cigarette, and then one of his own.

He said, "I ought to marry you, Mookie, now that half of Spain knows about us."

He meant as best he could to want to marry me, I saw that. I felt a little flip in my heart at the words, and I might have answered yes despite the fact that he hadn't phrased it as a question, despite the fact that the sex with Ernest was even shorter and sharper than it had been with Bertrand. But I saw that he didn't mean it in the way Bertrand had. I saw that he meant it in that easy way of a man making a promise he can't possibly keep.

I took a warm sip of the whiskey. I was just one woman in a long string of lovers he poured whiskey and lit cigarettes for, and took to bed only to climb out again and settle in with Pauline, in their shared bedroom in their mansion in Key West that did or didn't want a new patio, a saltwater pool, a wall around the whole property that would be no bulwark to Ernest's appetites.

I said, "I suppose a fellow as important as you are, Scrooby, does need two wives."

Ernest looked as if *I* were the one betraying us by having another lover.

"Pauline and I are through," he said. "We've been through for years. You've seen how it is, Marty. You were in Key West."

I closed my eyes to the Key West images: the talks in the garden, yes, but also the family around the table, Patrick's earnest face as he tried so hard to please his papa, and little Gregory hardly old enough to imagine a father who might not love his mama, even though Hadley and Bumby were proof of the thing.

"Pauline would have me in a cage for my entire life," Ernest said, "confined to the iron bars of cocktails and dinner parties and money and comfort no talent could survive."

But there were his sons.

And I'd done that before: I'd accepted Bertrand's proposal, and when his wife had refused a divorce, I'd been "Madame de Jouvenel" anyway. Bertrand meant it—I believe that to this day—but I learned my lesson but good from that love affair: a man who makes a promise he can't keep is just a man doing what men do, while a woman who accepts him is the worst kind of selfish scum.

I tucked my selfish-slimed heart back behind my bony ribs, and I said, "But there isn't a writer in this world who wouldn't swap places with you and your five hundred dollars per cabled story." Then, before he could turn the conversation, I set into the piece in front of us: a bit about the bombing of Madrid and the politics of the situation that was all news dispatch and nothing of the heart wrenching he'd written about Raven. The one thing that would distract Ernest from this marriage proposal he couldn't offer, even if I wanted to accept it, was criticism of his writing.

"This sentence," I said, and I read out a particularly good one. "Is it really as true as five minutes ago?" Undermining a line he was proud to have written and using his own favorite phrase to question it.

"Hell, Marty, you don't know what you're saying!"

He poured himself one whiskey after another as he berated me: How dare I question this? How dare I suggest I might know better than him about his own words? How dare I have an opinion about Spain that didn't line up square as the Lord's cross with his? His anger had nothing to do with the writing and everything to do with my spoiling his illusion of himself as a man who loved so passionately that he could set his whole life aside for a woman. He was angry that I'd backhanded his inane proposal, and he needed to off-load his anger without denting his pride, and my critique of his writing was the fighter I'd put into the ring for him to pulverize.

Paris, France

May 1937

"I've never read in public," Ernest told me. "What should I read?"

We were at the hotel in Paris, where we'd taken separate rooms for discretion's sake, but spent our days and nights together.

"Whatever you want to read, you silly Bongie," I assured him. "Don't you know you're Ernest Hemingway?"

It was rather adorable, really, how nervous the prospect of reading in public made him, his inability to face the possibility that even one person in the audience might fail to be moved by his words—although, of course, he wouldn't admit that. He couldn't say no to Sylvia Beach, though. When he'd lived in Paris as a young, unpublished writer, unable even to manage the small fee she charged to borrow books, she'd let him take for free any book he wanted, allowing him the self-education in literature he badly needed. Sylvia Beach supported writers: she kept a bunk on the upper floor of Shakespeare and Company, where you could sleep if you couldn't afford accommodations elsewhere, and a piano around which writers gathered to drink and smoke and talk. So the evening of the reading, we slipped from the wet Paris streets into the warm light of the bookshop on rue de l'Odéon, where Sylvia had arranged a joint reading with a poet, thinking that might put Ernest at ease. The chairs were already filled, with a spillover crowd standing about the store.

As Ernest hugged Sylvia the way he hugged old friends, or lady friends, anyway, the anticipatory chatter settled into expectant quiet. He sat at the table set up for him and laid the opening pages from his Cuban rumrunner manuscript before him. Sylvia said a few very kind words of introduction for a writer who, she said, needed none. Ernest looked up through his steel-rimmed glasses at the sellout crowd. I wondered if he saw *Ulysses* author James Joyce take a seat Sylvia Beach had reserved for him, in the back row.

"I don't know whether I can do this," Ernest admitted to the crowd.

Warm laughter. I'm not sure anyone believed him. He was Ernest Hemingway, after all. But his glasses were already fogging with flop sweat.

He read the opening paragraph slowly, in such a monotone that the old goober dread bubbled up in me. His protagonist was barely in the café in which the smuggler thugs would try to recruit him to run contraband when Ernest had to stop to wipe his glasses.

Several in the audience coughed into the quiet, but that might have been on account of the damp spring air.

He replaced his glasses and, gaze fixed on the manuscript, resumed reading.

After he finished reading the first page, he stopped to wipe his glasses again. My heart was aching for him. No one coughed this time, though.

Ernest replaced his glasses and looked out over the crowd.

"You can't say I didn't warn you," he said.

The crowd chuckled. Somehow, he still had their attention. Maybe it was the fascination of watching a great artist impale himself on the sword of their opinion or the specter of imminent collapse, or maybe it was the story, or maybe it was some of each. We do root for those we see struggling against their demons that so often resemble our own.

Ernest set the first sheet of paper aside and began to read from the second, his voice stronger now. He even looked up at the crowd now and then.

He was halfway down that second page—his rumrunner protagonist was telling the thugs he couldn't risk running contraband, that he made a living with his boat—before he was reading with actual expression. The thugs assured his protagonist that, with the to-be-ill-gotten gains, he could buy a new boat. The protagonist responded that he couldn't buy anything if he was in jail.

The audience chuckled at this last. Ernest looked up at them and grinned.

By the time the guns came out in the middle of the first chapter, Ernest was reading truly wonderfully, to a crowd awaiting every word. He read all the way through to the end of chapter four. When he finished—to great applause—Joyce nodded his respect, and got up and left.

Ernest sailed home the next day to Pauline and the boys, to fishing while he ought to have been finishing the novel he'd promised Max would be done months ago. I followed on the *Lafayette* to New York, arriving on May 23 to a throng of reporters at the docks wanting the scoop on what I'd seen in Spain—which was that the Republicans would win simply because they had an unlimited supply of guts. I stayed in New York to sort out a deal with William Morrow; the publishers wanted me to write a book to do for the Spanish what *The Trouble I've Seen* had done for the poor in America. I was intent, too, on convincing Mrs. Roosevelt to support bringing five hundred Basque children to safety in the United States, orphans with no hope of safety or security in Spain thanks to the Fascists and their German bombs. And I wrote her about Ernest's film, *The Spanish Earth*.

Ernest flew up to New York in June for the Congress of American Writers, at which we were both to speak about the march toward war. He picked me up on his way to Carnegie Hall, looking less healthy for his relaxing time in Bimini than he had for all the hard days in Spain. It was the dread of public speaking, I supposed, or the airplane booze he'd downed to ward off the collywobbles. Carnegie Hall held a lot more seats than Sylvia Beach's little Paris bookshop. Thirty-five hundred writers had crammed into them, with a thousand more outside the doors.

Ernest, whose glasses were fogged with sweat again, started slowly, his voice growing increasingly high-pitched, almost trembly, as he called for everyone to write truly, to write so that readers would feel themselves in the stories, to write only about whatever they believed to be the thing we ought most to care about. It was something, him so nervous and still giving everyone what for the way a preacher might. And the applause was wracking, everyone popping up despite the heat, stomping their feet and whistling and cheering as if Ernest were Babe Ruth returned to play for the Yankees.

I stayed after Ernest flew back to Bimini, to help with the editing of *The Spanish Earth* at the Columbia Broadcasting laboratories in the Studebaker Building on Times Square, where I was charged with the most important work: When we needed something to make the sound of a shell whistling, I made it happen with a deflated football and an air hose. My fingernails snapped against a screen for the rattle of bullets, not exactly Ernest's *racrong carong carong*, but surprisingly convincing. I snapped more frantically to simulate machine-gun fire.

I spent most of my time, though, sorting out how to get attention for the film, starting with Mrs. Roosevelt. She'd written that a mutual friend had been deeply moved by my speech at the writers' congress. When I felt discouraged, she admonished me, I should remember that we never know where the seeds of our own enthusiasm will find loamy soil. I replied extolling the moving details of *The Spanish Earth*: the plight of the Republicans fighting Fascism in Spain illuminated through the plight of a tiny village on a key supply road outside Madrid. It really was lovely stuff, the parallels and contrasts: The village fields were plowed by the peasants for food, while the Madrid streets were plowed by Fascist bombs. Where water ran in the fields, blood ran in the streets.

Hemingway returned only after we got the news from Spain that his German writer friend Gustav Regler had been seriously wounded and his Hungarian writer friend Máté Zalka killed while Ernest had sat in the sun with a big glass of his wife's good whiskey. There was no doing anything right for him after that. The film now had to be perfect; it had to rally American and European support for the Republicans, and it had to do it awfully damned quickly, which meant doing it Ernest's way and the rest of us be damned. When Joris Ivens kept insisting Ernest simplify the film's story—focus on the nobility keeping the land for leisure when it might feed starving peasants—Hemingway called the director a "little piss." "I'm the goddamned writer," Ernest told him, "and the writing is the story, and if you don't think I can tell a story better than you can, well then, you can go fuck yourself."

Ernest was less than thrilled with the plan to have Orson Welles do the narration too. "What the hell does a swishy theater kid know about war?" he groused.

Of course everyone knew who Orson Welles was. The actor wasn't a kid, even if he was only twenty-two, and he wasn't swishy either: he was six feet tall and two hundred pounds of solid, with the steamy good looks of the young Hemingway that had hung on my dorm room wall. Orson Welles had defied a government lockout to produce a prolabor operetta, and he was making two thousand dollars a week between radio and theater. The kid was smart, and the kid was damned good-looking, and the kid was a big success already, at half Ernest's age.

We were rolling the film in a darkened screening room—just enough light to be able to see the scripts so we could read along, there being no voice-over yet—when someone said, "Is it really necessary to say this here? Wouldn't it be better to just see the footage?"

Ernest, beside me, mumbled, "Some damned faggot who runs an art theater trying to tell me how to present war." He stood, his oversized shadow blotting out much of the film, which rolled on with silent images of soldiers dying in Spain playing on his body.

"Bug, don't be a fool," I said.

He stomped toward the kid.

The kid stood, his shadow casting onto the screen too, the images flickering across his tall frame as he took a half step back.

Ernest put his face right in the kid's space, and repeated, "What does a faggot like you know about war? Huh?"

The kid flapped his wrists, a gesture more dramatic in his shadow on the screen. "Oh, Mr. Hemingway," he shot back, "you're so big and strong, and you have so much hair on your chest."

Even I laughed. I couldn't help myself. The damned bit was funny as hell as it played out in the shadow on the screen.

Ernest picked up a chair—a chair, for pity's sake—and swung it at the kid.

That bit wasn't funny, but we all laughed—nervous laughter now—as Ernest, thank heavens, missed his mark.

The kid swung back at Ernest. He missed too, but that didn't stop either of them from trying again.

These two big bullheaded lugs charged at each other, their shadows casting across the projected images from Spain, where real men were fighting a real fight and dying for a cause.

Someone jumped up and raised the lights, so that the film and the shadows faded.

"Welles, you asshole," Ernest said, but he said it with a real laugh, and Orson Welles laughed too. Someone found a bottle of whiskey and some glasses, and we all got drunk together, Ernest toasting Spain and Gustav Regler and Máté Zalka, and even Welles. Ernest was never good at forgiving himself, but he was pretty good at forgiving anyone who would share a bottle of booze with him. He would forgive anyone who would support the *causa* and toast the memory of writers who were braver than he would ever be.

The White House, Washington, DC

July 1937

Ernest was in Bimini when the First Lady invited me to bring our little film to the White House: a screening for the president to be followed by a small VIP dinner July 8, which she couldn't have known was the day Ernest had been wounded in the Great War. The president, she wrote, would be pleased if Mr. Ernest Hemingway and Mr. Joris Ivens would accompany me.

Ernest flew to New York to make sure the film was just so before Joris Ivens and he and I—"trench buddies," I'd taken to calling us—headed with our film cans for the Newark airport. We checked in, and I dragged them to the airport buffet, where I ordered us each a fat turkey sandwich.

"The good Lord could be coming down to pass judgment," Ernest said, "and Marty would greet him with a spoon in her mouth."

I said between bites that, unless someone shot the whole White House kitchen staff, the food would be revolting. When they looked dubious, I offered to eat all three sandwiches myself.

"Dishwater soup, that will be the best of it," I said. "I thought I'd never again eat soup after I moved out."

"After you moved out? Of the White House, Stooge?"

It hadn't seemed so extraordinary to me that I had lived at the White House with the Roosevelts; things never do when you're young and don't know anything different, and it happened in such a roundabout way. I'd come back from Europe in late 1934 and talked myself into a job with Harry Hopkins at the Federal Emergency Relief Administration—seventy-five dollars a week plus a five-dollar per diem for food and hotels to snoop around the country. I was so outraged about the wretched treatment of the unemployed, though, that after a couple months I went back to Washington to quit, meaning to write an exposé. Hopkins refused to accept my resignation before I spoke with Mrs. Roosevelt, who, it turned out, had been reading my reports. She knew Matie on account of my mother's work for suffrage that had left me ostracized in the school lunchroom, so I supposed the name "Gellhorn" had caught her attention, although the First Lady's support for women journalists was by then already legend.

Mrs. Roosevelt arranged for me to talk to the president—over dishwater soup and chalk-dust veal. She seated me beside him at the far end of the dinner table, then shouted down to him, "Franklin, talk to that girl. She says all the unemployed have pellagra and syphilis."

"Which of course stopped the conversation," I told Ernest and Joris, and I took another bite of my turkey sandwich. "I'd be more help to the unemployed if I stuck to my job, Mrs. R. assured me, so I did, until I was fired—well, that's a whole other story—at which point the First Lady, worried I'd have nothing to live on, invited me to come live with her."

I thought it was quite champion, to be honest. I stayed with them for a few months, until a friend offered a quieter place where I could write my book.

"The president will have an opinion on the film, Bug," I said. "You'll listen politely, won't you? He *is* the president, and the point is to have the president screen the film, to have the press reporting that. When he offers suggestions, just remind yourself that he isn't a filmmaker, he's just the president of the United States."

Ernest picked up one of the sandwiches and eyed it warily.

"I've brought along my mustache and dark glasses, by the way," I said. "If you try to retire to the drawing room before we've hashed out the film, I'm as good with a cigar as anyone."

It was something to arrive at the White House with Ernest and our film that might rally the country to the fact that Spain was the last stop against Hitler taking all of Europe. Mrs. Roosevelt greeted me with a hug and a kiss. I introduced my trench buddies, and the president got a chuckle out of that.

Ernest settled from nervous into happy and nervous. He'd never been to the White House.

We handed the film over to the camera operator and, with two dozen other guests, made ourselves as comfortable as we could in the upright, round-backed chairs of the curtain-walled White House movie room.

Even as the lights were being brought back up, the First Lady whispered to me that she'd never believed all this State Department propaganda trying to paint the duly elected government in Spain as communist. The president excused himself for a few minutes as the rest of us made our way from the theater to the dining room: a Japanese gang conducting military exercises outside Beijing had had some mishap with a soldier, which led, in the way these things do, to mobilization for all-out war, and now the Japanese had taken a bridge the Chinese weren't keen to let them have.

The president rejoined us not long after we were seated at a single long table, with Ernest and Joris Ivens at his end and Mrs. Roosevelt and I at the other, and everyone else in between. After the first spoonful of soup, I mouthed to Ernest, "Dishwater," and he managed a nervous smile.

"The question," the president said, "is whether your film goes far enough in allowing the audience to understand the Spanish conflict."

I attended my soup and admired the new china Mrs. Roosevelt had ordered: white rimmed with forty-eight gilt stars set in a band of blue and lined with gilt roses and, in the midnight position, a gilt eagle with tricolor breastplate and olive branch. The president's words were something to consider. So often when you know a thing well, you can't see what others might fail to understand. You can't imagine that viewers, confused by the Catholic Church supporting Franco, might not see that he's the devil. You can't imagine anyone could prefer the admittedly more attractive and rich Fascists to the bedraggled but noble peasant Republicans.

Ernest set about lecturing the president as we soldiered on through a nicely wilted green salad and a healthy plate of rubbery squab. "All the nonsense against the Republicans, that's the Red baiters talking," he said. "The Spanish would wipe their country clean of the Fascists if we weren't making them fight with their hands and feet bound by all this neutrality . . ." He hesitated, groping for a word other than his usual "shit." "All this neutrality bunk," he continued. "We're neutral, and England is neutral, and France is neutral, and that damned Hitler says he's neutral while he sends planes and bombs and tanks to his Fascist pals."

The president assured Ernest that he was sympathetic to the Republic. "I cannot, however, single-handedly lift the arms embargo," he said. "I cannot ignore the Neutrality Act Congress just passed. I cannot ignore the request from the League of Nations that we remain neutral."

Waiters served the cake, which, having been sent by an admirer, was the only bit of the dinner or the conversation more satisfying than the china itself. Still, a well-placed article or two about *The Spanish Earth* being shown to the president might draw audiences to see it, and help them understand that what was at stake was democracy itself.

Pauline came up to fly with Ernest to Hollywood, where *The Spanish Earth* played to an A-list private gathering, to universal applause. The only thing about it, one prominent playwright suggested, was that Orson Welles's aristocratic narration was too smooth for the rough images of war. I don't suppose it took much to convince Hemingway to pop over to Paramount's Hollywood recording room and re-lay the track himself.

I returned from Washington to New York to work on my Spain book for Morrow, but the words that came were lousier and lousier. Hemingway had gotten into my brain, so that the words were Hemingway-esque, which was even worse than my own lousy brand of mud. I didn't know enough yet; that was the rub. I would have to head back to Spain to write this book, and before I could do that, I had to see Matie.

At the train station, I collected a ticket and the latest issue of *Collier's* to help pass the ride. There on the masthead was "Martha E. Gellhorn."

New York, New York

August 1937

Ernest returned to New York in August to give his editor the Cuban rumrunner book (with, thankfully, the cuts they had discussed). Perkins was in a meeting with another writer, Max Eastman, when Ernest arrived unannounced, but Perkins—not wanting to give Ernest a minute to again change his mind about the novel being finished—invited Ernest to join them. "I'm meeting with a friend of yours," Perkins said, never mind that Ernest and Max Eastman hadn't been friendly since Eastman wrote a critique of Ernest's nonfiction book about bullfighting, *Death in the Afternoon*, declaring it juvenile and without subtlety, written by a man who felt the need to convince the world he had "false hair" on his literary chest. The essay, "Bull in the Afternoon," had run in the *New Republic* and been reprinted in an essay collection that now sat in a jumble of Eastman's books stacked beside the black telephone, with the desk lamp shining brightly on it.

Sure, Ernest shook Eastman's thin, pretty hand, saying, "Eastman, old man," trying to ignore the sight of the essay volume, the damned critique.

Perkins breathed relief. He and Eastman settled back into their chairs, but Ernest remained standing. He walked to the window and looked out over Fifth Avenue. He told himself it was just a damned essay that no more than three pointy-headed intellectuals had ever read.

He returned to Perkins's desk to take a seat, but then changed his mind. He stood looming over them, not exactly meaning to loom, but not meaning not to either. With a grin that was meant to be playful but didn't quite achieve the goal, he began to unbutton his shirt.

"Look at this, Eastman," he said, thrusting out his chest, which was huge and suntanned and matted with dark hair. "Does this look like false hair to you?"

He laughed as if he were joking. He thought he was. He meant to be.

The two Maxes glanced at each other and laughed nervously.

"Why don't you show us *your* chest?" Hemingway urged Eastman.

Eastman glanced at Perkins, who was as much at a loss for what to do as Eastman was. He offered another nervous chuckle.

Perkins said, "Ernest—"

Hemingway interrupted, "Come on, Eastman, you old pussy. Show us your chest!"

Eastman stood. He loosened his tie and unbuttoned his top button.

"This isn't necessary," Perkins said.

Still, Eastman slowly unbuttoned his own shirt. His skin was pale, his chest hairless.

"What do you mean, accusing *me* of impotence?" Ernest said, again going for humor but now missing widely. "How many times did *you* jerk off last night?"

Eastman said gently, "Ernest, I didn't say a word about impotency." He nodded to the book on Perkins's desk. "You can read it yourself."

Max Perkins said, "Be reasonable, Ernest." He picked up the book and flipped to the essay, and began reading a passage in which Eastman did grant Hemingway a sort of courage—the courage to admit that he loved killing, that it allowed him to face down death. "This is you he's writing about, Hem," he said.

Ernest grabbed the book from Perkins and manhandled the pages until he found the other passage, the one about false hair. "Go ahead, read it to me, why don't you, Eastman?" he demanded. "Read it to my face."

Max Perkins said, "Really, Ernest," trying to calm him. Then to Eastman, he said, "Ernest has just finished a new novel."

"Have you? Congratulations," Eastman said, following Max Perkins's attempt to change the subject.

Ernest snapped the book closed right in Eastman's face, laughing as he caught Eastman's nose in the pages.

Eastman came up swinging.

As quick as anything, the two were wrestling each other to the floor, someone catching the telephone cord on the way down, sending the telephone and the books and papers and the lamp flying off of Max Perkins's desk.

Perkins scurried around the desk to save Eastman.

Eastman was on top of Ernest, besting him.

Perkins, imploring them both to be reasonable, pulled Eastman off of Ernest and put himself between them.

Ernest burst out laughing, as if the tussle had been in good fun, the way he had with Orson Welles at the screening of the soundless *The Spanish Earth*. A loss didn't count as a loss if it was all in good fun, even if a win always was a win. He picked up the telephone and set it back on the desk, gently replacing the receiver in its cradle.

Eastman said, "Who's calling on you, Max? Hemingway or me? This man is a lunatic."

Ernest went for him again.

Again, Perkins intervened, and Ernest, reluctant to have his own editor call the law on him, stood down. Already, his forehead above his left eye was beginning to swell.

"Now listen," Perkins said, "it will do no one any good for this to go beyond this room. Is that clear?"

Ernest returned to his editor's office the next day, and he apologized to Max Perkins, if not to Eastman. He was sorry, he said, if he and Eastman had broken the lamp—which he saw had been replaced. He said he'd gone out for a drink the prior night with the editor from *Esquire*, and the two had had a grand laugh over poor Eastman, whom Ernest assured him had looked far worse despite the purple goose egg on Ernest's forehead.

"It wasn't to leave this room," Perkins said.

"But it was only—"

"You can't expect Eastman to sit quietly while you put your own little version out in public for a laugh at his expense."

"My own little version? Christ, Max—"

"I'm quite sure Eastman would tell a different story if he were telling, which he isn't, Ernest. Not yet."

Ernest, somewhat chastened, said, "We should give Arnie the book. We'll give it to him and remind him mum's the word."

"Hemingway."

"I'll take it over to the *Esquire* offices myself."

Perkins lit a cigarette and inhaled. "All right. Sure, let's give him the book and ask him to keep it quiet," Perkins conceded, his words emerging in puffs of tobacco smoke.

In an attempt at humor and humility, Ernest took the essay-volume-turned-weapon from Max's desk and flipped to the offending page.

"Ha! Look at this, Max," he said. "You can see a mark from Eastman's nose on the page!" He laughed, oblivious to or ignoring the fact that Perkins didn't laugh with him.

Ernest picked up a pen and signed at the bottom corner of the page "for Arnold from Papa" and dated it.

"You can sign as witness, to make it official," he said to Max Perkins.

Perkins, somewhat reluctantly, signed too, and Ernest took the book to hand deliver it. At the *Esquire* offices, he wrote on the front endpaper—below where Eastman had signed and dated it the day of the fight and drawn, inexplicably, a six-fingered hand—that this was the book he'd ruined on Max Eastman's nose, and that he truly hoped Eastman would burn in a hell of his own making.

The story got out, of course, leaving Ernest little choice but to return to Perkins's office Friday, after Eastman had left for a weekend on Martha's Vineyard, to "make it right," as his editor put it. The way Ernest put it to me was, "Perkins told me 'no one has any right to humiliate a man like that, Hem'"—casting himself as victor, the one who left the unseemly brawl with his pride intact.

That was pretty much what Ernest said to the *New York Times* as well in his public "apology." "I feel kind of sorry," he was quoted in the papers as saying, but Eastman "shouldn't go around telling these lies."

Scribner would say nothing more than that it was "a personal matter between the two gentlemen."

Ernest, as he boarded the *Champlain* to return to Madrid, was hounded by reporters.

"The man jumped me like a woman clawing," he insisted. "I didn't want to hurt the poor schmuck. He's a sad old man."

When confronted with Ernest's quote, Eastman claimed to have declined to hit Ernest back, saying, "My dear old mama brought me up to be a better man than that."

Ernest had just finalized the Cuban rumrunner novel, now titled *To Have and Have Not*—not that that excused him, but if any writer is good in that moment of having to let go of a book, knowing all the wrong in it will be forever wrong, I don't know him. It ought to be such a glorious moment—a book is done!—but every glorious moment in the life of a writer is cloudy. Even the bits that are right in a book leave your soul ripped out of your chest and left on the pavement to be examined by every casual passerby. Ernest, after a start that left him the darling of American literature, had set his own bar so high that he couldn't possibly make the jump every time, but that didn't make missing it and having the critics slay him for it any more fun. And now it had been eight years since he'd brought a novel out.

To Have and Have Not was scheduled for publication October 15, an impossibly short two months away. His purgatory would be mercifully brief.

I sailed on the *Normandie* that August with Dorothy Parker and her husband, who were absolute dears, and the playwright Lillian Hellman, who eyed my tailored slacks and decent boots with her lidless eyes and asked if I meant to cover the Spanish war for *Vogue*.

"For *Collier's*," I replied, dismissing her crankiness as having more to do with having found her partner, Dashiell Hammett, in their own bed with a young starlet than with me. "I'm a war correspondent for *Collier's*," I said.

It felt so good to say it and mean it.

"Not that I don't think *Vogue* is awfully swell."

Madrid, Spain

SEPTEMBER 1937

The weather back in Madrid was splendid at first. We'd come the long way, touring the countryside with Herb Matthews in a Dodge truck, sleeping on mattresses in the truck bed and surviving on tinned salmon, ham, and coffee we boiled over villagers' open fires. We abandoned our truck to crawl uphill one dawn to a frontline dugout, where we lay on a straw floor, peering through a periscope to see sugar-beet fields warmed in the slant of morning light and, across the valley, five towers rising from within a walled city, and a looming outcropping of rock that was Mansueto, all of it heavily fortified, impossible to take. The going from Teruel had been even more brutal, on horseback with a cavalry escort up to the mountains, then down a steep ravine between Jucar and Huecar. We were so hot and dusty that, despite the nearness of the Fascist lines, we went for a swim. Ernest praised me for how tough I was about it all, and he seemed so proud, and I was a war correspondent for *Collier's*. I wrote my damned heart out, the real gen. I wrote my damned heart out, and, after we found our way finally to Madrid and the Hotel Florida again, I sent my pieces off and hoped to hell that people would read them.

Herb and Del had an apartment overlooking the Retiro Park, and Dorothy Parker arrived with her husband and a load of canned goods, but others we loved were gone; that was part of Bug's growing darkness—not just that they weren't there, but that they had abandoned Spain, or hadn't lived to do so. We went to a very sweet zoo with an elephant kept in an astonishing little Hindu temple, and to the flea market. We gambled at dominoes, and whenever the shelling started, we opened the windows to protect the window glass, and Ernest put Chopin on the Victrola—Ballade no. 3 or Mazurka in B Minor, op. 33, no. 4—at top volume. It almost drowned out the sound of the bombs, if you could keep yourself from listening too hard. But there was less and less to report, and Ernest was being paid so little by NANA compared to what he'd gotten in the spring. And of course there was the novel.

He'd been so sure *To Have and Have Not* was the best thing he'd ever written, his triumphant return, the way we finally convince ourselves about our new stuff so we don't kill ourselves in the space between when a book is written and when it reaches readers' hands. But the reviewer for *The Nation* found the book shockingly unprofessional. The *New Republic* declared it the weakest of Ernest's books, and the *New York Times*, finding it empty and mechanical and formulaic, declared that Hemingway's reputation was lessened with its publication. Sinclair Lewis wrote in *Newsweek* that Ernest needed to quit trying to save Spain and instead save himself.

I tried so hard to be sympathetic. None of us can stand to have no juice to write with, or to have what we've written pissed on, never mind both at once. I tried to focus Ernest on the few good reviews, and the good bits of the ones that weren't overall splendid. I tried to focus him on the cables from Max Perkins saying the book was selling terrifically. But I was increasingly a target of his crankiness. He didn't have Sidney Franklin to cater to him in Spain this time, and I wasn't the type to cook a big breakfast, or even get up to eat with him. He wanted people around all the time, and I liked a little quiet sometimes. And sex was always more difficult than it ought to be, more painful. Ernest seemed always to want it, every day and then some, and I wanted to be good to him, I did, but there were so many times when I didn't want it: when I was having my period, of course, although he insisted that was the safest time of all; when I had bathed and was nice and clean; even in the middle of the night, when he had had a nightmare and woke me to keep him company.

I had no juice to write with either; nothing happening to stir the juice, and it's a hard thing to be forever taking it from a crank and saying you love him anyway and trying to make him feel better when you're the dregs yourself. And of course there was the fact that those reviews of his book all came to him with letters from Pauline, that she was still being the good wife even though she must have been torn apart by its depiction of a marriage that must have looked to her very like her own.

Our solution was increasingly to drink too much and sleep too little and eat poorly, to have squabbles over everything from our sex life to the war to the writing itself, tearing at each other's egos in little bits. I tried not to think of the way Ernest had been with Pauline at that first dinner in Key West, the two of them sniping at each other over whether Ernest should go to Spain or stay home and love his family.

I turned to writing a long piece for *Collier's* that evolved into a meditation on the who and why of the soldiers coming to Spain from around the world. I began a new book, also about Spain. I started making plans for a lecture tour of the United States, to rally support for the cause.

"What the hell good will it do to abandon me here just to rant at a bunch of pansy-assed homebodies who don't give a damn about anyone who doesn't live in Poughkeepsie?" Ernest wanted to know.

"This agent tells me a lecture tour will raise money for the cause, and visibility too. And I'm chewing cement here is the thing, you know I am."

Neither the *Collier's* article nor the novel was shaping up to be anything.

"You can't whine about it, for fuck's sake," Ernest said. "A real writer never whines about the writing. A real writer sits down and writes." Never mind that he whined about the writing going so poorly for him too. Still, he did write. He was better at that, he was. He had no juice in the midst of those dreadful reviews, but still he got up each morning to write.

"Fine, go on your damned tour, then," he said. "I ought to go home to Pauline and the kids anyway."

"Sure you should," I said, even though I didn't mean it, that was just my own darkness talking—my own darkness made worse by my inability to sleep for Ernest forever waking me, by the sleeping pills that left me dull in the morning, by the forever thinking about the soldiers I interviewed. And there was the new play Ernest was writing, in which a rowdy American journalist hero—one who was just like Ernest right down to the love of raw onions and the nightmares, except that he was also a very noble secret agent for the Republicans—lived in rooms like ours with an American correspondent who went to Vassar rather than Bryn Mawr but had my blond hair and my legs and a silver fox wrap just like the one I'd purchased with some of my *Collier's* money, and who was an utter fool. He was calling the play "Working: Do Not Disturb," too, as if I were keeping him from working rather than working like hell myself.

One afternoon, we bumped into Lillian Hellman at the censor's office. The playwright had just arrived in Spain that very day, and was clearing remarks she was to give in a radio talk from Madrid that night. Ernest told her we were cooking up some beef he got from a bullring, and she'd better come, it was the only time she would see beef in Madrid. So she joined us at Herb and Del's penthouse, arriving with tins of sardines and pâté and the same bitterness to me she'd shown on the ship. She was treated to a rare piece of beef and an absolutely raw Ernest, and she promptly set to her chosen sport for the evening, which was to make me look ridiculous.

"You mean to go home to talk about what's already done when you might stay here and write about what's to come?" she asked, helping herself to more of the red wine, which was the only part of the meal other than her own canned goods she found tolerable.

My St. Louis manners were all that kept me from pointing out that I'd spent a helluva lot of time in Spain by then, and she'd just arrived, and yet she chose to sit here, drinking with friends, rather than having a look at a war she was to tell the world about by radio five minutes after she finished her sardines. A chauffeur was to pick her up from the apartment and take her straight to the broadcasting facilities.

"You can deliver passion in your writing about it, Lilly, sure," I said, "and maybe folks will read it, or maybe they'd rather read the funnies page. But it's something to call it out as special, to sell tickets and make it an event. It's something to hear about it from someone who's actually been here." Not going light on the "actually been here" bit, to tell the truth.

Ernest said, "And Marty here, she can quack as well as anyone."

He was drunk. He'd started drinking back in the room, and he'd tried to get me to drink with him, and he'd wanted to have sex too, but I'd only just finished cleaning up.

"I am an awfully loud duck," I agreed, trying to keep the hurt from my voice and remembering how hurt he'd been when I'd kept my clothes on rather than falling in bed with him. "And I can flap and I can fly."

"And lay rotten eggs," Ernest said.

Lillian yipped her thin, little laugh, with her thin lips and her gummy smile.

"Marty here has lost her cojones," Ernest said. "She wants to be seen as a war reporter, but she's afraid of getting hurt."

"Bug!"

"She means to go back to safety, to money grub at Spain's expense, telling everyone she's been such a brave girl and they should open their pocketbooks for her."

"It's for the cause," I said. "The money we're raising with the lectures will all go to the cause."

"Except the most of it that will pay for your first-class trains and your fancy hotels and probably a new fox stole."

We were saved from ourselves by the beginning of a bombardment, which we all rushed out to the terrace to see—all of us except Lillian, who sank into the sofa and buried her head between her knees, crying in fear.

The sight of the night bombardment was something, a fireworks show over the Telefónica, with shells bursting everywhere and the dust starting to kick up, reaching us even from the distance of the terrace. We didn't speak about it. We just stood there and watched the bombs fall until the apartment phone rang, with Lilly still trembling on the couch.

It was the radio station calling to say the broadcast had been canceled, as the streets weren't safe. She should tell the chauffeur when he arrived. But when the car showed up, Lillian gathered herself to go.

"Lillian, don't be an idiot," Ernest said.

"It may be my only chance to do this," Lillian said, as if she hadn't just been wetting her panties over bombs that weren't even hitting the building.

"Ah, a woman with cojones," Ernest said. "*You* won't head home the minute you've been fitted for a fur and shoes."

In the privacy of our rooms back at the Florida, I put on the Chopin mazurka Ernest loved, thinking it might soothe us both, saying as I set the needle to the record, "I don't blame you for being cranky, Bug. I know you're hurt about the reviews, but you can't—"

"I can't?" he said as the piano notes tinkled in their quick minor tone. Then, shouting, "I can't! I can't I can't I can't! That's all any woman is good for, to keep me from doing the things I need to do!"

I accidentally knocked the Victrola's arm, which skittered off the record and began scratching out an awful static.

He said, "You start all lovey and tender-taking-care-of-me, and the next thing I know your claws are all in my talent!"

"I do no such—"

"You do! You fuck my talent!"

I turned back to the Victrola, lifting the arm to try to save the needle, which was already ruined, thinking the only fucking I ever did was in service of his ego, to keep him from falling too deep into the dark sludge pit of having no war to write about.

He grabbed my arm so tightly that it hurt.

"Let go of me!" I demanded, pushing hard on his chest that he was so proud of, then raising my knee for his more precious parts.

He backed away faster than you would have imagined he could after all that booze.

"Your damned talent that you spend making a fool of me in your play?" I said. "Sure, that's talent, 'Working: Do Not Disturb.' A hero that is you all fine and noble, while the leggy girl that's me is the worst thing that ever happened to any man on earth."

He swung at me but missed, instead clipping the bedside lamp. It crashed to the floor in a terrible rumble of shattering porcelain and smashing shade and the tinkle of the light bulb going dark in a thousand pieces all at once.

We looked from the lamp to each other in the dim light.

"Oh shit, what kind of idiot Bug will I be without even a light to impale myself on?" he said.

And we started laughing, the fever broken.

"Be careful, Mookie," he said. "You don't want to step on that glass with your scarred little toes."

"I still have my shoes on."

"Damn, even your shoes? I've been trying to get you out of your clothes all day, and I've made no progress at all?"

We laughed again, and he came to me and kissed me.

"I'm sorry, Bongie," I said. "I'm a jungle beast, I am. I'm just a jungle beast and the juice is sour and I . . ."

I touched the side of his face. He was all scrofulous, Gellhorn style, and lovable, really, he was. And I knew how it was to have the writing terrors, and I said, "I do love your talent, Bug," which was the truest way I could say it. I loved his talent always, even when I didn't much like the rest of him. I wanted to be a part of his talent. I wanted to climb inside it and wallow in the good of his words. I wanted him to be writing some marvelous new *A Farewell to Arms* but with a Catherine who was the bravest girl he ever knew, braver than him, and me writing a *The Trouble I've Seen* about the fine people of Spain, and the two of us reading each other's work and talking about the writing, making it better together. I wanted the two of us to be climbing into bed at night and snuggling and kissing, and getting up in the morning with the juice to write, to make the whole world see that a bigger war was so close it was painful, that if they didn't pay attention to what was happening in Spain and what that madman Hitler was doing, and his buddy Mussolini too, we would all be done for but good.

The day before my twenty-ninth birthday, Ernest and I went down to the Fifteenth Brigade headquarters at the old mill at Ambite to celebrate the anniversary of the International Brigades' arrival in Madrid. We went with Herb Matthews and two poets we knew, and I wore woolen underwear for the onslaught of speeches and toasts, red wine, photographs, and film. When Bug took his glasses off for the camera, it touched me to see him be so publicly vain, and I thought I really did love him and he really did love me and it was just everything else going wrong—the Republican prime minister establishing a secret police with secret prisons and secret payrolls while the Fascists took all of the north of Spain.

Back in Madrid that night, we went from a street parade to a party thrown by some Russian friends who poured us too much vodka, and on to the Alianza to drink more and to sing and dance until three in the morning. Happy birthday to me.

I slept well past noon, and woke hungover, and not even the gorgeous flowers or the caviar and pâté en croûte Herb brought me that evening, nor the champagne and Château d'Yquem Bug opened, could relieve the pall of the news that greeted us: the word was out about Ernest and me back home. Matie would know. Pauline would know, too, if she cared to.

By the time Pauline cabled that she was coming to Spain for Christmas, it seemed hardly to matter. I supposed I ought to leave Ernest to his good, indulging wife. I supposed I ought to go home before my speaking tour to see Matie, to bask in the St. Louis horrors that beckoned now as some kind of relief. I thought I'd like to lie in bed and have Matie put her hand on my forehead, to go to Creve Coeur Park and read poetry. But St. Louis would be no good for me, and if I were reading poetry by a waterfall when another Máté Zalka died, I would never forgive myself.

So I stayed with Ernest, and I tried to hide the darkness away as Dad forever made it clear I should, the way Ernest often seemed to think I should as well. So many times I just wanted to curl up in bed and cry, like when the secret police came for Ilsa Kulcsar from the foreign press office, charging her with living with one man when she was still, technically, married to another (as if she'd pretended anything else), or when my Russian military adviser friend Mikhail Koltsov showed me the cyanide pill he carried always, lest he live to give the Fascists proof of Russian soldiers fighting with the Republicans. It had become impossible to look away from what I suppose we'd known all along but couldn't bear to see—that, indeed, the Republicans weren't any saints.

A few days after Pauline's cable, in the midst of another shelling, Ernest abandoned a lunch with the chief of the new secret police—a scoop for him—and hurried through the mud and splatter of shells to make sure I was safe.

"Marry me, Mookie," he said the moment he found me. "Tell me you'll marry me."

He meant it this time. He would leave Pauline for me. It was there in his big brown eyes and square, sturdy chin and furrowed brow, in the panic that he might have lost me before he could truly ask me to spend my life with him.

The thing is, you can't say yes to a man who has two young boys at home hanging in the balance unless you're dead sure, and maybe not even then. I ought to have said no from the beginning, but we were in Spain in the middle of a war, with all the needing to live every minute just in case there weren't many more, and I knew he would never leave Pauline without being sure of me, and there was safety in that. That was how I loved him. I loved him for his words and what they could do, how I could help him through it and he could help me—but without any threat to Pauline and Patrick and Gigi, or to his life back in Key West.

"You can't ask me that, Bug," I said gently. "It's not fair to ask me that when you can't mean it. It's not fair to Pauline or to Patrick and Gigi."

He flinched at the sound of his sons' names, but the certainty in his eyes didn't waver.

"It's not fair to me to make me be the reason for you leaving them," I said. "It's not even fair to yourself."

I left Madrid alone this time. I went to Paris, where I quickly became sick with the abundance of overrich food and the tasteless indifference to the plight of Spain by everyone I met. I retrieved my latest royalty check for *The Trouble I've Seen* from my French bank, and I divvied up the list of expenses I'd kept track of, and I sent my share to Ernest with a short letter saying that the royalties came from the best thing I'd ever written and paid for the best thing I'd ever done in my life, which was to go to Spain. I wrote him again from the *Normandie*, headed home in a foul cabin in which I was, nonetheless, trying to write. I wished a Merry Christmas to Pauline and him. I'd wanted it to be done one way or another, and now it was.

On a Lecture Tour in the United States

January 1938

"Both Sides of the World," we'd decided to call my lecture tour, which the Post Agency had booked for twenty-two cities. I'd thought folks might balk at a twenty-nine-year-old insisting on her view of how the world should be run, but crowds showed up in Milwaukee and Montclair, in Newark, at the Des Moines Women's Club, at the Sheldon at home. I tried to make each and every one of the people who attended—conservative Midwesterners and East Coast liberals alike—understand that Spain was the one single place in the world where Fascism might be wrestled down into the grave it deserved. Some audiences asked me silly things like whether I thought women should marry and why I didn't wear hats, and their obliviousness to what was happening in Spain was often astonishing. I wanted to put a copy of "Men Without Medals," just out in *Collier's*, in their hands, and say, "Look here, just read, for God's sake, will you?" and refuse to say a word until everyone had finished reading and looked up. It was impossible, trying to make people see before the end of a one-hour lecture what so few really cared to face.

At the Nineteenth Century Women's Club in Chicago on February 3, a woman in pretty pearls and steel-rimmed glasses came up to tell me how very much she'd enjoyed the speech. Grace Hemingway. I wondered how Ernest's mother could have kept hidden in her tidy white hair and generous smile the horns and fangs her son claimed for her.

In St. Louis, my morning copy of the *St. Louis Post-Dispatch* sported a photograph of Ernest at Teruel, wearing his glasses and his ridiculous stocking cap even though there was a photographer with a camera pointed at him. Vanity, where have you gone? He looked as tired as I felt, which was awfully damned tired; my hair was limp and thinning, my skin and my spirit wan, and I was losing weight like a boxer trying to move to a lighter class, but without the trying. Seeing the photo made me so sad to have left Spain and Ernest, who had by then come home himself. Max Perkins told me that despite all the rot in the papers about how happy Ernest was to be back with his family in Key West, all he really wanted was to return to Spain. Max was worried about him. Rumor was Ernest was drinking fifteen or more scotches a day, while Pauline carried on as if everything was just la-di-da.

I cut out the photo and wrote a note saying it would grieve me forever not to have stayed in Spain and returned to Teruel with him, and I mailed it off before I could change my mind.

On doctor's orders, I canceled the last few tour stops and settled in to Matie's care and to a new resolve to be a writer, and just that. Matie took me to Florida, for the warmth and the rest.

On March 4, Ernest came up from Key West to see us. "I've missed you, Marty," he said.

I said I hoped he had a nice Christmas with Pauline.

He said, "Pauline couldn't get papers to get to Spain."

"And you didn't join her in Paris?"

"No."

"But here you are, in Key West."

"Here I am in Miami, Stooge."

We were in Miami together—Matie and Ernest and I—when we heard the news that the Fascists, who had retaken Teruel just days earlier, were splitting the remaining Republican forces in two. The story was a half column buried on page 11. Ernest and I slept together that night, not for sex but for the warmth and comfort in our despair, and we stayed up half the night making plans to meet as soon as possible in Paris, to return to Spain.

Before we could sail, Hitler marched into Austria, crossing the border himself at his birthplace of Braunau to crowds waving swastika flags and cheering "Heil Hitler" in the streets. When the little madman himself stepped up to speak from the balcony of the Imperial Palace in Vienna hours later, he proclaimed to a square packed with enthusiastic Austrians the reunification of their country into Germany—the Anschluss—without anyone having fired a shot.

Ernest arranged a new contract with NANA and flew to New York—with Pauline, but I was tired of caring about that, tired of spending my energy on anything but my work. He sailed on the *Île de France* on March 18, while I arranged for *Collier's* to sponsor my trip and sailed the following week on the *Aquitania*. I shipped a car for us to use in Spain, and cabled Ernest to meet me in Cherbourg on the twenty-eighth. At the last minute, I added ten words to the cable: "If anything ever stops our working together, then future nix." The wording, I see in retrospect, was open to so many interpretations, and prescient too.

I arrived in France to find Ernest all wrought up about a piece Dos Passos had written for *Redbook* that Ernest had read on the ship.

"He hates the communists so much now that he's attacking—for money!—the good people of Spain. Honest ol' Dos Passos will knife you in the back for two bits," he said, "and your sister for four."

"Really, Bongie," I said, "does that matter now? The thing is the good people of Spain being slaughtered while the rest of the world buys tickets and popcorn." The Spanish Republic was in danger of collapsing within days. The world idled while Germany and Italy sent to the Fascists a new kind of bomb that exploded sideways to make sure as many poor sods as possible were killed. "You've got to do something, Ernest," I said. "You've got to yell at everyone until they help!"

He flew shortly thereafter to St.-Jean-de-Luz to call on the American ambassador to Spain, and maybe it was his doing or maybe it was coincidence, but days later the French opened their border to evacuate the wounded and promised to ship planes and artillery to the Republicans. Ernest caught a night train from there while I set off in the car, both of us headed back to Spain.

We met up again in Barcelona for the bad grub and dirty rooms of the Hotel Majestic. I did have my own soap, as always, which Hemingway declined to share even though there was no other soap to be had in the whole city, leaving the hotel maids with nothing to do but iron the dirty sheets and remake the beds with them. But Herb Matthews was there to help us drink away the bad news every evening, and to get up before dawn with us and set off across the pink-blossom-dotted hills, Ernest in his driving cap, Herb puffing on his cigar, and me holding tightly to a scarf to keep the dust from my hair in the open car. It was warm and muggy, but the thunder was manufactured, and I'd never seen a world so thoroughly destroyed.

Del rejoined us in mid-April—Good Friday, which was only good that year if you liked a four a.m. sunrise over refugees carrying almost nothing on account of leaving their homes in a terrible rush. We'd already spent days being strafed by Fascist planes as we wove between boxes of dynamite set to blow the stone bridges in the event of a Republican retreat. It was all so bleak, and yet we picnicked on mutton and tomatoes and onions at a communist headquarters in the middle of a vineyard, and when a shell landed not more than a football field away, someone said, "That sort of shooting isn't serious," and poured more wine. Hemingway was as happy in this bleakness as I'd ever seen him, and I felt happy too.

On the way to Tortosa on the Ebro Delta, Herb, Del, Ernest, and I watched for nearly an hour as twelve German planes flying in perfect formation bombed and bombed and bombed the same single company of Republicans, who had no antiaircraft with which to defend themselves. We crossed the swollen yellow river on a great steel bridge, and we turned left onto the Valencia highway, toward Ulldecona, wondering now where the war could have gone. Motorcycle couriers raced by, but even they didn't seem to have any idea what was going on.

We stopped in an olive grove with four other journalists as in the dark as we were, but a quartet of soldiers huddled over a map up the road enlightened us: the Fascists had broken through the government road, cutting off the Republicans. Not wanting to be trapped by the Fascists, we hightailed it back toward our sturdy bridge, counting and making notes as thirty-three silver Italian Fascist bombers flew overhead, again in perfect formation. A clear blue sky too. Fine bombing weather.

The sky in the direction of the bridge was soon clouded with smoke and dust. But with no alternative, we retraced the newly bombed roads to find our sturdy bridge now a pile of rubble largely buried in the rushing river. The only way across was a rickety footbridge soldiers were trying to fortify.

Del said, "It won't take the car."

Herb said, "Without the car, we're done for."

I said, "Those bombers could return any minute."

Ernest said, "We'll be the easiest target that ever was if we're crossing that bridge when they do."

A mule cart set off across the thing. We watched it for a minute.

We had no choice but to go, and to go fast.

Ernest and Herb climbed out of the car to lighten us, and Del let out the clutch, and we followed well behind the mule cart, which rattled the wood planks ferociously.

There was a hole nearly as big as the car in the middle of the bridge, out over the river. I tried not to look as we approached it.

I kept making notes, writing down each detail so I could write it well. I was Bug's brave girl again, and he was my funny trench buddy, and I was a good swimmer, I told myself. I was an awfully good swimmer.

Marseille, France

May 1938

Back in Madrid without, thankfully, having to survive a fall from that bridge or a dip in the river, I cabled *Collier's* that I meant to write a piece about the refugees we'd seen on the Barcelona Highway—a young woman with a canary, an old one holding a single chicken cradled like a child, a mother putting on makeup in a compact mirror for no reason I could imagine, but it seemed an act of bravery. They answered that the story would be stale by the time it could be published, and requested I go to France, England, and Czechoslovakia, for a take on the imminence of war. It killed me to leave a real war in Spain and decent people fighting for their liberty for something less, but all eyes were on the Sudetenland of Czechoslovakia and Hitler standing at its border. At least I had Ernest's and Herb's company as far as Marseille, on the south coast of France.

"Don't leave me for the Czechs, Mookie," Ernest said on our last night together. "They're just a bunch of lousy Germans who can live without you."

"The Czechs aren't the Hitler lovers the Austrians are, Bug," I said. "They're mostly decent folks who want to be left in peace."

"Come to Madrid with Herb and me."

"I don't have anyone to write for there. I don't even have the damned papers to travel back to Spain, and I sure don't have the stuff it would take to cut through the red tape."

"Let's go to Paris, then. What's Prague compared to Paris?"

"I want to. You know I want to," I said, which was both true and not. I felt the same darkness descending as he did, for Spain and for us, and I wondered if I would ever see him again if we split up now.

"The thing is the work," I said. "The thing is the work, which means you have to go to Madrid and I have to go to Czechoslovakia."

The work, for him too, would always be the most important thing. The work was the only thing that could keep the St. Louis horrors or the Madrid madness or whatever personal darkness you suffered at bay. But Bug's expression left me feeling disloyal to my favorite trench buddy. It left me thinking that I hated to travel alone, I hated to sleep alone.

"I suppose I could do the piece on France first," I said. "I could do the getting through France, and you could go to Madrid, and we could meet in Paris."

"Paris! We'll eat like pigs and drink champagne and make love three times a day. We'll write our novels, and everything will be fine."

"But I do have to go to Czechoslovakia, Bongie."

"You'll go to Czechoslovakia, and I'll pine for you, and you'll come back to Paris."

"And England," I said. "I also have to go to England."

"And fine ruddy England," he said. "Maybe Del will join us there. Maybe Herb too."

I set off through France alone, winding my car past new tanks on the roads in Burgundy and through new fortifications in the Alps, talking to soldiers and border guards and anyone with a sensible opinion about the threat of war between Germany and France. Ernest set off with Herb for Madrid, where he nearly took a swing at a reporter from the

Daily Worker in the lobby of the Hotel Florida just for poking at Ernest's commitment to anti-Fascism.

We met again in Paris, where I spent my days bothering every person in the know I could find (and I'd gotten pretty good at finding them) for my piece on the looming possibility of war with Germany, and my nights eating too much and drinking too much with Ernest. It was splendid until it wasn't, until I started making plans for Czechoslovakia.

"I'm going to fly, Bug," I said. "I'll leave the car here for you."

"You haven't even finished the French piece yet."

"I finished it. I sent it to *Collier's.*"

"It was a mess, you said it was, and they haven't run it. You can't send a thousand pages and ask them to reduce it for you."

"Not a thousand."

"'A five-foot shelf.'"

"I asked them to cable me comments."

Comments and money, because I'd given every extra cent I had to soldiers I'd met on the way out of Spain. They needed it so much more than I did.

"Why the hell do you want to rush off and leave me for some new piece when the French one isn't even properly done?" Ernest insisted.

"*Collier's* is paying me a thousand dollars per piece, Bug," I said. "My daily bread."

"Come back to Spain with me. I'll bake bread for you in Spain."

"They're already unhappy at how long the French piece took, which you know was because I couldn't bear to wave goodbye to Spain. I promised them the Czech article by June 18 at the latest, and the Brit one by July 10."

"Stay here in Paris. You can wallow in bed, and I'll be the good wifey-wife," he said. "I'll go out to the bakery and bring the daily bread back. Fresh baguettes. Croissants. That funny little breakfast loaf with the currants you like so much."

But even if I didn't want to go to Czechoslovakia—even if I didn't have a contract requiring me to—I couldn't let myself become dependent on a man still married to his wife, or even a man who wasn't. I wouldn't be the same me if I leaned on anyone but myself.

I said, "I don't know if the Hemingway family could take two good wifey-wives waiting for their lovers to return, Bug."

Maybe I meant to provoke him. Maybe I wanted to see him care.

"Be reasonable, Daughter," he said.

"I am being reasonable. It will be just a few weeks, and then I'll join you in Spain."

"We could just go home together," he said.

"To be in telephone distance of someone I can't telephone?" Thinking, *Sleeping alone while he sleeps with his wife.* "It won't be forever, Bug."

"Don't count on that!"

The sudden edge in his voice might have been simple concern for my life, but I could see in his moon eyes the hurt behind the words. I could see the impossibility of him committing to leave Pauline if I wouldn't commit to being the full-time wife he was offering to be, and the impossibility of me giving up my work or even just putting it second to his.

At the end of May, I set off for Czechoslovakia, and Ernest went home to Key West. I wrote to Matie about it. I wrote the day after he'd sailed that I believed he loved me and he believed he loved me, but I didn't think there was much to do about it.

At the Hotel Ambassador in Prague, home to every journalist come to witness Czechoslovakia's demise, I opened up my room to rid it of the impersonal hotel staleness, and I stood on the balcony amid the sounds of taxi horns and tram bells, the grind of wheels on tracks. The streetlamps came on as I looked across Wenceslas Square and its collection of stores announcing their wares in their funny, inefficient lettering, all those umlauts and accents and hooks. And a knock at my door announced my girlfriend from Madrid, Ginny Cowles, already in Czechoslovakia for the *Sunday Times*. She clicked into my room in her spikey heels and her gold jewelry and her discretion. She didn't ask where Ernest was, and I didn't offer.

She'd brought a pint of decent booze from which she poured us each a splash, and we stood together on the balcony watching the Czechs come and go, stepping right out across the trolley tracks without a thought about the trams.

"And to think, we gave up covering a real war in Spain for this," I said.

Ginny said, "This one will be real soon enough."

"All the brave Czechs at the border staring across the abyss at Hitler's Nazi flags in plain view," I said, "while the rest of the world dances the appeasement jig."

"Marty, dear," Ginny said, "you can't save Czechoslovakia by haranguing total strangers on the evils of Hitler."

"I don't intend to," I said. "I intend to save it by haranguing the Czech president into having some spine. *Someone* has to stand up to that vile little German who holds the lightning bolt to ruin us all."

And so we made the assault on Czechoslovakia together even more surely than we'd made the assault on Madrid. We watched the social democrats parade down the street, singing and cheering as they passed their president, who observed the whole four-hour-long parade with his cap respectfully in hand despite the sharp sun. We listened to all the insistence that Czechoslovakia had been free in 1490, when its famous town-hall clock first started marking time, and it was free now, and free it would remain.

We took a car out to Troppau, to see the women in the beet fields and the men making hay and, intermixed with the haystacks, pillboxes with soldiers and machine guns, and anti-tank weaponry. We went to

Pilsen to see the munitions factories in full swing. We went the forty miles or so to Theresienstadt and beyond, to see for ourselves the Nazi thugs lined up across the German border.

There were Nazi thugs aplenty on the Czech side of the border too, though, with Nazi flags displayed shamelessly in the windows in Odersch even as the Czech soldiers patrolled the streets. And the good non-Nazi Czechs had already begun leaving the Sudetenland, packing what little they could carry and setting off to join relatives in Prague or in Brno or in some other place of relative safety they might reach. I wanted to harangue them with demands to know how they could just abandon their homes before the fight was over. But it was a hard charge to make with half their neighbors already cutting flowers with which to welcome the Germans, and the rest of the world strolling by with faces turned away.

Ernest, on the way home from the airport with Pauline and Patrick and Gigi and a family friend packed into his Ford, drove into an absolute wreck of a vehicle belonging to a WPA worker, knocking it through the intersection. The jalopy flipped, but the driver somehow emerged, unhurt and shouting like a crazy man. Ernest matched the man's ire shout for shout, the two of them making such a spectacle in the street that a policeman hauled them both off. Ernest's lawyer (whom he'd portrayed as the shyster Bee-lips in *To Have and Have Not*) had to get him released, and in the end poor Patrick testified for his father, and the judge gave up on it all, and Ernest bought himself a brand-spanking-new Buick eight-cylinder convertible.

He added a window air-conditioning unit to his writing room over the garage in Key West and holed up there, away from Pauline's disappointment and the constant stream of tourists on the street beyond the new wall surrounding the house. He began to put together a story collection in which he meant to include his play about Spain with him as a spy-hero and me as a ninny, the thing he'd called "Working: Do Not Disturb" in Spain but now titled "The Fifth Column." He took to calling the gang working to produce the play on Broadway "the Jews." He squabbled with Max Perkins, who didn't think it a good idea to wedge the play into the story collection. He spent more and more time with the boxers at the Blue Goose Arena, where he claimed himself a one-time "amateur boxing champion," or the local paper claimed it for him without any support. Not even fishing on the *Pilar* improved his mood.

One night when he couldn't find a key to his writing studio, he waved a pistol around, then shot both the ceiling and the door lock, and barricaded himself in the studio. Pauline, unable to reason with him, took the boys to a friend's house for the night, then went to a party she and Ernest were to attend. When Ernest grew bored of waiting for her return, he found her at the party, where he thanked her for her fortitude by breaking furniture and punching guests.

My editors at *Collier's* hadn't run my piece on the state of denial in France yet ("too jumpy"), but they ran the Czech piece on August 6. It was a terrific spread, with photos of teenaged girls emerging from a gas-mask drill, and Czech munitions plants and soldiers. The country, no bigger than my home state of Missouri, was now surrounded on three sides by the German Reich, but no one was panicked. That was what struck me about the Czechs: they were just like a patient laid out on the table, waiting for Hitler to do his business.

By then, Ginny and I had been to England, stopping in every village pub from the Midlands to the Scottish border to harangue random strangers—criminally complacent fools who seemed to a man to squeeze their eyes shut against a war anyone could see was headed right for their white cliffs. I meant to take Ginny to see my writer-friend H. G. Wells, with whom I often stayed in London, but I made excuses lest I harangue him too, for his country's lifeless aristocracy doing nothing more than grasp tightly to their titles and their bank accounts while pretending Hitler didn't exist. I was getting awfully good at haranguing, to no good end.

I went down to Corsica to find some quiet in which to write, but I found only a man drowning on the beach. I returned to Paris, to a little room with a writing desk on a dead-end street near the Arc de Triomphe, where I settled into my fiction as the world settled into rumors of war. If Hitler was madman enough to bomb a city as beautiful as Paris, well then, the whole world was damned but good.

Ernest and his family left Key West shortly after his and Pauline's joint birthdays in July, heading for the L Bar T Ranch in Wyoming and a summer of rain and more rain. He read proofs for the short story collection, and Pauline read with him. He worried over what to do about *The Fifth Column*, deciding finally to ignore Max's advice about the play and include it with the stories. When he mailed the galleys back to Perkins near the end of August, his dedication read, "To Marty and Herbert with love."

By the end of August, Ernest was on the *Normandie* for Paris, to join me for a getaway to my favorite stretch of the French coastline between Le Lavandou and St. Tropez. NANA had called him back to cover the boiling brew that was Europe, and we were getting nearly as good at apologizing after we'd been apart as we were at arguing when together.

Le Lavandou, France

August 1938

Le Lavandou was just a charming little fishing village back then, with nothing to offer but the buoyant blue sea for me to swim in, clean sand on which to let the salt dry on my skin, and a big round moon reflecting on the Mediterranean to light our way home from the local bar in which Ernest and I spent lazy evenings drinking good, cheap rosé. That's where we were—at a table in the bar, listening to a local saxophone player accompanied by a pianist and trying to forget all the bad in the world—when we first heard the rumors that the French and English were scheming to hand the good Czechs of the Sudetenland to Hitler, in exchange for nothing more than a hollow promise of peace.

I packed up my swimsuit in my duffel and headed straight for Prague again, to harangue the new head of the US Foreign Service there, while Ernest, who might have accompanied me to report for NANA, went pheasant shooting in Sologne. Maybe he was tired of me, tired of my putting my work ahead of him when he had a wife at home who would always put him first. Maybe he didn't want to risk Pauline seeing our bylines from the same sinking ship. Or maybe he'd promised his wife that he wouldn't risk his own neck, a promise that would allow him to hide behind the welfare of his wife and kids. He wasn't a coward. I knew that. I'd seen him in Spain. Only it did hurt that he declined to go to a place to which any sensible correspondent would beat a path. It seemed the only reason he wouldn't go was that I did.

I hadn't seen my Russian friend Mikhail Koltsov since he'd shown me his cyanide pill back in Madrid, but he was sitting on the hard wooden bench at the Hradčany Palace in Prague when I arrived.

"Bonjour, étranger," he greeted me—"hello, stranger," but so much more inviting in French, the one language we shared.

"Bonjour, étranger," I replied in as flirty a tone as Mikhail had used. It would have bothered Ernest like hell to hear it, but if he'd come with me, I wouldn't be flirting. It passed the time. It relieved the burden. It made us feel that little bit better, to be suggesting an intimacy that neither of us really meant to act upon. And Hemingway had no claim on me. He had less than no claim.

Like me, Mikhail was anxious to talk with the Czech president. He'd been waiting there for four days already, and this day was no different; it was dark outside by the time we abandoned hope of getting an audience with the president. Mikhail helped me back into my silver fox coat, freeing my hair at the collar. I pulled the coat against the evening chill, and we joined the Czechs on the street, the two of us chatting in the beautiful round sounds of French as we walked together down the hill from the castle, through the Malá Strana Bridge Tower archway, and onto the cobblestones of the Charles Bridge. We stopped in one of the little bridge outcroppings, the old-fashioned streetlamps lighting our faces and the stone faces of the busts lining the bridge. Mikhail stood just that little bit too close for colleagues or friends.

I said, "He could use *Collier's* as a platform to win American support, if he would just talk to me."

Mikhail turned to the water of the Vltava River below reflecting the moonlight like a bomber in the sky. "The Czech president."

"If he would just talk to me," I repeated.

"There are Russian planes waiting at an airfield outside the city. If only he would fight, they're his."

I said, "I expect talking with me would be a little less threatening than allowing the Russian air force free roam in Czechoslovakia."

There were no good choices for the country, so we analyzed the bad ones over pilsners and a simple dinner at a crowded workman's cafe in the Old Town, between the bridge and my hotel on Wenceslas Square. Afterward, I had an urge to kiss Mikhail, not for the kiss itself but to stick that little claw in Hemingway's talent. At the last minute, though, I extended my hand, and said good night, and set off back to my stale hotel room and my balcony overlooking all the good Czechs trying to go about the everyday of living, even in the face of everything.

On September 21, the world abandoned the brave Spanish, declaring an unconditional withdrawal of the International Brigades.

On September 23, the Czech government ordered its citizens to mobilize for war. Waiters set down plates and vendors closed their news kiosks, almost a million men gathering their weapons and reporting for duty within a short three hours. Women stood in dry-eyed support as their men set off in tanks and trucks, on bicycles and by foot, to defend their independence.

Ernest cabled me that he'd gone from Sologne to Paris, where he was writing a short story for *Esquire* and hoping I'd return to him rather than stick around for a good old-fashioned Nazi drubbing. I cabled back that the good Czechs would help keep me safe until I could get back to him.

I was still in Prague a week later, when Hitler, Mussolini, Daladier, and Chamberlain huddled over the Munich Pact with their ugly black ink, abandoning the Czechoslovakian Sudetenland to the Nazis without giving the brave Czechs time to die for their freedom.

I got out of Czechoslovakia on the last civilian plane.

Paris, France

October 1938

Paris was changed that October. Everywhere posters called for *"pour sauver la patrie,"* to ready for the defense of the country. Ernest too was changed. His *The Fifth Column and the First Forty-Nine Stories* was published October 14, and he swore that even if he were kicked out of this world tomorrow, the stories all put together like that would make it all right. But again he saw the critics "ganging up" on him. We were in bed together, with sun streaming in through the tall windows. The room smelled of the coffee we'd nearly finished and the pastries I'd fetched for us from his favorite bakery, a last currant bun and half of a croissant all that remained on the tray on the clean white sheets. The morning sounds of Paris floated in through the window: the lovely roll of the language as strollers passed, the funny toot of Parisian car horns, the lap of the Seine. But all he could see were the reviews, pulled from a single envelope he'd insisted Max Perkins send.

"The *New York Times* is good, Bug," I said. Its reviewer had called the stories (with a few exceptions already published in magazines) still awfully good, and he was kind to the play too, which had yet to see a staging, the first producer having died and the second still struggling to find funding. This play was so close to Ernest's big, Buggy heart, though, and no one else much cared for it. *Time* called it confused. *The Nation* declared it almost as bad as *To Have and Have Not*, which they declared his very worst book ever (in case poor Bug had forgotten what they'd thought about it). "Melodrama," most everyone proclaimed.

"The collection is selling well," I said, stuffing my own hatefulness about the play down, knowing everyone assumed I was the girl who moved from one man to another and spent her spare time buying expensive silver fox furs while soldiers starved.

"It would sell better if Scribner would give it store space and run a goddamned decent-size ad. Pauline said it wasn't even in the Scribner store window on publication day!"

Pauline.

"Maybe she missed it," I said.

"She isn't the complete fool you want her to be, Mart."

I didn't want Pauline to be any kind of fool, nor did I imagine she was. Pauline was a smart enough girl that she might well have told Ernest his book wasn't in the window when it actually was, just to spoil his fun. But there was no saying that when Ernest was in a mood.

I said soothingly, "It's in the store window now."

"It should be filling the whole damned window. It should be lined up in shelves all along Fifth Avenue!"

"I'm sure it looks glorious filling the whole window, that beautiful cover with your name as big as a theater marquee."

"There's nothing to that cover, just my name and the title with a god-awful belt. You'd think the whole art department went on fucking strike just when the cover was to be done."

"It's a terrific cover. You can't walk past it without wanting to touch the red just to see it's real."

"And those damn Jews still can't get it together to put the play on the stage."

I took a last slow sip of my coffee and set my empty cup on the tray, measuring my response on account of his mood. "'The Jews,' Nesto?" I asked lightly, poking fun rather than condemning.

"The fucking Jews!"

"And yet here you are in bed with a Jew, you senseless lug."

"You aren't a Jew, Mookie. Jews don't have blond hair and legs like yours."

"You don't know anything about Jews, Nesto."

"I know those fucking Jews are making a hell of a mess out of my play!"

"Maybe your play is a hell of a mess to start with!" A low blow, I knew, but I was made such a fool in his damned play, and he refused to acknowledge that he'd done it, and one stingy little spot in my heart took some pleasure in the critics destroying it.

"My mother is half Jewish, and she's the most decent woman in the world," I said, unable to make myself take the mean words about his play back, thinking he'd left in all the laughs at my expense and taken out only the dedication to Herb and me. "My father was a Jew," I said.

"You're a goddamned God-fearing Christian, Stooge."

"The only god I fear is the one sitting on the fucking sidelines while Hitler takes us all to hell!"

Ernest rolled toward me, inadvertently knocking the pastry tray. I reached to catch it, but it was too late, the tray and the cups and the plate with the currant bun and half-eaten croissant fell to the floor. He looked at me, startled, then laughed. He was always quick to laugh at his own clumsiness, and in a kind way, in a way that let all the bitterness dissipate. Sometimes I wondered if he did it on purpose—knocked over lamps and spilled coffee in the middle of an argument to break the fever spell.

He touched a hand gently to mine. "I do love a woman who isn't afraid to sling a good, solid cuss," he said, and he laughed again, a further step back from the fight.

"Muck your mucking Fascist Jew hating," I said, falling into the way he took to editing his own work when no one would publish the real cusses.

He climbed from bed, collected the things from the floor, and set them back on the tray. "Muck my Fascist Jew hating," he agreed, standing there in nothing but his skivvies, offering me the retrieved pastries. "Have the currant bun," he said.

"I already ate mine," I said. "That one is yours."

"I want you to have it, Mook."

"You always save it for last."

"But I want you to have it this time."

"It's a good thing we already finished the coffee," I said.

He said, "It's a good thing the china hit the carpet and not the wood."

Ernest was still grumbling about the critics and the failure of the producers to get the play staged when we heard the news about *"La Despedida"*—the October 28 farewell parade in Barcelona for the International Brigades, which had been formally disbanded and were leaving Spain. The parade had been kept secret until minutes before it began, lest the Fascists bomb it, and still three hundred thousand people lined the streets. The Hungarian war photographer Robert Capa was there to photograph it, wearing an unprecedented suit and tie in honor of the soldiers. We felt sick not to be there too, to be made to wait for the letters and reports and newsreels. It drove Ernest back to Spain, and when he returned to Paris to celebrate my birthday on November 8, he was in an even bleaker mood.

We celebrated with a dim dinner and too much booze, and woke tired and bickering only to repeat the lousy day without even the excuse of my birthday—leaving us in a pretty bad state to hear the news coming out of Germany and Austria. Overnight, synagogues were burned to the ground and Jews evicted from their homes, their clothing and furniture flung out on the streets, shops looted. Reports were that fifteen thousand Jews had been jailed in Vienna alone. Others killed themselves rather than be taken away.

"We can't do anything about it with the journalism," Ernest said. "We may as well chuck the journalism in the waste bin."

"If we could get all the journalists in the world screaming in unison—"

"Not even then, Stooge. All the journalists in the world screaming in unison wouldn't shake off this damned determination to ignore Hitler in hopes he'll ignore us."

"We have to write it anyway. We have to go see it and write it."

"I tell you, it will do no good."

"But I have to write, Bug," I said. "If I stopped writing, you'd soon enough find me jumping from the Eiffel Tower in my best St. Louis hat, to see if I could fly."

"I have an idea for a story about a soldier fighting with the International Brigades in Spain," he said.

"For NANA?"

"A novel."

"But a novel, that could take years. We don't have years to make a difference."

"An American soldier in Spain," he said, and he set to writing it while I quietly made arrangements to return to Madrid. He would be going back to Key West for the holidays anyway, to see his sons—which of course meant seeing Pauline too. But I couldn't ask him to skip Christmas with his sons. He wouldn't love me if I asked him to, and I wouldn't love him if he acquiesced.

We bumped into Randolfo Pacciardi—the head of the Garibaldi Battalion who used to take me around the Madrid front on his motorcycle—in the hotel lobby a few nights later. He looked to be headed out for a spiffing time in his properly cut suit rather than the khakis and cap he'd worn in Spain. Civilian clothes. I was glad I'd never told Ernest about that ghastly back-seat business, Randolfo laughing that I was so brave at war and so scared of sex just because I declined to slide my hands down his trousers. That had been repulsive, yes, but it wasn't a thing to hold against a fellow who'd fought so well for Spain.

"Pacciardi, old man!" Ernest said.

"Hemingway! And Mademoiselle Gellhorn."

He kissed me on both cheeks in the French way, whispering in my ear, *"Ma chère amie, toujours aussi belle depuis cet épisode sur la banquette arrière."* My dear back-seat friend.

Randolfo had founded an anti-Fascist magazine, *La Giovine Italia*. "Maybe you'll write some pretty piece for me, Miss Gellhorn?"

"Marty here is covering all of Europe for *Collier's*," Ernest said, more proud than ever, and he launched into a tirade on the treachery and rot in Spain.

Randolfo listened politely but would not be goaded into maligning anyone he fought with, never mind that he'd been run out of his battalion when it was folded into a communist-controlled brigade.

Ernest said, "Sure, no one is a traitor, and no one is at fault, and Spain is lost, but let's not complain." He laughed to show he didn't mean it, even though he did, and Randolfo and I laughed with him.

Randolfo couldn't join us for a drink as he had plans, so we stood in the lobby for a long while, talking of all the brave men we'd known, memory after memory of men now buried in the fields of Spain. It was sobering. We'd experienced their dying one by one, that was hard enough, but here they were now, all stacked up to loss after loss after loss in one big unforgivable pile, and the war was over, and they'd died for nothing at all. Still the world lent no hand—not in Spain, not in Austria, not in Czechoslovakia, not in the Jewish neighborhoods all over the German Reich where temples were burning and men were disappearing. The world stood mute, leaving Hitler to his bullying ways.

"You won't go back?" Ernest asked Randolfo.

"To Spain? I am happy to die for the cause, but the dying for nothing at all is less appealing, yes?"

"To Italy, then?" I asked.

"I am afraid the same fate would meet me in Italy. I am not on Mussolini's favorite-persons list, you see."

He'd lost everything: his friends, his ability to fight, and even a homeland to return to.

Ernest said, "Well, Paris isn't a bad place to call home."

Randolfo, his tone heartbreaking in its bravery, said, "And yet it is not mine."

The moment we'd made our goodbyes and were out of sight of the former commander, heading upstairs to our room, Ernest leaned against the wall and, to my astonishment, began to weep.

"Bug?" I said.

"They can't do it," he sobbed. "They can't treat a brave man that way!"

And my heart broke again too, this time not for Randolfo but for Ernest, for his compassion and for his brave front as he'd spoken with Randolfo, and for everything *he* had left behind in Spain.

I put my arms around him, saying, "You're such a good Bug, you're such a good, generous man." And we stood together like that for a long, long moment, me holding him while he sobbed on the stairwell between a hotel room that was our home, and yet not, and a lobby filled not with fellow journalists like our friends in Spain but with absolute strangers. "You're such a good, generous man," I said. "I love you, Bug. I love you. I really do."

It was, I saw as I said the words, the truth. I'd been half in love with Ernest ever since I'd started reading his Raven piece, about the sightless, lipless boy back in that hospital near Morata. I'd been telling myself I loved Ernest Hemingway but that I wasn't in love with him, he wasn't mine and I wasn't his. I'd been telling myself he wasn't a man to fall in love with, that he was a man who could rip your guts out and leave them in the street to rot. But the truth was I'd been half in love with him all this time, at least half, ever since he'd written about Raven who wanted to call him Ernie, who wanted him to promise to return.

I had supposed when Ernest made his promise to that boy that it was one he wouldn't keep, one he somehow couldn't keep. But standing on that stairway holding Ernest while he cried for Randolfo Pacciardi, I saw that he *had* kept that promise to Raven. He had returned to visit the boy in the only way he could return: in his writing that brought the whole world along with him. And standing in that stairway holding Ernest's grief in my arms, I saw that I was in but good for the all of Ernest Hemingway.

PART III

Paris, France

November 1938

Two chapters into his new novel, Ernest declared it an untamable beast, as if the beast might be anything other than his own despair. He sailed on the *Normandie* for New York and Key West and the holidays with Pauline and the boys, and I returned to Spain, arriving in Barcelona on November 21 to write the piece about the Spanish refugees. I'd done the three pieces *Collier's* wanted on France, England, and Czechoslovakia, and sometimes we have to write what we have to write.

I palled around with Herb Matthews, still sporting his improbable peasant trousers, and with the photojournalist Robert Capa, whom I'd somehow not met before. Capa and I fell in like siblings, joking and bickering and having the most furious arguments about anything that might be argued in the moments when his camera wasn't in his hands, throwing words at each other that might hurt worse than the bombs so that there would be something more to worry about than the end of our lives. I told him his coat—a wide-lapelled camel hair with gaudy mother-of-pearl buttons—was a despicable thing to wear when all of Barcelona was freezing, and starving to boot. It was during an air raid, that conversation, and I let go of his hand long enough to pull my silver fox coat tighter around my neck as I said it.

"If I am to die in an air raid," he answered, taking my hand again, "I would like to be remembered most as a dapper dresser. Your problem is you care more about word choice than fashion. You think writing will bring an end to suffering. You are more stupid than a herd of mules!"

"You self-congratulating little cynic!" I laughed. "Never mind that you're just here to make your own fame and fortune on the back of the poor Spanish!"

It was all in jest, and yet it poked at something that was true: that his pictures and my words—the only weapons we knew how to fight with—were lousy worthless against Hitler's guns and planes and men.

I stayed in Barcelona and wrote about the refugees until I was too tired in the head to write anything but sludge, even with Robert Capa and Herb Matthews to shame me into writing my heart out as best I could. I had no heart left. My heart was already splattered all over the streets, rotting with the corpses in the bomb craters everywhere in Spain.

There was nothing to do then but go home and find a quiet place—a fiction-writing place, perhaps Bug was right about that—where I could sort through the voices battering my heart. I left with Robert Capa, who was as sick and exhausted as I was, and if Ernest wanted to make a fuss over our traveling together while he was sharing Pauline's bed, that was fine with me. We headed for Paris, where we each hoped to find a way to let our badgering voices speak to the world. I hoped only that my words might speak in the way that his photos really did, despite all my saying how silent they were.

Matie and my brothers and I, along with my older brother's family, spent Christmas together in St. Louis, with Ernest calling from Key West so often that I forever had to be vigilant for the telephone's ring.

"I should have done it as a novel rather than a goddamned play," he said, all torn up about *The Fifth Column*. "Those hacks in New York are making it so cheap we're going to have to mark it down to the 4.95 Column. They want to make the thing a foolproof success, by which they mean 'take out anything that hasn't been done before.'"

"It is a lot of money, Bug," I said. Fifty thousand dollars.

"They've spent as much on a helluva lot of lesser plays."

It was all such a mess: his mess of a play, our mess of a relationship, and, worst of all, the mess of Spain, which daily brought increasingly bleak news. I felt the darkness of that stirring the words in my head, making everything I put on the page the wrong dope.

Ernest pleaded for me to meet him in New York, where he was going to spend a week revising the damned play himself. Matie pleaded for me not to go, invoking Ernest's wife and his children, asking whether I was the kind of woman to come between a man and his family.

"You don't really even want him to leave his family, Martha," she insisted. "You'd regret it if you were the cause of that."

"If it wasn't me, it would be someone else, Matie. It always has been."

"And that makes you feel better?"

She took a letter from the secret drawer in her desk—the hiding place she'd used so often as a suffragette scheming to make public statements and arrange protests. The letter she handed me was in my own handwriting, from Paris the prior May.

"I want you to read it carefully, Martha."

"It's my own letter, Matie! You don't think I know what I wrote?"

"I want you to read it carefully."

I took the thing from her, and I read it, to indulge her.

"What does it say about you and Ernest, Martha?"

"It says he loves me but there is nothing to be done about it. I don't need him to do anything about it, though. I don't need him to leave his family. I don't need to be a wife. I have enough on my hands being a journalist, and I'd be such a rotten wife, Matie, you know I would."

"It says he loves you, that you both believe he loves you," Matie said gently.

"I do believe it," I insisted. "And so does Ernest."

"And yet it says nothing about you loving him."

I read the letter again.

"Are you sure you do love him, Martha?" Matie asked. "Because this time it's different; there are children involved. If he loves you beyond all measure, and you love him in the same way, and there is nothing left of his marriage, well then, maybe. But this time there are children whose needs must be put first."

Not saying "selfish scum"—that was my father's phrase—but meaning it, or nearly.

"This time you'd better be awfully sure of your own feelings," Matie said.

New York, New York

January 1939

I arrived in New York on January 14 only to wake up the next morning to screaming headlines: "Hemingway by K.O. in Big Night Club Card." Some fool at the Stork Club had rubbed a hand over Ernest's face, saying, "Tough, eh?" and Ernest had socked him good, and now the newspaper couldn't help but work in a reminder of Ernest's fight in Max Perkins's office almost two years before. Still, for Ernest and me together, New York was like Paris, only more so. We went everywhere together, with only Matie's admonition to spoil it. We even went to a showing of *The Spanish Earth* with his and Hadley's son joining us by cab from the ferry.

"Bumby," I said, immediately kicking myself. I'd reminded myself a thousand times to call him "Jack," because, really, what teenager cares to be known by his baby love name, and a bumbling one at that? "I'm Marty," I said. "It's so nice to meet you, Jack. I feel I know you from all the pride your old father here likes to spill about you to all of us who know him."

The poor kid just gawked at me as if I were a mirage, which maybe I was if you'd just come down to New York from some boys' prep school where the closest you were allowed to a woman was a glimpse of some old schoolmaster's wife.

Ernest said, "Shatz here"—*shatz* a German word meaning "treasure"—"is down from Storm King School up near West Point, where not only is he the best damned boxer in the place, he's also the best damned student. First in his class, and second in the whole outfit. That's his mother's influence, of course. Hadley is a fine mother even if I'm something to cast out with the rotten fish and wilted lettuce. My influence would have Shatz here drinking rum by the gallon and cussing out the headmaster."

While Bumby rooted around in his chest for his own voice, Hemingway danced a boxer dance and poked at him playfully, telling me what a fine fisherman Bumby was too, and what great friends he was with Edward Albee's son. "You know Albee, the playwright?" Ernest said to me. "Maybe I should get him to give what for to that gang pulverizing *The Fifth Column*."

Bumby fell into play-boxing with his father, then said, finally, "Some of the ponds at school have trout."

"Rainbow trout?" I asked.

"Brook trout! And the streams have brookies too. But some of them also have rainbows. Do you fish, Miss Gellhorn?"

"I would certainly love to fish with you, Master Hemingway!" I said, and he blushed from one ear to the other all the way across his grinning face.

Bumby hardly touched his dinner at the Stork Club for being so busy trying to impress his father and me. We talked about the word out of Spain—Robert Capa had gone back and Herb Matthews was still there; they'd fled Barcelona when the government abandoned it on January 22—which left me without much appetite myself, the guilt of being warm and well fed while my friends were still in Spain doing what I ought to be doing myself.

"Capa's editors at *Life* arranged to get him out with the Americans, but the idiot refused," I said. "He said he'd take his chances with Herb and the others, never mind that he has no goddamned passport."

Bumby giggled at my swearing, which of course provoked me to swear more. "If my swearing means I'll go to hell," I whispered to him, "well then, I'm sure there will be better fucking conversation there than in heaven, and if it's a little warm, I'll just take off my fur."

As we put our coats back on and braced ourselves for the cold night, Ernest asked his son, "Well, how do you like Marty? Should I keep her?"

Bumby said, "I'll take her if you don't, Papa!" and we all laughed.

He wasn't Pauline's son; I suppose that was part of his easy acceptance of me into his life. He was used to a woman other than his mother having his father's affections. Maybe I wasn't even the first of his father's extracurricular loves he'd met. Children do get used to their parents ceasing to love each other as long as their parents love them, and Ernest did love his children, he would always love them. And maybe I hadn't been quite sure when I wrote that letter to Matie, but I did love Ernest, and I would love his children too.

The Hemingway and Pfeiffer families were to gather in Key West in early February for Patrick's confirmation. Ernest's mother was coming, and Pauline's parents and her uncle Gus, who was forever giving Ernest and Pauline everything they needed and then some. Ernest thought I should come down for the confirmation; he tried to convince me of it one of our last nights together, as we browsed Fifth Avenue shopwindows full of clothes and shoes and jewelry, furniture and linens.

"Mouse adores you as much as Bumby does," he insisted. "And my mother went on forever about what a fine job you did in Chicago on that little speaking tour."

I said, "That 'little' speaking tour was twenty-two cities, you know."

"Your big speaking tour."

"And Pauline would love to see me at her son's confirmation?"

"Let's go to Cuba, then," Ernest suggested. He'd gone to Cuba by himself before, on the *Pilar*; he liked to get away from the crowded life Pauline had gathered around them in Key West, which was no longer the sleepy place they lit on originally for the quiet that allowed him to write. Cuba offered both excuse and access: he could be in Key West in just a few hours, and back again as quickly, but no one from Key West would come to him.

"Whatever in the world would I do in *Cuba*, Bongie?"

"I have enough stories for a new book, nearly. The three *Esquire*s and the *Cosmo*—the way I wrote it, not the way they twiddled the thing. And 'Landscapes with Figures,' and three long ones I want to write, one about Teruel and another about the storming of the Guadarrama pass, and one about an old fisherman who fights a swordfish all alone on his boat for days only to have a shark eat the thing because he can't get it into the boat. That last one could be the ticket, it could make the book, but I need to go to Cuba and go out on a skiff, to make sure I don't give the reader the wrong dope."

"The 'wrong dope'?"

"I do begin to sound like you, don't I?"

"We're two strands of the same rope, all twisted together now, Bug. I wonder that we don't hang ourselves."

"Cuba, Mookie. When all the time you spent risking your ass in Spain only to have the whole thing go to rot is muddling your brain, the sun there will bake most of the rot out of you, and the rum will sterilize the rest."

We'd stopped in front of a shopwindow view of a table set with lovely china and pretty napkins, wineglasses, candlesticks, silver knives and forks and spoons and serving bowls and platters, everything so perfectly matched that it gave me the jitters.

"I need to write, Ernestino," I said. "The only thing that bakes the rot out of me is the writing."

"They want me to do these lectures in New York and all over the goddamned place, but I'll tell them I'm not free to lecture."

"You don't need the money?"

"I'll tell them nicely, in case I need the money later, for writing the novel. In case I can't make the stories into a book. I'll tell them I can't do the lectures now but I might do them later, and we'll spend our days in Cuba writing and our nights drinking rum and making love."

I put a finger to one of the letters on the store window. "How many nights, Nesto? So I can plan."

He set his hand over mine, and we stood looking from the dark sidewalk into the brightly lit display dining room. "A whole lifetime of nights, Mook."

"Cuba," I said. A chance to drag our relationship out in the bright light of daily life, just Bug and me in private, which was something we would never find anywhere in the United States. Not with his fame. Not with the glut of photographers looking to make a living capturing people like us for scandalous headlines. We could try a more normal life together in Cuba without him having to leave his children's mother. Matie had said it true: If Ernest loved me beyond all measure and I loved him in the same way and there was nothing left of his marriage, well then, maybe. But if Ernest left Pauline for me, I would be beholden, and I was no good at being beholden. I was lousy at being a wife who always put her husband before her writing. I was better at selfish lover, selfish scum.

"I'm afraid of the writing, Nesto," I confessed. "It's all roiling my gut like hell: the pages behind me, the ones ahead."

"You've been out of the sun too long, Mookie," he said. "Come to Cuba with me."

Cuba. Writing in the daytime and drinking rum at night. Sharing a bed and all of it in a regular way. Seeing if our motors could run together on the plain juice of daily life, without the chaser shot of war.

Key West, Florida

JANUARY 1939

Ernest flew back to Key West on January 24 for the family doings. He called me five days later, answering my "hello" with "Yeats is dead."

"I'm sorry, Bug," I said.

"Maybe we shouldn't wait," Ernest said. "Maybe we should go to Cuba now."

A line from a Yeats poem came to mind, about making the iron hot by striking rather than waiting for it to heat up. But I answered gently, "It will be just a few more days, Bongie, and there's Patrick's confirmation."

After we hung up, I went to my mother's bookshelves and pulled down a collection of Yeats's poems, and I paged through to find one I'd learned of from Teachie at Bryn Mawr, about treading softly on others' dreams. I supposed Teachie would die before I did, as my father had, as Matie almost surely would too unless I could manage to get myself killed at war.

Ernest's mother—who had stayed at Key West's priciest hotel on Ernest's dime for Patrick's confirmation—returned to Oak Park, and

Ernest caught the next ferry to Havana. He'd settled into rooms in the Sevilla-Biltmore by the time I arrived, and taken a room for writing at the Ambos Mundos—a corner room with floor-to-ceiling windows, louvered shutters, and a fabulous cross breeze, with a balcony and a view of the cathedral, the harbor, the sea. "Both worlds," the hotel name meant. Old and new. Cuban and Spanish. Married and not. The telephones standing silent, no ugly ringing of interruption. No letters or bills. No children or wife or pet raccoons. Just fishing tackle and old newspapers and canned meats at one hotel, and a typewriter, ribbons, and a grand supply of paper at the other.

I dropped my bags at the Biltmore and walked to the Ambos Mundos, where I took the black wire cage of an elevator up to the fifth floor. I found Ernest stretched out on the bed in the alcove of his writing room, reading over some pages. A half-eaten twelve-pound ham and an empty bottle of rum sat on the bedside table. The sheets were a mess despite the availability of maid service, and the sink in the john was covered with hairs.

"Hemingstein," I said.

"I knew you'd get here, Daughter, because I arranged that you would."

"Hemingstein," I repeated, laughing now at the reference to my arrival in Madrid that first time, "it's one thing to live in squalor in the middle of a Spanish war, but this is pathetic."

He patted the bed beside him, and I stretched my legs alongside his and allowed myself to be pulled into his big bear embrace, his arms around me the way I loved them.

"I did wash my clothes for you," he said, nodding to spare khakis and a shirt drying in the fresh air of the balcony, and moccasins drying on the windowsill.

I said, "You are such a pig, Bug. An adorable pig. A talented pig. But really."

"I'm writing, Mookie."

"You can't allow a maid in for five minutes?"

"The maid was here yesterday."

He meant to finish some stories for a collection that would pay his bills while he dug into a new novel. He was working on a story about a brave young man filming the Spanish war.

"He sounds like you, only better," I said.

"Is there a man better than I am?" he asked.

"What about the Cuba story you're here to research? The one about the fisherman and the shark."

"After this war story I'm writing. I'm calling it 'Under the Ridge.'"

I also meant to write about the Spanish war, a novel, but I soon abandoned it for one about a young American journalist witnessing the fall of the Czechoslovakian Sudetenland to Hitler.

"A beautiful blond with legs up to her shoulders, I should hope," Ernest said. "And as brave as you are."

I did draw on my own experience in Prague, but my journalist protagonist was far more noble than I was. She was trying to help the Jewish and anti-Fascist refugees in Prague who had been ordered to return to the Reich and its concentration camps. For me, though, it was one thing to write journalism pieces from a place full of great friends with the same reason for being there as you and very little alternative, and it was another to wrestle the abomination that was a novel into submission in a characterless hotel in a warm climate, in a country at peace. Yes, maybe it was the pent-up desires of a decade spent living in hotels in Europe. Maybe it was the irresistible charms of Cuba, or the need for something more than a hotel room in which to test our love. Or maybe it was my excuse for avoiding a story I couldn't manage to begin well. Whatever the reason, while Ernest settled in to his writing, I set mine aside and began a daily perusal of the Havana newspaper advertisements for real estate.

"Look, Bug, this one has a tennis court and a pool," I said, thrusting the advertisement at Ernest, who looked up from his journal at the Ambos Mundos bar, pencil in one hand and a beer in the other. I wore no stockings, no hat, nothing more than a plain cotton shift that would have scandalized all of St. Louis and the better part of Missouri. But this was Cuba, and as near as I could tell, the Cuba rules had never been drawn up.

"And a mango grove, Bug," I said. "It has a mango grove, so we'll have everything we need."

"Except booze and typewriter ribbons," he said.

"Except booze and typewriter ribbons," I agreed.

He grinned and said, "Well, let's go see it, then, Daughter."

We collected the car and rambled off out of Havana, through the slums on the outskirts of the city and the unbearable stink of a tannery, to banana and coconut farms where children merrily made their way home from school.

"It's quite a drive," Ernest said after what really was just a very few minutes.

"But it's quiet and the air is fresh."

"Except that awful tannery stink," he said.

"But here, Bug. You'd like to write in a place where the air is this fresh, wouldn't you?"

San Francisco de Paula, a little town not far from the center of Havana.

A friend of the owner's family met us at the front gate and unlocked it, opening the way to a tree-lined drive. Inside the gates, the gardens were crusted over with empty booze bottles and rusted cans. The paint and the tennis court vied for the honor of being the most horrendous, the tennis court really just a fenced-in collection of every variety of weed the little town had to offer. The sludge in the pool was worse than the sludge in my brains had ever been. The place had been built fifty years earlier by a Catalan architect in the wake of the death of his two sons—I was glad to hear the boys hadn't died there—and it hadn't been lived in for so long that it was steeped in the smell of rottenness. Inside, the walls were nasty with a hideous black mold.

"This makes your habits look almost respectable, Bug," I said.

But I fell hard for the good of the place: the high ceilings and the abundant doors and windows, the arched passageways and tile floors. From the high ground of the house, you could see all the way to Havana, fifteen miles to the west. Just out the windows and doors, brightly flowered bougainvillea and jacaranda I dubbed "the *flamboy-antes*" even that first day were fighting to pull the garden walls down.

"Oh, Bug, don't you love it?" I said.

"You can't be serious."

"The tree at the front steps, though." A ceiba so beautiful that the natives must have considered it a shrine. "All those orchids growing on its branches like a crowd of exquisite subjects flocking to the plainest of queens . . ." And there were hummingbirds too, and eighteen kinds of mangos. "And the name: Finca Vigía. I only wish the ancient watch-tower still stood to climb. Wouldn't that have been a space where the writing juice would run?"

"A hundred a month, Stooge? Look at this place, for Christ's sake."

"I am. I am looking closely at it, Ernest Hemingway. And I am falling in love with it."

"But a hundred a month!" he repeated.

"You pay sixty dollars just for your writing room, never mind the rooms you live in."

Never mind the $1,000 per month maintenance of his Key West house.

A hundred a month—I could cover that myself for a while with the money from my *Collier's* pieces.

"I'll take it," I told the man showing us the place. "You tell them I'll take it. Don't you dare show it to another soul."

Havana, Cuba

February 1939

"No telephone," Hemingway insisted.

"Don't be silly, Scrooby. What would Matie do if she couldn't call me?"

"It will ring us right out of our writing."

"It will be my telephone. You needn't give the number to Pauline."

"No radio," he said.

"But how would we get the news, Bug?" The US newspapers came by mail boat, which took days.

I found a painter to whitewash the walls, two gardeners to retrieve the place from the weeds, and a man to drain and clean and refill the pool, trying to make the Finca Vigía habitable while Ernest wrote from his hotel-room office those last weeks of February and into March. He finished "Under the Ridge"—a blatantly anti-war thing in which a correspondent bearing a strong resemblance to Ernest was filming something very like *The Spanish Earth*—and he turned to another story. He was almost always at the typewriter, and almost never writing by hand, a sure sign that this new story was going well.

We were sitting together on the bed in his office one afternoon in early March, our legs stretched alongside each other as we read our pages, when I set my manuscript aside and picked up the first page of his. He didn't object. I read the first few lines. A story set in Spain, in a forest, during the war. Not the one he'd started in Europe, but not so different either: an American fighting with the Republicans in Spain.

I closed my eyes for a moment, remembering the oiled roads he wrote of, the streams and the mills and the dams, and all the boys who died in Spain, grown boys fighting the war and little boys whose grandmothers held their hands as bombs fell in the streets of Madrid.

He'd already been revising. He'd struck the first-person plural and penciled in the third personal singular, trading "we" were lying on a forest floor for "he." I read on, the rest of that page and the second and third, where the original typing switched to the third person.

"Why do you put a space before the commas and periods and dashes?" I asked, thinking I might never pick up my own sloppy, sludgy pages about the Czechs again.

"It's the French way."

"Only for two-part punctuation. A semicolon. An exclamation mark."

He looked up at me, uncertainty in his brown eyes and furrowed brow. He so hated to be wrong.

"A Spanish war story," I said. "A story about the Republican attack on the Fascists in the Guadarrama Mountains? The La Granja attack?"

"Yes."

"So I know how the story ends, then."

He didn't respond.

I said, "But that was in May." May of 1937. "After we'd come back to New York for the writers' conference. You weren't there."

"I have the bombing on the Tortosa road to call on for the sounds and the smells and the rest of it, the details," he said. "I have all the International Brigades we did meet. It's easier sometimes to take what you know along to something you need to explore. To write what you almost know rather than what you know too well to truly see."

"It's stunning, Bug," I said. "It's a stunning opening."

"Do you think so, Mook?"

I stroked his hair, which was thinning. Gray was creeping into his beard too.

"The repetition: he lay, he lay, he could see, he could see," I said. "It oughtn't be so beautiful, but it's incantatory. Almost biblical."

"I didn't think I was ready to write it."

I set the pages aside, and he did too, and we made love. It was so easy to love him when he wrote like that. I could love a man who wrote like that forever, couldn't I?

While I continued organizing the work on the Finca Vigía—picking out paint colors and finding someone to rid the place of the flying white ants that came in the windows to chew up my moldings—Ernest decided it would be a fine time to take a break, and he went off to fish. Before he returned, I'd hired a houseman named Reeves and arranged to restore the tennis court with crushed coral limestone bordered by bamboo. The gardeners had cleared foliage enough that we could see the Havana lights. And Hitler had decided it would be a fine time to take the rest of Czechoslovakia, which he did on March 15—news which, as I'd lost the battle of the radio, we only happened to hear while in town for drinks.

I thought I ought to go, but even without the overlord of my new possessions, there was no getting into Czechoslovakia now. I was left to curl up in my new bed in my new home, with Bug and my novel set in Prague that now would have no hope of saving the Czechs even if I could ever make it jell.

With the work on the Finca Vigía still at full tilt, Ernest decided he ought to go back to Key West for a few weeks to see Bumby, who was coming down for his Easter break.

"He could come here," I suggested. "We could have a grand time here."

"I have some business to take care of," Ernest said.

"Of course," I said.

"Don't be like that, Mook."

"Like what, Bug?"

He called from Key West several times a day, interrupting the little writing I was getting done between overseeing the house restoration. He called to make sure I'd seen the news that Franco had declared victory in Spain. He called to tell me who had been hired to translate his stories into Russian. He called to tell me Pauline thought "Under the Ridge" was his best story ever—this in a late-night call that left me imagining him and Pauline sitting in bed together, his pages the only thing between them.

"She says it's better than 'Hills like White Elephants'!" he said.

"How nice that you're sharing your story with Pauline," I said, wondering how far Pauline might go to flatter him. Ernest always thought the thing he'd most recently finished was his best ever, but "Under the Ridge" seemed to me to rely too heavily on the reader believing in the hero's political convictions, which I wasn't sure Ernest himself believed.

"Pauline is the best copy editor I know," he said.

How very convenient it must be, I thought, for him to have a triple-purpose appliance: copy editor and bed- and ego-warmer all in one.

"What about the other story, the long one?" I asked. "The La Granja attack one that starts with that amazingly incantatory opening."

He'd only just started the thing March 1, but he'd had fifteen thousand words before he'd left for Key West. Fifteen thousand words, and it was the beginning, the hardest place to get them.

"It's only begun, and it's already too long to sell anywhere."

"Maybe it's a novel, Bug."

"I can't afford to write a novel. Anyway, I can't write anything here, with people coming and going and not a minute to myself."

"It would make Max happy to have a new novel from you."

"I was a hundred ninety-eight pounds this morning," he said, calling up the image of him padding barefoot across the wood floor of the bedroom he shared with Pauline to his bathroom overlooking Whitehead Street. It was a measure of his mood, his weight. Under two hundred pounds meant he was happy. Was he happier with Pauline than with me?

"I'm sure you look awfully fine for Pauline and her Key West horde," I said.

"Mookie," he said.

I said nothing.

"I've been reading Scott's *Tender is the Night*," he said. "It's amazing how excellent it is."

He'd still been here in Cuba when he stumbled on a copy of Scott's story about a psychiatrist and the patient he marries. I was surprised he'd never read it, given what good friends they'd once been and how closely the book explored the problems in Scott's own life: the villa in France, the crazy wife, the husband's turn to alcohol.

"Do you really think he's done for writing novels?" I asked, glad of skirting an argument when I was in Cuba and Pauline was with him in Key West.

"I always had this stupid little-boy feeling of being better than Scott," Ernest confided. "Like a tough little bully lording it over the sissy."

"The very talented sissy."

"This *Tender is the Night* is so good it's frightening. Reading it makes me want to give up the stories and do a novel again."

"You can do that," I said. "I'm telling you, the new story you're writing, Robert Jordan at the La Granja attack, it's a novel. You know it's a novel."

"But I need the damned money."

I thought to say I had money, but he hated Pauline's money—or her uncle Gus's that they depended on. Ernest's royalties were substantial, but he seemed to think it was Pauline's family money that poisoned him, that without it he would chuck the Key West mansion and the fancy parties and he would be a better writer and a better person in the bargain. I didn't want him to hate even the little money I had compared to Pauline. And I supposed the only thing worse than being dependent on him was having him dependent on me.

"Max could give you an advance," I suggested. "Tell him you're working on a novel."

"I can't make the dough as fast as Pauline spends it. I need to sell the stories for the money. I ought to go to Hollywood and write crap for the money, like Scott does."

"Come back to Cuba, Bongie."

"This place is overrun with tourists thanks to that damned new road," he said. "The fishermen here are no longer anything more than props to photograph."

"The visitors are looking for the rumrunner and the thugs from *To Have and Have Not*, and for you, Bug. Ah, but for the days when no one could get to Key West except in private yachts!"

He laughed—at himself, or at Pauline's money, or both.

"Come wake to the birds in the ceiba tree and the flamboyantes out the window, Bug. Fall asleep to the wind rattling the palms. It's quiet here now. Quiet and bare and clean and empty. I swam in the pool today. I just stripped off my clothes right on the patio and dove in."

Yes, I knew what he liked. I knew what Pauline couldn't offer with the children there, although Pauline was a smart girl, she might manage things awfully well after the children went to bed.

"In broad daylight," I said. "The sun warm on my bare shoulders and legs, on my bare bum."

When Ernest returned to Cuba, he brought the *Pilar* with him, and although he kept his hotel rooms in Havana and his wife, he woke in my bed at the Finca Vigía, in a room that was bright with yellow tiles and southern light. He woke that first morning at sunrise, and he went straight to his medical scale—one I'd had delivered while he was in Key West because I knew he liked to weigh himself every morning. I watched in horror as he noted his weight in pencil right there on my newly painted bathroom wall, at shoulder level where the tile gave way to fresh paint.

"What the hell, Nesto! The damned wall isn't even dry!"

"But it's only pencil, Stooge," he said, smiling a goofy smile that wasn't exactly an apology. "You might worry when I start using pen. That will mean it's gotten awfully hard to get rid of me."

I smiled. I could smile. He'd brought the *Pilar* to Cuba.

"I'll pay for this," he said.

"For the damage to my wall?"

"And the rest of it. Even your houseman."

"I can take care of myself," I said. "And Reeves as well." The responsibility for my own keep brought with it the need to write, to earn a living, and I liked that. I liked having the absolute right to keep my career when Ernest might have me set it aside to tend to him.

"We'll split the expenses, then," he said.

"But you have your room rent."

"I'll let the rooms go."

I wondered what he would do about an address for Pauline and the boys to write to, but I supposed he could arrange to continue collecting his mail at the hotel.

"All right," I said. "We'll split the expenses."

"Fifty-fifty, except my booze," he said. "I'm the master of my own booze, and I won't be negotiating it with anyone."

"Fifty-fifty, except for your booze," I agreed.

"It's settled, then, Mook," he said, and he put his typewriter on the desk right there in my bedroom—in our bedroom—and he pulled on a pair of pants and, still bare-chested, he rolled a fresh sheet of paper into the carriage.

"And maybe you ought to pay for your own typewriter ribbon and paper, along with the booze," I said. "I don't know if I can afford to subsidize anyone writing as damned fast as you are."

He said, "Write faster, then, Daughter," and he began his two-fingered peck at the typewriter keys.

Ernest was as useful around the house as a stuffed rabbit in those early days, leaving me to finish all the purchasing of comfortable chairs and good, strong reading lamps, garden benches, the mixings for Papa Dobles and the glasses to serve them in, which I found finally at the ten-cent store along with plates and linens (table and bed). He left me to hire the cook and the maid, and to show them how, exactly, he liked everything. But he was writing so beautifully that I couldn't bear to suggest he do anything else.

I settled in to writing my journalist-in-Prague novel too, sometimes outside in the bamboo grove or on the bougainvillea-covered terrace, where I thought perhaps I ought to hang a plaque thanking *Collier's* for its donation to provide me this paradise. I set up an office in a second bedroom off the east end of the living room, with a view only of a courtyard where pigeons liked to gather, a room to which we eventually moved our huge double bed since I was the later sleeper. I remembered the first place I'd called my own, for four dollars a week when I was a cub reporter back in Albany. It felt shameful to be so well off in such a ruined world, but I consoled myself that soon enough my money would run out and I'd have to set off to cover the misery again.

The Finca Vigía, San Francisco de Paula, Cuba

April 1939

The Spanish war story Ernest had started just before he left for Key West—the La Granja attack story with the incantatory opening—consumed him. At the end of each day, he counted his words and shared his progress: five hundred words or more. Me, I was dizzy and ill just vomiting out a few words a day, fighting off abandoning the book only with thoughts of the poor Czechs now enduring Nazi boot prints not just in the Sudetenland but all over all their lovely earth, Hitler's thugs having taken Prague in mid-March and the vile little man proclaiming his greatness from the very castle where I'd flirted with Mikhail Koltsov. I had none of the magic Ernest did. Each night I read his pages, words as clear as water and carrying like the music in a story so moving that it made me want to toss my own pages into the sea.

"Your juice is running like you just harvested the whole grove of mangos all at once, Bug," I told him one night as we walked hand in hand along the Prado in Havana, where we sometimes liked to go after a good day. We'd written until two p.m. We'd played a bit of tennis. I took a dip in the pool while Ernest watched from a patio chair, pretending to read. Then Ernest shed his shorts and T-shirt for decent slacks and a collared shirt, and I pulled on his favorite little black dress, my hair still wet.

"The whole world is going to drink this novel of yours up in one big gulp," I said as we strolled.

"Are they, Mook?" His eyes as wanting-to-believe as the puppy we passed on the wide boulevard, the little dog playing under an oak tree beside an old lady reading a newspaper she'd bought from the news-and-lottery-ticket boys.

It might have made me jealous, how beautifully Ernest was writing, but how can you be jealous of something as gentle and soothing and good as the wind blowing in the palms outside our bedroom window?

"The damned critics will ruin it," he said. "The damned critics are out to slay me."

I pulled him closer as we walked, letting go of his hand to take his arm and leaning my head on his shoulder. "Not this one, Bug."

"They don't know the real gen when they see it."

"They'll know this," I said, trying to push out the one bit of uneasiness I felt, the little fear that he might stick a knife in me with Maria, the Spanish girl his Robert Jordan hero falls for, the way he stuck a knife in me with the Dorothy ninny in his Spanish war play. "Don't think about the critics," I said. "Just keep on pouring the juice until the jug is empty. Do you know how it will end, the old miracle?"

"Do we ever really know how a thing will end until it does?"

A flock of negritos circled in the sky above us, little black finches looking for just the right laurel tree in which to settle for the night.

He said, "Do we even know how *we* will end?"

I said, "Sure enough we'll end up dead like everyone does. The timing is the only thing."

"And what you do with the time."

"And what you do with the time."

"We write well together, Mookie."

"We write well together, Bug."

"Let's go out on the *Pilar* tomorrow, after we're done with the writing."

"I could swim while you fish."

"You'll scare the poor fish with your goggles, Stooge! You scare me!"

I wore motorcycle goggles when I swam in the sea, so that I could make friends with the bright, tiny fish trying to avoid the larger ones Ernest liked to catch.

"I thought you liked the goggles," I said. "I thought they were sexy."

"You're sexy in them," he said. "It isn't the same thing. You aren't more sexy in them, you're just sexy enough to still look sexy in hideous goggles."

"That might be the swimsuit," I said.

"That might be the swimsuit. I like the swimsuit, although I like even better the little black dress," he said, fingering the fabric. "I like taking off the little black dress. Why don't we go home now, and take off the black dress? Then tomorrow we can go out on the *Pilar* with the sexy goggles."

"Let's have dinner first," I said.

"Let's have a drink at the Floridita," he said. "And then we'll go home and take off the dress."

"A drink and some dinner tonight," I said, "and tomorrow we'll write as well as we wrote today, and we'll pack a picnic supper and spend the evening on the *Pilar*."

Ernest received a cable from Pauline that May suggesting he come to New York for the Joe Louis–Tony Galento heavyweight match, for Patrick's birthday.

"You should go," I said. "Mousie would be so pleased."

But the cable was too late. He couldn't get a flight that would reach New York before the fight and the birthday were over.

"She might have told me in time for me to be there," he said. "She goes about doing whatever she damned well pleases, and no writer in the world could write fast enough to keep up with her spending."

He and Pauline were already arguing about the boys, whom she had taken to New York to outfit for a summer camp she'd arranged without consulting him. "I thought I was so good not to bother you," she'd written. "Also, sweetie, I didn't just shove the children in camp to be rid of them as you seem to think." But after the plea for his company for Patrick's birthday, he didn't hear from Pauline for such a long time that he finally called her, only to find that she had experienced some rectal bleeding while in search of a summer rental in Nantucket (the cost of the Key West mansion alone not high enough, apparently, he said). She'd returned to New York for a battery of tests.

Ernest made arrangements to fly to join her. I divvied up our expenses as I had after Spain and counted myself glad that I was independent, that I would never burden anyone else with whatever summer house I might want to rent.

"Here's the split," I said. "The final accounting in case you don't come back."

Before he could get away, Pauline's tests all came out negative. "Just a burst vein in her tight ass," Ernest joked.

Pauline suggested she and Ernest go to Europe together with a grand little group of friends; she thought it might be the last chance to go before war broke out. "*Our* last chance to go," she wrote. He responded that Hitler knew there was everything to gain with war scares and nothing to gain by war, but if the German leader kept lighting matches to show how many powder barrels he had open, something would blow. He declined to go with her on the excuse of his writing, though, and she sent the boys off to summer camp and sailed for Europe with her pals. She wrote that she wished he were coming, and she sent along a clipping of a stout old couple, the man in a kilt, boarding a ship, saying by the next opportunity to go they'd look like the enclosed. "Don't worry, sweetie, and write well," she wrote. "There's nobody like you."

She had already spent everything in their joint account by the time she sailed.

Ernest set about selling the film rights to *To Have and Have Not*, to raise the money to cover Pauline's trip.

Ernest wanted to spend his fortieth birthday that July 21 writing his novel.

"It's nothing, a birthday," he said the afternoon before. "If I can write a good novel, that will be something to celebrate."

"You're writing a very good novel, Bongie."

"I have to write a good one."

"A horridly scrofulous novel, on grey paper with blunt type."

He laughed, and he said he could tell Matie's arrival was imminent, and I closed my eyes for a minute, remembering how much I'd loved climbing on the tram on sunny afternoons, hauling sandwiches and eggs and lemonade and Matie's volume of Robert Browning to the lake at Creve Coeur.

"You're sure you don't mind her coming on your birthday?" I asked, not that there was much to be done about it now if he did. Matie was to arrive in Havana the next morning, and it had taken me all I had to persuade her to visit Ernest and me.

"The only thing sweeter than having one Gellhorn here to celebrate my birthday is having two," he said. "But she won't mind if I write?"

"Matie will mind if you *don't* write, Bug. She wants to be no trouble. She wants us both to write."

We went out on the *Pilar* only after we'd finished the writing that day before his birthday. I said we could fish, I would fish with him, but he said the fishing was only for Saturdays and Sundays now, that he couldn't have the temptation of fishing luring him away from his writing. So we took books to read and a picnic dinner with a prebirthday cake I'd made myself, not a terrible cake. We floated on the water and read for what was left of the afternoon, just sitting side by side on the deck with our books open and the quiet lap of the sea against the hull. When the sky bruised up and the light grew long, we set aside our reading and poured ourselves a bit of good red wine, and spread out the picnic and the cake.

"Some days the going is so tough," he said.

"I know, Scrooby, but it really is a horridly scrofulous novel."

"Do you think so?"

"The passage with Robert Jordan talking with the old Spanish lady—"

"Pilar."

"Right, Pilar." Like his boat. "Where Robert Jordan is talking to Pilar about his father—it's so funny and moving at the same time, Bug." It was a brilliant passage, really. Jordan explains to the old Spanish woman, Pilar, that his father, a "Republican" back in the United States, had shot himself. Suicide. The old woman—thinking a Republican in the United States was similar to the Spanish Republicans, the bravest of whom would kill themselves rather than give up information to Fascists—asks if Jordan's father was tortured, by which she means by his political opponents. And Robert Jordan agrees that, yes, his father was tortured—by his own demons, but he doesn't tell her that. How could Ernest take something as bleak as a son talking about his father's suicide and make it funny?

"It's so funny, and it's so moving, and the funny doesn't cheapen it," I said. "The funny takes it to another level. It makes it even more moving."

Ernest basked in this for a moment. It was what he liked to hear, the specific ways in which his work was extraordinary. It's what all writers like to hear.

He said, "I've never written harder nor steadier."

I said, "I'm good for you that way."

He took a sip of his wine and a bite of the cake and he looked across the water, as if to judge whether he needed to tend the wheel.

He said, "I mean to jam it through before war comes."

"I know, Bongie. I know."

"The war is coming, and it's going to be like no other."

"There's no stopping it. No one listens."

I wondered if we would go ourselves, eventually. I wanted to go. It was what I did best, it turned out, writing about war.

I said, "So the thing to do until then is write our novels."

He said, "This novel is the most important thing I've ever done, Rabbit."

The nickname sat between us as we stared out at the soft light bluing the water, the sun below the horizon now, but with a residue of light lining the far edge of the sea. Rabbit. It was what Bertrand de Jouvenel used to call me, his love name for me. It was what Ernest's new hero called Maria, the Spanish girl in the novel. Sure, one of the characters in my own novel shared some characteristics with Ernest, and another experienced some of the things I'd experienced in Prague. But Rabbit? *Conejo*, Robert Jordan called the girl. In Spanish—a language Robert Jordan must have known pretty well, since he'd been a Spanish professor before he joined the Abraham Lincoln Brigade to fight in Spain—rabbit was slang for "cunt."

Home in bed together, the birthday cake brushed from our teeth and our faces, and only the sex to be done with, Ernest said, "We could do this forever, Mookie. We could spend our mornings writing and our afternoons playing tennis or fishing, and our evenings eating in Havana or on the *Pilar* or right here, at our own scrofulous table."

"Scrofulous, Gellhorn-style."

"Our magnificent, with overtones of delightful, table."

"And a pinch of silly."

"Maybe without the silly. Scrofulous, Hemingstein-style: magnificent with overtones of delightful, but no silly."

"You and I and your family," I said matter-of-factly. It didn't bother me, really, but I thought he shouldn't pretend.

"You and me and the boys, when the boys are on vacation from school."

"You and me here, at Finca Vigía?"

"Or wherever else you'd make me move my typewriter," he said.

"And your scale."

"And my scale."

"We'd have to stay here, Bug, on account of your daily weights on the wall. We could take the scale anywhere, but if we left here we'd have to leave behind the wall."

"You and me here at Finca Vigía. Mr. and Mrs. Heminghorn."

"Mr. and Mrs. Gellingway."

He laughed and he said, "I'm forewarned, aren't I? I'll be known as Mr. Bug Bongie Stooge Snorter Gellingway!"

He pulled me to him, and we snuggled the way I liked to snuggle, just together, just close.

"I'll make it right with Pauline when she's back from Europe," he said. "Mouse and Gigi will be at camp, so I can make it right with her and then pick up Mouse and Gigi at camp and take them out to Wyoming, to the L Bar T, and I can make it right with them there. Bumby is going out west with Hadley and Paul. I could have him meet me there too."

"You're sure, Bug?"

"I'm sure, Mookie. Aren't you?"

The Finca Vigía, San Francisco de Paula, Cuba

July 1939

Matie arrived at ten thirty the next morning, Ernest's birthday, for a two-week visit. When he finished writing for the day, he drove my mother all around the island, showing it off to her and showing her off to his friends. We had a birthday dinner in Havana, with most of the talking done by Ernest and Matie. He loved my mother even then, loved her more than me, I sometimes thought—and with good reason, as she was far more lovable. But much of what they talked about was me: what I'd been like as a girl, and how I took that with me everywhere.

"That's Matie's fault," I said. "She's the one who dragged me to suffragette marches in my formative years."

"Seven thousand women," Matie said proudly, wading into the long-form version of the suffrage protest at the Democratic Convention in St. Louis, in June of 1916. Woodrow Wilson was standing for reelection, and he was progressive except, as so often is the case, when it came to women's rights. Matie, the president of the St. Louis Equal Suffrage League, organized a protest, placing and paying for ads calling for participation. "Well, we knew how to organize by then," she said.

"We'd managed two years earlier to get fourteen thousand names on a petition to put suffrage on the Missouri ballot. But the South Side brewery wards were afraid women would vote for prohibition, so they voted against suffrage and for the drink. We lost three to one. But three to one, that's halfway there."

"Matie," I said, "I'm sure Ernest—"

"Hush, Daughter," Ernest said. "You mother is telling a story."

"Don't say I didn't warn you," I said.

"A year later," Matie continued, "St. Louis got the 1916 Democratic Convention, with the president in attendance—the gift we needed. We lined all of Locust Street from the Democratic Party headquarters in the Hotel Jefferson to the convention in the old Coliseum, the route every delegate had to walk to get from his bed to cast his vote. Seven thousand women from all over the country stood silently in proper white dresses, wearing yellow 'votes for women' sashes and holding yellow parasols in a 'Golden Lane for Suffrage'—a walkless, talkless protest to make the point that we had no voice."

"And you were holding a parasol, Daughter?" Ernest asked me.

Matie answered, "At the Art Museum at Nineteenth and Locust, we made a tableau, one woman representing each of the forty-eight states and the territories, with each woman dressed in white, gray, or black to represent whether the state had granted women the vote, or partial suffrage, or, like Missouri, obstinately refused to budge."

I said, "The ones in black had nifty chains on their hands, to make the point so subtly."

Matie said, "We had a Miss Liberty wearing a crown and holding a torch high for the whole time the delegates to the convention walked past us. And down in the front, two little eight-year-old girls . . ." Matie smiled at me then, as she always did when she told this story.

I said, "I represented the future of women voters—without a parasol, much to my eight-year-old disappointment." And I laughed, and Ernest did too.

"A scrofulous representative of the future of women voters," he said.

"Scrofulous, Gellhorn-style," I said.

"With a pinch of silly," he said.

"With a big dollop of silly!" Matie said.

"The most unlikely bit of that story, Edna," Ernest said, "is that our Marty could stand still for any amount of time, much less silently."

He and Matie both tumbled into laughter. I liked to see them laughing together. I took it as a sign that Matie was all right with Ernest and me. She might not approve of us living together at the Finca Vigía, but Ernest kept his address at the Ambos Mundos; he kept the veneer of propriety that gave Matie comfort.

"What was that other girl's name, Marty?" she asked.

"Margaret? Maude? Her last name started with a *T*, I think."

Matie said, "Well, little Miss T. stood quietly anyway."

Early the next morning, Matie and I went for a walk in the gardens.

"We might pick some flowers for a vase on the dining room table," I suggested.

"They're to be seen, not owned, like every beautiful thing in this world," Matie said, just as she used to back in Creve Coeur Park when I was a child. "You're such a beautiful girl, sweetheart," she said as we walked along, smelling the flowers but leaving them be. "You could have a nice, handsome young man all to yourself."

I leaned over to smell a flower, wanting suddenly to snap its stem, to snap a dozen stems and put them in a vase on my desk, to keep all to myself.

"He has children, Martha," she said. "Not just a wife and an ex-wife, but children."

"I love his children, and I love that he doesn't need to have children with me."

"This didn't end well before, Martha." With Bertrand de Jouvenel in Paris, she meant. "This has never ended well."

We took Matie fishing later that day, and Ernest landed a 525-pound marlin. He himself had weighed 202 pounds that morning—he had to get down from that, he said, faulting my not-so-delicious prebirthday cake and the birthday dinner as he noted his weight on the wall. He'd written sixty-three thousand words of his novel. He had, as yet, no title.

The following Monday, July 31, I banged out the last words of my journalist-in-Prague novel, which I was calling *A Stricken Field*. I read some of the pages to Matie with all the pride and joy and relief that comes at that moment when you've finished writing and no one has yet declared the thing sludge, and you haven't just the moment before read Hemingway. I told Matie I thought I would take the thing to New York myself, and then *Collier's* wanted to send me to the Soviet Union. I told Ernest the New York bit, but not the rest, not yet. He was kind enough not to point out that what I'd finished was just a draft, that it wasn't close to New York ready, a fact I would come to realize myself after that first bit of euphoria.

Ernest wrote his sons at camp late that August that Otto Bruce would pick them up and bring them on the train to Wyoming, where he would meet them. I didn't know what he'd arranged to "make it right" with Pauline, and I was reluctant to ask.

He and I crossed from Cuba to Key West—in a sea so rough that Ernest had to stand all night to keep the boat right—to find the Whitehead Street house empty except for the peacocks and a gaggle of their chicks. We drove on to St. Louis, where he dropped me to visit Matie and prepare for my Russia trip while he carried on to Cody, Wyoming, for a visit with his ex-wife, Hadley, and her husband, Paul.

When Hitler marched his filthy boots into Poland September 1 and all of Europe went to war, I was still in St. Louis, having had to postpone my Russia trip on account of a bad flu. Before I would be well enough for the assignment, though, the Soviet Union—which had stood with us against the Fascists in Spain—attacked Finland, and took Lithuania, Latvia, and Estonia, leaving only the poor, brave Finns holding the line, and the assignment to Russia no longer on offer for me.

Ernest and his boys were at the L Bar T when the news of war came. Pauline, newly arrived in New York from her European extravaganza, flew to join them, arriving in the rain with a sore throat and a fever. It was awful, by all accounts. It came to a head somehow when Pauline went to unpack her clothes and found the buttons of one of her new Paris suits had melted into a waxy mess—a discovery that left her bawling dreadfully while poor Mouse tried to comfort her.

Ernest had Otto Bruce take Mouse and Gigi and their mother to her parents' home in Piggott, Arkansas, and he called me.

"Well, it's done," he said.

"The war," I said, afraid to take any other meaning before it was offered.

He said, "Yes. And the other too."

The Sun Valley Lodge, Sun Valley, Idaho

September 1939

With copies of *A Stricken Field* in Matie's hands and in the mail to Teachie for safekeeping (both sworn not to show it to a soul), I flew to Billings, Montana. Ernest picked me up in a convertible overloaded with guns and fishing rods and sleeping bags, and we set off together the five hundred miles over unpaved roads beyond Craters of the Moon National Monument, in a darkness so complete that anyone with any sense would have turned back, headed for the Sun Valley Lodge. The new mountain resort near the whopping metropolis of Ketchum, Idaho, improbably offered fine dining and dancing to big-band music, along with hunting and fishing, tennis and horses in the summer, skiing in the winter, two gorgeous circular swimming pools from which steam poured upward when it was chilly, and none of the crowds to go with such a swanky resort as yet.

We settled into a two-room corner suite with fireplaces and mountain views—room 206—and into Ernest's life. We wrote in the mornings, and hunted duck and pheasant or fished in the winding creeks when the work was done. We took horses up into the mountains, along with sandwiches and a bottle of wine. We had dinners with Fred Spiegel, who'd driven ambulances with Ernest in Italy and whose family owned a catalog business out of Chicago that had been terrifically successful despite the Depression. Fred's wife was swell, and so was Tillie Arnold, the lodge photographer's wife. I was glad to have women friends, glad Sun Valley was that kind of place, where little notice was paid to differences in social standing that might well have separated us in Chicago or St. Louis.

When my editor at *Collier's* called to see if I might go to Finland, I wasn't sure. I did want to cover the poor brave Finns holding the line against Russia; I did want to understand how the good Russians I'd known in Spain could be part of something so brutal. And it would have been silly to turn down the money, especially with Ernest having to enlist Pauline's own family to try to get her to be sensible about the financial end of their split. Ernest had been more than generous with Hadley, giving her all the royalties from *A Farewell to Arms* and Bumby all the support he would ever need, but Hadley had had nothing, while Pauline could make King Tut look like a pauper if only she would be reasonable. The thing about leaving Ernest for Finland, though, was that he did so poorly when left on his own.

As we lay in bed, looking out the window to the moonlit mountains, which made me think of the mountains where I crossed the border into Spain, I said, "The Russians and the Finns toe to toe at the border, Bug," trying to tempt him into getting NANA to send him to Finland too.

He twirled a lock of my hair, still damp from an evening swim. "You don't much care who is fighting as long as there is someone at it, do you, Mook?"

"The same could be said of you."

"But I like my fighters contained in a boxing ring."

"You don't, though. You're just like me, Bug. You could come too. We could go to Finland together."

"I have the novel to finish."

Outside, the moon was tucking itself in behind the mountains. Good night, moon.

"Is this something you really want to do, Mookie?" he asked. "If you really think so, you go and I'll stay, and I'll join you if I can, and if not we'll meet back home."

"Back home at the Finca Vigía."

"Back home at the Finca Vigía. With this little *Collier's* egg laid in your nest, you'll be able to settle in to write stories without a worry. You won't have to do the journalism anymore."

"But I love the journalism."

"You won't have to leave me if you don't want to. And if you do, I'll wait quietly at home, like a good wifey-wife."

I looked to a sky thick with stars over sharp mountain peaks, trying to gauge whether he meant it or was just being as reasonable as I'd had to be for the whole of our relationship.

"I hate to leave this paradise, Bug," I said.

"It's an awfully fine place, isn't it, Mookie? We might have our wedding here."

"After the divorce is final."

"In the spring. It will be done in the spring, and we'll have a fine, big wedding, and when *Collier's* asks you to run off and abandon me, you'll have the excuse of being married."

"I'll say my husband and I work together."

He laughed and he said, "Yes, I believe you will."

By the time my travel papers came through, though, his tone had changed. "What old Indian likes to lose his squaw with a hard winter coming?" Smiling as if he were joking but with a hangdog look in his eyes.

Tillie Arnold thought it foolish for me to leave. "What if Ernie changes his mind, Mart?" Ernie, they liked to call him at the Sun Valley

Lodge, which reminded me of Herb Matthews in Spain, and that boy Raven at the hospital in Madrid.

I said, "Then I'll have been glad to know he's that fickle before it's too late."

Her question did give me pause, though. I thought to tell her about the money, that we needed the money, but Ernest would have hated that.

"I can't possibly pass up the opportunity, Tillie," I said. "Anyway, it's in my blood, and I have to do it. But I know I have you to tend to Ernest for me while I'm away"—words I casually worked into a conversation with another friend too, making light of it but leaving no doubt that I was relying on them to keep him busy enough that he wouldn't look for anyone new. And as we were saying our goodbyes before Ernest took me to the airport, I hit the point one final time. "You two keep an eye on this clown for me, will you?" I said. "Remind him to bathe and shave every now and then."

"Never you mind, Mook," Ernest said. "I'll be a very good boy while you're off covering the war." And he was, I suppose, although even before I set off out of Hoboken on a Dutch ship, he'd rechristened our rooms "Hemingstein's Mixed Vicing and Dicing Establishment" and reverted to poker and craps. He told everyone who would listen that he was "stinko deadly lonely," but he kept writing. When Ernest was writing, nothing got in his way.

For my part, I mingled with anxious passengers heading home to Europe—forty-five on a ship built for over five hundred—all of us eating boiled cardboard and sleeping on pygmy beds with mattresses of nails. We kept queer hours. Who could sleep on a ship that routinely passed by dead bodies floating about in their life vests? (Life vests inappropriately named, I thought, but I didn't dare say it aloud.) Who could sleep while negotiating seas thick with the new German magnetic mines, the ship's radio forever rattling with the news of sinkings even in the neutral zone? There was no way to claim one's neutrality to balloon-sized mines floating in the choppy water. There was no way even to see them in the fog.

Somehow, I arrived in Antwerp, and flew out the next morning—November 29—to Stockholm, and then on to Helsinki and a hotel room with a view of the blackout paper securely taped over window glass. I cabled Ernest and Matie both that I'd arrived safely. The next morning at precisely 9:15, before I'd even managed breakfast, the warning sirens sounded the approach of Russian planes.

Helsinki, Finland

November 1939

The Russians bombed the Helsinki airport that first morning, but the planes over the city itself dropped only leaflets saying, improbably, "You know we have bread. Why do you starve?" The clouds settled in then, and the Finns went about their business as if the cement sky could protect them from a Russian air base only fifteen stinking miles away.

I was taking a late lunch when the planes came again, unseen on account of the clouds until they dived and dumped their bombs. I'd never felt that kind of explosion before, not even in Spain. I'd never seen that kind of smoke rolling right down the street.

People yelled, "Gas!" and of course I'd left my gas mask back in New York. I was done for. I pulled the little passport picture of Ernest from my purse to say, "Goodbye, Bongie." I wished I had a photo of Matie too. I felt like I'd always worried I would end up feeling with Bug—with my guts ripped out and tossed into the street. It was the damned Russians doing the stomping, though, and in stomping on my guts, they would stomp Bug's too.

But no one was coughing the poison-killing-you cough. The whole damned attack was all over in a minute, the planes gone and no one dying from the poison gas, which wasn't gas at all but only rubble dust from the bombs.

I took my bar of soap from my pack, and I washed the war from my skin, and I dried the soap and put it back in my pack, feeling as alive as anything. God, I did love covering war when it wasn't killing me. I could write a thousand words in five minutes and I could make it jell, I could make every word of it something to pay attention to.

I set off through glass-strewn streets with two Italian journalists, one of whom looked very like Randolfo Pacciardi, but both of whom were Fascists my old back-seat friend would have despised. There were so few journalists in Finland that I had to take the company I could get. We found big apartment buildings burning like the fires of hell, and the Finns marvelous about it, not crying or running but rather leaning their backs into dousing fires and digging out.

The few foreigners remaining in Finland took to panicking and shoving off any way they could. There were no planes and the Russian fleet was blocking passage by ship, but they left Helsinki for safer ground. A friend who wrote for the British papers banged on my door at two a.m. one morning, saying, "There will be gas in the next few hours, love. Best skedaddle with me now." I'd already arranged to go out to the countryside at seven thirty with my Italian pals, though, and that was soon enough for an eight thirty bombing; I told him a girl needed her beauty sleep, and I didn't wake again until eight fifteen—at which point I did hurry like hell. I was the only one left in the hotel except the good concierge, who of course wouldn't leave until the last guest had. My Italians, who'd been waiting for my call to wake them, fetched me for a walk in the countryside in the snow. There was no gas that morning either, it turned out, despite all the scurrying about to get out of its way.

I wrote Ernest that I loved him like a mad hatter, and that the book was the thing, that he was me and his book was my book and nothing mattered more, and he was to keep writing and I would do my business here, and I would get back as soon as I could. I suggested he open the Cuba house as a Christmas present to me, and I would come wallow in the sun and be glad to be home. I'd be there by the end of the year, I promised, and if I wasn't, he could abandon me for some more loyal love.

Ernest wrote Max Perkins that I was getting shot in Finland so he could finish his book. He wrote the Spiegels after they left Sun Valley that he couldn't eat or sleep for worrying about me. And he left Sun Valley himself for the holidays in Key West, ignoring Pauline's warning that he wouldn't be welcome even for Christmas with his sons.

I took the letter President Roosevelt had given me instructing everyone to step aside and let me go wherever I wanted to go, and I set off for the front. A chauffeur in military garb drove me out over icy roads and mined bridges, through unending forests and always with the flashes of guns like fireworks in the predawn dark. It was the first big night operation of the war, and I had the orchestra section to myself, serenaded by Finnish pilots hardly out of their school uniforms, and in the company of captured Russians too. That was something. If I had to be in a bombing zone, at least I was getting a story no one else would have—a war in the arctic, where the weather was your friend or your enemy. Three million Finns defending their homeland might have some tiny chance against 180 million Russians fighting only for two lousy strategic positions, if only the weather and some awfully good luck might turn up for the Finns.

Well before Christmas, I was back in Helsinki with the goods to write three terrific pieces—and no way to get home.

Ernest arrived in Key West to find that Pauline had sent away the help and set off for New York, leaving the boys in the charge of a nanny they abhorred. Their mother had told them to wait for their father to fetch them for Christmas in Cuba but hadn't bothered to share the plan with

Bug. He stayed long enough to pack up his belongings, everything but his French racing bicycle in the basement—one of the his-and-hers bicycles he and Pauline had ridden on the dirt roads of the French Camargue for their honeymoon, now rusting beside its mate, the wheels melting into the stone floor. He stored everything in the basement of Sloppy Joe's, and by Christmas Eve, he and Bumby, Mouse, and Gigi had loaded the Buick onto the ferry to Havana.

I was eating in a Helsinki restaurant with only a paperback propped up against my water glass for company when an American military attaché I knew asked to join me.

"Anyone with any sense is leaving this place, you know that, right?" he said.

"And yet here you are having this dreadful fish. It is fish, isn't it?" I poked at the food, longing to be on the *Pilar* again, swimming in my silly goggles while Ernest fished. You know when you leave to cover war that just because you get there doesn't mean you'll get home, but you can't think about that or you'll never go. You go, and you pretend bravery even to yourself, insisting on going back to sleep when you ought to leave for the countryside in case of gas, because if there's a risk of gas, what the hell are you doing there? Yet you have to be; it's what keeps you alive. It's hard enough for a man in this business, when the whole world expects you can cover a war. A woman has to fend off the doubts of the whole world along with her own certainty that she is in so far over her head that her lungs are filling. A woman who wants to be taken seriously has no choice but to brave the possibility of gas.

"So what keeps you here?" I asked.

"Me?" he said. "Oh no, I'm not staying. I'm evacuating on a flight to Sweden."

"There's a flight to Sweden?"

"Sure there is. Tonight. You want to come? I'd have asked, but I didn't think—"

"Christ, yes!" I answered before he could say anything about maybe there not being a seat for me. "Don't you move. Don't go away."

I abandoned my plate and rushed out of the restaurant, returning in minutes with my pajamas and a bottle of whiskey.

He laughed and he said, "You've been through an evacuation before, I guess."

I said, "I am a pro."

I spent Christmas in Sweden, writing my damned heart out while I waited for a ship to Lisbon, Portugal, where I could catch the Pan Am Clipper to Cuba with my tush intact, my pride in full bloom, and my promise to be home for the new year kept. I was still in Sweden when I got the news that Gustav Regler, our German novelist friend from Madrid who'd taken a bullet in his back while trying to stop the Fascists in Spain, was being held as an enemy alien in France.

The trip to Paris was no picnic, I can tell you that. I arrived feeling like a used tissue, grimy and abandoned. But the city, all dusty white with a powdered-sugar covering of snow, was reviving.

I harangued everyone I could collar to free Gustav Regler. I waved my letter from the president around as if it were the French constitution and I the duly elected president. All those administratoramuses did listen on account of the letter but with pasty expressions and flaccid promises to "look into it"—as if "it" were a pair of eyeglasses they might put on their ugly noses to see the thing reasonably. They could not have cared less about a German communist, even an anti-Nazi one who'd nearly died trying to save Spain.

There was nothing more to do but give all the cash I could spare to Gustav Regler's wife and assure her that I would sit on the steps of the White House with a protest sign draped over me until Roosevelt insisted the French set her husband free.

I cabled Ernest that I was on my way. Only I got tripped up about a visa to Portugal—the same delay and delay and delay as when I'd tried to get from Paris to Spain that first time. And when that was finally sorted out (after more waving of President Roosevelt's letter), it wasn't clear the French airlines would fly. By the time I got to Lisbon, the weather I'd so counted on in Finland had turned true enemy. The Clipper had stopped running, even those big Pan Am flying boats unable to get anywhere on account of the weather. "ASHAMED DISAPPOINT YOU," I cabled Ernest. "MISERABLY UNHAPPY." It was January 2, 1940. A new decade had begun, and I was alone in Lisbon, my sole companion the promise I hadn't kept.

The Finca Vigía, San Francisco de Paula, Cuba

January 1940

I arrived back in Cuba, finally, to the sea a calm azure and the sky a sharper blue dotted with puffs of soft white, and to Ernest looking an absolute mess. I'd been a little crushed when he hadn't been there to greet me from the flight, even though I'd told him to stay home and write and I would come to him, I would find him as I did: sitting in his club chair by the drinks cart with his first scotch of the day, counting the words he'd written. But it wasn't his first scotch, I didn't think, and his hair was long and scraggly except where it wasn't, where it seemed thinner than when I'd left. His rope belt was tied around a larger girth—weight gain I hoped I'd find recorded on my bathroom wall, but looking at the slop of him, I feared I might not. He hadn't showered, perhaps not for days.

"Bongie, you can't find your way to the barbershop without me?" I teased, offering my warmest smile as I dropped my pack on the floor and pulled the door closed behind me.

He looked up at me. He didn't smile. He said, "I won't have it cut until the novel is finished."

I went to him and kissed him on the cheek above the scruffy beard.

"We're becoming superstitious?" I said. "Because that sounds to me like an excuse to bother me for leaving you alone on New Year's Eve."

"Two months and sixteen days."

"I know, Bug, I know," I said, moved by the precision of his words. I couldn't have said how long we'd spent apart, with so much going on that one day bled into the next. But then he was a counter, a keeper-tracker of numbers. His weight every morning, even when he was hungover, even when it was much higher than he wanted to know. His daily word count each afternoon over his first scotch. He had taken to reporting both tallies in letters to anyone who would listen. Max Perkins worried this daily counting suggested Ernest might end up in a loony bin, but if your roots were in journalism that had to be cabled at a cost of so much per word, it made sense to be in the habit of counting. And it gave Bug a sense of control over the things he struggled to control: his weight, the progress of his writing, my absence from him.

"I didn't mean to be gone so long, Bug," I said. "You know I didn't."

"You stopped in Washington."

"That was for Gustav Regler. You can't fault me for that."

"You stopped in New York."

I took in the room around us, supposing the whole of my Finca Vigía would look a mess too if it weren't for Reeves and the rest of the staff. But the French doors gave up clear views to the gardens, the books tidily lined the shelves, my club chair cushions were freshly plumped, and the drinks cart sported at least as many bottles as it ever had. If the pool pump was on the fritz, well, the pool pump was a full-employment opportunity for the next-door neighbor boy who took care of it.

"I stopped in New York only for a minute, only to praise the gang at *Collier's* so they would keep hiring me if . . ." If Ernest's novel wasn't finished and published in pretty short order; he had no income while he was working on the novel except a bit of royalties from earlier books that went to Pauline. "If we want to go somewhere to do the journalism again," I said.

"Two months and sixteen days, and me in the middle of a novel that was going so well."

I gently fingered his unruly hair. I meant to love even the things he did to vex me.

"The book is everything to me too, you know that," I said, wondering if he was growing his hair because of the balding, because the balding made him nervous in the same way that Yeats's death had. "It's part of the reason I went to Finland, so we'd have money while you write the book."

He took his nearly empty glass from the drinks cart and poured himself a healthy dose of booze, straight up, and slumped back into his chair. I was too tired from the travel to drink, but I poured myself a glass of the damned stuff and came and sat on his lap, and clinked my glass with his. I removed his glasses and kissed him real now, a long kiss on the lips I'd so missed. He tasted of the whiskey, which might have been better than if he hadn't.

"Don't be a silly Scrooby," I said. "It's done and I'm home."

The sun settled behind a cloud, dimming the room and the glasses in our hands, the alcohol, and Ernest's face as he studied me. It was a look I recognized, a decision to roust himself from his crankiness.

"I think 'silly Scrooby' suits me," he said. "I thought you loved 'silly Scrooby.'"

I laughed, and I said everything suited him, and I set my drink on the cart and gently unbuttoned his shirt to slide my hands over his sturdy chest.

"I need a shower," I said in my huskiest voice. "Want to join me?"

We were still lying on the warm, after-sex messy sheets, when he said, "You won't leave me again, Mookie." Not a question, but not exactly not one.

"I won't leave you ever again until the book is done."

He grinned and said, "Unless I tire of you and boot you for someone with blonder hair and longer legs."

I didn't think he meant the words to hurt the way they did, not consciously.

"I won't leave you unless you tire of me and throw me off the *Pilar* to the sharks," I promised.

"You and your silly swimming googles," he said.

I stood and went to his writing desk, took a piece of paper and a pen, and dated the page. I wrote "GUARANTY" in large block letters at the top, and I put it in writing: I, the undersigned Mrs. Martha Bongie Hemingstein, guaranteed never again to brutalize him in any way, not with weapons or words, and I recognized that such a fine writer as himself could not again be left for two months and sixteen days. I signed it and I put two lines for the witnesses, under which I wrote "Judge R. R. Rabbit" and "Judge P. O. Pig."

And we had a good laugh, and I wrote a second guaranty, promising that after we were married I would never leave him for any reason, and a third that I would never divorce him as long as he was a good boy.

There were eight huge pink orchids growing out of my ceiba tree at the front of the Finca, and Ernest was averaging five hundred words a day and weighing under two hundred pounds within weeks of my return. He was searching the Bible and Shakespeare and the *Oxford Book of English Prose* for a title, daily coming up with one that was just the thing only to toss it away the next morning. The weather had turned cold—nothing like Finland, but Ernest hadn't been in Finland. He took to writing in our nice, warm bed in the mornings, whether I was awake or not.

One morning I woke to find him standing at my desk, with a letter I'd gotten from Allen Grover in hand.

"Bug?" I said. "What are you doing?"

"You didn't tell me you saw Grover in New York on your way to Finland."

"What the hell, Hemingway?" I said. "You're reading my mail?"

"Why didn't you tell me you saw Grover?"

"I most certainly did tell you."

"But not this way. Not the two of you at his apartment, listening to the radio."

"He had a radio. Of course I listened! How else was I supposed to get news of the world?"

I threw off the covers, climbed from bed, and took the letter from him. "Do I read your mail, Hemingway?"

"I don't get mail from men I've been to bed with."

"No, only wives and ex-wives."

"I'm happy to have you read my mail, Mook. I have nothing to hide."

"Nor do I," I said, feeling violated even though it didn't matter, I really did have nothing to hide.

We played tennis most afternoons, and we cut back on the drinking, confining ourselves to one good Saturday drunk a week and not much else. He needed a night to let off the steam lest he overheat in the writing and blow the whole thing to bits, he said. So we'd go into town and start with absinthe, followed by a good bottle of red wine at dinner and, when we were already starting to be pretty juiced, vodka with the pelota players. Ernest did pretty well at the handball game even drunk, although none of the players was sober, there was that. Then we'd finish off with whiskey and soda, and, more often than not, wake the poor souls who lived on the streets we wandered with our singing. We tended to sing with strangers and whores, and none of us could carry a tune.

If it was a lot of drinking, at least it was just the one night each week, and we could sleep it off on Sunday and be back at the writing Monday. While I was in Europe, Ernest had gone out drinking nearly every night.

On March 8, Duell, Sloan and Pearce published my journalist-in-Prague novel, *A Stricken Field.* The day before it was published, Mrs. Roosevelt, in her My Day column, recommended it as an important book, even using the *m* word: "masterpiece." The *New York Times*, on the morning the novel was released, called it taut and engrossing, and praised my choice to tell the story as fiction, saying if I'd written it any other way it would have told only part of the story. The *Herald Tribune* put it among the year's most powerful books, even if the review did mention some unevenness. But all that goodness was undone by what Allen Grover—my old pal who'd just weeks before visited us at the Finca, drinking our booze and impressing our Basque friends with his physique—allowed in the pages of *Time*.

In the guise of a review of my novel, what *Time* reviewed was my private life. They started and ended with Ernest, my "great and good friend" whom I'd returned from Finland to visit in Cuba where, they assured readers, Ernest Hemingway was living—living in *my* damned home, but never mind that. The nasty piece ended with a footnote suggesting the dreadful Dorothy Bridges character from Ernest's Spanish war play was inspired by me, as if any character so vacuous needed inspiration from any real woman. The whole thing was so tawdry that I wanted to stick Grover's head in a great big bucket of manure and slowly drown him there.

"I told you Grover was a Jew," Ernest said.

"A *Jew*, Ernest?"

"You know what I mean. In the Shakespeare sense. A bastard who visits on the pretense of being your friend, only to mine your private life and throw it to the goddamned wolves."

I dialed Grover's number and, at his hello, demanded, "Did you come down to visit us just to confirm that Hemmy and I were an 'us,' so your magazine could drag us through the muck and take Pauline and the boys along for the slimy ride? I don't even care for myself, but now those sweet boys are going to hear about it from every damned schoolmate who gives them the stink eye, when Ernest would have had the entire Easter vacation to help them understand."

"Martha—"

"Ernest has been writing a book that is the next coming, I swear it is, it's the kind of book only a brain as finely tuned as his could give us. But such a finely tuned brain is a delicate thing, and now you've yanked his head up from it on account of a tawdry magazine that would sell a friend's privacy for a lousy buck. And he's writing the ending too, where even the best writing can fall apart and leave the writer with nothing. Even a writer like Ernest can lose a book at the end if some filthy magazine makes too much trouble."

"But I didn't—"

"That was no review at all! That was a personal assault worthy of the Hearst papers, a personal assault in the guise of a review that cheapens us all, not just the Gellhorns—God, poor Matie! Do you see what you've done to my mother, who is going to have every old biddy in St. Louis waving this in her face? Her daughter's life played out in print like some sorry movie with the kind of dismal ending every cheap tart deserves, or that's what they'll think, them and their puny little quick-to-judge minds."

"Martha, be reasonable."

"Not just us. You've ruined everyone who tries to do this, who tries to write. You've cheapened it all, every bit of the goodness that writers do."

"Really, Mart, I don't think you can put the demise of literature on seven hundred words on page eighty-two."

"I counted you as a friend, but, oh boy, was I mistaken. You're a backstabber and a money-grubber and a phony and a spy for the lousy side of this stink."

"But I didn't know anything about it! I swear, Marty—"

"How dare you drag Mrs. Roosevelt's name into it just to make it a bigger story, the First Lady wrapped up in a scandalous love affair involving the world's most famous writer?"

"*I* didn't drag anyone," Grover insisted. "I'm *not* the dragger."

"How dare you drag Bertrand's name into it, just to put a point on the scandal, to lay the blame for Ernest's broken marriage at *my* feet, as if I wouldn't have lived happily ever after as Madame de Jouvenel if Bertrand's witch of a wife hadn't insisted on keeping her husband and her lover both!"

"I swear, Mart, I had no more idea of the piece than you did until I opened my copy."

"Sure, and it's my lousy luck that Tom was away. He would have stood up for me. He would have been all over your lousy bastard of an editor to pull the piece. Any damned friend I have in this world would have shown some loyalty and put their fucking resignation on page one before they'd let this rotten stink run. But you—"

I slammed down the receiver. He'd made a fool of me, but, sure, I could survive that; I might even forgive his magazine's trash of a piece with its making me out to be a whore and finding the filthiest photograph of me to run with it. But he'd made a fool of my writing, or he'd let his magazine do it, painting me as a pathetic hanger-on, with no talent beyond a savant ability to attract the attention of talented men. As if *The Trouble I've Seen* hadn't gotten me on the cover of the *Saturday Review of Literature* before I'd ever met Ernest. Unlike Ernest, *Time* assured its readers, my legend was larger than my work.

The Finca Vigía, San Francisco de Paula, Cuba

March 1940

Mousie and Gigi, when they came for their Easter break, quickly settled on calling me "The Marty." Mouse instructed us to call him Patrick now that he was eleven. He and Gigi palled around in matching checked shirts, Patrick reading away whole mornings by the pool with me—mornings when I was meant to be writing, but, as my partner in crime, he swore not to rat me out even under pain of the rack or water torture or being denied a new book. He measured everything he read by whether it was longer or shorter than his father's *Green Hills of Africa*, which wasn't *Middlemarch* or *War and Peace* but was a lot of pages for an eleven-year-old who might just as likely read comics.

Gigi did not insist we call him Gregory but did make us play dice with him, and for money too. He wooed the dice, blowing on them and saying, "Come on, baby, one more little fever," which I was to understand meant he wanted a pair of fives, but to be honest I was working so hard at suppressing giggles that it might have meant something else altogether. He never played if he didn't feel hot about the game, and a nickel was all he would risk even at his hottest, throwing sevens and elevens at will. He was a funny boy who, when he wasn't wild with gambling, sat quietly watching mother hummingbirds make their square little nests and tend their eggs.

Bumby joined us in early April. Watching him swim and fish and shoot, I imagined how Ernest must have looked when he was sixteen and handsome and strong. Bumby was already into the business of a high schooler planning for college, so we had long, chummy talks about exams and schoolbooks and college boards. "The Bumble," as I took to calling him, was to be in a play at school, so you could often find him belting out lines in various teenaged versions of adult emotions. He hit his *t*'s, though, and he would be heard even in the last row of the theater, no doubt about that.

Ernest and I spent our mornings writing, or Ernest wrote and I snuck off to read with Patrick. I'd written exactly one story since I'd come home from Finland. On a good morning, I managed my five-finger exercises, little bits that didn't have to be anything at all as long as I was writing something: a character sketch or a description of a place, a snatch of dialogue unencumbered by actual plot. I wanted to be lost in the throes of a fine, big story, like Ernest was with his Spanish war book. He took no note even of his sons—who were only visiting for a few weeks, for heaven's sake—until he'd finished his writing for the day and counted his words. He believed in himself and his work as surely as if he were the good Lord himself writing on stone tablets. I'd have given my left leg, and my right one too, to write with that kind of assurance. But it was so ghastly hard to write without the threat of a bomb falling on my head. It was ghastly hard to decline *Collier's* repeated offers to send me off to have bombs dropped on me in Europe. "No way, no how," I assured Ernest. "I promised to stay here with my Bongie Pig, and I can keep a promise as long as it doesn't involve me flying an airplane myself from Portugal in Atlantic storms on New Year's Eve."

"Or even if it does, Mrs. Hundred-Thirty-Pound Pig."

He'd roped me into his obsession, weighing me on his scale every morning.

"Even if it does, Mr. Woppenstein Pig," I said, not feeling piggish but understanding that he did and that he wanted my company in this as in everything but his writing. "I'll be your good wifey-pig, and I'll read every word you write, and I'll proclaim each one stinking brilliant, you know I will."

"You make me so happy, Mrs. Heminghorn Pig," he said. "You make me so damned happy, so able to write."

But there was no offer of pages to read as my reward. The closer he got to the end of his novel, the more reluctant he was to share it. He took to burying his new pages in a desk drawer under other papers, like some rodent stocking up for winter. I imagined he laid a hair across the drawer like a bad British spy so that if I passed the desk too enthusiastically he could prove that I'd been snooping. And our whole life now was about his writing. I couldn't write crap in the peace in which he loved to write.

It was my own fault. Where he had gobs of discipline, I had great clots of sloth. I could learn from the way he sat down every morning to write. But I needed to be excited about a thing to do the writing. I needed to go out and find some ghastly trouble and stew myself in it night and day, collecting it all in notebooks for after the excitement was done. I couldn't write the way Ernest wrote, taking a pile of clean white paper on one side and rolling it through a typewriter and stacking it neatly on the other side, day after day after day without any excitement at all to bring the juice on. So my whole life boiled down to helping him and trying to write without the juice. My life boiled down to waiting for Ernest to be finished with the book so that it would be my turn, and we could sign contracts with NANA and *Collier's* and set off toward something dangerous and awful and terribly damned fun.

But I was happy to share his family. Afternoons and evenings, Ernest and the boys and I played tennis, and we were marvelous tennis players, or we thought we were. We fished on the *Pilar*. We shot birds. The boys took me as part of their gang, as obedient to their father's wishes as they themselves were, and I took them as part of my family, and I thought this was just the perfect way to be a mother, with boys who were already nice boys with little chance of ruin by a reckless mother, with none of the body misshaping or bad-child risk that might come with a Gellhorn brood.

One night not long after Bumby arrived, when the house was put to bed and Ernest and I were snuggled together, me going on about the grand shooting we'd all done that day, I asked if there wasn't a lighter gun for poor Gigi.

"A lighter gun than Mousie's?"

Gigi didn't yet have his own gun, so he used his brother's. The poor kid had to sit and balance that heavy thing on his knees just to aim it straight.

"He topples backward from the recoil every time he shoots, Scrooby! It's all I can do not to laugh, but of course that would be the end of his affection for me."

Ernest laughed and said, "But Gigi wouldn't take a smaller gun if we had one to give him. His manhood would be questioned by a smaller gun."

"His eight-year-old manhood?"

Ernest laughed and laughed.

"You do like them, don't you, Mook?"

"I do love them, Bug. There are no finer boys anywhere on this big earth. You produce a fine brood, you do, Ernest Hemingway."

He said, "We might have a daughter someday. I'd like a daughter."

I lay perfectly still for a moment, listening to the breeze in the palm outside the open window. "A daughter, Hemmy?" I said finally.

"One who would grow up to have golden hair and long legs, long brains, and pluck to spare." He stroked my hair. "One who would be a better shot than her mother, though!"

We might name her Abigail June, I thought to say, but still I could not say the name of that poor baby being denied syphilis treatment for want of twenty-five lousy cents per shot.

The next evening, when we went out for target practice on the negritos that sang so gloriously as they headed from the fields to the laurel trees in Havana, I shot a hawk. He was a beautiful creature, and I was sorry the moment I saw him drop, even while Ernest and his sons cheered at my prowess with a gun.

The Finca Vigía, San Francisco de Paula, Cuba

April 1940

Hitler stomped into Denmark and Norway with no fight from the Danes and next to none from the Norwegians that April. Ernest and I only learned of it four days later, when the newspapers arrived on the mail boat. That was fine for Ernest, who was in his novel and who wanted no distraction. Me, I put maps up on our walls so I could keep track of the war as carefully as Ernest kept track of his word count and his weight and, now, my weight too.

I read the news when I was meant to be writing. I wrote letters. Every time I tried to write fiction, I was left wanting to chuck it all and run off to Europe, where the danger was real and the writing would be about something bigger than myself. That was all trying-to-be-too-damned-noble, of course. I wanted to go to war every minute I was writing just so I could run about with the other overwrought loonies and think myself sane. I wanted to go to war so I wouldn't have to learn and think and write and discipline myself into five hundred words a day.

On May 10, Germany invaded Belgium, France, Luxembourg, and the Netherlands. That worm Neville Chamberlain resigned as the

British prime minister, and Winston Churchill stepped in. When I came home from the mail boat with the newspapers—May 15, the news old and stale and still stinking lousy—Ernest set his writing aside, and took the papers, and read.

"Fuck this whole fucking Nazi mess," he said, and he left without telling me where he was going, although not in a huff.

He came home a bit later with the radio I'd been nagging him to allow me to buy.

"So we can have the war news screeched loudly and to the minute," he said.

It was a pretty radio, a Detrola in the shape of the arch of a stone cathedral, with a beautiful, warm clock face; inlaid wood trim and turned-spool feet; and a sturdy speaker and dials. As he set it on our living room bookshelf, by the door where there was a plug and it would be just out of the sunlight, he said, "You need to write some happiness, though, Mart. If you write only disaster, you'll soon become disaster girl, with a byline everyone will put down on account of not being able to stand a world so bleak."

I turned on the radio and began searching with the dial.

He said, "They'll charge you with the great sin of manufacturing catastrophes just to have something to write."

I found a station—CBS, with Elmer Davis delivering in his warm Hoosier accent the news of May 15 as it was happening: General Winkelman surrendering Amsterdam to the Nazis, who had also crossed the Meuse River into northern France, while, in America, we worried ourselves with some new kind of stockings made of nylon rather than silk.

"Christ," I said.

"Christ," he agreed.

We talked for a long time about the war, then, and what was to be done about it, whether Roosevelt would take us into it, and whether we thought he should. We were a country of fools like everyone else, we decided, and so of course we would get in. It was just a matter of when.

"Clearly, I don't need to manufacture disaster as long as that brute is running roughshod over all of Europe," I said. It was evening and we were having dinner, neither of us having written another word. We'd brought our plates to the club chairs in the living room, and we were listening to the evening newscast, more or less the same news: Amsterdam and France, and the new nylon stockings.

"What the hell is nylon?" Ernest asked.

"They use it to make toothbrushes."

He laughed because we needed to laugh. He laughed, and I laughed, and he poured us a second drink, and he said, "If you ever wear toothbrushes on those legs of yours, Mook, I will definitely toss you off the *Pilar* to the sharks."

"Don't be silly, Bongie," I said. "I don't wear stockings at all."

After the news was over and Ernest had turned the dial off, I said, "We should be there, like we were in Spain."

Ernest said, "After the book is done, Mookie. It's almost done. There will be time after that. There will be more than enough war to last."

Outside, the negritos were singing their way back to Havana. Perhaps a hawk somewhere too, one I hadn't killed.

I supposed Ernest was right about the risk of my becoming a disaster-girl writer, so I put together a proposal to write a happy bunch of pieces that would be nearly as vacuous as nylon stockings. Local rabbit hunts in Cuba, or eighteen ways to cook cassava, or the lodge dances with our very rich and very famous Sun Valley friends. When my editor at *Collier's* replied that there was too much going on in the world for anyone to be writing about the life of a vegetable, I signed my response "the lucky vegetable."

Several times a day, I turned on the radio, and updated my wall maps.

After just two days, Ernest stomped in from his writing desk, demanding, "How am I supposed to write this damned book if I'm forever bothered by the news?" He pulled the plug, silencing Edward R. Murrow and his *World News Roundup*.

"It's a bother, I'm sure, Hemingway," I said calmly, "to be troubled by the news of the French dying en masse trying to defend what's left of the free world while we sit here drinking daiquiris and catching trout."

He looked hurt. Well, I'd meant to hurt him. All that was going on in the world, and still every morning he got up and weighed himself and pulled on his pants and sat down to write.

He gathered himself the way he could, though, and smiled sheepishly, and stuck the plug back into the socket. He turned the volume down just a little. "Not trout, Mookie," he said lightly. "Trout are freshwater fish."

"How the hell would I know? It's not like I ever catch a damned thing."

"But you don't care to, Mook," he said gently. "You never care to."

I turned back to my map, pulling a pin and sticking it fiercely into a new position. I didn't begrudge him his magic. I loved that he had the magic; it was when I loved him most, when he had the magic and the words were coming, and he couldn't be bothered with anything else. But there was no me in his magic, and the way the magic came to him wasn't the way the magic came to me. I had to go out and find it. I had to live *in* the world, not holed up in a quiet corner with a cook and a pool and cats to rub against my legs. I had to live in the world, and if there was trouble anywhere in it, I needed to have my boots filthy with it, to be stewing in the trouble until the words boiled out of me.

Ernest watched me as I moved my map pins: the British and the French troops falling back toward Dunkirk. I squared my shoulders, lest he think he might come to me and touch me. I would collapse if he touched me, or I'd belt him, or both.

After a moment, he muttered to himself that all writers were crazy, but none more so than the female kind, and he went back to his desk and wrote much longer into the day than usual, while I spent the afternoon writing with the radio on, producing only four lousy paragraphs that I tore up in the end.

When he was done writing for the day, he poured himself a drink as he always did, and he counted his words as he sipped it, and when he was done counting, he squirreled away his pages, as he now did at the end of each day.

"I might ask Pauline to read the draft when I'm done with it," he said at dinner that night.

I chewed a lousy bite of roasted potato going to mush in my mouth.

"If you can get Pauline to read it, Scrooby, well then, have at it," I said as lightly as I could manage after a full day of fuming at the news while Ernest's typewriter hummed happily in the other room.

"She's a fine editor," he said. "She may be the best editor I know."

I set my fork down slowly. I was tired. I was cranky from the writing or the not writing, and I was cranky from the war that *Collier's* was forever dangling in front of me, but I'd promised when I'd come home from Finland that I wouldn't leave him again.

"Fuck you, Hemingway," I said finally. "Fuck you and your fucking secret manuscript and your stingy love. Go back to Pauline if you want to. Let her spend all of your money and all of hers too on a life that means less than nothing. Poland burns and you put a marshmallow on a stick and throw a damned party. Amsterdam burns and you take the party onto the canals. Paris is going to fucking burn, and when they tell us about it on the radio, you'll just turn the thing off and go back to banging your damned typewriter keys, one more lovely paragraph about a war that's already lost. You do that. You do that with Pauline. I don't give a shit."

I stormed out, and I walked and walked, and I walked farther and faster, the humidity and the exercise plastering my cotton dress to my bare legs. I walked until the anger settled into something tolerable, until I'd decided the thing to do was to wire *Collier's* that I would be in New York in two days, ready to head for Europe and the war.

When I came back to tell Ernest I was leaving, he was gone.

Fine, let him go off on a big stinking drunk with anyone who would drink with him, and since he was forever proving his manliness by standing everyone for drinks with money he didn't have, he would have company the whole night long and I wouldn't have to put up with him in my bed. I stripped off my sweaty dress and dove in the pool, and I swam naked until I was cool all over, until I was shivering from the cold.

Ernest had better sense than to climb into my bed in the wee hours when he came home that night. When I awoke, hungover with sadness, he was asleep in the bedroom he wrote in, but he'd left a note beside the radio. It didn't say "GUARANTY" on the top, but it allowed that he was thoughtless and egoistic and even mean-spirited, that he had been for the whole of the last year or more, that it was due to the pressure of the book, which had to be good or he was finished. He wrote that I didn't have to marry him if I didn't want to, that he wouldn't blame me if I didn't want to go through with it. He wouldn't want to marry a selfish ass like himself either, but he loved me and he knew he would never write the same without me. His writing would always be mine even if my writing was no longer his, he wrote. He signed it, "your Bongie who loves you, even if you no longer want to marry him."

The note sat atop his Spanish war manuscript. He'd settled on a title: *For Whom the Bell Tolls*. It came from a meditation written by John Donne, which he'd included below the title.

I sat in the club chair, with the radio silent and the booze bottles corked, and I read the opening I'd read in the hotel room in Havana fourteen months earlier, and the next chapter, and the next. I read and I read, and when Ernest came in, I looked up at him and I didn't say a word. He would know by the fact that I was still sitting there—in the same house with him even after the prior night—how good the writing was.

I read all morning and all afternoon and into the evening, laughing out loud at the funniness, even the funny passages like the bit about Robert Jordan's father being a "Republican" that I'd read before, and wondering how he could make a story truer than true when it was all made up, and only a little uneasy, still, for whether he would ruin me through Maria the way he had but never would admit to with Dorothy from the Spanish war play.

He left me there to read in quiet, staying in the bedroom where he liked to write but not even banging on his typewriter keys, not coming out even for a drink at the end of the day.

The light in the room was fading when I came to chapter twenty-six, to a passage in which Robert Jordan admonishes himself not to kid himself about love, that most people just aren't lucky enough ever to find it, and he had found it with Maria, and whether it lasted or it didn't, it was a true thing and he would be lucky even if he died the next day.

I found Ernest stretched out on the bed in his office, with the carbon copy in his lap. I climbed in beside him, and he set the carbon on the nightstand and put his arms around me. I tucked my head under his chin, and I lay there shivering, the way in his novel Rabbit lay next to Robert Jordan the night they first met.

"I'm lucky even if I die tomorrow, Bug," I whispered.

"Whether it lasts just through today or whether it lasts for a long life, Mookie," he said.

"You've never written better," I said. "Not even the piece about the boy from Pittsburg."

"Raven," he said.

The boy in the hospital in Spain, whom he'd promised to revisit, but had only ever done so in the piece he wrote. I supposed he was visiting Raven again in this new novel. I supposed he was revisiting the boy he, too, once had been, a boy young and foolish enough to put his life on the line without any real idea what it meant to die.

The Finca Vigía, San Francisco de Paula, Cuba

June 1940

The living room ceiling of the Finca Vigía collapsed that June. Ernest and I just looked at the mess: soggy plaster on the club chairs and on the booze on the drinks cart and on my precious radio and on my map. He picked up a bottle of the best scotch we had, and he brushed the plaster from the thing and splashed it into two fairly clean glasses.

"Life with you is interesting as hell, Mrs. Pig Disaster-Girl," he said, handing me a glass and kissing me the gentle way I liked. "And I wouldn't trade one ceiling-collapsing day of it for a whole century of warm writing. Do promise you'll marry me, will you? I know I've been a horrible pig. I know that. But I'll be better, I promise I will. I'll sit with you every night and listen to the disaster war news, and I'll be all for going to see it ourselves if you'll just let me finish the book. I'll crawl through the mud with the soldiers again, and I'll watch you be braver than anyone, and I won't even lock you in your room. But stay with me until I finish?"

"Only I have to go to New York, and get Matie."

"For just a few days."

"Yes, only for a few days."

The boys arrived the next morning for their summer visit, and it rained, and it rained, and it rained. Ernest, buried in his book, hardly looked up to notice his boys, or the war, or me. He was writing so well, though. He was writing brilliantly.

The day I left for New York, the Germans marched into Paris. I called Ernest to tell him, unsure whether he would have heard the news without me there to turn on the radio.

"Ginny just flew from London to Paris, to cover the fall of the city," I said.

"She always was crazy as a feral cat," he said. "And I know about feral cats too." He'd collected them at the house in Key West, and now he was collecting them at the Finca Vigía. He would hear no word against them despite there being more than we could afford to feed.

I went to Washington and spent a little time with the Roosevelts, then collected Matie and returned to Cuba, where the mangos and alligator pears were thick on the trees and the male pigeons courted the females, who, being fewer in number, could be as picky as they chose. It was all easier somehow, for the five weeks we had Matie for company. The visit started with my mother eyeing the car, which had suffered its fourth accident in my absence. Ernest simply assured her he would get a new car with the proceeds from his new novel. I started a piece on the Nazis in Cuba; two thousand Germans were in the country, and I'd had run-ins enough with some of the local Fascists to know they were not all Germans of the likable type. When we were done writing each day, we took Matie out on the *Pilar* to watch marlins playing in the water like little boys, or like fighter planes. We all found it restful, even when a whale shark as big as the boat swam right up to us, its gargantuan mouth (twelve feet if it was an inch) open wide and quite perfectly terrifying.

"You only need worry, Edna," Ernest assured my mother, "if you're a sardine."

One afternoon when Ernest hadn't shown up two hours after he was to meet Matie and me for lunch, I knew exactly where we'd find him: on his favorite seat at the left-hand corner of the bar at the Floridita, with the fans turning overhead and the bartender serving daiquiris.

"What the hell, Hemingway!" I said when we found him leaning toward the cool seafood display case, yammering on to some poor patron on the next barstool who, on account of his fine listening skills and manners far better than Ernest's, was left with no chance to get in a word.

Ernest looked up to Matie's and my reflection in the mirror over the bar.

"You can stand me up," I said, "but I'll be a hideously rotund piglet before I'll have you stand up Matie!"

Around the bar, people chuckled, those who understood English did, while those who didn't asked each other, *"¿Qué dijo ella?"*

Ernest looked from me to Matie, who was suppressing a smile.

He excused himself to his bar companion, saying loudly enough that no one in the bar could mistake his words, *"Como puedes ver, tengo algunos problemas . . . Culpa mía sí, estoy en un lugar de problemas aquí—de mi propia hater, pero no por ello dejan de ser problemas."* As you can see, I'm in a spot of trouble here—of my own doing, but trouble no less.

He set a few bills on the bar to cover his drinks and his friend's, and a healthy tip.

"Forgive me, Edna?" he said. "I'd like to say I'll never do it again, but your daughter is so beautiful when she's self-righteous that I can't always help myself."

The drinkers laughed, and Ernest and Matie laughed, too, and my mother said to me, "Not just any garden-variety ugly, fat piglet, Martha, but a hideously rotund one?" And she and Ernest laughed even harder, Ernest putting his arms around me to hug me so that his chest and stomach rattled against me as I stood stiffly, not amused.

"I'm sorry, Mart," he whispered into my ear. "I get carried away about the book. I'm a pig, I know I am, but I don't mean to be, and I'll try better, and anyway, I'll always be *your* ugly, fat pig."

"Hideously rotund," I said. "Pig*let*," I said.

He laughed, and, without letting go of me, he leaned back to have a look at my face. "I'm not that bad, am I, Mookie?"

"*Hideously* rotund," I insisted.

"All right, then," he said. "Hideously rotund. I'll always be your hideously rotund pig."

"Pig*let*," I said.

"Piglet," he agreed.

On good days, Ernest would let me read his pages. On very good days, he would let Matie read them too. Matie, after she'd finished reading some of the chapters one afternoon, said, "I feel so sorry for him."

"Sorry!" I said. "How can you feel sorry for a bear of a man who has been an absolutely smashing success and is so sure of it that he'll blurt it out with the first hello?"

Matie frowned and said, "But of course you can't see it, because you're so deeply in it yourself."

"He's writing such a damned gorgeous novel, though, Matie. A novel that's truer than this very minute."

She said, "Do you suppose he's as certain of that as you are?"

"Listen to him, Matie! He badgers every poor, unsuspecting bar patron who happens to take the stool next to him about how brilliant the book is."

"Yes, you do see why, then, Martha," Matie said. "And there's what he's writing about too. The father."

I didn't see, but I saw that she thought I should, that if I couldn't see what she saw in Ernest's writing—or in Ernest himself—it exposed something about me she didn't want to know, and maybe I didn't either. She let it go and so did I, or I tried to. But her words stayed with me, and each time I read Ernest's pages, after I'd had the breath knocked out of me by the first reading, I read a second time. And I began to wonder why, when he was so sure of it every night, it was so hard for him to share his pages. I began to see the fact of his own father winding through the story, the fact of Ernest, like his character Robert Jordan, not wanting to do what his father did, and struggling against it. Making fun of the father's suicide in that early dialogue with Pilar that was so damned funny, and broke your heart even as you were laughing. Now, in the latest pages, he sketched at the edges of what it meant for a father to kill himself. He'd never said straight what a selfish bastard his father must have been to kill himself, but there it was, leaking out in his novel that was meant to be his masterpiece. And a few paragraphs later, as Robert Jordan worried that he would be charged a coward, he told himself straight out that that's what his father was, a coward who let his wife bully him.

His father's Civil War revolver, that's what his character Robert Jordan's father used to kill himself. A Smith & Wesson, like Ernest's own father had used to shoot himself in the fall of 1928, just after Ernest had moved from Paris to Key West with Pauline, after Patrick was born and *A Farewell to Arms* was published and his bully of a mother returned the copy he sent her with a note that she would not have filth in her home. If he would write a book that wasn't full of filth, she would be happy to have it, his mother wrote him. Ernest had been only twenty-nine.

"There isn't much to the girl, is there?" Matie said. "In Ernest's story. The story is so real and Pilar is so real, and Pablo and Anselmo and even the Gypsy, even Robert Jordan, although he's a bit heavy on the hero side, isn't he? Everyone is so real except the girl, the 'rabbit.'"

"Maria?"

"The girl is all love for him and nothing for herself, all docile and compliant, and that's what he wants, that's love to him. A damaged child with no desire in life but to adore him."

"That's what Robert Jordan wants?" I said, trying to understand what Matie was saying. "Or Ernest?"

I wanted to ask her then what was wrong with me, why I couldn't be happy in bed. Why was it that the best of the bed stuff was when it didn't hurt too much? But how could I ask that of my mother, who never spoke of sex except once to say it was to be endured? Whom I suppose might have had the same thing wrong with her. It would be an easier conversation with Ernest than with Matie, except that I couldn't tell Bug, after all this time of lovemaking together, that as he had been meaning to make me happy, he had been making me hurt.

The Finca Vigía, San Francisco de Paula, Cuba

July 1940

Ernest wrote the ending to his Spanish war novel, *For Whom the Bell Tolls*, in one big 2,600-word day, July 11, and if it wasn't a hell of a chapter and a hell of a book, well then, you could tell him so and he would assure you that you were wrong. He was no good for writing at all the next few days, but he finished the first draft of the thing for all intents and purposes, writing the epilogue—or something more like a rough outline for two chapters that would wrap up the story—on his forty-first birthday, July 21. It was a big book: two hundred thousand words.

To celebrate, we went shopping in Havana and had a fine Basque fiesta at the Beach Club, and we were unbearably happy. We would have married right then and there if only Ernest's divorce from Pauline had come through.

Ernest took the manuscript to New York a few days later. He holed up in the Hotel Barclay with an electric fan blowing directly at him in an attempt to stave off a brutalizing heat wave as he revised the manuscript. The printer was setting the novel for galleys as fast as Ernest let the pages go. On Wednesday, July 31, Max Perkins was banging on Ernest for more pages, as the printer had only one day of work left to set. The next day, Max begged him for another two hundred. Ernest rarely left the hotel room. The publication date was set for October 14—less than three months from the date he'd finished writing the first draft, when it usually took a year or more from a book's final draft to get it out.

As soon as the last page was sent off to the printer—again with the epilogue to come—Ernest boarded a Pan Am Clipper for home. Matie and I met him at the boarding dock. Before we'd even said a proper hello, he handed me a little box.

"Open it, Rabbit," he said. "Open it here. Open it now."

Inside was a diamond and sapphire engagement ring.

"It's . . . damn, it's beautiful, Bongie," I said, wanting to touch the stones nestled on the bed of velvet, and yet reluctant to. "It's awfully big," I said.

He said, "Go ahead and bite the stones, Stooge."

Matie, standing beside me, put her hand on my shoulder and squeezed it lightly, her silent call to consider what I was about to say, or what I was about to do. The gems were the real deal, sure, but Ernest wasn't—that's what my mother's gesture meant. Ernest was still married to Pauline, and I'd done this before, I'd agreed to marry Bertrand de Jouvenel when I might have known his wife never would let him go.

I gently unloaded the ring from its slot, with Matie's hand still warm on my skin.

"Don't be silly, Bug," I said as I slid it on my finger. "I know this is the real deal."

The Finca Vigía, San Francisco de Paula, Cuba

August 1940

It's always a moment, the first time you see your galleys for a book, your words set in leaded type in some fabulous font the way readers will experience it. The galleys for *For Whom the Bell Tolls* arrived by airmail just about as quickly as Ernest himself did. He was as happy as could be to be going over them, even with the notes from his publisher and editor suggesting changes.

While he finalized the book, I tried to find my way out of a bit of a box Ernest had gotten me into with Charlie Scribner. Ernest meant to help me; he thought if I had a contract for a book, I would sit down and be disciplined and write. So he'd huddled with Charlie, and the two of them had come up with a madcap plan for me to do a new novel with Scribner—never mind that I had a perfectly good relationship with my publisher, Charles Duell, who might hate me personally for all I knew but did love my writing. Charlie Scribner might love me personally, but I would never know if he loved my writing or only meant to keep Ernest happy.

We made plans to go to Sun Valley in the fall. Ernest and I would cross over to Key West and drive up to St. Louis, where he would drop me for a visit with Matie and drive out to Idaho to meet the boys, with me joining them later.

"If the divorce comes through, we can marry right there, in Sun Valley, Mook," Ernest said.

"Bug, we can't marry while Mousie and Gigi are in Idaho," I said. "Not even with Bumby there."

"Not with the boys there but after they go home, Mrs. Bongie-Piglet. We can stay as long as we want and do whatever we want after the boys leave."

Ernest kept reaching new financial settlements with Pauline all that summer. He negotiated through her uncle Gus, who assured him with each new deal that she had agreed, only to find she'd told her lawyer to demand more money. Ernest accused her of trying to put him out of the book business, because of course he couldn't write novels if he was forever having to make a buck to cover a monthly check she didn't even need. She insisted on keeping the very expensive Key West house even though she'd shut the thing up and moved to an equally expensive place on Telegraph Hill in San Francisco, with views of the bay and the new Golden Gate Bridge. Unlike Hadley, who had given Ernest up to Pauline without much fuss, Pauline meant to keep him from having a dime to enjoy life. It made me hesitate to marry anyone, watching how rottenly one person could try to make another pay in stocks and bonds and houses and furniture for having fallen out of love.

"With the book done, we could go cover the war," I said. "After the boys go back to school."

"There are still the galleys."

"Don't be silly. The galleys will be done before the boys leave. After the galleys are done and the boys leave, we could go to the war."

He said, "The book won't be released until October."

I said, "After the book is released in October, we'll go to war."

"It will be a nice long war," he said. "There'll be plenty of time yet to get ourselves killed, don't you worry about that."

Ernest asked my mother that evening, "Edna, what is this fascination your daughter has with carnage and pestilence and butchery? Just what I had in mind—for our honeymoon, she means to have me abandon my own writing to follow her off to war."

"*Collier's* wants me to go to China," I explained to my mother. Japan and China had been at it in a more serious way than usual since the Marco Polo Bridge incident a few years back, when we'd been at the White House to show *The Spanish Earth* to the president.

"Or, perhaps more truthfully, your daughter wants to go to China for *Collier's*, and *Collier's* is still making up its mind about whether to send her or some lesser journalist," Ernest said. "I fear you allowed Marty here too much Somerset Maugham, Edna. She imagines China as exotic buildings and women wrapped in vibrant silk, splendidly suited European men arriving in rickshaws at European bank buildings on the Bund."

And the funny little wooden boats called "sampans," which sometimes gathered together in little villages. There was no place I could imagine would be more enchanting.

"Me," Ernest continued, "I know only that my uncle, a missionary in Shaanxi Province, cut out his own appendix while on horseback on his way home from meeting the Dalai Lama."

"Oh, bother," I said. "You're just bitter because Matie here handed me Maugham's novels while your mother made you drop your allowance in the collection plate to save the poor heathen Chinese."

"My uncle Willoughby," he insisted. "My father's brother. 'Hunter of Wolves,' that's what Hemingway means in China. And my cousins taught me how to sing 'Jesus Loves Me' in Chinese."

"You'll *have* to come with me on this assignment, then, Bug, so you can do the singing for me. Do they have guitars in China?"

"*If* you get the assignment."

"I'm sure they'd give it to me if they knew it meant you singing about the Lord our God in words the good people of China would understand."

The next day, August 23, I sat down and wrote Charlie Scribner that he was a sweet man to offer to be my publisher. It was a long letter, trying to explain that I couldn't accept his offer but in a way that would leave him relieved rather than insulted. I wrote that I would do anything to earn a living if I had to: I would scrub floors or write corset ads, which I'd spent more time than he would like to know doing (the corset ads, not the floors). I wrote that I just couldn't write a book for money; I never could make the juice run unless I believed awfully in a thing. If I needed money, I would write for *Collier's*. They were after me to set off for the wars, and I looked forward to that. I loved that and Ernest did too, and that was the plan after the book was done—to head off to cover some war together. The only question was where.

That night, the letter mailed, I dreamed I was drowning in a tub of lard that was, like the silk dresses the Oriental women of my youth wore, crusted on the outside with sapphires and diamonds.

Charles Scribner sent Ernest a copy of the proposed cover for *For Whom the Bell Tolls*, which Ernest liked well enough, although the bridge was the wrong kind of bridge; it was a stone and wood bridge, whereas the bridge in the novel was a high-arching, spidery metal bridge of the kind that might be blown without an abundance of dynamite. The truth is there is always a bridge that is wrong on the cover, and no one ever much seems to care that the damned thing is wrong as long as it's evocative enough to cause a reader to pick up the book and turn to the first sentence. I'm quite sure that if it would entice readers, the bridge on the cover would be gossamer threads that would be blown away in the wind with no dynamite at all.

Ernest, being Ernest, made a drawing of what the bridge ought to look like and sent it to Scribner, along with a picture of bells of the type that might be tolling in Spain.

He worried his heart out over that bridge, in a happy way. He worried over the whole long list of Charlie's and Max's suggestions. He worried whether he should make his journalist British rather than American, on account of avoiding a libel suit from a real American journalist the character may or may not have been based on. He worried whether there were too many obscenities on some of the pages, "obscenity" being the word he was using again and again as Scribner was unwilling to publish a "damn" or "shit" or "fuck." In *A Farewell to Arms*, they'd been unwilling even to print "balls" if it meant something other than round things with which one played games of the nonsexual sort, so this time he'd stuck with the Spanish, *cojones*; they either hadn't known what the word meant or had chosen not to fight that battle. His editor, Max Perkins, was the kind of man who wouldn't swear even when two of his most important authors were swinging at each other in his own office, even when brutal Germans were hanging Nazi flags all over the most beautiful city in the world.

"If that is civilized, then, damn, I want no part of it!" I said.

Ernest said, "If I put something in the book, then it belongs there, and Max and Charlie can go obscenity themselves if they don't want to publish it that way. A book is a whole thing, and if you start chipping out bits of it, or even chipping off the edges of some of the bits, well then, you would have a different thing."

They all worried over the fact that the Republicans didn't look any better than the Fascists in the novel on account of one awful scene in which some Republicans dragged the town's Fascists from a church into the square for the sole purpose of brutally beating them and then pitching them off a cliff. It's such a long scene it would be pretty unbearable even if it were the Fascists being so cruel, which it wasn't, it was the men we all admired.

Ernest's answer was that Max should simply not send galleys to anyone on the left who might object.

Max sent a set of the galleys to the Book-of-the-Month Club, along with a note that two short chapters comprising an epilogue of about fifteen hundred words would be added to tie up loose ends—chapters, he assured them, that had been written but which Ernest wanted to hold on to until he'd had a chance to read the galleys from start to finish. Ernest was sure Book-of-the-Month would reject the book. He consoled himself with all the books he was sure they wouldn't have liked: Steinbeck's *The Grapes of Wrath*, Richard Wright's *Native Son*, Dostoyevsky's *The Brothers Karamazov*, Flaubert's *Madame Bovary*.

On August 26, Perkins wrote to tell Ernest that *For Whom the Bell Tolls* would be the November Book-of-the-Month Club selection. They planned to print a hundred thousand copies. Scribner would publish as many or more.

That same day, Ernest packaged up all but eighteen pages of the galleys and airmailed them back. He still wasn't happy with the epilogue, which he'd rewritten and rewritten and rewritten. He wrote to Max that, in his own mind, the book really ended with Robert Jordan feeling his heart beating against the pine needle forest, right where it had begun. The epilogue seemed like going back into the dressing room after the fight.

He was like a horridly caged bear after he sent that letter. He revised the epilogue he'd now convinced himself the book didn't need, only to tear it up and start a fresh approach, and then another. He was a beast to me in the process, the way so many of us are unkind to the people we love when we're letting go of a thing we've worked so hard on, when if we just had, say, another five years, we could make the thing a masterpiece, but our time is up. Nothing I could do or say was anything but dead wrong and vile and mean-spirited, even when it was only to ask if he'd like a cup of coffee or a glass of booze.

"I'm not your fucking punching bag, Nesto!" I objected one night when we were well into the booze. "You'll always be writing something, and if that is forever going to make you too cranky to be nice to me, then fuck you."

It was the worst time to hash out anything, when we were in the booze, but the only time we did it—exploding about the different ways we wrote or failed to write and the way we did one thing or another around the house, the way we drank too much (my complaint) and had sex too seldom (his), all with an undertone of the difficulty of the divorce from Pauline.

I left him to do as much drinking as he pleased, and I went off to bed thinking that if he wouldn't be nice to me before we married, I couldn't see how he would be after I was his captive wife. Thinking I didn't really mean what I'd said, it was only the booze talking, the booze and the darkness of not writing. Thinking it was the booze talking for him too, the booze and the darkness about the book being just at that point where the writing is about to be judged. Thinking I ought to go back and climb in his lap because I knew it wasn't me that was the problem, it was the book, but the book wouldn't fight back, and he needed someone to fight back.

By morning, he'd have forgotten about the fighting. He always did. So I tried to forget it as well. We were good for each other, Bug and I, as long as we weren't both dealing with the darkness at the same time.

I found, the next morning, a copy of the latest draft of his epilogue shredded into little squares, which he had left on the drinks cart next to an empty bottle of scotch. He'd gone back to working after we'd argued, in the middle of the night and full of booze.

Beside the scraps of the former epilogue, he'd propped a folded piece of paper with my name written on it. He'd been no good company while he was writing this beast of a thing, the whole eighteen months, he wrote, but would I please be a good Bongie and try to remember how cranky *I'd* been with *A Stricken Field* and what a good boy he'd been about that? He wrote, "If you don't mean to marry me, for God's sake tell me with time enough to accept it before I have to take the *Pilar* across to Key West by myself. Don't leave me with all that time alone and far too much to think about."

I reread the note, trying to sort out what he meant by it, nervous about what he might mean. He ought to be so happy, with the book done and the thing so brilliant. But I knew how it was. I knew how the darkness came. I knew the emptiness that was left when you let a thing go, the limbo before you knew how one thing might do and were on to the next.

He had such high ambitions. He only wanted to write something that would win "that thing," which was how he spoke of it when he spoke of it, which he didn't much do for fear of jinxing himself.

I felt a little sick, reading the rest of the note. I felt like I ought to be a better person, more understanding.

He closed it by saying Mr. Scrooby now referred to himself as "us." I wondered if he'd used that nickname for his penis with Pauline too, or with Hadley. I thought I ought to be more like Hadley always had been, concerned only with Ernest's life and not with her own even before he'd ever published anything, before anyone else knew that he was Ernest Hemingway who only wanted to write well enough to win the Nobel Prize.

The next morning, Max telegrammed that he agreed they should print the novel without the epilogue. *For Whom the Bell Tolls* was done.

The Sun Valley Lodge, Sun Valley, Idaho

September 1940

It was a lovely thing, to stand on the diving board in fresh, clear, if slightly thin, air, with the steam pouring around me and the white-capped mountains in the distance, and the Sun Valley Lodge's clean, fluffy white towels always waiting in generous piles atop the fence posts around the pool. Ernest and I had stopped in Key West on the way, to select the half of the books Ernest was to get under the settlement he'd finally reached with Pauline and to pick up a new Buick convertible for which his editor had sent an $890 check directly to Muhlberg Motor Company, charging it against his advance. I'd stayed a week in St. Louis with Matie. But now we were writing in our suite or on our private wooden sun terrace each morning. I was helping Ernest read through a new set of galleys for *For Whom the Bell Tolls*, as well as trying to get my stories just right for *The Heart of Another*, a collection Scribner was going to publish. Ernest had finally convinced me that Duell, Sloan and Pearce hadn't so much put my prior books up for sale as locked them in a damned vault.

Our afternoons were full of shooting and fishing and riding with Ernest's sons, and having long conversations, especially with Bumby. Ernest was hell-bent on convincing Bumby to take a year off after he graduated from high school the following spring.

"College will always be there," he told his son, "and a man might as well catch a steelhead if there's only one life."

The military draft had been reinstituted, and as much as the rich and glamorous in Sun Valley tried to ignore the war when they weren't making money on it, it seemed only a matter of time before American boys would be in it too.

We all read books that Ernest had Max Perkins send us, and we rode horses, and when we weren't playing tennis with the boys, we were playing with Gary Cooper and his wife, Veronica Balfe—"Rocky"—swapping partners sometimes. Ernest had known them since Cooper starred in the 1932 movie version of Ernest's in-love-with-the-nurse novel, *A Farewell to Arms*.

"Cooper would make a top-notch Robert Jordan, don't you think so?" Ernest said to me after one particularly spirited game in which Ernest and Rocky had prevailed, much to Bug's glee. We were dressing for an evening of eating and drinking and dancing to Glenn Miller's swing band, and entertaining Ernest's Hollywood agent, Donald Friede, who'd come to talk about the film rights for *Bell.* I agreed Cooper would be terrific, and while I was at it I noted that Ernest might ask Gary where he bought his clothes, as he always looked so sharp.

"That's his face you're responding to, Mrs. Bongie," Bug said. "All the silk ties and slim-cut jackets in the world won't make my face look like his. It would take the TB to slim me down to his weight, and he'd still have that goddamned face."

"But I love your face, Mr. Bongie," I said, and I thought of the photo of him I'd had on my dorm room wall at Bryn Mawr. He'd been as handsome as Cooper in his youth, and he wasn't two years older, but

Cooper's face remained smooth and his body slender, his hair still full so that he looked years younger than Ernest.

Still, even in a room with a movie star like Gary Cooper, Ernest was the one people circled around. He had a way of looking at you with those big brown eyes that made you feel like you were the most important person in the world, and his voice was still soft and warm, and he told such great stories, in a shy way that was absolutely lovable when he hadn't drunk too much.

Ernest liked to go shooting with Cooper, whom he conceded was a better shot with a rifle ("probably on account of he doesn't drink as much"), although he claimed he was better with a shotgun so it was overall a draw. I had no claim to match Rocky with any gun whatsoever; she was a damned skeet-shooting champion. I did like her immensely though. She seemed so happy with Gary. She seemed someone I might turn to for happiness advice. So one afternoon when she and I were shooting pheasant some distance from Ernest (who was helping Gigi handle his gun without having to sit), I asked her if the lack of privacy bothered her.

"But of course that's why Mr. Harriman invited us here, to have our photos taken to promote his new little resort," Rocky said. "He's bent on having it rival the Swiss Alps, and who wouldn't want to hobnob with the likes of Gary Cooper and Ernest Hemingway?"

"What Averell Harriman is bent on is the side benefit of increasing ridership on his Union Pacific Railroad," I said, "but, Rocky, that's not—"

"I was being flip, Mart. We're all here to have fabulous sex with our husbands night and day, of course. This place is just lovely for that, isn't it?" She laughed delightedly.

I laughed with her, wondering, Did she really enjoy sex?

"I don't mean that kind of privacy," I said. "I don't love being followed around by photographers, of course, but . . . what I meant was . . . well, does Gary ever . . . ?"

Gary was always so well presented, so charming and solicitous. Ernest was charming and solicitous too, but he wasn't above skewering even his friends in his books, even his lovers in his plays. He wasn't above taking all our lives and our vulnerabilities and laying them out in order for readers to have a good chuckle at our expense. Gary didn't write, that was part of it. But Gary wasn't a man who would ever read Rocky's mail, even when it came from a former lover, if she had former lovers, which maybe she didn't; they'd been married for decades. So maybe that was explanation enough. Maybe Gary had been married for decades while Ernest's two marriages had collapsed. Maybe that was why Gary Cooper could trust his wife and leave her mail unread.

A flock of doves rose up, flushed by the dogs, and we raised our guns and shot. Rocky got two at least, while I missed every one. I hadn't really been much for hunting even before Sun Valley, ever since I'd seen that beautiful hawk I shot in Cuba fall in service of nothing more than my pride. But a few days before, in a horrific outing that reminded me of Pablo's men massacring the town Fascists in Ernest's novel, our little posse shot five hundred rabbits, which, through Ernest's organization, we'd cornered against a canal so they had no escape. The farmers had complained of the rabbits ruining their crops; that was the excuse for it. The boys weren't there that day, at least.

"Well, it will be different in China," I said. "No one in China will have a clue who Ernest and I are."

"Really, Marty, you aren't going to drag Ernest to China," Rocky said. "Even Gary says the poor man is exhausted from writing that book."

She reloaded her shotgun.

"Ernest is resting *now*," I said. "And he likes to cover war as much as I do. We're war correspondents; it's what we do."

He'd promised that after he finished the book we would go off to cover some war together like we had in Spain, with nothing but the work and the good we could do and no one prying into our private lives every moment, wanting to photograph us for the morning papers as if our lives were anything to write about. But now that it was finished, he bounced back and forth between reneging—which sometimes led to knock-down-drag-outs about whether we'd ever made this deal—and phoning my editor at *Collier's* to insist I would cover China better than anyone and ought to be given the damned assignment, already, what was he waiting for? Ernest was funny that way. He would get it in his mind that he wanted to live life one way, and then he'd get it in his mind that he wanted to live entirely differently. I suppose we all do. I suppose we all bumble through life far more randomly than we like to think.

"Can I ask you a personal question, Rocky?" I asked.

"Well, sure, I suppose I don't have to answer if I don't want to."

"It doesn't hurt?" Thinking of what she'd said: *fabulous sex with our husbands night and day.*

She said, "What doesn't hurt?"

A young boy's voice called out to me across the field then, Gigi shouting, "Look, Marty! I got one!"

Rocky and I both laughed delightedly. "That boy is such a doll," she said. "I'd like to arrange a marriage between him and my Maria." She laughed again; her daughter was just a toddler. "All Hem's children are dolls, aren't they? Just like their daddy."

We were still in Sun Valley when Ernest received the first copies of *For Whom the Bell Tolls*. With all those people around, with his own sons and with movie stars and famous writers, he might have wanted to show it to everyone, but he took the package and he took my hand and he pulled me back to our private suite.

"Open it, Mookie," he said, handing the package to me as if it were a present bought specially for this day.

"I can't open it, Bug! It's your book!"

"Your book is mine, and mine is yours," he said. "Open it."

"I—"

"Open it, Mrs. Heminghorn Pig!"

I slid the end of the package open and pulled out the volume. "It's a hideously fat book, for sure, Mr. Pig!" I said. "Look how fat it is! Feel how much it weighs! You have to be a pretty important book to be that fat."

"We'll have to put it on the scale back at the Finca!"

"You'll never get under two hundred with this in hand," I said.

He laughed and laughed. He was so pleased.

"I love thy bridge on the cover," I said, mimicking the way his Spanish characters spoke.

"Dost thou?" he asked. "I don't know. It's—"

"It's a very fine bridge," I said. "They fixed it just like you told them to: metal and spidery."

"With some distance for the perspective."

"With some distance."

"Open it, Daughter," he said. "Open the book."

I opened it to the verso and the title page.

He stood right beside me and reached over and turned the pages, to the dedication: "This book is for Martha Gellhorn."

"Oh, Bug," I said, and I stood there looking at the black letters on the white page, and it was hard, suddenly, to get a decent breath into my chest.

"It's our book, Mookie," he said.

Sun Valley, Idaho

October 1940

After Bumby and Mouse and Gigi left Sun Valley, Ernest and I rode up the Middle Fork of the Salmon River, twenty-three miles of trail that took a week to cover, and none of it much less than straight up or straight down. I was tough about it (although not half as tough as the horses), finding little comfort other than the bar of my favorite soap I used faithfully in the clean water of the streams. But the outdoors seemed to calm Ernest. He let up on the drinking some and even seemed open to coming to China with me if I got the *Collier's* gig.

When we got back, I was sick as hell with a nasty flu.

"Next time we'll take the horses up on the ski lifts," Bug suggested. But laughing only made me ache more.

Collier's had given the China assignment to someone else, it turned out. It already made me sicker than the flu to sit idle while Quentin Reynolds wrote about London as if the bombs were dropping on him alone, and now I'd be left to Bucharest or some even smaller corner of trouble. But I'd take that. I didn't much care as long as someone gave me an assignment somewhere.

Ernest was in serious negotiations with Paramount for the film rights to *For Whom the Bell Tolls*. Dorothy Parker, who might write the screenplay, arrived in Sun Valley in mid-October to chat with him. On the whole I thought Hollywood was crap for serious writers, but I loved her humor and Ernest did too, or said he did, although he thought someone else would be better for the screenplay, someone with cojones. He had cojones himself when it came to the film rights: he'd just turned down $100,000.

"Not *enough,* Scrooby?" His entire earnings for the prior year had been $6,000, which just paid Pauline's $500 per month if you didn't back out taxes first.

He said, "My friends on the coast tell me they can get us more, Mart."

"You might lose the deal altogether, though. Aren't you afraid of that?"

"We can always take the offer," he said. "They've already shown us they want it badly enough to pay a hundred thousand dollars, and we haven't yet admitted that we want the money badly enough to sell for that."

"But, Bug, people change their minds. People get their backs up and when they decide 'fuck you,' you can't always lure them back to the table, and we don't even need money for anything but books."

"And places like this."

"Don't be silly, Bongie; this place isn't costing us a cent."

"We need a new icebox in Cuba," Ernest said. "I'd like new binoculars and a sleeping bag. And there's the Finca Vigía, and food and booze."

"The booze bill, that is a big one," I agreed, managing a laugh even though I felt like hell from the damned flu. "But between the book and a hundred thousand dollars for the movie, we'd have enough for a helluv an icebox and the rent and the rest of it even if neither of us ever did another journo piece again in our lives."

The book wasn't even published yet, but the Book-of-the-Month Club had decided to double its first printing to two hundred thousand copies. Scribner, too, was already going back to print.

"Not the rent, Mook."

"Your half of the rent."

"Not the rent, Mook," he repeated, for no reason I could imagine, unless he was trying to say that after we were married I would be expected to cover all the rent for the Finca, rather than just my half.

"All joking aside, Bug, with a hundred thousand dollars, you could write novels for the rest of your life and pay Pauline and never have to worry about any damned thing you want in this whole world."

"Except the booze," he joked.

"Yes, well, Bongie, but you prefer the cheap stuff, and I can go without."

He wrote to Friede the next morning that he had damned well better take the $100,000.

After Max Perkins sent him thirty advance copies of the book, Ernest sent the first one to Scott Fitzgerald in Hollywood, inscribed "with affection and esteem," then hired a boy to package the others and mail them to the people who might do the book the most good. When Scott wrote back admitting to envy, Ernest read the note aloud to me. And he couldn't wait for the reviews to arrive by post then; he called a reporter friend of his and made him read the first reviews over the phone. I listened as Ernest gleefully asked, "He said that? Read it again." Quite some time into the call, he handed the phone to me and made the poor fellow read the reviews a second time. The *New York Times*, using Ernest's favorite word of praise, "true," called it the best book Ernest Hemingway had written, and the *Saturday Review of Literature* deemed it one of the best novels of the decade.

Ernest's divorce from Pauline became final November 4. We called Matie with the news, Bug with the phone first, answering her hello with, "Hello, Mother! It's done, finally, and I'm all set to marry your marvelous daughter, and all we need to complete the deed is your lovely presence. I'm arranging for you to fly in tomorrow morning."

The two spent several minutes negotiating Matie's flight schedule, with the result that Matie would arrange her own flights to come that Wednesday, which she insisted was the soonest she could get to Sun Valley.

Matie's first words to me after Ernest handed over the receiver were, "Martha, do you know what you're doing?"

"Yes, of course," I said with more bravado than I felt. I meant for my response to sound to Bug like the answer to some other question: Did I have a dress to wear? Did Ernest have a proper suit?

"I thought from our conversations while you were here in September and from your letters since then that you were going to wait," Matie said. "I thought you would give it some time. I thought you were having second thoughts. You *were* having second thoughts." She put the receiver down—the long-distance charges be damned—and returned a minute later to read to me from my own letters: my feeling trapped, my preference for engagement over marriage, my fear of what marriage with Ernest would mean. She said, "You write that you have no privacy, and that you have to do things for Ernest's sake that you don't want to do. Nothing matters more to you than getting this *Collier's* assignment to China, that's what you write here. And if you get it, it will be a showdown, because Ernest doesn't want you to go."

"A helluva showdown"—that was what I'd written.

I did like being engaged. Being engaged made me feel forever young. I didn't know how I could marry, though. That was what I'd written. I'd written that I loved Ernest but I didn't know how I could be married to him.

All that letter writing, though, had been before the dedication in *For Whom the Bell Tolls*.

I said, "Well, of course we'll wait until you get here, Matie," not wanting to give Ernest even a hint of what Matie was saying, or what I'd written her.

Ernest, after we'd hung up, said, "We can do it twice. We can quietly marry this afternoon, and when your mother arrives, we'll pretend we haven't already done it, and we'll do it again."

"Bug! We can't do that!"

"I'll get Cooper to put on a dog collar and do the honors the second time."

"Really, Bongie."

"Your mother might have been here already."

"Don't be silly. It isn't like we've been able to marry for more than a minute."

"She might have come and waited."

"She came and waited in Cuba."

He groused about that, but he agreed, finally, to sit tight until Matie arrived. He did leave me feeling, though, that I was making him wait until New Year's Day to tear off the Christmas wrap.

Matie took her time getting to Sun Valley, but wasted no time when she got to the lodge. She sat us both down in our suite with its view of the snowcapped mountains, and she laid out in detail all the reasons we ought to wait.

"It won't look right, the two of you marrying with the ink on Ernest's divorce barely dry," she said.

Ernest said, "The fact that Pauline was a selfish bitch and dragged it out forever is no reason for Marty and I to wait."

"Ernest, really," Matie said with a pointed look at me, "you can't talk like that about a woman you loved enough to marry. And there are the children to consider. The children need time to get used to this."

"The boys love Marty," Ernest said. "If I don't tie your daughter down pretty quickly, Bumby will move in on his old papa and try to steal her away from me!"

"Really, Ernest, be serious," Matie insisted.

"I am being serious. You should see how he moons around Marty! The more she swears, the deeper he falls."

"There's the drinking," Matie said. "There's the arguments and the crashing cars and the storming out on one another. The both of you. Your tempers."

Ernest crossed his arms over his chest, his face losing the glow of good-willed tolerance.

"Martha will never be a decent wife, Ernest," she said.

"Mother!" I protested.

"But you won't, Martha. You don't even want to be. You'd rather go off to the Burma Road than get married."

"And I'm smart enough to know not to put her to that choice," Ernest said, trying to be light about it, but still with his arms crossed.

"He's coming to China with me, Matie," I said. I'd gotten the *Collier's* assignment after all, and Ernest had finally given up on trying to talk me out of it and instead arranged to do some pieces for *PM* magazine on China so he could get a visa too.

Matie said to Ernest, "You haven't been a bachelor in twenty years, and it terrifies you."

"Matie!" I slid one hand across Bug's folded arms and took his hand in mine lest he take a swing at my mother, even though I didn't actually think he would.

"Neither of you has thought this through far enough even to know whether the law here will recognize Ernest's divorce from Pauline." Matie's voice was calm and matter-of-fact. Not "Ernest's divorce," but "Ernest's divorce from Pauline," as if to suggest to us both that Pauline was the real wife, or perhaps that this wasn't the first time he'd left a wife, and perhaps it wouldn't be the last.

"In Idaho?" Ernest said.

"Not every state recognizes the legitimacy of a divorce granted in another state. It will do you no good to try to marry in a state where you think you're divorced but the state disagrees. Think of how that would look in the headlines."

"Is that what this is about?" Ernest demanded. He stood, suddenly as angry as I'd ever seen him, at least when he was sober. "This is an ambush?" He looked to me now. "You've dragged in your mother to suggest maybe we can't even do this, is that it?"

"Ernest, be reasonable," Matie said.

Ernest stormed out of the suite, slamming the door.

"Matie, he dedicated the book to me," I said quietly, lest he might be standing on the other side of the door, listening.

"That isn't a reason to marry him, Martha."

"I can't *not* marry him now, Matie," I said, beginning to cry. "He dedicates the book to a woman who stands him up at the altar? Think how humiliating that would be for him."

"Just put it off, Martha. Just give it time."

"How can I do that, Matie? You've seen how he is. I could hardly make him wait for you to arrive. He's no good at waiting when he wants a thing. He's no good at getting less than exactly what he wants exactly when he wants it."

"But, Martha—"

"I do love him, Matie. I do love him. And he does love me."

"That doesn't mean you should marry him."

"You'd rather I live in sin?"

"I would."

"Mother!"

We both turned to a sound beyond the door, but it was just the maids passing and disappearing.

"He's going to go to China with me, Matie," I said in a lower voice. "How many men in this whole world would set aside their own ambitions even for a minute to let me follow mine?"

Matie said, "You can live in sin in China as easily as you can in Cuba."

"Mother."

"Maybe the divorce isn't effective in Idaho. You might buy some time just by making sure of that, at least."

Ernest left me a note that night, charging me with ratting on our plans. He'd conceded to everything I wanted: the quiet wedding with no church anywhere in sight, just a justice of the peace. No press but Robert Capa, whom I adored and who adored me and would never let anyone run trash about us with his photos. The trip to goddamned China when he'd like to go home and start a new book. He was giving me everything I wanted because the only thing he wanted was for me to be happy, and what I was giving him in return was a good, sound busted heart.

The apology was all on me this time. I found him in the bar, and I told him Matie was just being a silly Mother-Bongie worrier, and of course I had no intention of ratting on our very finely made plans. I was sure the laws of Idaho wouldn't get in our way, but we could sort that out the next day. I had a drink with him, and another, and he told me I'd better keep loving him, as he'd already bought me a Winchester double-barrel shotgun for my thirty-second birthday, just two days away.

"What would I do with a double-barrel shotgun bought for a gal who decided she didn't love me anymore?" he said, and I saw the darkness and the hurt awful in his eyes.

"Bug, I do love you," I said. "I do love you, and I understand you, and you understand me, and we deserve each other, the good and the bad."

I kissed him, there in the bar, trying to make a chip in the darkness.

"If we can't find a justice of the peace to marry us in Idaho, we'll just go to some goddamned other state," he said.

"Of course we will, Bongie," I said.

And when he ordered another drink, I put my hand high on his thigh and I caressed him, and I told the bartender not to bother with the drink, that I had other plans for him. I said it with just a hint of sexy, so that Bug would feel the pride of having a woman he thought was more beautiful than she actually was declaiming publicly that she wanted him in her bed. Just a very small bit of sexy so that anyone who might hear would still imagine me a good woman rather than a slut.

"Well, all right, then," he said. "All right."

We climbed in bed back in our suite and we made love, and it wasn't any better for me than it ever was, but I let him think it was like I always did, and he held me afterward like I liked him to. This would be enough, I thought. There never would be any more for me than there ever had been with Ernest or any other man, but that was my own difficulty, that didn't have anything to do with love. And after he was asleep, I climbed from our bed and went into the sitting room where Matie had tried to talk us out of marrying. I opened the curtains to the moonlight on the mountains, and as I watched the stars make their slow, steady progress through the black of the sky, I let the tears come.

The Trail Creek Cabin, Sun Valley, Idaho

November 1940

Robert Capa arrived in Sun Valley the day after Ernest threw me a birthday party at which I'd somehow managed to drink the least of anyone and yet suffer the most. He came to shoot a picture biography of Ernest for *Life* magazine. He stayed for our prewedding party at the Trail Creek Cabin, a little log cabin where we had a simple gathering with dinner by candlelight and dancing. It was just Matie and a very few friends, and Capa standing on a barstool for a good angle on Ernest, who looked handsome and happy in a jacket and tie. Spent flashbulbs popped off the camera like shells from the big guns in Spain. We both loved Capa, so it was okay, really, it was.

We were married on November 21, a Thursday. It was a short ceremony officiated by a justice of the peace, as I'd wanted, although no one would take seriously my desire to be pronounced "writer and writer" rather than "husband and wife." The deed was done in the dining room of the Union Pacific Railroad some seven hundred miles down the tracks, across the state line into Cheyenne, Wyoming, where Ernest's divorce from Pauline was recognized. We celebrated with a quiet dinner—roast moose—and it was only after Ernest was asleep that night that I allowed myself to cry again. Maybe they were happy tears or maybe they were sad tears or maybe they were simply tears of relief; I no longer knew.

We went to New York after the wedding, to arrange the details of my trip to China. We were headed back to Cuba when we heard F. Scott Fitzgerald had died of a massive heart attack, at the age of forty-four.

"Christ," Ernest said. "Christ."

Scott, only three years older than Ernest, had drunk himself to death, that was the truth of it.

I thought Ernest might want to go to the funeral, but the news left him too depressed to want to go anywhere but home. So we returned to the Finca Vigía, where the orchids hung like ornaments from the ceiba tree, the crystal on the drinks cart sparkled the sunlight into rainbows, and the pool pump was again on the fritz.

For my Christmas present that year, Ernest had arranged to buy my beautiful Finca Vigía outright, with $12,500 of the proceeds from *For Whom the Bell Tolls*.

"Twelve thousand dollars!" I said. "But, Bug, you didn't think it was worth even a hundred a month!"

He said, "I wanted you to know this would be your home forever, Mrs. Hemingway."

We were done writing for the afternoon and I was swimming in the pool while Ernest sorted through the mail one afternoon in January—the two of us chatting at the same time about our plans for the China trip—when he opened a large brown envelope and extracted the first issue of *Life* for 1941—the issue with Robert Capa's photos of us in Idaho.

"Here we are, Mook!" Like a kid. "Come see!"

I swam to the pool's edge and hauled myself out of the water, dripping my way toward him as he flipped the cover (Katharine Hepburn looking glamorously upward) and began searching for the spread with Robert Capa's photos of us in Idaho. And there it was: a full half-page photo of us looking awfully damned happy.

"Don't drip on us, Bongie!" Ernest exclaimed. "You'll look beautiful anyway, but I'll look awfully goofy with my face made all wavy from pool water dripped on the page!"

"You look so handsome, Bongie," I said, and he did, both in that big photo where he was looking at me like I was the top prize he'd just won at the carnival game booth, and in the smaller photo below it, the two of us perched on the railing of our sun terrace at the lodge.

As I registered the title of the piece—"The Hemingways in Sun Valley: The Novelist Takes a Wife"—he turned the page to a short bit on *For Whom the Bell Tolls* run with six terrific pages of Capa's Spanish war photos, and then to a full page photo of Ernest showing off a pheasant he'd shot.

"I look silly holding the bird like that," he said.

"Don't be ridiculous, Bongie," I said, blinking back the memory of all those dead rabbits this dead bird provoked. "It's the hair that makes you look silly. But look how silly my hair looks in the first photo!"

He laughed, and he kissed me, putting his hand on my hair so that it came off wet. I dried his fingers gently with my towel, and he turned the page again, to photos of Gary Cooper looking very like Robert Jordan from the novel, and a young Ingrid Bergman (who'd been a star in Sweden but had appeared in only one American film). Cooper hadn't yet signed to play Robert Jordan, nor Bergman Maria, but the movie rights had sold for the $100,000 Bug had insisted Friede accept, along with a bonus of up to $30,000—ten cents for every copy of the novel, which was selling like frozen daiquiris in hell.

I flipped back and read the captions carefully, then the quarter page of opening text. I'd published three books and had a fourth coming out the next fall. I'd been a war correspondent for *Collier's* in Spain, France, Czechoslovakia, and Finland. I was under contract to cover the Chinese army in action for them, an assignment that would take me to Hong Kong, China, Singapore, and the Dutch East Indies. Still, Ernest was "the great American," while you had to read the very fine print under the smallest of the photos for any suggestion that I was anything more than Ernest Hemingway's bride who aimed her new double-barrel shotgun well enough to make him proud.

PART IV

Hong Kong

February 1941

Let's just say we made it to Hong Kong. We'll skip the stopping in Los Angeles on the way to talk with Gary Cooper again about playing the lead in *For Whom the Bell Tolls*, and the lunch at Jack's in San Francisco to meet Ingrid Bergman. We'll skip the bit about the luxury cruise on the *Matsona* from San Francisco to Hawaii, all the way tossed about the ship like Ping-Pong balls in a spirited volley. We'll skip all the draping of leis and the swarming of greeters and the hordes of photographers in Honolulu, and smiling until our faces hurt. Also the relative privacy of the Pan Am Clipper flying boat, the glorious night's rest in Guam, and the second Clipper, which splashed down in an overcast Victoria Harbour, from which we were ferried across to Central Hong Kong with its colonial banks and expat mansions and the Hong Kong Hotel, complete with ceiling fans and antiques and squishy leather chairs straight out of Somerset Maugham. Ernest and I were there for the journalism, but all of wealthy Hong Kong gathered each Saturday night to dine and dance at the hotel, and I did love to dance.

A second role had been added to our itinerary not long before we left: President Roosevelt asked us to observe closely the politics of China—in particular the relationship between Chiang Kai-shek's Kuomintang, the Chinese nationalists who controlled some of the south of the country, and Mao Zedong's communists, who controlled the north. The great bulk of the country was already in the hands of the Japanese, and the two warring Chinese factions were meant to have set aside their civil war to cooperate against them, a condition of their US aid. The alliance, though—if it had ever existed—was going sour. Chiang Kai-shek was rumored to be talking about making peace with the Japanese in order to gain time to rid China of Mao and the communists.

"So the president wants us to spy on our Chinese allies, that's about the sum of it?" Ernest said.

"'Espionage,' Bug," I answered. "It's so much lovelier a word than 'spy.'"

The president had had us briefed by the secretary of the Treasury and the general manager of the Rubber Company of the Far East.

"If we don't stop the Japanese in China," the latter told us, "they'll move into the Pacific, to take over the world's rubber supplies."

"Bad for your business," Ernest said glibly.

"No rubber, no tires," the man responded. "No tires, no trucks, and no airplanes, no way to defend ourselves."

Ernest said, "Which would be very bad for business all around."

Hong Kong, once we'd hoisted ourselves up from the squishy Somerset Maugham chairs at the hotel and wandered beyond Pedder Street and the mansions, turned out to be a dump of a place nailed together with odd lots of rotten wood, surrounded by the Japanese, and throbbing with Chinese refugees. Ernest, so good with languages, learned within a Hong Kong minute to order a rickshaw in the local slang so we could ride comfortably through the awful poverty. There were brothels and mahjong betting parlors and street sleepers. There were opium dens in which Chinese paid ten cents for three pills and a space in the tiers of hard bunks—cheaper than food, and it dulled the appetite. There was everywhere the vile odor of night soil, human excrement put out to be gathered by old women who tended, each time the air-raid sirens sounded for a blackout drill, to drop their collecting baskets and run. But the worst, always the worst, were the children. A twelve-year-old boy made the rounds to the bunks to see if users had overdosed. A girl who couldn't have been nine, and with the side of her face burned in some way you didn't want to imagine, carved balls within balls of ivory, three months to make one little trinket that would end up forgotten at the back of a desk drawer halfway across the world.

The trouble with me and my bar of soap, Ernest insisted, was that I assumed the Chinese judged the world the way I did, that whatever made me glum must make them so too.

"If it's as bad as you think," he said, "wouldn't they be shooting themselves? They're having kids, Mook. They're lighting firecrackers every night."

He knew all about the firecrackers. He set them off in our hotel room until I put my foot down about it. He drank and swapped tall tales with a jolly entourage of British officers and pilots, Chinese generals and millionaires, and a crazy Australian in the Hong Kong Hotel lobby. He went pheasant hunting. He bet on the horses at Happy Valley with nothing to show for it but a tweed coat with a deep inside pocket and such complicated buttons that it was, he swore, pickpocket proof.

Me, I flew to Lashio, Burma—the end of the Burma Road built by the British to get supplies to the Chinese army. I didn't have papers to go to China yet, but I had a flight, and that seemed enough. We left at four in the morning, in little visibility to elude a Japanese army that was more than happy to point its guns at a little China National Aviation Corporation DC-2 with canvas seats and a cabin that wasn't pressurized. We flew sixteen hours—fifteen hundred miles at seriously freezing altitudes and with no real navigation, with hail pummeling the wings so violently that it left passengers vomiting. The pilot, an Indiana boy who liked to make puns, opened his window to judge how fast he was going and, to pass the time, told me of a similar flight in October that had been brought down by the Japanese. The Japs had killed the pilot, nine of the fourteen passengers, and a twenty-five-year-old stewardess making her last flight before her wedding day.

Indiana had to get a fix on the flare pots meant to mark the landing strip in Chungking to land us, in weather so soupy you might have served it at the White House and garnered praise for the brilliant new chef. We had a quick breakfast there, then set off for Lashio, the weather along the gorge of the Burma Road so bad that my arms began twitching. My head was so soft that I admitted to the pilot that I might burst into tears for no reason.

"That's on account of the lack of oxygen at this altitude," he explained. "If I take us any lower, the downdrafts in the gorge will take us all the way down."

The next morning, we waited for the word that the Japanese had finished their morning bombing, then took off again, flying low along the Burma Road this time to land in Kunming on the China side of the border, a big walled city so thoroughly bombed that it was something to see even if you'd witnessed what the Russians did to Finland or the shelling of Madrid. The townspeople, when we arrived, had formed a mile-long bucket brigade, passing water from hand to hand to put out the fires, while women hobbled on bound feet after their children or dug through the rubble that had been their homes.

By the time I returned to Hong Kong and Bug three days later, the press were reporting that Ernest Hemingway and his new wife were in town to research a novel. We went about the city as if we really might be setting a novel there, happy to avoid stirring up interest in the intelligence we were meant to collect.

"Who would ever set a novel in a place where they spit so much?" I asked Ernest. There were slimy blobs of mucus everywhere you went, and always people adding to it.

"That's the tuberculosis," he answered.

When I looked appalled, he said, "I thought you knew. Honestly, Mook. I thought you were handling it awfully well."

"No rubber, no tires," I muttered to myself.

We moved to the Repulse Bay Hotel, a quiet place outside the bustle of the city, which was even more English than the Hong Kong Hotel, if you overlooked the barbed wire stretching across the sand between the veranda and the South China Sea and the pillboxes and barricades meant to guard against Japanese invasion. Tuxedoed waiters poured tea and served pink gins to all the beautiful people who languished in wicker chairs, and no one spit—although on a walk to Aberdeen to have a look at a sampan village, we did pass a woman vomiting blood.

"The cholera," Bug explained as he took my arm and hurried us off. "This is what you meant for our honeymoon, isn't it?"

He began to oversee the boiling of our water and arranged extra vaccine shots, while I husbanded my shrinking bar of jammy French soap. I filed a story with *Collier's* about Hong Kong, which my editor cabled was beautifully written but not quite exciting enough—a problem he would remedy in the opening paragraphs. I filed another about the heroic CNAC pilots like the punny one from Indiana. Ernest gathered a new gang of friends with which to drink, including a redheaded Virginian on his way back to Washington, DC, from China, where he'd been laying out flight routes. When he left Hong Kong, he took with him an envelope from us to deliver to the US Treasury secretary, setting out the little bit of intelligence we'd gathered in our first five weeks in Hong Kong, as we waited for our permissions to tour China itself to clear.

We were pretty thrilled the night we were called, finally, to report for our flight from Hong Kong to Namyung. With some luck, we would make the short flight over the Japanese and the mountains to join the Chinese army in the Seventh War Zone. War was harder than you might have imagined to find, the Japanese having overrun the best three-quarters of China and not, apparently, in need or want of the rest. We waited in the cold at the airfield, armed with flea powder, mosquito nets, and bedrolls, and what Ernest deemed to be enough whiskey to last us, and quinine too. After a good long while, the flight was canceled, as the weather would make landing impossible.

We did manage the flight the next day, though, the weather having cleared enough for us to land but not so much that our little plane couldn't use the cloud cover to hide from the Japanese. We arrived in the pouring rain to meet our political escort, our transport department escort, our interpreter, our driver, and a tubercular mechanic. The seven of us squeezed into a Chevy, which would turn out to have exploding tires, and we set off down a long slug of boulder-studded mud. We were not to worry, Mr. Ma (the political escort) assured us: deluxe accommodations awaited us in Shaokwan.

The Chinese version of "deluxe," it turned out, included two wooden benches for sleeping, a single brass bowl filled with murky water, two kerosene lamps, a hole-in-the-floor toilet, and mosquitos enough for Ernest and me both, with some to spare, despite the cold.

"'The Light of Shaokwan,' indeed!" Ernest said.

"Are we to wash our faces and brush our teeth together in the same bit of water?" I asked him.

"Mrs. Bongie," Ernest said, "if you even dream of brushing your teeth in this, you are a bigger nutcase than I give you credit for."

I took my soap from my pack, held it to my nose, and inhaled. "No rubber, no tires."

"Cheer up!" he said. "It's a fine honeymoon you've arranged for us!"

We were, at least, only one hundred miles from Japanese-occupied Canton, and perhaps fifty from the front.

He opened one of the whiskey bottles, took a long pull, and handed it to me. *"Ganbei!"* he said.

"Ganbei?"

"Bottoms up, Mrs. Bongie-China-Saver-Heminghorn."

"Gellingway," I insisted.

"Mrs. Bongie-China-Saver-Gellingway."

I rushed about Shaokwan collecting the political information I needed for *Collier's* while Ernest made rousing speeches and traded flowery toasts made with a yellow "rice wine" kerosene. Three days in, we pushed off with Mr. Ma and the gang for a closer look at the war, traveling in an ancient truck through limestone mountains and grassy valleys to the North River, a wide, muddy thing so like the Mississippi River that I was reminded of that dreary hat I'd tossed out the train window, to land not in the water but on the homebound track.

We boarded a rusty Chris-Craft motorboat driven by a bearded old fool who sat cross-legged at the helm, smoking a bamboo pipe and spitting out the window. It was the only motorized boat on the river, we were told, and, no, we shouldn't worry about the rope pulling a sampan behind us, dragging right beside the motor, or the boy bailing the Chris-Craft hourly to keep us from sinking. A contingent of teenaged soldiers had boarded the sampan, already crowded with the driver's family and a screaming baby, leaving us only the sloping roof of the Chris-Craft itself on which to sleep. We poured some whiskey into a thermos of boiled water, and we wedged ourselves securely between boat hooks and coiled ropes, and we settled in to the view: temples built improbably high on the cliffs, egrets and ducks, and men on the bamboo-edged shore pulling junks upriver by rope, singing as they worked. Despite the abundance of sun and the flies and gnats, which gave way to mosquitos as evening colored the sky, we were better off than we would have been in the dank, damp sampan, where we would have had no choice but to share our whiskey.

The boy, between bailings, routinely tested the water depth with a pole, but still we ran aground several times in the dark. Mercifully, we tied up to a sampan village, charming boats gathered together in a friendly little cluster.

Ernest called out as welcome, "You folks have any cholera we haven't found already?" sending the poor Chinese scampering inside their little boats lest this crazy American brute do them harm.

"Bug!" I scolded.

"Didn't you see the black flag?" he demanded.

"Don't be silly. Our good hawking captain has better sense than to tie us up with a cholera quarantine."

Ernest slept while I lay awake listening to the talking and the laughing and the sucking, the nauseating spitting, until finally it was something close to quiet for perhaps three hours.

By the light of dawn, Ernest pointed out the black flag. "A dose of cholera included in the honeymoon suite at no extra charge!"

Farther down the river, we went ashore in a downpour to join a platoon of soldiers awaiting us with horses so small that Ernest could touch his toes to the ground from his mount—a convenience, he claimed, as he weighed as much as the horse. The soldiers took us to their division headquarters, where soggy paper banners greeted us with "Welcome to the Representatives of Righteousness and Peace" and "Democracy only Survives Civilization," whatever that was supposed to mean. A white-gloved general saluted us, and his shoeless orphan soldiers schooled us in the weaponry and activity of the Twelfth Army Group holding this front. It was cold and wet and miserable, with no actual fighting. The most noteworthy thing that happened was that Ernest refrained from strangling me in the middle of the night.

The next day, we rode up through rolling hills to dirty little villages with peasants struggling to work their plows in the gray mud, each village separated from the next by a vast emptiness that made getting anywhere impossible. We found generals happy to drink our whiskey, but not a drop of war. The Japanese had better sense than to want this bit of land where the peasants had already burned their own crops twice rather than leave them to the enemy.

"Just shoot me now and put me out of this misery, Bug," I said one night after we'd finished our single bowls of inedible rice and settled into our hard wooden-plank beds, my stomach no better than it had been all the long trip.

He said, "But it's a terrific honeymoon, Mrs. Pig. They threw in the tuberculosis and the cholera both—such generosity."

"Oh, go suck an egg, Mr. Pig," I said.

He laughed and he said, "Ah, what I wouldn't do for a decent egg."

"No rubber, no tires," I reminded myself.

He said, "Good night, Mrs. Representative of Righteousness and Peace."

I said, "Good night, Mr. Representative."

He said, "I do love you, Mookie."

I said, "I take you on the grandest adventures to the most romantic places. Who wouldn't be wild for that?" And then after a moment, "I love you too, Bug."

"But not enough to share your soap with me?"

"I promised to love and honor," I said, "but I said nothing about obeying, and I certainly did not promise to share my soap."

I'd climbed a ladder to a bamboo tower that was the only place a woman could relieve herself in the thousand-year-old Chinese village in which we'd found ourselves—clay huts emptying into muddy streets, our bed a stone floor in the company of flies and mosquitos, and our whiskey gone—and I was setting about my business (which would be conveniently collected in a not-particularly-sweet-smelling five-foot Ali Baba jar beneath me, for fertilizing crops) when a hammering on the nose cap of an unexploded Japanese bomb began. The air-raid signal.

I looked down to see the peasants scattering out into the rice paddies. In the distance, someone plowed the mud with a scrawny buffalo.

Ernest waited at the bottom of the ladder, grinning up at me. "You might have used the rice paddy."

"Can't you see I'm busy here?" I demanded.

"Best of Chinese luck!" he called up, and he disappeared into a doorway, leaving me to my fine view of a squadron of Japanese planes passing mercifully high overhead.

"That would have been something," Ernest said afterward, watching as I descended the ladder. "The intrepid war correspondent killed in the line of duty."

"I was in the middle of something, and anyway, you can't expect me to duck for cover at the first suggestion of fighting we've seen, even if it was a mile overhead."

We set off not much later on our little horses, Mr. Ma giving us a broken-English tutorial on the Japanese air force. He took us up the Hill of Heroes, from which we watched through binoculars what purported to be a battlefield conveniently in full action for us, Chinese soldiers with rifles, machine guns, and mortars in khaki camouflage scattering toward a tree-lined Hill of the Unknowns, entrenched with Japanese. The general who stood observing with us was a real general, to be sure, even if he spent more time hosting drunken banquets than he did leading soldiers, or even visiting them. The soldiers were real Chinese soldiers as well, although they wore shoes, which ought to have made us suspect. What the real Chinese soldiers were so bravely marching toward, though, was not the Japanese army but rather a mock Japanese camp. The real Japanese were another ridge beyond, far enough away for the exercise to be all smoke and explosion without an ounce of threat to life.

"Bug," I said, "I think we're done here."

"Without actually seeing the war beyond this staged bit, Mrs. Bongie? And, sure, you've gotten sick, but I haven't yet, and even for you there's still the cholera."

We watched for another minute, the soldiers moving so surely in their fake assault.

"Cheer up, Mook," Ernest said. "You've done your bit like a champion. You can't be blamed if there's no war to be seen."

Wong Shek, China

April 1941

After a rainy stop in the village of Wong Shek, with the usual Chinese officers hosting the usual extravagant banquet—competitive wine drinking and toasting of soldiers, none of whom were invited to the party—we headed back the way we'd come on our toy ponies. The send-off at the Chris-Craft was as extravagant as the drunken bacchanal the night before, made all the longer by a two-hour wait for a missing soldier who was to travel with us. And the return trip was even longer and more cursed than the trip in had been, all of it for nothing more than so many sodden nights and dreary days, and a single fake attack. We consoled ourselves with the promise of our accommodations in Chungking—the private home of a Chinese diplomat we were to be given on account of my being friendly with the Roosevelts, in the city that, being the working capital of free China, must have something to say for itself.

"A real bathroom and real beds," I said.

"Clean sheets. Hot food. Mosquito nets."

"Or, better yet, no need for mosquito nets."

The prospect got us through forty-three long hours on account of the rope attaching us to the motorboat getting caught in its propeller, bringing us to a dead stop, and a flood on the road to Shaokwan that necessitated us carrying on in the boat. I covered the greasy sampan bunks with Keating's powder. We ate almost nothing, but Ernest found us a bottle of pink wine, which we drank from our collapsible cups atop the boat, watching the crew work to untangle us.

"Bug, what's that in the bottle?" I asked as he tipped the last bit into my cup.

"In what bottle?"

"In the wine bottle, Bongie. It looks like . . ." My stomach flipped up inside itself: it looked like a snakeskin.

Ernest said, "Well, if he looks like a snake, it's because he is a snake, but don't worry: he's too dead to have drunk much." He grinned at me. "If you vomit, Mook, I'm afraid I'll have to write a piece about it." And while I was still too busy being revolted to say a word, he said, "I thought you'd prefer it to the bird wine. I couldn't tell whether the cuckoo bird in that bottle was alive or dead. It's hard to tell with bottled birds, and anyway, the snake wine is said to stop hair from thinning. I might take a bottle home for Perkins."

I set my collapsible cup on the boat roof beside me. He finished his own glass, then set to drinking mine.

We watched as our crew finally untangled the rope from the propeller and the motor leapt back to life. This had been, I thought, both the longest and most interesting twelve days of my life.

"Finally. The worst is over," I said.

"You go on hoping," Ernest said.

What followed was twenty-five more hours in the absolute filth and cigarette stench of a "first-class" train compartment to Kweilin—a place of magically rounded mountains and romantic mists and a hotel with the promising name of "The Palace," which had fine porcelain toilets unconnected to actual plumbing, dead bedbugs smashed to the wall, and live ones everywhere else.

"If only I had a pistol," Ernest said.

"Don't be silly," I said. "Those bugs are too slow to be a challenge."

"Ah, but they're tiny—that makes 'em tough to hit."

I used the last of my Keating's powder on the bed. Ernest assured me that the floor would be the safer bet.

We delivered a message for our plane to fetch us in Kweilin, only to find two days later that the message had made it no further than the man to whom we'd handed it. The plane that finally did come to take us to Chungking, a Douglas DC-3, was carrying Chinese cash in stacks so large and worthless that we sat on them the whole flight. The path from the airstrip to the long-awaited diplomat's house was a long, impossibly steep stairway to a muddy collection of drab cement buildings and shapeless shacks. But then there was the house: large and lovely and welcoming.

We opened the door and stepped into a sitting room with varnished tables and plush armchairs and sofas—and three Chinese thugs who squinted at us through a drug-eyed fog. Every bit of the place was filthy with their hair oil and their hair. The sheets and pillowcases and the pink satin bedspread were as stained as the sofas, and the fine porcelain toilets were overflowing.

"No rubber, no tires," Ernest said, and he laughed. What else was there to do? "What say you we see if there's any decent booze at that bar we passed?"

He must have found someone to speak to before we went out to the bar, because while we were drinking someone changed the linens and cleaned the bathroom. They didn't, unfortunately, clear out the thugs, who, we concluded, were there to spy on us as surely as we were there to spy on them.

The next morning, we met the Chinese finance minister, who insisted on keeping us company for breakfast, lunch, and dinner, often bringing along a wife whose black satin dress buttoned from collar to knee with button-sized diamonds. She had ruby and emerald buttons as well, but no sapphires, as they wouldn't stand out against the velvet.

We lunched with the Chinese president, Chiang Kai-shek, and the beautiful Madame Chiang, a couple everyone in America felt they knew on account of the two being *Time* magazine's People of the Year a few years back. Madame Chiang came to the door to receive us without the fanfare of servants announcing us. She wore a Chinese dress and diamond earrings and no more than a hint of lipstick on a face that was cream colored and oval, and absolutely smooth. Her English was a damned sight better than my own thanks to a father who'd been educated in the United States and her own years at Wellesley, and she chain-smoked like I did, menthol cigarettes she kept in an ebony case. She translated for her husband, who honored us by receiving us without his teeth—a dubious honor if not an outright affront, it seemed to me. Still, our simple lunch turned into a three-hour interview, and we returned the next day for a tour of their private air-raid shelter and a further chat with Madame Chiang, this time in stone chairs in a sunken garden just coming into spring.

The whole encounter left me uneasy, though. I suspected Chiang himself understood our English perfectly well, that the language barrier was a charade the two used to allow them to communicate in a language we couldn't understand. They grilled us far too intently about what aid the Russians might be receiving from the United States. And while they called their Japanese invaders "a disease of the skin," they called their Chinese communist allies "a disease of the heart"—by which they meant the greater threat to their personal power, which was of far more importance to them than improving the lot of the Chinese people, or even ridding their country of the Japanese.

The worst of it, though, was that when it came to writing about them, we had to stuff down our disgust at "the Empress of China," as Ernest dubbed Madame Chiang, and her Chinese-leader husband, and present the two tyrants as bastions of a democracy they had no interest in. It wasn't that I wrote anything untrue but that I chose the convenient truths and discarded the rest. They were a corrupt pair, but they were allied against Hitler and the Japanese, and if I hadn't seen on my own my patriotic duty to present them in the best possible light, my editors at *Collier's* would have made sure I did.

For the same reason, I couldn't write at all about the one person I found to admire in China, which was the communist leader Mao Zedong's second-in-command, Chou En-lai. We'd been brought to him by a woman in a man's hat and trousers who approached us in the Chungking marketplace and, after we'd wandered the city long enough to slip our minders, blindfolded us and put us in a rickshaw that took us to a small, whitewashed room with nothing but a table, three chairs, and Chou En-lai himself. Chou was thoughtful and eloquent, intelligent and charming. He was perhaps the only person we'd met in China who gave two whiffs and a puff for the good Chinese. But we couldn't write about him at all, lest any good thing we might say cause a rift between the two Chinese factions, which needed to stay united to defeat the Japanese.

I managed in Chungking to contract China Rot, which, in case you don't know (I didn't), is a nasty business in which the skin between your fingers oozes yellow pus and blood. It's contagious as hell, and the treatment involves a thoroughly disgusting-smelling ointment and gloves of the type you might wear if you were welding, or stoking a coal fire, or hoping to win the Miss Ugly Contest with your hands alone.

"I warned you not to wash," Ernest said.

I was so sick—with the China Rot and the dysentery and the vast abyss between what I saw and what I could report—that I couldn't make a scheduled flight to Chengdu. Ernest made the trip for me, and returned with photos of a hundred thousand workers building a mile-long airstrip in Szechuan Province, to receive B-17 bombers it was our understanding Roosevelt never meant to send to the Chinese, who, at any rate, had no pilots who could fly them. The Chinese peasants were building the airstrip from nothing and with no machinery, using manpower alone to pull concrete rollers weighing three and a half tons.

"Don't count China out yet," Ernest said, and he told me enough about it for me to add a few paragraphs to my *Collier's* piece.

We began to put together what we knew of China for the debriefing: that for the cost of two battleships, we could fund the Chinese for another year of war they might otherwise not survive, time we could use to build our own naval fleet for the inevitable dual-ocean war; that a Chinese civil war was inevitable but might be postponed through dialogue between Chiang and Chou En-lai; that if we were going to send planes to China, we ought to send pilots to fly them. Our information seemed unlikely to make any difference. America was growing increasingly isolationist in our absence, gathering for anti-war demonstrations and peace rallies, and by and large sticking foolish heads in American sand.

I was still wearing the damned China Rot gloves when we left China, flying from Chungking to Rangoon, Burma, where I would carry on alone to tour efficient naval installations in Batavia in the Dutch East Indies and luxuriously disastrous ones in Singapore. Ernest had just poured a full measure of gin into his collapsible cup when the flight turned into a helluva flight, with the wings surely about to break off and a crash inevitable. I gripped tightly to my seat with my awkward gloves, racked with guilt that I'd nagged Ernest until he'd agreed to join me for this nightmare when he might have been back in Cuba working on a fine new book. Ernest held his collapsible cup of gin as if it were the chalice that would save us.

When the plane, by some miracle, found smoother air, Bug smiled happily. "I didn't lose a drop! The gin shot out of my cup and hit the roof, but I caught it on the way down."

I laughed and laughed. "God, no wonder I married you," I said. "World champion gin catcher that you are."

I reached out to touch him, to say all the things I'd been thinking as the plane bucked.

He said, "Don't you dare put those diseased hands on me!"

I looked at him, shocked, and we both laughed again, and he said, "And to think, I might have made the mistake of borrowing your soap. You did leave that thing back at that dump of a house, didn't you?"

"The soap?"

"The diseased soap."

"Of course," I said. And I shifted my pack away from him lest he catch a whiff of the warm honey smell of acacia, and I remembered that day in Madrid, the miracle of the branch of fresh yellow blooms in that hospital where Bug never did like to go.

The Finca Vigía, San Francisco de Paula, Cuba

June 1941

Despite it being far and away the critics' favorite, *For Whom the Bell Tolls* did not receive the Pulitzer Prize. It was a rough blow, especially as the committee declined to honor any book of fiction that year. It wasn't that another book had been judged better. It was that Ernest's book had been judged not good enough.

"If I'd won that thing, I'd think I was slipping," he claimed, and he took to disparaging Max Perkins for having sold only half a million copies of the novel in six months, sure that if Max had really been supportive, it would have sold even more and, anyway, why hadn't Max airmailed him updates, it being only eight days from New York to Hong Kong by airmail. I felt so bad for him that I didn't even give him what for for having written to me while I was in Singapore that he had three Chinese girls in his hotel room and knew exactly what to do with them. Maybe he did and I was a fool, but I'd seen the spread between Hemingway the man and Hemingway the myth, and I knew how dark he got when left alone.

On the way back home to Cuba, we stopped in Key West for Patrick and Gregory, on summer vacation again, and for the *Pilar*. Ernest sailed across, fishing on the way, while the boys and I flew ahead to a home with a leaky roof, a broken pool pump (again), and an insurmountable mound of mail in which, somewhere, there was a check for Ernest's royalties for the half-million copies of *Bell*.

I turned my attention to putting the finishing touches on the stories to be included in *The Heart of Another*, a ghastly, boring task of weeding out enough commas to fill that five-foot Ali Baba jar back in China, and to writing a piece for *Collier's* about the Nazis in Cuba, only to have my editor respond that the piece I wrote, which was the piece he had asked me to write, wasn't at all the piece he wanted to have. Bug talked about writing his memoirs, a chance to pay back Gertrude Stein for that nastiness about him in her damned *Autobiography of Alice B. Toklas*, he claimed. But the idea seemed pretentious even to him, and anyway, he wasn't done living, and he'd only ever threatened to resort to memoir when he couldn't find the juice to write anything else.

Nothing I could say would dig him out of the hole he insisted on continuing to dig that summer. Every cent he made went to someone else, he complained, mad about the taxes he would have to pay thanks to the great success of *Bell*, and intent on staying in Cuba long enough to claim nonresident status in the United States to minimize them. "When war breaks out and anyone asks whether I did my part," he said, "I can say I paid for the whole damned business." He fumed at Scribner, which had deducted from his royalty check the full cost of defending a spurious plagiarism suit. He obsessed about the *For Whom the Bell Tolls* movie. He reread and reread and reread the very few reviews that hadn't praised the novel, careening between wanting to tell the bastards a thing or two about writing and wondering if they were right. When he was in his cups, he said he had no better book in him than *Bell*, and if it couldn't win him anything—despite all his success, he'd never won a prize for his writing—he never would.

I was both relieved and worried every time he took the *Pilar* out, his mood whenever he returned ruled by the size of the marlin he'd brought in. He spent the days when he wasn't on the boat listening to my radio, torn between relief that the country was finally realizing we couldn't just stick our heads in a bucket and worry for Bumby. The military draft at this point only applied to twenty-one to twenty-eight-year-olds, and Bumby was only seventeen, but he would be eighteen in October, and if we entered the war, who knew what might change?

On Labor Day, we gathered around the Detrola to hear the president's radio broadcast: "We shall do everything in our power to crush Hitler and his Nazi forces." Three days later a German submarine fired two shots at one of our destroyers, the *Greer*. The torpedo missed, and the event was reported as a case of mistaken identity. I was recovered from the China trip by then and already sick again of watching the world going to hell while Ernest and I sat in Cuba getting drunk and indulging in loud, furious rages at each other.

I said, "Maybe writing something about it will make a difference or maybe it won't, Bug, but we damned well should try."

"What happened to being done with travel? What happened to sitting in one place for five minutes and writing a decent book?"

"I'd be happy to sit in one place for five minutes! You're the one dying to pick up and move to Sun Valley."

"To see my sons!"

"They couldn't come to Cuba?"

"But Christ, you love Sun Valley, Mart."

"But I don't, Bug. Have you not heard a word I've said about it all summer? I hate that place like holy hell. I'm nothing but your wife, and I'm bored with myself there, more bored even than I am here. It's dull as pavement and twice as heavy on my soul."

"You don't even think a journalist changes anything," he said.

"I want what we had in the beginning, Bug. I want to be a part of what *happens*. Nothing *happens* here."

"Plenty happens. And you don't really want war."

"I do, though, if it's there anyway. I want explosive and loud and hard and laughing."

"And dead, Mart? You want dead?"

"Yes! Yes, fucking yes. I would rather be dead from something exciting than dead from boredom, wouldn't you? I hate this faint goodness in me that's all I can find in Sun Valley. I would rather have China Rot miserable than Sun Valley bored."

"You aren't that much of a fool, Mart."

"Yes, I am! Yes, I fucking am!"

"Oh!" he said, surprised as hell. He grinned his goofy grin and he said, "Well, that's a different perspective on this."

We burst out laughing and he said, "I hadn't realized I'd married an absolute fool."

"Well, what a fool you are for not realizing it, then, Bongie," I said, and we laughed and laughed. What else could we do?

"You were so fond of that China Rot ointment and those gloves, Mrs. Bongie, I do remember that."

"It's just that there isn't a single bottle of wine in this place with a snake in it."

"Don't be silly, Mrs. Bongie Wine Drinker Fool, you never did like the snake wine. It was the bird wine you were crazy for."

"And the bedbugs," I said.

We talked about the bedbugs, how Ernest had wanted to shoot them, and about the thugs with their hair oil when we thought we were getting a diplomat's house, and about Antoine de Saint-Exupéry handing out grapefruits at the bottom of the stairs at the Florida in Madrid and Lillian Hellman sticking her head between her knees while the rest of us watched the night bombing from Del's balcony. It was all funny in retrospect, viewed from a safe, beautiful house in safe, beautiful Cuba, with everything you needed and no threat to your life.

"You were sweet on Lillian, that's what I remember," I said.

"Ah, I was only trying to keep your attention, Mook."

It was the way these arguments ended again and again, the way we blew off the stink of the juice not flowing, not for either of us. There was nothing but misery and darkness when the writing wouldn't jell, unless we could pull ourselves out of it and make each other laugh.

We determined, finally, in a fit of reasonableness, that a break would do us good. He would go on ahead to Sun Valley and his sons, and I would stay alone at the Finca for a week or two.

I said, "You can call me when the snake wine has arrived from China."

"You can bring the grapefruit," he said.

We went to bed then, and we made love, and if it wasn't amazing, it didn't hurt much, and we curled ourselves around each other and fell asleep, and we slept late the next morning, and we didn't either of us even try to write. We went out on the boat, and we fished, and Bug nearly caught an eleven-foot marlin, two hundred pounds if it was an ounce and a fair match for Ernest, but it bested him. We laughed about that too, about losing such a mighty and beautiful fish, and we felt better for the fish having won its freedom despite our best efforts, and for knowing we could still love each other even when neither of us could make the writing jell.

Sun Valley, Idaho

October 1941

I arrived in Sun Valley after our break from each other, resolved to cast off my anger and trouble-seeking and hell-on-wheels and settle down to the piles of clean white towels on the fence posts around the circular pools and to our room (not our usual suite but a simpler one, Averell Harriman having now made enough of a success of his new venture not to need to have photos of us to attract a crowd). Robert Taylor ("too thin to be given much weight," Bug declared) and his wife, Barbara Stanwyck ("damn ugly, but damn smart"), were keeping Ernest company in the usual shooting and riding and partying at the Trail Creek Cabin, along with Robert Capa and Gary and Rocky. The director Howard Hawks was there to discuss Gary playing Robert Jordan in *For Whom the Bell Tolls*. Hawks had brought along his striking young wife, "Slim," who was either completely taken with Ernest or doing a terrific job of pretending to be for the sake of getting him to agree with the director.

The talk was largely of the war. "We'll find it under the Christmas tree," Ernest liked to say, "or wake up New Year's morning with an unshakable war." He was sure it would start in the Pacific, never mind that it was the Germans who were whacking us, shooting at another of our destroyers so that President Roosevelt had to order the Navy to destroy on sight anything in the waters necessary for our defense.

Still, our own lives went on as ever in Sun Valley, with Jack and Gregory and Patrick joining us, and Ernest and I being kinder to each other with the boys there, and Bug trying very hard not to worry about Bumby and the draft.

The one bright spot in that fall was the publication of *The Heart of Another*, my story collection Scribner brought out on October 27. When the first copy arrived, we took it out onto our terrace, and we sat in the warm sunshine with the long view of the plains and the mountains and a very good bottle of cold champagne.

"Oh, Bug, it's the most beautiful book in the world, isn't it? Isn't it the most beautiful book you've ever seen? Of my books, I mean. Yours are always beautiful."

He raised his wide, flat champagne glass and said, "To you, Mook. Aren't you glad you broke with Dull, Slum and Pus? Didn't I tell you you would be?"

He'd bothered poor Max Perkins, who was now my editor too, over every detail of my book, the way he did for his own. He'd even taken charge of my photo, supervising my hair and my makeup and my clothing, and taking the photograph himself.

I said, "It's a much better cover than Elizabeth Bowen's new one, isn't it?" Bowen was a British writer who had inherited an Irish estate she rarely visited and was married to a man who, it was whispered, was about the only man in England with whom she never slept, but she lived in Oxford, and she knew everyone, and her latest short story collection, *Look at All Those Roses*, was getting a lot of attention. The *New York Times* suggested it ought to be read "prayerfully."

"It's a fine cover, Marty, but not half as gorgeous as your author photo."

I said, "No bridge, though. Not a stone one or a spidery metal one," and we laughed, and I said, "Do you suppose a book without a bridge on the cover will sell?" And we laughed again, and we drank more champagne.

I said, "It usually makes me sick, Bug, this part. It always makes me sick that what's inside will be disappointing, that I thought it was one thing all through the writing, and then it will all be something else, a disappointment."

Like *What Mad Pursuit*. I didn't like even to say the name of that damned first novel. I liked to think it didn't exist, that Dad never saw it, never told me how vile it was.

"It's a fine book, this one," Ernest said. "You'll be proud of it, always. Only you'll regret it isn't written by Martha Gellhorn *Hemingway*." He laughed as if he were only joking, and he drained his glass of champagne.

"But Bug, you do understand that, I know you do. Even publishing as Gellhorn, everyone thinks you've written it for me. They think Bowen and Kay Boyle and Katherine Anne Porter are great talents, when they only make a thing out to be a big mystery and then it all comes to nothing, they just leave you wondering what the hell that was all about. They're the little literary darlings, while I'm just under your Svengali spell. My style is 'aping into mush'—that's what that cad from the *New Republic* says."

"You're a fine mush, Marty, but you're no ape," he said, and we laughed again, and he refilled his champagne glass, then tipped the bottle to mine to top it up.

"Didn't Gigi shoot well today?" he said.

"He always does," I said.

"But today especially."

It had been a dreadful day for shooting, actually. There were ten thousand ducks, but they were high as bombers. Only Gigi hit anything.

"Today especially," I agreed. "But really, Ernest, does Elizabeth Bowen write anything other than the same cross-class romance that women have been writing for a hundred years?"

"She does all right," Ernest said.

"You don't know how it is, Ernest. You're like a boy with a new bicycle when your books come out. I'd like to be that way. I'd like to be something other than all scared inside, and regretting."

I opened the book to the title page, the letters slanted gracefully forward, with finely drawn shadow lines on the *T* and *H* and *A*: *The Heart of Another*. My name all in capital letters, which I liked although I was a little sad that my *A*'s weren't the *A*'s of the title or my whole name the font of "Charles Scribner's Sons," my favorite of the letters I suppose because they weren't quite right, and they were beautiful in their wrongness. I really was beginning to perhaps wallow in smuggery when I turned to the table of contents and looked down the list of stories, the sick gloom edging into my gut at the sight of "Slow Train to Garmisch."

"I ought to have left out 'Slow Train,'" I said. "I ought to have written something else."

"You'll do better next time. You'll do it sharper and tighter."

"Yes, I'll do it better next time."

"But you're happy with this one."

"It's just a book of stories about people, about the human heart. But that's the only thing that really lasts, isn't it?

"It's a fine book, Marty."

"It's a fine book, I know that."

"It's better than this last one of Fitzgerald's, not to speak ill of the dead, but really, if I die with a book only half finished, do us all a favor and burn the thing, will you? Old Scott still has the technique and the romance, but the dust has been off that butterfly's wings for a good long time now even if the creature will still move."

"You'll be more famous than Scott ever was, Bug," I said.

"His first two were okay, they sold okay, but what did he write after *The Beautiful and Damned*? That crazy thing about the bootlegger."

"*The Great Gatsby.*"

"Gatsby, the not so great. That book hasn't sold more than twenty thousand copies, that's what Perkins told me. It's only still in print because they can't sell the damned copies they have. And *Tender is the Night* sold even less, only twelve thousand. And he never won that thing either."

That thing being the Nobel, or perhaps the Pulitzer. It was a way Bug consoled himself. Well, he hadn't won any major award, but then, neither had Scott, not even for *Tender is the Night*, which Ernest truly admired.

"Hollywood ruins a writer," he said.

I poured him another glass of champagne and then raised my glass and clicked it, searching for words to move him away from the subject of Scott before he sank into it. It made him dark, thinking that Scott and James Joyce and Thomas Wolfe were all dead. It made him dark that the three of them were now being spoken of as literary gods in that way one only gets when no longer here to enjoy it. Scott's books weren't selling any better than they had before he died, but two issues of the *New Republic* were dedicated to his memory, and one of the writers Ernest had satirized in *The Sun Also Rises* had written that Scott was always trying to promote Ernest as the genius when it was Scott himself who was the genius—or that's the way Ernest read it. It oughtn't to have mattered; Ernest had such a huge audience for his books. But it's a funny thing about writers: If we sell well but don't win awards, then we act like the sales are all that matter, but we know in our secret hearts that it's the awards that do. If we win awards but don't sell, well then, we can see that all the awards in the world mean nothing since we're supposed to be moving hearts, and you can't possibly move a heart that never picks up your damned book.

I said, "Thank you for helping Max do such a beautiful job on my book, Bug."

He looked to the mountains as he sipped his champagne. "We'll go out tonight and get happy drunk to celebrate."

"I wonder if the thing to do isn't to stay in and have a fine time together, just us and Mr. Scrooby and no hangovers in the morning. Then maybe I could write."

"It's the book coming out, Mook. No one can write with a book coming out."

"I'm becoming a measly good wife, and there's nothing for me in that. Why don't we go to Europe, Bug?" I said.

He wasn't writing anything either, really, and his book had been out for a year by then.

He drained the last of the champagne and went to pour more, but the bottle was empty. "We ought to have another bottle," he said.

"Really, let's think about it. About Europe," I said. "It would give us the juice again. It would help us find the juice to write something grand."

"It's a damned thing, this war bit, Marty. Neil and Sheepshanks and Johnson."

Neil and Sheepshanks and Johnson were journalists who had taken it when a shell hit their car in Spain, near Teruel where Ernest had been but on Franco's side of the fight.

"Yes, I do know that. Of course, we'd—"

"There'll be more too," he said.

More journalists dying in this new war.

"But it's—"

"It's not even our war, Marty. What's the point in dying for someone else's war?"

"But Spain wasn't—"

"We'll go out and get happy drunk and celebrate, and in the morning we'll write. With both our books out now and that done, we'll write sharper and truer. That's what we'll do, Mook. That's the thing to do."

A few weeks later, we got the news that Ernest was to be given his first prize ever: the Limited Editions Club's Gold Medal, to be presented by Sinclair Lewis. We'd planned to stay in Sun Valley until early December, then drive through Indian country—Utah and Arizona and Texas—to the Gulf on our way home to Cuba. But the trip really didn't matter, and I said I could make the arrangements for us to go to New York for the award ceremony.

"You don't like New York," Ernest said.

"But this is different, Bongie. This is your swanky award. It would be lovely to go for that."

"We'll not change our plans for an award that doesn't matter."

"What do you mean it doesn't matter, Bug? It's a fine award, and Sinclair Lewis will speak all gushy over you before he puts the thing in your hands. Think of that. Sinclair Lewis, who is only the first American ever to have won the Nobel Prize in literature."

"I'll have Scribner send a stenographer, and we can read about it."

"But, Bongie, we could fly to New York for the ceremony and come back if this driving trip means that much to you."

"We'll not change our plans," he insisted. "I've already written to Max that I've promised you this trip to see Indian country, and I won't go back on my promise."

"Promised *me*?"

"He'll send a stenographer, so we won't miss a word of the ceremony, and I'll go up and fetch the thing when I'm there on some tax business I have to attend to after the first of the year."

Texas

December 1941

Ernest and I sat in a scruffy little bar just over the border into Texas, drinking daiquiris on a hot afternoon and talking about cows, when a young boy came into the bar, the dust kicking up into the bright sunlight in the doorway.

"La guerra! La guerra!" he called.

"What's he saying, Bug?" I asked, knowing in my gut what the boy was saying but unable to believe it even though we expected it. It was impossible that this poor kid who was far too young to have any idea what his words might really mean could be bringing us this news.

"Boy!" Ernest shouted. *"¡Chico!"* But the boy was running to the man behind the bar, rattling excitedly in Spanish, and the bartender was already turning the radio to the CBS Sunday news program, *The World Today*.

We listened, disbelieving. Every person in the dark, little bar listened.

"The fucking Japs have bombed Hickam Field and that naval air base at Pearl Harbor," Ernest said to me.

The attack had to have come from aircraft carriers, someone on the program was saying. The Japanese had taken a great risk in the attack.

It wasn't clear yet how much damage they had done—how many ships had been sunk or damaged, how many planes had been destroyed from the bombing of the airfields. They didn't yet know how many were wounded, how many parents would be opening telegrams in the days to come.

"This is how we get into this war?" I said, remembering the planes wingtip to wingtip on the tarmac when we'd gone through Hawaii on the way to China, and so many ships all packed into the harbor with Japanese fishing boats slithering around them. It was the military's favorite system, Ernest had said: get everything packed into one place in order to get the whole lot wiped out.

John Daly, the CBS radio host, was now reporting that at KGMB, the CBS station in Honolulu, the sound of antiaircraft was incessant as perhaps a hundred planes continued to attack.

Bug looked up at me, his face pale despite all the time in Sun Valley, his eyes red and watery. "Bumby," he said.

His son, a freshman at Dartmouth despite all Ernest's attempts to get him to take the year off, had turned eighteen on October 10.

We spent Christmas in Cuba with Bumby and Mouse and Gigi. We finished our tax returns and we wrapped presents, and Ernest took all his fear for Bumby out on Max Perkins. He wrote angry letters chastising Scribner for failing to send a stenographer to record Sinclair Lewis's damn speech for the Limited Editions Club award Ernest couldn't be bothered to collect. Even after Pearl Harbor, he charged Scribner's failure to commit the speech to paper as the most horrendous thing that ever happened in the whole dang world. I steadfastly avoided the subject, which was ungenerous, I know, but it was tiresome, hearing repeatedly how Lewis's speech was the only thing Ernest got from the book and now he never would be able to read it. Not that he cared for himself, mind you, but he'd sure have liked his children to be able to read Lewis's remarks. "If they'd sent a damned stenographer they could have made a truckload of money publishing the speech and done me some good in the bargain," he said over and over. "I wired asking them to do it, for God's sake." And my pointing out that he did have the medal itself only drew irksome insistence that the damned thing was a reminder of how thoughtless his publisher was.

It was my fault sometimes too: if I hadn't insisted on that drive through Indian country, he was quite sure he would have gone. Well, I hadn't given a hoot about the trip. *He'd* used the trip as an excuse to avoid something that would make him uncomfortable. He was oddly and lovably uneasy with public accolades. But there was no saying that. So I just listened, and when I was the target of a tirade, I ducked as best I could and resolved to make him go the next time, even if it wasn't the Pulitzer or the Nobel.

We did buckle down to write in a way we hadn't done since Ernest had finished *For Whom the Bell Tolls*. I started a simple, unambitious novel that had nothing to commend itself except that it was what I could write. Ernest began some stories, which he set aside to write an introduction to an anthology titled *Men at War*. And we entertained more visitors than ever. Howard and Slim Hawks came to talk about the *For Whom the Bell Tolls* film, and Ginny arrived in her gold jewelry and her spiked heels and her swanky Boston accent that were all even more out of place in Cuba than they had been in Madrid, and more welcome too.

The moment we opened the Finca door to Ginny, she demanded to know what I might be doing about the war.

"Really, you do mean to go cover it now that we're in it," she repeated again to both Ernest and me over drinks in our living room.

"They're refusing to accredit women," I answered before it could grow awkward with Ernest.

"Never mind that we were responsible for every good bit of work to come out of Spain," she said, touching my arm and laughing. And then, with an apologetic glance at Ernest, she said, "The three of us, I mean."

Ernest poured himself another from the drinks cart, and freshened Ginny's and mine, and started in on a reminiscence of one of the morning breakfasts Sidney Franklin used to make.

"Sure, that was great fun," Ginny said, "but the question is what are we all going to do now?"

I said, "It's complicated."

"Of course it is, I know it is, that's why I'm here," Ginny said. "Well, of course I came to see you happily married and all that. You know I love you both and wish you the best."

"Even if you did write that book about us," Ernest said, referring to Ginny's *Looking for Trouble* about all the correspondents together in Spain.

"I was more than fair to you in the book, Hem," Ginny said.

She'd stayed in Europe since Spain, for the most part, covering the war. She was a roving correspondent for the *Sunday Times* of London, moving about Europe to see the lights go out one by one. She'd been in Berlin when Germany marched into Poland. And what I'd heard about Paris was true: she'd arrived when the Germans were just seventeen miles outside the city and everyone else was fleeing toward the South of France, which was still free at the time. But now that we were in the war, the rules for which US citizens could go where had changed, and for all her gallivanting around on behalf of British newspapers, Ginny was still an American.

"I'm sure you're already working your influence with the Roosevelts to get a spot for yourself, Marty," she said. "I thought I would see if you couldn't get me a dance card too."

With a glance at Ernest, I said, "Well, it's complicated in a lot of ways."

"You got to China, though. Rumor has it you not only got there, but you got everywhere you wanted to go, that the president gave you a letter demanding everyone in the whole world had to take you wherever you wanted to go and tell you whatever you wanted to know."

Ernest said, "Yes, and the damn thing prohibited anyone from giving her the China Rot too, and we see how that went."

He told her all about my contracting that god-awful fungus, and the gloves and the ointment. He poured himself another drink, and refreshed Ginny's and mine, and he made a lewd joke about how we'd had to have sex with my hands far enough from him to save him from the stench.

Ginny mercifully skated past the joke as if he hadn't said it.

"But really, Marty," she said, "when did you talk to Mrs. Roosevelt? Or did you talk to the president himself? How long do you suppose it will be until your accreditation comes through?"

I could hear in her voice the desperation I felt. I thought of Josie Herbst, who'd gone to Spain to escape a failed marriage, but I was only just married, and Ernest was faithful to me when he might not be, and that meant something, for him to be loyal. It wasn't all on Bug either, this not going to war. There was a part of me that was reluctant to open myself up again to the possibility of snake wine and China Rot.

"Ginny," Ernest said, "are you losing your touch? It hasn't been three years since you could bat those dark lashes of yours at some poor unsuspecting minister of propaganda and end up in an intimate chat with Il Duce himself."

"Sure I can still do that, Hem, but I have to get close enough for them to see my lashes. It's fine for you; I'm sure you're already packing your bag for the next ship to Africa. But Marty and I have to get close enough for someone to see us flirt."

Ginny and I were alone the next day when she again brought up the subject.

"*Collier's* has contacted me about doing something for them, sure," I admitted.

"You have to start now if you want to get in this thing," Ginny said. "The US military has its hands in, and they're making it clear they think war is no place for a woman."

"That's the thing, though. No one will let us anywhere near the front, Ginny, and I haven't got any sideshow where I might go unnoticed as a woman, and it's too late for me to change my sex, however much I might like to have done it when I could."

Ginny didn't laugh. "But if we don't step in now," she insisted, "there will be no place for us to step into, Marty. You know the Roosevelts. You're the best one to raise it."

I thought of Ernest and me in China, how good he was even when it was unbearable, *especially* when it was unbearable. If I just kept working on him, now that we were in the war, he would want to go. But I couldn't explain that to Ginny any more than I could have explained about that stupid argument we'd had the night before she arrived, one that erupted out of nowhere but ended with him blaming me for having missed the Sinclair Lewis speech again, and me saying I was so sick of hearing about that damned speech, and him slapping me. It wasn't much of a slap, but it made me so mad that I slapped him back, except he backed up and I missed, and the whole thing was so funny that we'd ended up laughing about it together, thankful to be laughing.

"When anything happens and Ernest and I want to go very badly, then I guess maybe I can arrange it," I said. "But what sense is there in fretting about it in advance? It's going to be a nice long war, and they're eventually going to want to make it popular, and they'll sure as hell need us then." Which was what Ernest had taken to saying to me.

The Finca Vigía, San Francisco de Paula, Cuba

January 1942

I spent the rest of that winter writing dreadful poop and overseeing a drunken gardener, a crazy maid, and a cook who liked to announce the moment our guests were seated for lunch that there would be no meal today. Ernest repeatedly assured me that a writer needed a house in which to write and this was just the cost of having it. He spent the time writing slightly better poop, and badgering everyone involved in his war anthology to get it right, and worrying not one moment about the garden or the house or the meals except to feed the cats—so many now that when he brought the salmon out to feed them, they swarmed like snakes in a pit. And all the while the Japanese dominoed down the Far East, encircling Hong Kong, bombing the Philippines, taking Thailand, the Dutch East Indies, Burma. I wanted nothing more than to throw two clean pairs of panties, a few tins of meat, and a bar of soap in a pack and head off to war.

The threat of Nazi submarines in the Gulf of Mexico also grew—Operation Drumbeat, their target the bauxite coming from the British and Dutch Guianas in South America, although we didn't yet know that. No bauxite, no aluminum. No aluminum, no airplanes. No airplanes, no way to defend ourselves.

By May so many ships were at the bottom of the Caribbean that shipping along the north coast of Cuba was halted until convoys could be established. Late in June the Navy called for patriotic yachtsmen and small-boat owners like Ernest to chip in their boats and their crews to the effort to root out the submarines. Ernest began working with the first secretary of the American embassy to try to get the *Pilar* involved. At the same time, he enlisted the oddest collection of bartenders, pelota players, wharf rats, and priests to his "Crook Factory"—furtive-looking strangers forever in our garden, and sometimes moving into the house—to collect intelligence on foreigners who might be working with the Nazis in Cuba. The Crook Factory's most enthusiastic activity in the service of the war effort seemed to me to be drinking our booze, but the new US ambassador to the island included Ernest's spy reports verbatim in his own to the State Department, or so Ernest said. And I did like the impromptu dinners with the gang from the embassy.

The boys arrived on the Clipper, and we celebrated Patrick's fourteenth birthday with a jolly little party in which Ernest tried to pretend he wouldn't prefer all his sons to stop aging long enough for this war to be over. Bumby, visiting for ten days between his spring and summer terms at Dartmouth, had joined the Marine Corps Reserve, which would allow him to finish college if he could do it in two and a half years, after which he would train as an officer.

With the boys and the Crook Factory chaos and the cats all in our little six-room house, everyone coming and going at all hours and always this hokey secrecy and everyone refusing to bathe for fear of washing off their manliness, I was left with no quiet to write, and Ernest too was left far less well off than he imagined. We had frightful rows about absolutely everything. About money. About sex. About whether we were entirely too slovenly or entirely too compulsively clean. We argued about whether we were writing and why or why not, and whether we were writing what we ought to be. I thought we should go to Europe or the Far East to cover the war rather than dying of boredom on this unchanged little island while all of Rome and the rest of the world burned. But I was selfish scum, somehow, to want that. I was such selfish scum that one night, in front of poor Gigi, Ernest screamed at me, "You dry, little cunt! I'll be read long after the maggots have finished with you!"

Unable to get accredited to cover the war in Europe as I was still, unfortunately, female, I pitched an idea to *Collier's* to cover the U-boat war in the Caribbean—an assignment that exacerbated Ernest's crankiness. He still hadn't received clearance to use the *Pilar* to hunt German submarines. My tour was delayed by hurricane warnings, but I finally set off on a thirty-foot, single-sail potato boat with a barefoot crew and no life preservers or navigation equipment. I took with me not much more than a supply of canned beans and crackers, a Superware Sanitary Pail (yes, for that), an umbrella, writing supplies, a copy of Proust I would ultimately pitch overboard, and a heart that rose like those lovely negritos that roosted in the Havana trees.

The first day, I was eaten alive by a swarm of red ants that had climbed aboard for the journey, and in fighting them off, I lost my umbrella to the sea. By the end of the second, I was sunburned all to hell, at which point torrential rain soaked me while a crazy sea left me queasy and hanging on for life. But I settled in, finally, moving along the islands, sometimes swimming naked among hummingbirds flitting in the palms. I saw no German submarines even when I flew on patrol, but I did visit an internment camp in Haiti where Germans worshipped Hitler as surely as if they were Nazi generals, never mind that they'd left the motherland so many years before that they could only have learned about the master race in a correspondence course. I survived three horrific days of hurricane weather before finding my way to Suriname in the Guianas, where I talked myself in and out of restricted areas, dressed for a dinner served in a gold mine in the jungle, and visited a French penal colony where poor, dead-eyed skeletons in striped pajamas cut wood until they collapsed from exhaustion or disease.

I was doing my bit for the war with *Collier's*, and Ernest was carrying out his intelligence work and making short patrols within easy reach of Havana while he waited for Navy Intelligence to clear him for longer ones. He was editing his thousand-page war anthology meant to inspire would-be soldiers, and reviewing the movie script for *For Whom the Bell Tolls*. Absent from each other, we wrote gushy letters and missed each other miserably, except for one or two letters written when Bug was in his cups.

He took his sons with him as crew to investigate alleged German sympathizers resupplying submarines, sending Patrick and Gregory into a cave no one else could fit into, a suspected drop point—which I would have told him was lunatic if I'd been there. If the space was that small, how could it be used for a drop point, for heaven's sake? But I wasn't there, and maybe he'd figured out for himself that it wasn't dangerous and only let his sons think it was. They were his sons, not mine, and anyway, little Gigi, at nine, beat twenty-four grown men in a shooting contest, so maybe he was better equipped than anyone for the job.

Ernest's crew began target practice in the Gulf Stream, using machine guns and hand grenades and satchel charges. He monitored coastal traffic, investigated floating debris, and looked for U-boats on the surface, although of course U-boats rarely surfaced when he was out, the *Pilar* not being outfitted for night patrols.

I soldiered on, hampered by censorship rules that left me in the dark about everything, including the seventy-one ships sunk in the two months I toured Haiti, Puerto Rico, St. Barts, Antigua, and the rest. Without Ernest to convince me to be reasonable, I continued on to South America, where I set off in a hollowed-out log to explore the far reaches of the Saramacca River. I was stoned by villagers. I broke my wrist. I contracted dengue fever, my ankles so swollen that I assumed I had elephantiasis that was permanent.

"Who knew China Rot would ever look so good?" I asked Bug when I was safely home again at the Finca. The cats had taken to leaving their business wherever they happened to be, but the gardener had managed despite his drinking, the cook brought me soup that tasted divine after the travel slop, and Ernest was grateful to have me home again.

I wrote two pieces for *Collier's* about my adventure. Bug wrote heartbreaking letters to Bumby about things like how to swing his arms when he tackled—he was on the Dartmouth football team—when what he really meant to say was how loved Bumby was and how much his father couldn't bear that he would go off to war. It was a comfort to us both to climb into bed together every night and settle in to love again, and to wake in the morning and step onto Bug's scale, and write our daily weights on the wall, side by side.

I went to New York for a bit that October, where I had my hair cut and curled by Monsieur Jacques from Paris after many long phone consultations with Ernest about exactly how he would like it. I had dinner with the editor of the *New Yorker*, who was a terrible bore but an important one, and with Dorothy Parker, who was, as always, funny as hell. "I love you because your feet are so cold in my bed," Bug wrote me, "and because you're the bravest and most beautiful woman in the world." It left me both wanting to rush immediately home to him and wanting to stay away longer so he would continue to write letters like that.

I spent a few days with the Roosevelts, where I came down with such a nasty cold that they stuffed me in the Lincoln Bedroom and fed me their dishwater soup but would not bend to what I'd really come up from Cuba for, which was to persuade the president to change the rules forbidding women correspondents to cover the war. I'd have settled for him making just one little exception for me, to be honest. I wouldn't even have to abandon Ginny, as she'd batted her lashes in the direction of someone who'd found her a position working in London for the American ambassador.

I returned to Cuba in a bit of a temper, to learn Ernest had finally gotten clearance to change the *Pilar* from a fishing boat to a Q-boat. After spending all of November having her deck painted green and outfitting her, he set off with his pals for a shakedown training cruise, leaving me to evenings steeping myself in the novels of Henry James and days reading everything I could find about war. I meant to be ready when the president changed his mind.

In the quiet of having the Finca all to myself, I had the floor repaired where the roots had pushed through it, and planted orange and lime and fig trees, and breadfruit, and I tossed everything I'd written since our honeymoon in the bin and started a new story. It wasn't much, just a very small thing about a trophy mistress of a rich white planter, a mulatto girl who falls in love with a teacher. I worked on it for three solid weeks, and at the end of every day I felt exhausted and full of love for the human race, and I saw then how Bug felt on the days he was writing so well, like he was on some beautiful drunk and so happy to return to the cups every morning. There was nothing that could bother me then, not the cats and not the rowdy return of the Crook Factory and Ernest's nagging about the money I spent on the floors when he'd spent more on booze alone, never mind the cost of equipping and manning the *Pilar*.

"It's just a tiny story, perhaps forty thousand words if I'm lucky," I said one night as I was in the bedroom and Bug in the adjoining bathroom, putting paste on his brush.

"A tiny story can be a big story too," he said.

"It will be too long for a story and too short for a novel."

I pulled off the shift I was wearing and threw on my nightclothes, hurrying to cover myself. It was a hot, muggy night, good for sleeping naked, but I didn't want what came with that.

"A novel isn't made by so many words, Mookie," he said in his gentle voice that left me feeling a little guilty about not wanting to have sex. "A novel is made by so much story."

"But if it's only forty thousand?"

"*The Sun Also Rises* was only sixty-seven."

"That's almost twice as long."

"That one of Scott's about the bootlegger, I think that was barely fifty thousand," he said, pulling his shirt over his head so the words were muffled.

"*The Great Gatsby*? But it didn't sell anything, Bug."

He stood there in his shorts and sandals, with his chest tanned from the time on the boat and the shirt still in his hands. "Just keep writing, Mook, and don't think about it when you aren't writing. If you think about it, you lose the thing you're writing before you can go on with it the next day. Don't write until you're empty; leave a little bit inside you at the end of the day, and then come play tennis with me or swim, and drink and make love to me, and let the well refill while you sleep."

"Just write and enjoy the writing."

"And don't forget to get the weather in the book."

I put paste on my toothbrush, saying, "The weather is important, I know," thinking of the difference it had made in Finland, three million Finns trying to defend their homeland against one hundred and eighty million Russians with the cloud cover hiding the Russian planes until they were right on top of Helsinki. In the end the Finns had had to give the Russians what they wanted and then some in exchange for peace.

"Bug," I said, "when I was in Washington, I tried to get the president to clear the way for us to cover the war."

"But I'm *fighting* the war, Mookie. Isn't fighting the war better than just writing about it?"

"But I'm not, Bongie. I'm just arranging menus and playing tennis."

I turned to see him sitting on the bed, looking happy enough, still, his shirt beside him and his sandals still on his feet, which were dirty with the day.

"You're hardly back from your submarine and bauxite tour of the Caribbean and you want to leave me again already?" he said lightly.

"I didn't see anything there. I didn't see a damned thing."

"But we went to China for you, Mart. Is that what you want again? To go off and get the China Rot? You were miserable that whole damned trip."

"I wasn't, though, Bug. And that was almost two years ago."

"I went on the damn Indian country tour and missed the award ceremony and the Sinclair Lewis speech for you, and still it's all about what you want."

"For me? That trip wasn't for me."

"I sure as hell didn't skip out on hearing Sinclair Lewis laud me for my own sake."

"You did, though, Ernest. I don't know why, but you did." I knew I shouldn't say what I'd so often thought, that I should stick the damned toothbrush in my mouth, but I was so tired of being blamed for his skipping out on that speech, tired of his carping about how no one had cared enough to transcribe Sinclair Lewis's praise of him. "Because as happy as you are to praise yourself, you're awkward at hearing others do it?" I said. "Because the award you were being given was beneath you turning up to accept it? I sure don't know, Hem, but I said a thousand times that we should go to New York, and you're the one who insisted on sticking to the travel plans, and what the hell does it matter anyway? Before the damned trip was over, we were at war."

"Well, that's revisionist history if I ever heard it."

I slammed my toothbrush against the sink edge in frustration, the paste flying into the sink and onto the vanity and the mirror. "You're not even going to be here; you're going to be off submarine hunting. What the hell does it matter where I am if you're not here?"

"You don't think it's a bit of a distraction to have my goddamned wife getting her goddamned tush shot all to hell?"

"Is that the problem, Hem? You're worried you'll have to climb into bed every night with something with no lips to kiss, like that kid back in Spain?"

"Christ, Marty!" He pulled his shirt on again and headed for the door and town and his drinking pals, turning to say on his way out, "For God's sake, Mart, you've just started a fine new novel. There'll be plenty of war left for you after your book is done."

After the front door closed behind him, I went to the drinks cart and poured myself a big glass of booze, and I sat by the pool in the steamy darkness, wondering how a good conversation about the writing had turned so bad, and how I'd ever imagined I could tell him about trying to enlist the president to help me get accredited. Help us, I'd said, but Ernest could be accredited in five minutes with no more effort than picking up the phone.

"I wouldn't hold you to loving me if I got myself blown up, Ernest Hemingway," I said to the clean water in this swimming pool I'd retrieved from sludge. I tried to remember that, how happy I'd been to find this place, how much I'd wanted to spend my days making a home. "I'm smart enough to know you'd be no good at loving a girl you no longer found beautiful."

Which wasn't fair—I told myself that as I drained the drink and set the empty glass at the edge of the pool, and stood and pulled off my nightclothes, and dove into the water. But anger and frustration do that, and I wasn't any fairer in my anger and frustration than Ernest was.

After Christmas, I went to St. Louis to visit Matie, who was sixty now and facing the seventh anniversary of Dad's death. Ernest and I, with all the distance between us, wrote apologetic letters and resolved to love each other better. We did love each other. We did know that, and that was the hard part. The rest of it was just sorting out how to live together, the two of us each temperamental in our own way, sure, but we wrote so well together, and we were passionate about the same things, and we loved to fish together and shoot and play tennis and cover war. The rest of it couldn't possibly matter as much as it sometimes seemed.

I headed home to see him before he set off on his first official patrol in the *Pilar*—a patrol in which they were pretending to be a scientific expedition but were in fact, essentially, bait to draw German submarines up out of idle curiosity to see what this little boat was. I was caught in a snowstorm at the airport in Chicago, unable to get back to Cuba in time to see Ernest before he set off. When I did finally get home, I was relieved to find that Ernest's patrol allowed him to come and go. What he was doing scared me to death; it made me crazy with worry, the way, I could see now, the madness had come over him when I went off on my little potato boat. Of course he'd been crazy with worry all that summer, and so crazy with relief when I came home that I got the brunt of that as well. I resolved to try to keep that in mind, to forgive him for it and to forgive myself too, and to try not to let my worry make me as crazy as his made him.

The Finca Vigía, San Francisco de Paula, Cuba

April 1943

Ernest and the *Pilar* had only just returned for repairs and supplies when a U-boat hit a Norwegian freighter off the Atlantic Coast and, two days later, sank an American tanker—all while we went out drinking with the pelota players. I began again to badger the gang at *Collier's* to send me to England. The Caribbean wasn't where the war was; it was where some little drop of the war had splashed. The Germans appeared to have given up bombing the British Isles to smithereens, but still they were a good bit closer to the war than Cuba, and I knew they wouldn't send me closer.

The *Pilar* went back out on May 20 in what Ernest was now calling Operation Friendless in honor of one of the cats. I was left to write out the weekly menus and supervise the gardener, lest the great hunks of flowers in my trees and my blooming lilies be chopped to pieces in a drunken rage. But I was left, too, to the quiet of my story that was too long for a story and too short for a book, and which was going gloriously well. I didn't know it myself, but Ernest told me so, and he had told me often enough that my stuff stank when it did that I knew to believe him. I sent him the new chapters as I finished them, and he critiqued them the moment he got them and sent them right back. He wrote me letters almost every night too, delivering them and the manuscript pages to the mail boat each week when it came by Cayo Confites, where the *Pilar* was based, so that they reached me in bulk.

In June, Ernest was involved in a hunt for a U-boat off Cayo Fragoso, a sixteen-hour patrol. They gathered information for planes dropping depth charges and "mousetraps," with the end result so much flotsam and oil that there was little doubt the submarine had been destroyed. The channel went silent—no more late-night German chatter. Still, when one of Ernest's crew came to collect Patrick and Gregory, at the Finca for their summer visit, I could hardly believe it.

"Don't be foolish; they're only boys," I said in a whisper and well out of their earshot, wanting to remain the good Marty.

"Ernest's boys," he answered with a certainty that left me sure Ernest had anticipated my objection and would brook no disagreement.

"Gigi is only ten!" I insisted. "Even Patrick is only fourteen!"

I might have slept at their door to keep those boys safe, but they would have climbed out the window and swam half the Caribbean to be with their father.

In the quiet of having the Finca to myself, I finished my novel. June 27, 1943. It was a thoroughly respectable ninety thousand words after all, wanting only a title. I was enamored of "Share of Night, Share of Morning" from an Emily Dickinson poem. Ernest wrote suggesting Ecclesiastes and Proverbs, and worried how readers would take to a mulatto protagonist now that it was so thoroughly done as to be impossible to change.

With the book finished, I was lonely. The first thing I did was write Ernest a long letter, one I worried would make him angry because I tried to explain myself to him, which really was meant to be an apology for how hard I was to live with, how I complicated his life. I wrote it at night, and maybe I should have written it in clean daylight, but I wanted him to see inside me, to know how thoroughly I abhorred the woman I had become. I needed to shuck off all the safety and the earned wisdom and be a fool again, rid of the brutalizing influence of being married and owning a home and having to keep my edges polished and my voice low. I needed to be young and poor and loving him like I had in Madrid.

At least I had a visit from Matie to look forward to, and, as I hadn't seen her in six months, I was keen to be with her and love her and be loved by her. I threw myself into getting the Finca in the finest condition it ever had been so it would be the pleasantest place on earth and she would never want to leave. I had the house painted a scrofulous smoky pink, her room fixed to maximum coziness, and the pool cleaned extra specially so that it looked like the fountain of youth. I imagined us taking long walks together, reading poetry and having picnics like we did in Creve Coeur Park, but without the overhang of having to go back to the St. Louis dulls.

Ernest responded to my letter, asking me not to give up on him. He was dreaming of sleeping with silver bears, and surely that meant he ought to come home. After he sank one more submarine, he'd help me get wherever I wanted to go in the war.

The permit for the *Pilar* expired July 4, and on the ninth, Ernest received coded orders telling him his patrol was over even though he hadn't ever gotten his last sub. He limped home with Patrick and Gigi to join Matie and me, and if it was crowded with all of us in our little house, it was such a happy crowded that I wondered if I would ever want space again.

Ernest promptly ordered a new marine engine for his patriotic little boat, and he read my finished manuscript and, finding it far short of commas, took to adding them for me. He was a good new Bongie after his submarine hunting, so nostalgic for all the friends he'd taken to bits over the years that he even wrote some of them to apologize. He really was trying to be nonrighteous and nonbragging. After some long talking, he even saw the sense of me going off to be a war correspondent with *Collier's*. We settled it that, if *Collier's* could fix it, after he got his new engine and his new orders for the *Pilar*, I would go to London. I let my editor know, and for good measure I wrote Ginny too, asking her to keep me in mind if the ambassador meant to hire anyone else.

Patrick and Gregory and I, with the help of the embassy crowd, put together a party to celebrate the *Pilar*'s return and Ernest's birthday, his forty-fourth. We gathered at the Club Cazadores del Cerro to shoot the most bizarre assortment of pigeons, quail, dead guinea pigs, oysters, and one huge moro crab, which we saved for Ernest's last shot. After the shooting—and a fair amount of drinking to go with it—we returned to the Finca for a pig roast and more drinking, but not so much that we got more than happy drunk.

With no patrols to go on and no writing done in well over a year, though, Ernest quickly grew sour. With my own book done and a war to be covered that I couldn't yet get to, despite *Collier's* efforts to get me accredited now, I grew sour as well. We did our best, but our best often ended in tussles over money and housekeeping, the cats, the self-aggrandizing, and the booze.

Ernest and I went into Havana for dinner one night, with Ernest drinking beforehand in a way that even Gigi had mentioned to me. Gigi was trying to sort out this drinking thing as his father, inexplicably, had begun to allow the boys to drink with us. That night, I suggested we let our chauffeur drive us to dinner so we could have a nice drunk and get home without any new dent in the car.

"I never drink so much that I can't drive, for God's sake," Ernest said.

"We could stay home and have something here," I suggested. "It would be cheaper." He was always on me about the money I spent.

"You're such a fool about the money," he said. "You watch every penny, and then you spend a fortune polishing the floors."

"Replacing the floors, Bug. Tree roots were coming up in the middle of the living room." Never mind that while I was writing pieces for *Collier's* to earn a decent living, he'd dug a great big financial hole with his submarine hunting and his expensive new engine for the *Pilar*. But you couldn't talk sense with a man who was sure his sailing excursions, whatever the cost, saved the free world. So he drove us into town himself.

As Ernest kept drinking and drinking at the restaurant, I discreetly signaled the waiter to shut off the booze. The good man got the message, but after Ernest's glass sat empty for a minute and a half, he stood and called to the waiter, "Where the hell is the service here?"—leaving the poor fellow no choice but to bring him another.

As we were leaving the restaurant, walking out the open doors into the warm air of the street, I said quietly, "I can drive, Bongie. Would you like me to drive?"

"I'll drive," he said.

The valet hopped to fetching the Lincoln as people on the street turned to gawk. People always turned, because Bug was Ernest Hemingway and they knew that now, even here in Cuba. I was careful in public to call him Bug or Bongie or Rabby rather than Ernest or Hem, but still there was never a place where we weren't Mr. Hemingway and his wife.

"You ought to let me drive, Bongie," I whispered.

"You think I can't drive?"

"We've had a nice time, haven't we, Bug?" I said in my most soothing voice, although we hadn't. "I'm happy to drive. I don't mind driving, and I haven't had quite as much to drink as you have."

"You think I can't hold my drink?"

The people who had been looking turned away, embarrassed to overhear.

"Of course you can," I said gently. "I just think you ought to let me drive."

"I sure as hell can drive my own fucking car."

"All right," I said. "All right."

When the valet pulled the car up, Ernest just stood looking at the thing, too drunk to recognize it as his car or to remember that he had to climb in if he wanted to go anywhere. The valet held the door and looked to me rather than hurrying around to open the passenger door.

I climbed into the driver's seat, saying, "Come on, Bongie. Let's go home and cuddle in bed."

"Get out of my fucking car!" he shouted. "Get out of my fucking car, you dry, little cunt!"

People turned toward us again, but there wasn't the awe or the respect that was usually in the faces of the people who so often gaped at us. There was horror, and there was judgment.

Someone said, "*¿Necesita ayuda?*" Did we need some help?

I said quietly, "Come on, let me drive us home, Scrooby." Scrooby, with the suggestion of sex—Mr. Scrooby—that so often appeased him.

When he didn't respond, and still with all those people watching, I said, "Sweetheart."

His eyes narrowed in that way they did, that moment when what might still have somehow been saved as a happy drunk gave way to the darkness. I saw it coming, but I didn't turn away. I don't know why I didn't, except that it seemed important for me to keep looking at him; I thought if I just kept steady, he would see what a pig he would be if he carried it through, a public pig, and he never was that. He could be cruel in private now, when he was drinking, but he was never less than charming when there were people to see him, to judge.

"You're drunk, Bug," I said quietly, keeping my gaze fixed on his, sure that if I kept my pride and kept facing him, he would see how much it would humiliate me for him to hit me in public, how much it would humiliate him too, and he wouldn't do that to me, he would love me more than that, he would care about me and about us more than that. "Come on," I said gently, "let me drive us home."

He cocked his arm back.

Still I didn't look away. Maybe I could have. Maybe I should have. Maybe I should have backed down and scooted over and given him the wheel. But it seemed if I did, it would be letting go of the last scrap of me that I had. And it all happened so quickly anyway. He slapped me. A fierce whack across my cheek that stung like hell.

I turned the key and shifted into gear without taking my gaze from his. I didn't say anything. I just kept looking at him, and I took my foot from the brake, and I put it gently to the accelerator, and I drove his precious Lincoln Continental slowly but surely forward.

As the bumper and the front hood hit the tree, I tried to fix the sound of it in my mind, like the *rong cararong rong rong* of the machine guns. Not crunch, exactly, but something like that. *Runch?* The chrome of the bumper folded in toward the metal of the car body and the venting grates and the beautiful whitewall tires Ernest so admired. Not hiss, but just an almost-silent *ssss* as the radiator collapsed toward the engine block, the car not warmed up enough to produce much steam.

Yes, I thought. Runch *and* ssss.

I calmly turned the key to kill the engine. Not click, but *tik,* a short, little sound without the *c* to soften it.

I opened the driver side door—thunk—and climbed out—*chhhh chhhh*—as my practical flats slid onto the pavement.

I left the car door open, the key in the ignition.

"All right, Hemingway," I said. "Fine. It's your car, then."

I walked away, setting off toward home in the darkness, trying to ignore all the sounds that followed, the spectator sounds that were a chaos of *"Coño,"* and *"¿Viste eso?"* and *"Hijo de puta,"* and, above it all, Ernest shouting drunkenly, "You stupid bitch! You stupid bitch!"

He wouldn't remember any of it in the morning, I told myself, my anger spent now in the crashing of the car, which, of course, I shouldn't have done. I was becoming as crazy as he was with his obsession about finding submarines. Or maybe I'd always been as crazy. Maybe I was the crazy one and it was me that was driving him to it, rather than the other way around.

If we were lucky, he wouldn't remember any of it in the morning, and I wouldn't remind him. I'd say that we'd had a little accident, and wasn't he a good husband to stay and tend to the car while he sent me home. In that way, we would get past this. I'd stick it down inside me where it wouldn't hurt for too long if I didn't let it, and all he would remember would be a grand dinner and a happy drunk and a little accident that might, at least, convince him to let Juan drive us into town next time. If he did remember, well, his darkness was the kind that let go in the morning. It was only my darkness that held on to things, that began to form a tidy little pile of bitterness at the edge of my heart.

The Finca Vigía, San Francisco de Paula, Cuba

August 1943

The car was not yet repaired from our "little accident," which Ernest had, indeed, been too drunk to remember, when my editor at *Collier's* called. He didn't have anything yet, but he might be able to get me accredited to London if I came up to New York.

"I might go with you if it wasn't all propaganda," Ernest said over a good, big breakfast on the patio by the pool the morning I was to leave. He was waiting for new orders, still intent on sinking one last German sub. Rommel had been run out of North Africa in May, and now we'd taken back Sicily and were bombing the hell out of Nazi ports and factories. Even if the Germans could keep building subs enough to spare a few for our neck of the woods, they'd have a damned hard time getting them in the water, much less all the way across the Atlantic. But Ernest was obsessed with those subs that no longer existed. I'd learned to raise the topic of going to war before he started drinking. The drink brought out charges that I was picking fights just to justify wanting to leave him behind. "You've turned into a fucking prima-donna writer, abandoning me when I have important business to do, never mind that I spent half the last year tending to you and your novel." But he was good about it—even all for it, really—when he wasn't drinking. So I ignored his drunken petulance and organized this trip to New York to check the galleys for my novel, and to follow up with *Collier's*.

"You're such a rare, great writer, Bug," I said, one ear to the front of the house, where my bag sat by the door, waiting for the car that would collect me for the trip. "You're such a rare, great writer that whatever you think about becomes a great book without you having to live it first. I'm a lousy writer—"

"You're a fine writer, Mook. You've written a fine new book, and you're proud of it or will be if you allow yourself the luxury. You're too fine a writer for the hack job of journalism even if it weren't going to be censored into propaganda."

The sun was warm on us, and the flowers lovely, the morning not yet too hot.

"Sure, I'm a fine writer, then, but I can't write the way you write. My writing is like colonic irrigation, things rushing in and out. I never can make anything into a book except by going out and seeing it and recording the details, the *rong cararong rong rong*. I need to go to war if only to have something for a new book, Bug. And anyway, I know I'll write the news true, and if I don't go for *Collier's* they might send someone who won't."

He said, "Why don't they send writers over, not as propaganda correspondents or to write government pamphlets, but just to have someone write it truly afterward, even if the truth can't be told right away? Maybe I could get them to make a category like that for me, so we could be together. The British are using writers that way, and artists too. Maybe I could get a job with the Brits."

I said, "Then we could be together and happy like we were in Spain."

He said, "We were happy in Spain, weren't we?"

"We belong to each other, Bongie."

"But I can't go anywhere until after we've cleared the Caribbean of German subs."

"Someday the war will be over, and we'll have a wide life ahead of us," I said.

"Will we? I wonder if this one will end before we're too old ever to have a bit of fun again."

"If it doesn't, I'll try to be jolly and beautiful for you even when I'm old."

He said, "You'll always be beautiful, Mrs. Bongie."

The car arrived, and I stood and leaned over him and kissed him, long and slow and loving. "Be careful of the sun, Bongie. I don't want you to become Anselmo." *Viejo*, he called the character in *For Whom the Bell Tolls*: the old one.

"Ah, Mook," he said, standing too. "I'll never be Gary Cooper, even if I clean up and put on a fine suit. You knew that when you married me."

I slid my arms around him and looked straight into his sad eyes. "I'm going to try harder to be a nice Mrs. Rabby. I know I've been an awful Mrs. Rabby, but I can do better, only first I need to do this or I never will be able to."

"I haven't been a good Mr. Rabby," he said. "I haven't protected you good, and I've been scoffing, which is the worst, I know, but you do know I admire you, Mook. I admire you and respect you, and as of this date and this hour I will not be scoffing again."

"Don't miss me too much," I said, and we kissed long and slow and lovely again. "I won't be gone long."

"I know. But living alone makes me jumpy."

"It makes me jumpy too, but maybe you jumpier."

"I'll have the wigglies for company." One of his nicknames for the cats.

"Yes, but don't sleep on the floor with them, Bug. It isn't good for your back."

"I'll read them your letters. When you make it to London and to beyond London and I forget the secret code, I'll have them remind me."

"But don't forget the code, really."

"A visit to Robert Capa means you're in Africa," he said. "One to Herb Matthews means Spain."

"Italy."

"I was testing you, Mrs. Bongie."

"And you'll come if the submarine hunting is finished before I get back?"

"But it won't be. We'll be out for two or three months this time, as soon as we get the new orders. You won't be gone that long."

"But if it is."

"If it is, sure. If the submarine hunting is done before you climb back into our bed here, I'll come to London and climb in your hotel window and be wild with you."

I arrived in New York feeling fat and jowly and old-looking. I set about seeing doctors and dentists and getting vitamin injections, and having my shoes rebuilt so they would stand up to war. I had my hair cut and colored, too, just the way Ernest wanted it: short and tawny brown, like Maria in *For Whom the Bell Tolls*. And while I didn't much care for all the boring doing-about of New York society, Mousie came down from boarding school, and that was fun.

Everything was going snappily for the book too, which I'd finally titled simply with my protagonist's name, *Liana*. Or everything was going snappily except the prepublication notice that referred to me only as "the wife of Ernest Hemingway" and the photograph Max Perkins had chosen for the cover, which made me look as old as I felt. Still, those were little things that didn't matter, and all the things that mattered were lining up well: the Book-of-the-Month Club was considering it, and Paramount was talking about a film, and the Theatre Guild was interested too, although its snooty manager was so lordly and condescending about my "miscegenous love story" and so certain no audience would like it unless I made my protagonist lily white that I really did want to rub her I-know-everyone-worth-knowing-and-let-me-tell-you-about-it mouth in hot peppers.

Three weeks into September, my papers for Europe still hadn't come through. I moved from the Berkshire to smaller, cheaper rooms at the Gladstone, where I made a little nest for myself with photos of Ernest and the cats and the Finca. I knew by how very much I missed him that all the bickering didn't mean anything. It was just the detritus of my long months in the sea of my novel and his long months in the actual sea.

I started going down to Washington for the weekends, where on Saturday evenings the Roosevelts introduced me to every ambassador in town, and on Sunday nights Mrs. Roosevelt cooked scrambled eggs.

All the while, Ernest and I wrote the dearest letters. I wrote about the *Bell* movie, which I saw almost the day I arrived so I could assure him that the critics were wrong about it, that it wasn't the political mess they made it out to be. The handsome Gary Cooper and the beautiful Ingrid Bergman were so clearly the good people of the film, and the Fascists, even if they weren't called that, were as unattractive as all bad people in film are made to be, and anyone could tell the difference. The film was long, sure, but it was long because it was important, and if they would only let people smoke in the theater so they wouldn't have to go for three hours without a cigarette, then no one would think it too long at all. Only the color was bad, the color did bring out the fake a little, the makeup and the sets, which would have looked more real in black and white. But audiences were wild for color, and at least Ingrid Bergman as Maria did look astonishing with her short tawny hair and blue blue eyes.

Ernest wrote me that he was glad about the film and that I was a better judge than any lousy critic. He shared all the good stuff of

Bumby's visit to the Finca, now as a lieutenant in the military police and off to his first duty station, at Fort Custer in Michigan, thank heavens. After Bumby left, Ernest wrote that he missed Bumby and me both so dreadfully that he might die of sadness. I wrote that I couldn't be a part of that kind of painful death, that I was sad with loneliness too and he mattered more to me than anything in the world, and if he truly couldn't bear it, I'd call it off with *Collier's* and come home to him. But he was still expecting permission to operate the *Pilar* in the Caribbean again, using Guantanamo as a base this time.

At the end of October, I boarded a Pan Am Clipper for London via Bermuda and Portugal and Ireland, with a promise of a war correspondent credential when I arrived. *Collier's* had commissioned me to write one long piece and as many one-thousand-word ones as I cared to, on the lives of specific people. It was the easiest writing for me, these personal stories, and I was glad to be at the edge of war, poised to move right into it if only I could find a way to get beyond England, which was as far as I was accredited to go. The journey took twelve days, but I was so smashingly happy to be going off to war that I went dancing with anyone who would dance on the stopovers, and wrote Bug all about it, and wished he'd come with me.

London, England

November 1943

My old friend Allen Grover, whom I'd excoriated over the *Time* magazine piece on *A Stricken Field*, made it up to me by pulling every string in his entire closet of sweaters to get me two weeks at the Dorchester in Park Lane. London hotel rooms were nearly as rare as pleated women's skirts (which were banned on account of the waste of fabric), with so many journalists back from North Africa or on leave from the Italian campaign, or biding their time in London awaiting the next phase of the war, which surely would be France.

Ginny took me to breakfast the morning after I arrived—not much of a breakfast due to the rationing, but I fell upon it and upon her, wanting to know everything she knew. It made me ashamed of myself. It made me want to trade my practical shoes for her spiked heels and gold jewelry and Boston vocabulary. It made me want to have dyed my hair dark instead of tawny, and never left the war.

Ginny went with me to arrange for a uniform—with a patch on the left jacket pocket, *C* for correspondent—and to pick up my accreditation papers. That was something, to get my pass, with my photograph and my fingerprints and in the blank for grade, "Accredited War Correspondent."

"It says here I'm a captain in the US Army, how about that?" I announced with glee. We were on our way back to the Dorchester, Ginny's spike heels clicking along through the busted pavement, her shorter legs matching me stride for stride in the brisk autumn air.

"Which will gain you exactly one benefit," she said. "It will save you from being shot by Germans who will otherwise imagine you a spy."

I grinned and I said, "I do like the way you think, Miss Cowles: we sure can't be captured by Germans on this side of the Channel."

"Well, you're an optimist," Ginny answered. "Clearly you're the new girl. Give it a month or two, and if you're still so sure of that, I'll see about having you committed as a lunatic."

"You think I'm crazy just because I figure we'll either convince them to let us tag along on the invasion of France or we'll figure out how to do it without their say-so?"

"I think you're crazy to be so certain that we won't be captured by Germans here in England, Mart," she said, and she laughed her proper little Boston laugh.

We were almost back to the hotel, when I said, "Martha G. Hemingway."

"Pardon?" Ginny said.

"Martha G. Hemingway, that's who it says I am. The real me reduced to a single letter and the most important bit of me now is that I'm someone's wife."

She put her arm in mine, and we walked on together for a quiet moment, past people hurrying up or down from the subway or selling newspapers or conducting busses—so many of them women, with all the young men now in uniform.

"Well," Ginny said, "I'm thirty-three and unmarried. If you want to swap names and positions, let's talk. But I should warn you Virginia isn't my real name any more than Hemingway is yours."

She pulled her own credential from her pocket and handed it to me. It read "Harriet V. S. Cowles."

"Harriet!" I said. "'Harry,' that's what I'll call you from now on!"

"Harry Virgin," she said, and we laughed and laughed.

God, it felt good to be at war, or close to it.

London in war was a different place than I'd so despised six years earlier, when it had been only on the verge of war and trying to imagine it wasn't. All of Paternoster Row, the center of London publishing, was reduced to jagged edges of partial stone walls, as were a dozen of the most beautiful churches. The rationing was wearing everybody thin too, and the only spots of color on the otherwise drably garbed populace were the burgundy linings of the nurse's cloaks and the dark-cherry and sky-blue trimmings of the parachute regiment. It all added up to the most beautiful London I'd ever seen.

Ginny and I went out together every day. I called her Harry, and she called me Mutt, and it was something to have a close pal like that, someone who wasn't your husband to talk to about anything that was on your mind. I talked about Ernest, not the whole difficult meal, but a nibble or two at the edges, like with wanting still to be Gellhorn. And I began to imagine that when I went back to Cuba I might try to take Ginny with me, that with her as company, like in Spain, Ernest and I might love each other more easily.

The Dorchester, where the *New York Times* had set up shop, was the place to be—that or the Savoy, where the *Herald Tribune* had its offices. Ginny and I gathered most nights at one or the other with the journalists in town, to eat what little there was and drink whatever booze we could find. Ginny took to introducing me to everyone I didn't yet know: a Hungarian novelist whose *Darkness at Noon* had made him a famous son of a bitch rather than just a garden-variety one; the British writers Evelyn Waugh and Cyril Connolly, who seemed somehow not all-wool; and a fellow headed to Algiers, where he was poised to be the French ambassador as soon as there was a free France to ambass. The ambassador-to-be stopped by Ginny's room with his wife one evening when Ginny was already in curlers and cold cream, but she invited them right in, and we became instant lifelong friends.

I met *Life* correspondent Bill Walton and the novelist Irwin Shaw, whom I lumped together on account of the two of them forever skulking around the same gal. The gal was Mary Welsh, an American who wrote occasionally for *Life* and *Time* and was forever showing up braless and in thin sweaters to advertise how chilly it was with all the coal going to the war effort, and who was rumored to be sleeping with Walton or Shaw, or perhaps both. Her husband, the perfectly splendid Australian journalist Noel Monks, had been in Spain with us, the first correspondent to reach Guernica after the Fascists bombed it to hell. I thought if this Mary Welsh was going to carry on behind her lovely husband's back, she might at least be discreet.

Someone in the assembled gang was forever asking about Ernest and wondering when he would join us. I didn't mind it from friends, but I wondered if the new people who liked me did so on their own judgment or only because Ernest had chosen me. I supposed they saw me as I might have seen myself had I been meeting me for the first time—as the very ordinary wife of an extraordinary man.

The reporting was different than in Spain, it was. That was Ernest's argument for staying in Cuba: gloom and doom was frowned upon, and of course being accredited meant submitting all your copy to the censors, who, after years of war, were practiced at the art of saying no even to the most reasonable reports. But my copy for *Collier's* wasn't the war propaganda Ernest had disparaged (how far and fast our troops were going and the way we were slaughtering the Germans and the Italians, as if there was not a bit of them slaughtering us back). The censors didn't bother me much.

I went to Lincolnshire for a piece on the absurdly young boys of the British Bomber Command. Less than a quarter of them could expect to survive the war, and they knew it already; it was thick in their private jokes and their slang and the way they waited so intently for the drone of returning aircraft even when it wasn't their turn to go. As I watched them, I thought of Bug's piece back in Spain about the boy Raven from Pittsburg who'd lost his eyes and his lips. I thought to apply to go on a bombing run myself, but I wasn't that brave.

When I got back to London, even before I'd finished the piece on the bomber crews, I learned that a shy, young Scot I'd befriended had not returned. I was haunted by thoughts of him as I wrote, and I cried and cried when I was done writing, and I wrote Bug a letter saying what a deep impression those boys had made on me and how impossible it would be to understand if I hadn't met them myself.

I wrote a story that three Polish men in London told me, about secret schools that had operated in Warsaw, educators who taught one hundred thousand Jewish children in violation of the law, with no doubt that they would be shot if caught. I wrote about fourteen-year-old boys who were working in factories so that older men could fight, and Dutch refugees who now met in a London club, and doctors in a burn unit in Sussex determinedly trying to save soldiers and bombing victims from the fate of Raven from Pittsburg who'd fought in Spain. They were all terrifically compelling stories, and I was glad to write them, but, except for the bomber command, it wasn't really war reporting. And even the bomber command piece was only like accosting a passerby on the street for five minutes, with no possibility of settling in for long enough to understand them deeply and truly. The censors probably would have stricken out the more deeply and truly anyway, but at least I would have tried.

I wrote Bug long, affectionate letters saying that everyone asked about him, and of course I agreed that he was of best use where he was now, but, really, if that changed he would come, wouldn't he? He would understand the war better than anyone, and write it better, and without him writing it, no one would see it as clearly as it was. I even suggested he pitch a series of stories to *Collier's*—never mind that that would undermine my position with the magazine. I would have said anything that might persuade him he ought to take a share in this.

In January, *Liana* was published. The movie and theater deals hadn't come through, but the reviewers were absolute darlings. The *Washington Post* said I'd come of age artistically. The *New York Herald Tribune* talked about the novel's "splendid sultry grace." And no one but no one said anything about miscegenation, or even found fault with my mulatto protagonist.

In the middle of the month, Ernest wrote me that after his current patrol on the *Pilar* was over, he would batten down the boat and the house and come to England. I wrote him that I was leaving London "to visit Herb Matthews"; I'd found a pilot to smuggle me to Algiers, where I would stay with the ambassador-in-waiting Ginny had introduced me to, and see Bumby, who would be on leave there for the weekend. From the north of Africa, I could cross to Italy, where the Allies had gone ashore in September and had ever since been meeting fierce resistance. But I could come back to London or he could come "visiting with me," and if he would let me know when he was coming, I would arrange it all. I couldn't have been happier.

Italy

February 1944

On the roller-coaster roads of Italy, it seemed forever to be hailing on us, and I was dodging American military press officers, who would have taken me into custody and sent me home had they realized I was there, to boot. A French transportation officer took me under his wing, driving me through rubble pile after rubble pile of what had once been charming little Italian villages, with mines occasionally detonating around us, and burned-out trucks and dead animals and blood-soaked bandages everywhere. We joined a regiment of Sardinian soldiers transporting supplies to the Allied troops at the front and bringing back the dead, which they tied on the backs of their mules. We visited a tent hospital, and spent a night in a cellar with an American major, a French doctor, a dinner of military rations, and music on the radio from Berlin. We dodged shells from German batteries, and watched Allied planes bomb Monte Cassino, and I went in search of Ginny Cowles, who had abandoned her job in London and was dodging the military police as much as I was or more, having found her way to the American sector in Italy. I wrote like hell too, and it was some of the best writing I had ever done, stories about these brave boys who deserved to have their courage recorded in the headlines, who deserved to be known and applauded, supported, remembered.

I might have stayed there forever if not for Bug, but despite his January letter saying he would be coming to join me, the letters that followed were increasingly morose. The day after he finished his tour, he wrote that it was done and said again that he would join me in Europe, but this time he claimed himself an old horse forced over the jumps. He made out that it was my fault that he'd ended his patrols and that I'd deprived him of a novel about it in the bargain because now the journalism would erase what would be a very fine story from his head.

He demanded by cable whether I meant to be a journalist or a wife in his bed, and he began to charge me with abandoning him these five long months, never mind that the entire time I'd been gone, he'd been out on the *Pilar,* or preparing to be, waiting to be—more than happy to abandon me if I'd stayed in Cuba. The specific choice of the word "abandon" from a man who could choose his words was not lost on me either. His divorces had both been granted on grounds of abandonment, although it was Ernest who had done the abandoning of Hadley and Pauline. I couldn't believe he could mean it. That was just the darkness talking, the darkness or the booze or both. He'd said he was coming, and when he did it would be like Spain again: good and accomplishing and loving.

March began without any word that Ernest had gone to New York yet, and it would take him two weeks in New York to get travel papers.

He closed his next letter "So long, Bong," with a finality that was despairing. I read it standing with my back against a good tall boulder, with the *rong cararong rong rong* of machine guns not far ahead. I slid down to sit, and read it all the way through again, looking for other words or other meanings, a suggestion that he was just trying to provoke me. He was reneging on his promise to come and trying to make it my fault.

I folded the letter into the tiniest square, and I tucked it into the back pocket of my trousers, trying not to think this might be the last letter I would ever get from him, working out how long it would take me to get back to Cuba, and knowing it was too long. Was there already another woman in my bed? There wouldn't be, of course there wouldn't be; there was no one in Cuba to entice him. But there had been that woman he'd had the affair with before he met me, the one who used to drive too fast in those stupid games of chicken that The Swede had told me about. She was from Cuba, the wife of a wealthy American living in Cuba, who maybe lived there still or maybe didn't but maybe some other beautiful, vulnerable woman did.

I would go back to Cuba now, I decided.

But there was no point in going back to Cuba to straighten us out. I loved him and he loved me, but I couldn't live his life there, or I couldn't live only his life there without some of my own life living too, and he wouldn't live mine or even let me live it. Wouldn't or couldn't, the result was the same.

A few days later, *Collier's* devoted a column to me in which Bug described me as a journalist who got to a place, got the story and wrote it, and came home. The coming home part was the best, he wrote. And something about the words made me think that it wasn't over at all, that if I went back for him, I might blast him from Cuba and bring him back with me, to the only kind of life where we had ever been truly happy together for more than a few weeks at a time.

The Finca Vigía, San Francisco de Paula, Cuba

March 1944

Ernest was impossibly changed when I got home to Cuba. After always weighing himself and marking his weight on the wall every morning, trying to stay very close to two hundred pounds, he was now a good 220, and with a beard peppered gray. I told him he looked marvelous, but the truth was the beard and the weight made him begin to look like an old man. My beautiful Finca was a mess too, full of drinking buddies who never bathed.

He was perfectly lovely and admiring when we were in public, telling everyone I was his Marty, and I'd just come back from covering the war, and wasn't I as beautiful as I was smart? But he would wake me in the middle of the night to rage at me like some beast caged to craziness, faulting me for everything in the world he could find that was wrong when what he was really angry about but wouldn't say was that he hadn't uncovered three dozen German submarines. He'd spent so much money on the *Pilar* that he'd run through even the movie money from *Bell*, and had to ask Max Perkins to advance him $2,000—money he would be owed as soon as the sales of cheap editions of some of his books were published.

"The goddamned government thinks I ought to pay for the whole goddamned war with my taxes alone," he ranted.

"Honestly, Bug," I said, "a person can't owe more taxes than the money he makes."

"What the hell would you know about it? Five hundred dollars every month to that bitch Pauline whose daddy owns one half of America and her uncle the other half. The boys' schooling. This place you can't even be bothered to come home to."

"The Finca is bought and paid for," I reminded him.

"Not the chauffeur and the cook and the maid and the gardener."

"For which I pay half, and I didn't ask for the chauffeur or the cook."

"I'm not the one buying every piece of furniture on the island, paying to have the place painted that ridiculous pink."

And of course all that submarine hunting cost nothing, nor your good, solid year of hangovers, I thought. But I didn't want a knock-down-drag-out. I was exhausted from the trip—exhausted the way a person is after she's been running on war adrenaline for months and no longer is. And it wasn't exactly fair anyway. Ernest actually had received a very lovely letter from the ambassador commending him for his highly confidential—and risky—intelligence activities. He was beautifully unaggrandizing about it too, asking our editor at *Collier's*, whom he did tell about it, not to tell anyone else. He ought to have been happy, with that honor and with his book having sold three-quarters of a million copies, more than any other novel except *Gone with the Wind*. But none of that improved his mood for more than a minute, and then he was back to the foul, berating, blaming, waking-me-up-to-rant brute I no longer recognized.

It didn't help that Bumby, his own son, said that I was now the writer in the family. Bumby was only being kind to me, but it didn't help at all.

Word started getting back to me about tawdry stories Ernest told when he was out drinking, stories about me that his bar buddies liked to repeat all over Havana. He wrote Matie the most humiliating letter too, telling her he thought I was paranoid but then had decided after all that I was just plain selfish and spoiled.

"My mother?" I said.

"Is it too much to want a wife in my bed at night and not somewhere else having higher adventures than mine at so many thousand fucking bucks a pop?"

It was outrageous, him calling me out for the money I made, which was much of what we had to support us, but I bit those words back, saying instead, "What could you possibly have expected Matie to do except call me up concerned that you might already have buried me under the pool pump, Bug?"

"I thought she might talk some sense into you! I thought she might tell you to give up the bitchy, selfish-scum business and be a wife!"

Selfish scum. He knew exactly how devastating those words would be, and he said them anyway.

"No matter," he said. "I'm leaving for Europe."

"Bug," I said, thinking just for that minute that maybe there was still something to put back together, some little piece of our love that could survive this.

"I've signed up to do a piece for *Collier's* on the RAF pilots."

"Collier's?" I repeated. "But, Bug." I swallowed down the fear and rage and despair. "*Collier's* can only have one war correspondent."

"The military doesn't want women in Europe."

"They don't, sure, but that didn't stop me from getting to Italy."

"You suggested it, Mart. You suggested I pitch the series to *Collier's*, and I did."

"Well, yes, but—"

But that was when I was still in Europe and wouldn't have to find a way to get back there; I could have stayed and figured the work part of it out somehow, like I had in Spain, in Czechoslovakia, in China. That was before, when I thought there was something left to save, when I would have given up even my own position as a journalist for him to join me.

Ernest said, "You were the one who hooked me up with that Roald Dahl."

"The air attaché at the British embassy."

"Right. I set it up through him, like you suggested. Like I said, the piece about the RAF pilots, like *you* suggested, Mart."

"About the night raids in Germany."

"The piece you damned well beat me into doing! I wasn't the one who wanted to go; I wanted us to stay here. But, no, you have to do it your way. So I'm fucking doing it your way, right? They've got me on a plane to London."

"But you could write that piece for anyone. You could write it for NANA. You could have any job you want."

"You told me to pitch *Collier's*. It was your fucking idea. Your. Fucking. Idea. Are you reneging on it now, for Christ's sake?"

"But I've written twenty-six pieces for *Collier's*. I've hardly written for anyone else in seven years. And you could write for anyone." Repeating it and repeating it, unable to demand he back out of the assignment he'd already taken, and at my suggestion too—I couldn't deny that. But hoping to God he would volunteer to back out of it.

"I leave for New York April 23," he said. "I've arranged the tickets."

"April 23?" I repeated.

"You won't be satisfied until I've been killed at war, so, fine, I'm off to do it for you. A man with three kids can't leave them with nothing just because his wife is crazy as hell. But you won't let it go until I've done it, so I've got us tickets to fly to New York and on to London to get myself killed."

Got *us* tickets. So he did mean for us to go back together, then. He did mean to sort this out somehow, and if he did, well then, that was okay. It was what I'd been asking for, the two of us going off to war, where we could be happy together again.

The problem, of course, was how I would get from New York to London. I could still write for *Collier's* from London, if not as their war correspondent, if I could get back to Europe. But Ernest hadn't actually sorted out how I would get beyond New York. He'd managed to find himself a seat on a seaplane to Shannon and then on to London, but it had been arranged by the British military, and, he assured me, no women were allowed on board.

The first thing we did after we checked in to the hotel in New York was put my name on the American Export plane passenger list for another flight. Hemingway, not Gellhorn, on the idea that it might matter. But there weren't many other flights, and I kept being shoved further and further down the list in favor of someone with more reason to be on it than being the wife of Ernest Hemingway. I couldn't get another position as a war correspondent myself on such short notice because I was a woman and one thing had become very clear: no women were going to be allowed to cover the invasion of France, whenever it did happen. The rumor was that even Helen Kirkpatrick, whom the US newspapers had elected as their single representative on the committee planning the invasion press coverage, would not be allowed to go.

I went down to Washington for a weekend at the White House on the excuse of getting the president to put in a word for me. Ernest was very busy, and I said of course he ought to stay in New York. The truth was I didn't really imagine I could ask the president to bother about my flights, I wasn't that ridiculous, but I needed a break from the stress of trying to keep a happy face. Bug did still love me, I knew that, and I did still love him, and maybe we weren't wrong for each other. Maybe it was just the time, the stress on his part of having a wife in London where folks were dying every day from the bombs, and all the panic on my part that I would miss the invasion of France.

I returned to New York before the end of April, writing Mrs. Roosevelt how refreshed the weekend had left me. If I missed the invasion, I assured her, well then, Ernest could tell me all about it—as if it weren't only the want of getting to Europe to experience the invasion firsthand that kept me dragging my broken soul out of bed. There was nothing for it, for a wife to be wanting the job her husband had. I'd seen that reproach even in the First Lady's eyes, and if she thought so, then everyone would, especially as what Bug was telling anyone who'd listen was something close to true—that I was such a good wifey-wife to have seen that he ought to go to London in my place.

I made a backup plan, thinking maybe this could be like Spain, with Ernest going ahead but me getting there too, and him squaring everything away for me in the meantime. With Allen Grover's help, I arranged transport on a Norwegian freighter carrying dynamite, a twenty-day passage that left New York before Ernest's seaplane but would get me to London two weeks after him. Bug saw me off—me and forty-five Norwegian crewmen, only two of whom could cobble together a short sentence in English, and me with just three Norwegian expressions I'd jotted down in my notebook before we left: *vennligst* for "please"; *takk skal du ha*, which seemed to me a helluva lot of trouble for "thank you," but I did want to be polite; and *kan jeg få en drink?* Bug had suggested that last one, which is exactly what it sounds like, and mercifully easy to remember.

"Travel safely, Mrs. Bongie-Pig-Welcher-Heminghorn," Ernest said.

Welcher, slipped occasionally into my nicknames lately, even though I wasn't welching at all: he had my spot at *Collier's*. But we did that, we called each other names we didn't really mean: Mr. Hideously-Fat-Pig. Mrs. Warp Fathouse. Mrs. Representative of Righteousness and Peace. And Ernest was good at war. He'd been good in Spain. He'd been so much better than I in China. And he was going to Europe because I wanted him to.

"Travel safely, Mr. Bongie-Pig-Submarine-Snooper-Gellingway," I said, and we kissed one last time. "I'll see you at Big Ben."

On a Dynamite Transport Crossing the Atlantic

May 1944

We traveled in a convoy, for protection from German subs, in a fog so thick that the old boat blew its foghorn night and day, proclaiming to all wandering in the fog around us, "Hell, don't run into us! Don't you know how easily we go boom?" As you can imagine, since the ship was a dynamite transport, no smoking was allowed on deck or anywhere else. The sweet captain made a small exception for me, allowing me to smoke in my cabin as long as I did so over a big bowl of water. I kept so close to that odd ashtray that there was no relaxation in it, but still I smoked my two packs a day.

As you might not have imagined, there were no lifeboats on the ship, and only sludge for food, and shockingly little booze.

The first week, the fog never lifted except occasionally just enough to show how wobbly the convoy was getting with no one able to see anyone else. The days all blended into the nights and into the days again. It was freezing as hell, but still I made myself walk around the deck for a few hours between my long sleeps, trying to amuse myself by making up stories, and taking skimpy notes in a journal. I read too—a first novel written by a boy I knew in St. Louis, and *Lady Chatterley's Lover*—and I wrote letters. I spent a little time every day with the captain, cobbling together little bits of conversation and glad of the company. It wasn't as lonely as it sounds. It was sleepful and healthful and thoughtful and writingful and readingful, and nothing-to-do-ful, which I needed more than I had realized.

At the end of that first week (which might have been six days or eight days or ten, it didn't much matter), the fog lifted to reveal the most dramatic icebergs, not just tidy little peaks rising from gray sea but monstrous bird wings and soaring arches and giant whale tails, and one block of ice that looked quite a bit like Ernest's good friend Mr. Scrooby in repose. I watched the boats of the convoy lining themselves back up into a nice tidy order in the sunlight, and I wondered if there was enough sunlight in the world to line Bug and me back up like that. I felt so ashamed and guilty, because I had thought and thought and thought about it all that time I was walking and watching the sea, and I never could see that there was. He was a rare bird, wise and wonderful, and a glorious writer, but he was bad for me.

He was bad for me, or just wrong for me, and maybe it had never worked, or maybe it had worked in the beginning, and I was the one who'd changed. I didn't want to break his heart, and I didn't want to break my own heart either, but I couldn't think of him anymore without the dread and the darkness. I needed to gather up what was left of myself and glue it back together with whatever sticking paste I could find, filling especially the cold, hollow dead spots, and I needed to try not to let it all get wet again until I was good and solid, and maybe not even then.

Liverpool, England

May 1944

I rose at four in the morning the day we were to reach England, even though I'd been up late the night before writing a story. My mind, after the icebergs, overflowed with stories, all that emotion and love and loss pouring out of me through the only exit I allowed it, for what good was crying too much over something that was done? It was the way stories came to me, not during a thing but after, as I was letting go. I stood in darkness that morning and watched the land emerge from the night, and I felt gloriously free, suddenly, and nearly happy, and resolved. There was nothing left to do but the landing at Liverpool and the train to London.

Ernest had been in London for two weeks, time enough to check into the Dorchester Hotel, in the very room I'd vacated for all I knew. Already he'd managed to land himself in St. George's Hospital—not to report on the war wounded but as a patient himself. I learned of it from journalists at the docks in Liverpool. Apparently the first news had reported him dead, news I was grateful not to have heard.

By the time I arrived in London, the story of Ernest's little escapade was everywhere: he'd gone to a party at Robert Capa's place in Belgrave Square and then caught a lift back with another partygoer, who, being as drunk as Ernest or even more so and driving at three in the morning and in the blackout, had promptly crashed them into an emergency water tank at Lowndes Square.

I found my husband sitting in bed in his hospital room, turban-headed in gauze and surrounded by champagne and whiskey and by pals keeping him company in the drink: Robert Capa, whom I still adored despite his hosting the party that left Ernest in this state, and Irwin Shaw and Bill Walton and that American wife of Noel Monks's who wore the sweaters with nothing underneath. I watched from the hallway, wondering how none of them—not his drinking buddies and not even the nurses hurrying to and fro out in the hallway with me—had the sense to suggest that a fool with fifty-seven stitches in his head and a concussion and two bum knees in the bargain might better lay off the booze for a day or two. But no one could tell Ernest Hemingway how to live if he didn't want to hear it, or, mostly, even if he did.

"So I'm sitting on the plane and we're waiting for some last passenger to show," he was telling the gathered apostles, "and this actress gal—I'll remember her name in a minute, I would have it, but this damned bandage is sucking the juice from my brain, or maybe it drained out with the blood. God almighty, who knew a head could bleed so damned much from a little bump on the windshield?" He laughed, and everyone laughed with him. "So this actress gal, who apparently thinks a schedule is nothing and the whole world is built to wait for her—"

"Don't I know some women like that?" someone interrupted, and everyone laughed again, even the sly little Mary Welsh.

"Is there any other kind of woman?" Ernest said, and again everyone laughed. "Except you, of course, small friend," he said to Mary Welsh.

Shaw and Walton looked from Ernest to Mary Welsh, and I did too. "Small Friend" or just "small friend"? But Ernest was forever calling his friends by nicknames.

"So this pretty lady comes up the boarding stairs, finally, with a little box she's carrying so carefully you'd think it was filled with Baccarat champagne glasses filled to the brim with Dom. Well, it turns out—whatever her name—it turns out she's taking hard-boiled eggs to her favorite ration-deprived Brits, and they're frozen so they'll last the two days it takes to fly across the Atlantic, right? Eggs on a goddamned flight across the Atlantic, can't you see it? The first rough air we hit . . ." And he started laughing, and everyone laughed with him, and I stood watching it all, remembering that turbulent flight in China.

"You ought to have offered to hold them for her, Bongie," I said. "You who can catch booze on the bounce off an airplane ceiling right back into your highball glass without losing a drop." God, what a funny moment that had been.

He looked up at me, his expression that of a boy caught in a misdeed, something more than the drinking, which he wasn't embarrassed about even with all those stitches. Everyone else looked too, and Robert Capa grinned a welcome.

I said, "I leave you alone for two weeks, Ernest, and you turn into a Turk?" and I laughed, trying to make light of it all.

It struck me then, the guilt in his eyes. I hadn't been able to fly with him; I'd been left to three weeks in the fog on a dynamite ship because his plane would take no women. And yet here was this funny story about this egg-carrying actress on the plane.

He quickly gathered himself and said, "I knew you'd get here, Daughter—"

"I've just come off three weeks on a dynamite ship that threatened to blow up all the way across the Atlantic," I interrupted. "You might think twice about claiming to have arranged that for me when you flew here on a lovely airplane." Only barely able to keep from sticking his nose in the fact of that damned actress.

"I was going to say," he said to everyone else in the room, then back to me, "that I knew you'd get here, Daughter, because this time *you'd* so nicely arranged that *I* would."

Being kind in public.

I went to Ernest and kissed him on the forehead below his bandage, relieved not to be humiliated in front of all these people and doing the wifely thing so as to avoid humiliating him.

"You see what a thing a marriage is, friends," he said to everyone else. "My wife can laugh at me, but I'm not allowed to laugh back."

Everyone laughed, but not so comfortably now.

You might have thought the room would have cleared for a wife who hadn't seen her husband to have a few minutes alone with him, and Capa did stand to go, but Mary Welsh took a bottle of booze and refilled Ernest's glass, and Shaw and Walton stayed with her, and Ernest didn't ask anyone to leave.

It was just as well. I couldn't possibly tell Ernest while he was in the hospital that he no longer had to worry about a wife who laughed at him. I wondered if he saw the truth in my eyes, and I supposed he might. I supposed that was why he kept his little entourage around him—because he saw what might come if we were left alone to get it all over with. And I thought of that poem Matie and I used to read by the waterfall at the lake at Creve Coeur, Browning's "Life in a Love":

> Escape me?
> Never—
> Beloved! While I am I, and you are you,
> So long as the world contains us both,
> Me the loving and you the loth,
> While the one eludes, must the other pursue.

I made the excuse of exhaustion on account of the travel, and I returned to the hotel room I'd taken, my own room under Gellhorn rather than Hemingway. I could be the good wife for a day or two more while Ernest was in the hospital, but I would do it in my own space and in my own name.

London, England

June 1944

After two days of Ernest humiliating me in front of his drinking buddies whenever I visited him at the hospital, reducing me to tears and embarrassing our friends, he arrived back at the hotel room, apparently surprised to find no evidence of me there.

"Mookie," he said when he called my room.

"Ernest," I answered.

"My head hurts, Mook."

"You can't keep crashing it into things and expect it to remain your friend."

"But I haven't ever crashed my head before, except that once in Paris when I pulled the skylight down on myself. Remember that?"

That had been with Hadley, or maybe Pauline.

"There's that scar under your beard too," I said.

He laughed and said, "You can't blame me for that one. That was that damned horse in Wyoming."

It had bolted through a thicket with him in the saddle. That too had been before me.

"Oh, Mook," he said. "I'm a faithless dolt, I am. But I have a very scrofulously comfy bed in our very comfy room, and where are you?"

"Bug," I said. I looked out the window, to the spring green of Hyde Park. No one was strolling, only people hurrying one way or the other, or that was the way it seemed. I just didn't know where to begin, and I knew this wasn't a conversation I should start over the phone, with Ernest alone in a cold hotel room and just home from the hospital too.

"Sure," he said, "sure you need a quiet place to write. Okay. But you'll forgive me for being such a bad Papa Bongie, won't you? I know I've muffed it miserably."

"Damn, Bug," I said, wanting to ask about the actress on the plane when he'd told me it would take no women. Wanting to hear the actress was just a fiction. But it wasn't the kind of detail you could make up: an actress carrying frozen hard-boiled eggs on an airplane across the Atlantic. And it didn't matter, really.

"I've made us a reservation at the Grill Room," he said. "I'll come collect you."

I said, "I hear they have terrific boiled eggs."

"Boiled eggs?" he said. "Well, I don't know about that. But if there are boiled eggs to be had in London, I suppose they do."

"Bug," I started, "Bug, I . . ."

"I'll come collect you," he repeated.

"I need to finish what I've got in the typewriter," I said. "How about eight o'clock?" He could pick me up, and that would give us some time alone together, and I needed the time alone with him to lay it all out, to make him see that we weren't good for each other, that he was good, and I was good, but we were lousy as hell together.

"All right, sure. Eight," he said. "I'll collect you for dinner at eight, then, Mook."

I finished my writing—notes about my funny conversations with the dynamite-ship captain and smoking over that bowl of water, and how London had changed even in the few months I'd been away, or maybe it only seemed to me it had, having now the perspective of Italy. After I was done, I cleaned up, and then I waited.

When Ernest didn't show up and didn't show up, I began to wonder if I'd misunderstood. But, no, he'd been very specific about "collecting me" for dinner.

I called his room, finally. When there was no answer after I let it ring and ring, I imagined him sitting in the restaurant downstairs, drinking already, I supposed, wondering if I'd stood him up. I must have misunderstood.

I went on down to the hotel's restaurant, telling myself we could talk afterward if I could keep him from drinking too much. He was there, at the table he'd reserved for us, his broad, hunching back to the door. The bandages were gone, but the long shaved patch in his bullheaded noggin matched the white of his sideburns and beard, which were just visible, and the stitches looked dark and angry. He was laughing—the harsher laughter that signaled he was heading beyond happy drunk, if not already there. Bent toward him across the table, attentively laughing, was a small, curly-haired brunette with sharp eyes the blue of her thin sweater that shared every detail of Mary Welsh's breasts.

I slipped away quietly, and I found Ginny, and we curled up in her room where Ernest wouldn't find me if he came looking, and I wouldn't have to know if he never did.

London, England

June 1944

For three long days, Ernest and I communicated only through notes passed through his brother, sixteen years Ernest's junior and presumably on his way to the invasion of France with the army, although of course that operation was hush-hush. Ernest bounced from blame to remorse to heartbreak and anger. I tried to keep my responses measured, with little success. He was seeing Mary Welsh, or he wasn't; what did it matter to me? But pride is a funny thing.

On the fourth morning, I awoke to a shadow looming in my doorway, saying, "It's happening, Mart," in a familiar voice.

Ernest? But, no, his last note had said he was leaving London for a bit.

I said, "Don't be silly, shadow-man, waking up good Christians like this."

"No, really," the shadow said, disappearing already as I scuttered out of bed.

Ernest's last note. He was *Collier's* war correspondent now.

I dressed quickly and hurried to the Ministry of Information, where a hundred of us were ushered into a conference room lined with armed military police, the doors locked behind us.

"This is awfully cloak-and-dagger," I said to the chap beside me—an Australian reporting for one of the Sydney papers, whose editors were so pissed with the censors that they'd run pieces with blank spaces to show how much text was chopped. I tried to imagine how that must have looked, a diversion to keep my mind off of Bug.

At the front of the room a staff officer said, "This is it."

A corporal passed a handout—a communiqué from Eisenhower—as the staff officer outlined the naval and air operations for the invasion of France, which had just begun. I listened like hell while reading the sheet at the same time. I'd like to say my insides hadn't gone all crunchy, but the one thing I do stick to is the truth, even if it's just my own truth I can tell.

"You'll have a half hour to write your copy," the staff officer told us, and he pointed our attention to the typewriters they had on hand for us. "You'll file them here, in this room, and you'll turn them over to the censors here, and when the censors are done with everyone, we'll send them off with military police dispatch riders, who will deliver them to the cable companies. You'll wait here until the military determines the news can be released and the cables are gone."

"You'll be handing the news-breaking to the damned Krauts, that's the dinkum oil!" my Australian-journalist companion objected.

"Yes, we will do," the staff officer agreed.

"But the Germans will control the story," the journalist insisted. "They'll tell it like they've won the battle even if we take Paris by midafternoon."

"The Germans will be kept in the dark as long as possible," the staff officer said. "They won't have a way to know what we're hitting them with or where until they're hit."

Every journalist in the room mumbled frustration in the same accepting tone.

Me, I grabbed a typewriter and pounded out a thousand words a minute. I had sludge for brains, though, and it was all drivel. You can't write the real stuff when you're locked in an airless room a whole channel away from what you're pretending to cover. You can't write the real stuff when you're only making words out of someone else's words.

When I had the best I could do in front of a censor and his blackout marker, I flipped my blond hair and smiled. "So what was your personal brand of heroism before the war?" I asked him. Yes, I'd learned well from Hemingway, who would have laughed if he'd seen me flattering the guy. But if this really was it, Bug was on a ship headed for France. And this was it.

The censor was done butchering my words, and the military police dispatch riders had set off, and I was jotting in my journal for my own sake when one of the officers announced, "In just fifteen seconds the invasion news flash will go out into the world."

9:31 a.m.

He raised his arm, and when he dropped it, the MPs unlocked the doors, and we went out into a brand-new world.

I told my taxi driver the news. He didn't believe me. I talked to some colored soldiers at Westminster Abbey. An old woman selling Red Cross pins. I was getting scared by then, afraid for Bug, who had no right to my heartache, but still he *was* my Bug and I was his Mookie, and it wasn't like he'd taken *my* particular spot on that crossing ship. No women journalists had been allowed to be part of the invasion reporting. Nineteen women accredited to cover this war, at least six of us with more experience than half the men, for pity's sake, and all of us barred from doing our jobs for no reason but our sex.

Bug on his way there, though. Bug who would scoff at me for wallowing in self-pity on account of rules that could be broken. He might already be in France, getting the real juice, the story from the ground. He might already be taking another bit of shrapnel in the leg in this Second World War, to add to what he'd collected in the first. Bug could be brave; I'd seen that. He could be the old Hemingway if he wanted to be.

I headed for the south coast of England, for one of the embarking ports, making my plans as I made my way, to hell with the rules.

I suppose I did look around for Ernest when I arrived at the coast. I suppose some part of me wanted to see him safely back in England, while a bigger part was afraid to see him return so quickly to safety when there was a war to report. If his flirtation with Mary Welsh hadn't already collapsed our life together, his walking away from covering this invasion when I'd been denied the chance surely would.

At the docks, an MP stopped me, wanting to know my business. I'd anticipated this. I pulled my press credential from the damp wool of my uniform and handed it to him.

"I'm to interview the nurses before they set off," I said, nodding toward six nurses boarding a painfully white ship that sported bright new red crosses when every sensible ship on the water was some shade of gray a German bomber might just miss.

"A lady journalist," the MP said.

"Here to cover the women's angle, the nurses and the Red Cross gals."

"All right, then, but don't dawdle. You don't want to end up in France yourself," he said as he handed my credential back.

The ship's deck as I boarded was a chaos of boxes of bandages and plasma bottles, canisters as big as beer kegs filled with blood. Everywhere, the crew scurried about, moving medical supplies to the operating room, blankets to the hundreds of bunks that would cross the Channel empty, but would not return that way.

I found a loo before anyone could determine that I had no business on the ship, and I locked myself in.

In the dark of the bathroom, I thought of the soldiers already on the French coast, already dying, and Ernest there too. I took three deep breaths in the wet-wool stink of the tiny bathroom, thinking with any luck I'd be there soon, and trying to silence the gut crunchiness, longing suddenly to be hiding with my thirteen-year-old best friend in the abandoned coats outside our fortnightly ballroom dancing class back in St. Louis. As I listened in the darkness for the ship to weigh anchor for the French coast and the war, I tried to imagine Bug as a boy like those boys who never did ask me to dance. I tried to imagine Ernest Hemingway as a boy who imagined himself a boy still, another boy I might forgive.

After we'd cleared the harbor and I was sure they wouldn't turn back on account of one stowaway journalist, even a female one, I emerged from the loo. It was rainy and cold, and I was afraid as hell, and I joined everyone else in sweating out the fear with healthy doses of whiskey.

At dawn, we sailed to the Normandy coast, the first hospital ship to arrive. No one gave a damn who I was—not the merchant navy men or the doctors or the nurses, who were all American and just arrived from home—as long as I kept my guts inside me. We were all far too concerned with the planes overhead, and the gunfire, and the shells bursting in the water around us, and getting the job we'd come to do done.

We anchored at Omaha Red, where bulldozers scooped through the sand to detonate mines while guns fired at Germans on the high bluff and the swollen gray-skin sacks of what had once been American soldiers floated by. Landing craft began pulling up to our ship, delivering the wounded. The operating rooms on board kicked to life.

I organized two cabin boys in bright-red jackets to make corned beef sandwiches for anyone able to eat. I carted water. I translated for French soldiers who could still say what was wrong with them, and commanded *"ruhig"*—"quiet"—to the German POW wounded whenever the doctors asked me to.

That night, the crew paid me the kindest thank-you I could have imagined, taking me ashore with an ambulance crew to collect casualties, whom we would take back to the ship at first daylight. We waded through waist-high water and hiked up a narrow path cleared of mines, with red flares lighting our way. The world was rich with the smells of sweet grass and cattle and gunfire and burning rubber, and overrun with the sound of gunfire, *racrong carong carong*.

Our path led to a village where even the church had collapsed like a paper bag. Lines of Germans—scrawny, undersized members of the "master race"—marched off to POW enclosures and to their fates without the bother even of having to answer my questions on account of the Geneva Convention prohibiting me from haranguing them.

We loaded bandaged and bleeding and burned boys onto stretchers and carried them down to the beach. We brought up more empty stretchers and returned again.

Not long after dawn, we boarded the ship again and set off back toward England, trying to keep our cargo alive long enough to get them proper help.

Back in London, in reward for my work and for risking my life, I was taken into custody by military police and confined to a nurses' training camp outside London. If I behaved myself, they might allow me to cross the Channel again when the nurses in the camp were ready to go. If I didn't behave, I'd be shipped back home.

To be honest, that arrangement didn't suit me.

After I'd finished two long pieces for *Collier's*, one on the hospital ship and one on the German soldiers I'd been unable to question, I quietly rolled under the perimeter fence of the nurses' training camp and found my way back to London, where I began searching for a way to get back to the war.

I wrote Matie, wanting her to know I was okay and that I was looking for a way to get to Italy. Not even a sleepy censor who might not see that I had no clearance to go anywhere, though, would let through specific plans for anyone to go to any specific location, lest the Germans learn that the soldiers they were shooting at were actually there. So I wrote Matie that women correspondents here were being treated too much like violets and so I thought I'd be better off returning to my old haunts, where I'd been before I went home to Cuba. I kicked myself for not establishing a secret code with her like I had with Ernest, and hoped she would know that "old haunts" meant Italy. I told her Ernest had gone in with the first invasion wave, and he'd been very brave, and I wasn't seeing much of him as he had masses of his own pals, but I was happy as a goat.

The fact is I was dead tired and sad as hell. I'd been stripped of my military accreditation, my travel papers, and my ration entitlement on account of having stowed away on the ship, and I had no way to get anywhere. But I struck up a friendship with an RAF pilot who was returning to the Italian front, who knew me only as Marty and not even as Gellhorn, much less Hemingway. I made up a story about a fiancé in Naples. I did feel a little guilty about suckering the poor kid, but it got me to Italy.

There, I joined a band of Polish soldiers who'd been the heroes of Cassino and weren't much bothered by an American gal breaking rules.

I spent the next month of the war foraging for ducks and geese with the Poles, liberating bottles of Chianti, swimming when we weren't warring, and trying to make the soldiers famous. In order to do so, I got very good at sweet-talking every wireless operator I could find into helping me get my work back to the United States, never mind that every one of them might as easily be arrested for helping me as I might be just for doing my job.

Collier's was happy to run my pieces, just as they'd run my D-Day bits despite my trip to get them being unsanctioned. My D-Day piece ran with Ernest's, in an issue with his name on the cover as their special correspondent and a photo of him surrounded by laughing soldiers on the crossing boat. His beard in the photo was so long he might easily be mistaken for St. Nicholas, and he held a pair of binoculars in his hand as if to scout the enemy positions himself. His face was carefully turned, but still the beginning of the scar where his stitches had been was visible. I wondered if anyone had honestly managed to be that jolly on their way to war. And then I heard the truth about his piece: despite its self-aggrandizing suggestion that it might just have been Ernest himself who'd led the soldiers on his landing craft to recapture Fox Green beach, the details about the landing boats being shaped like coffins and the shells sounding like a punching glove, Ernest hadn't actually gone ashore at all.

He'd crossed on the *Empire Anvil.* He'd climbed down from it onto one of those coffin-shaped landing craft with his throbbing head and his swollen knees to accompany the soldiers to the left flank of Omaha Beach. The landing on Fox Green went dreadfully, though. The weather was so lousy that the platoons got separated before they reached sand, and the soldiers were easy targets for German machine guns.

Ernest, the moment German machine gunners found his landing craft, dropped flat to its hull. He clung to the boat's bottom as the soldiers climbed out and ran for it. He stayed in the landing craft as it retreated. It took him to another ship that was already headed back to England, the *Dorothea Dix.* He arrived back in port on the south coast the very day he'd left.

From there, he took his war correspondent accreditation that was denied me, and he returned to the Dorchester Hotel in London, where he remained in a comfortable suite for the next five weeks while 156,000 Allied troops battled stiff resistance across fifty miles of French coastline, facing down German machine guns to take the beaches, and then the cliffs, and then the hedgerows of Normandy.

Maybe if I'd gone that first day, maybe if I'd lay flat in the landing craft as the *rong cararong rong rong* of machine-gun fire tried to end my life, I would have returned to London too. But I hadn't gotten the opportunity to find out, and now I never would.

Paris, France

August 1944

I was with the Eighth Army in Italy, which was beginning its offensive on the Adriatic, when I heard the Allies had reached Paris. I hitched a lift on a plane to Lyon, and from there caught a ride with four intelligence officers headed for the city on the Seine, where I'd left so many friends years before. We had a wreck on the way, throwing me from the jeep and breaking one of my ribs, but we pressed on and reached Paris. Ernest was already there, in a room at the Ritz, with Mary Welsh down the hall.

I took a room at the Lincoln, careful to avoid him, and went out walking through a city so largely unchanged that it made me weep. Sure, the Parisians were hungry and cold, there being not much food and even less coal or gas. But the buildings stood unharmed, and the bookstalls on the Seine still offered everything from Sophocles to Gide. The chic Parisian women looked as impeccably coifed as ever, with only their shoes, now wooden soled rather than leather on account of the shortages, much changed. If one thing was missing that had only recently been in abundance, it was anyone who would own up to having ever said hello to a Nazi, much less cooperated with them.

In the small world of the journalists in Paris, though, it was impossible to avoid Ernest and his drinking parties, and anyway, there was no war to cover in Paris. It had moved on, and I needed to as well. I headed off to Brussels with the troops, leaving Hemingway to tell his stories of how I misused him to his drinking pals.

To Bumby, whom I had loved and still did, Ernest wrote that he would trade his equity in me for two nonbeautiful wives who might occasionally go to bed with him. He wrote to my mother that he no longer wanted his life smashed up by heartlessness, carelessness, ambition, and selfishness.

I returned to Paris once more that fall, and he invited me to dinner. I accepted, thinking we might hash out the details of the divorce I kept asking him for in letters that brought no response.

He dragged everyone he knew along to join us and spent the evening disparaging me so vilely that his entourage melted away out of embarrassment.

I suggested, when finally we were alone, that it might be best if we divorced. He had been going around with Mary Welsh for some time by then.

"You bitch," he responded. "You selfish, scummy bitch."

Robert Capa came by my hotel room later that evening, to find me sobbing so fiercely for want of what to do that Dad, may he rest in peace, would have been appalled. Capa had been playing poker and had heard from some of the gang who'd slunk away from our dinner that there had been trouble.

"Hey," he said. "Hey."

He stayed with me and brought me glasses of water and tissues, and took the grubby ones away until I'd spent myself.

He lit me a cigarette then, and said, "Phone the Ritz and ask for Mary Welsh."

"Ask for her? Why would I want to talk to—"

"When Ernest answers," he said, "I'll tell you what to say."

I followed Capa's instructions right down to reciting to Ernest the specific details of his relationship with Mary. When Ernest began to rant so loudly that Capa too could hear him, Capa said, "Go ahead and put the phone down now, Mart. I'm your witness. It will be all right."

Hemingway and I began divorce proceedings not much later, citing as grounds that I had abandoned him. It would mean that he would get all of the things of our life together, including the Finca Vigía that I had put my heart into making our home. But I didn't want it anymore. I didn't want anything at all except my name back, and some way forward past the sadness.

I saw Hemingway only twice after that. Once, in the midst of the Battle of the Bulge, he showed up at the bar of the hotel I was staying in, apparently for the sole purpose of haranguing me in front of everyone about how stupid I was about war and how selfish, even though by then I'd given up everything to him. I left and went to bed early, only to awaken in the middle of the night to a pounding on my door. When I looked through the peephole, Ernest was standing there in nothing but his long johns. He'd inexplicably pulled a bucket over his head and was wielding a mop.

"Hemingway, you're drunk," I said through the closed door. "Go to bed."

The second time, he came to my room at the Dorchester in London when I was down with the flu, to finalize the divorce. By then, I'd seen Dachau, and I'd been left with no doubt that I'd done the right thing to come to the war, even if it had cost me my marriage. I suppose I understood, too, that my marriage could not have been saved even if I'd stayed in Cuba and tried to be the Mrs. Hemingway Ernest thought he wanted me to be.

For a time, I tried to get Ernest to send me a few of my things from the Finca Vigía, but I suppose he meant when I agreed to sign the divorce papers saying I'd abandoned him that he really would like to keep my letters from my mother and my panties and my photographs. I wasn't always as upstanding as I'd like to have been about it. In frustration, and trying to enlist Max Perkins's help in getting Ernest to send me some papers I needed, I wrote that I hoped my ex-husband weighed three hundred pounds, that he was a pig, and surely if there was a God he would punish Hemingway by making him fat.

For a time, friends liked to bring me little bits of gossip about his life: that Mary Welsh was in a state because although our divorce became final just before Christmas of 1945 and her divorce from Noel Monks was final too, Hemingway had not yet married her; that he kept my photograph in the bedroom at the Finca Vigía, explaining to Mary that Bumby and Mouse and Gigi wouldn't understand if he took it down; that he told Mary he wanted a daughter with my blond hair and long legs, and berated her in language that was familiar to me; that he had a new maid he called Martha, although that wasn't her name; that long after Mary Welsh finally became the fourth Mrs. Hemingway, in March of 1946, he would show up drunk at one place or another to rail against the fact that I'd abandoned him, or to crow about how he'd left me, or to tell tawdry stories that reflected well on neither of us. I never wanted to hear about him, and I told everyone so—sometimes rudely, I'm afraid—even though, as careful as I was not to disparage him in public, I did sometimes let loose on him with Matie or with Ginny Cowles, with whom I wrote a play about our time together in Spain.

Although I'd somehow always managed to keep my lovers as friends, I shut Ernest out of the life I constructed. I covered what was left of the war. I settled afterward first in London, then in Washington, DC, where I spent far too much energy spewing my rage against that pig Joseph McCarthy and the lackey senators doing his bidding. I published another novel, an indictment of war titled *The Wine of*

Astonishment, again with Scribner, in 1948. The next year, I adopted a son, and through him I learned the truth I'd long suspected: that I made a horrid mother. I moved to Mexico, and Italy, and Kenya. I returned to England. I had a few major love affairs and a few more minor ones, and a dreadful time with a real romance that I nonetheless don't regret.

Ernest peeked back into my life in a small way in May of 1953. Matie and I were packing up the house at l'Olgiata, moving like the nineteenth-century rich to a house I'd taken on Lake Garda for the summer, when she told me Ernest had sent her a manuscript. *The Old Man and the Sea.*

"He writes me sometimes, still," she said.

I sat on the trunk I'd just jammed closed and pushed back my hair, frizzy from the humid Italian air, or from the white heat of writing all day, or from both. I had a new book coming out from Doubleday that summer, a collection of stories titled *The Honeyed Peace*. The only way I knew to hold the dragons of dread at bay, still, was to write like hell.

Matie said, "Well, I sent it back, of course I did."

"You sent it back!" Feeling all shredded inside at the words, despite everything. "Mother, you can't have."

"I already have a copy of the book itself, and the manuscript was all marked up. I did tell him how much I enjoyed it."

"Matie, he didn't mean for you to read it, for pity's sake. He meant to . . ."

"'Saddle me with the burden' is, I believe, the phrase you're looking for," Matie said.

"Grace you with it. Honor you."

"But then I'd have responsibility for the thing, and who could I leave it to when I pass but you, sweetheart?" Leaving me to wonder if Ernest had thought that through, if he'd wanted to saddle me or honor me or grace me, ultimately, with the manuscript he'd started at the Finca

Vigía when we'd lived there together, the novel that had won him not just the Pulitzer but also "that thing."

I did cry when I heard that news—that Ernest had finally won the Nobel. October of 1954. I was married to Tom Matthews by then. I wasn't in love with him, precisely. I didn't pretend to be, not even to him. But he was such a good man, and I'd known him most of my life, and his wife had died, leaving him with three grown sons and a teen-aged boy, and my own son needed a father and a stable home at that point more than I needed to be husband-free and able to roam. We bought a six-story house in Chester Square, in London, next door to my dear old "Harry Virgin" companion in crime, Ginny Cowles. I was as consumed with chintz patterns and carpeting as I had been at the Finca Vigía, with Ginny to shop with as we had in Spain but no more help from Tom than I'd gotten from Ernest. Still, I was writing, pieces for the *New Republic* and the *Atlantic Monthly*, which I sometimes composed as I stretched out in the hot sun on some terrace, wearing nothing but a straw hat.

Ernest didn't go to Stockholm to collect his Nobel Prize. He was recovering from injuries sustained in two separate plane crashes and a bushfire accident, or so the newspapers said. But he'd been reported dead in one of those crashes too, so you couldn't always believe what you read when it came to Ernest Hemingway. The American ambas-sador accepted the prize on Ernest's behalf, and read aloud a speech Ernest had sent. It made me think of Max Perkins failing to send a stenographer to record the Sinclair Lewis speech Ernest had forever moaned about. Perkins himself had been dead for years by then, of pneumonia in June of 1947.

Ernest's luck still held—that's what he said in response to those rumors of his death. And maybe it did, but it seemed to me that all he'd written in the years since the war was the postwar romance *Across the River and into the Trees*, which the critics roundly cited as the last gasp of a formerly great writer, and the tiny, little *The Old Man and the*

Sea, which, while hailed as Ernest Hemingway's triumphant rebirth and printed in its entirety in a single issue of *Life* magazine, was the story he'd described to me even before we first went to Cuba—the old fisherman who fights a swordfish all alone on his boat for four days and nights only to have a shark eat the thing because he can't get it into the boat. Like with *For Whom the Bell Tolls*, what had started as a story had grown into a book.

I wondered if Ernest still called the Nobel "that thing," or if he would now that he had it. I wondered if winning it might finally bring him the peace I never could. I thought of writing him, sending my congratulations, but I was afraid of what might spill out if I opened that wound. Maybe he was right that I was too small and selfish to be married to such a big talent. Maybe he and my father were both right, that I was too selfish ever to be a proper wife, no matter how good the man.

I thought of writing him again in 1959, after Fidel Castro took over Cuba and Ernest and Mary were left scrambling to get out. I wondered what Reeves would do without my beautiful Finca Vigía to care for, and whether the neighbor boy, who would be grown by then, still tended the pool pump. I'd always hoped to see again my flamboyantes and my ceiba tree, to swim in my pool to the sound of the negritos. I hadn't realized I'd held on to that hope until I saw with the fall of Cuba that I never would dive into that cooling water again.

Ernest and Mary moved to Ketchum, Idaho, a place that for me would always bring memories of that copy of *For Whom the Bell Tolls* dedicated to me, and Matie trying to persuade us to live in sin, and Ernest and I dancing at the Trail Creek Cabin with friends just before the justice of the peace declined to pronounce us writer and writer. I heard from friends that Ernest had grown paranoid with imagining that federal agents were following him, poring over his bank accounts, bugging his home and his car and reading his mail all on account of his ties with the now-communist Cuba. Years later, a 127-page FBI file started in the 1940s would show his fears to be more justified than any of us imagined, but at the time he was committed to the Mayo Clinic in Minnesota for psychiatric care. He attempted suicide several times while there. He received electric shock treatment. When he returned home, he couldn't remember anything well enough to write.

I wished I had sent those letters, of course, when I heard the news that Ernest had shot himself at his home in Ketchum, Idaho. July 2, 1961. I suppose it's what I might do as well if ever I found myself unable to write; I suppose that was the little bit of common ground on which Bug and I had built our love, or whatever it was that we shared all those years. He hadn't used the Smith & Wesson his father had, the same gun Robert Jordan's father in *For Whom the Bell Tolls* had used; that particular gun had been locked up in a safe-deposit box somewhere, well out of reach. Instead, he'd used his own favorite gun, a shotgun like he'd given me for a wedding present back in Ketchum, that Robert Capa had photographed me shooting for that spread in *Life*: "The Hemingways in Sun Valley: The Novelist takes a Wife."

AUTHOR'S NOTE

As might be expected for a story that begins with one clandestine relationship and ends with another—and involving people as famous as Martha Gellhorn and Ernest Hemingway—the many sources I turned to in the writing of this novel often differed on even the simplest of things, including who was where when. I sorted through those discrepancies as best I could, with the intent of being as true to the facts of their relationship as possible. I have long been an admirer of Martha Gellhorn and her work. I became, in the course of writing about Ernest Hemingway and despite his flaws, a great admirer of him as well.

Sources I relied heavily upon in writing this book include *Travels with Myself and Another*, *The View from the Ground*, *The Trouble I've Seen*, *A Stricken Field*, and *The Face of War*, all by Martha Gellhorn, as well as the extraordinary reporting Gellhorn did for *Collier's* (some of which is reprinted in her books). Also essential were *Gellhorn: A Twentieth-Century Life* and *Selected Letters of Martha Gellhorn*, both by Caroline Moorehead, and *Nothing Ever Happens to the Brave: The Story of Martha Gellhorn* by Carl Rollyson. Gellhorn's letters to Eleanor Roosevelt and Pauline Hemingway informed the early chapters in Key West. Specifically, for Gellhorn's time in Spain, I turned to her "Only the Shells Whine," "Men without Medals," and "City at War"; *Looking for Trouble* by Virginia Cowles; *The Starched Blue Sky of Spain* by Josephine Herbst; notes from the period written by Ted Allan and posted online by his son at normanallan.com, and *The Spanish Earth* film. Amanda Vaill's *Hotel Florida*, which became available only late in the process of this novel, was a great resource for helping me sort out this complicated period; I wish it had been available earlier. I read "Come Ahead, Adolf!" and "Obituary of a Democracy" for Gellhorn's time in Czechoslovakia; "Slow Boat to War" and "What Bores Whom?" for her crossing in the dynamite boat; "Blood on the Snow," "Death in the Present Tense," and "Bombs from a Low Sky" for her time in Finland. For their "honeymoon" in China and the Far East, I turned to Gellhorn's *Collier's* pieces "Fight into Peril," "Her Day," and "Fire Guards the Indies," as well as "Mr. Ma's Tiger" in *Travels with Myself and Another* and Peter Moreira's *Hemingway on the China Front: His WWII Spy Mission with Martha Gellhorn*. The latter was also helpful for the scenes of Hemingway and Gellhorn's wedding, as was "The Hemingways in Sun Valley: The Novelist takes a Wife" with photos by Robert Capa from *Life*'s January 6, 1941, issue. "Messing around in Boats," also from *Travels with Myself and Another*, helped me understand her time exploring the Mediterranean during World War II. For her time in Europe during that war, *The Women Who Wrote the War* by Nancy Caldwell Sorel was an additional great source, along with Gellhorn's "Visit Italy," "The Bomber Boys," "Three Poles," "The First Hospital Ship," and "Hangdog Herrenvolk." The story of how Gellhorn first meets Eleanor Roosevelt draws from her introduction to her writing from the 1930s in *The View from the Ground*.

Michael Reynolds's *Hemingway: The 1930s* and *Hemingway: The Final Years*, Jeffrey Meyers's *Hemingway*, and James R. Mellow's *Hemingway: A Life without Consequences* were my starting points for Hemingway, along with *Ernest Hemingway: Selected Letters 1917–1961*, edited by Carlos Baker, *Hemingway in Cuba* by Hilary Hemingway and Carlene Brennen, George Plimpton's "The Art of Fiction" interview of Hemingway in the Spring 1958 issue of *The Paris Review*, "Hemingway in Cuba" in the *Atlantic*, and of course his novels and stories, particularly

For Whom the Bell Tolls. "Hemingway's Spanish Civil War Dispatches" by William Braasch Watson in *Hemingway Review* illuminated the background of his writing from Spain, including the NANA cable, and was another great source for the time Hemingway and Gellhorn spent in Spain. For the scene with Jack Hemingway in New York, I drew from *A Life Worth Living: The Adventures of a Passionate Sportsman*, by Jack Hemingway and Geoffrey Norman. Michael Parkinson's 1974 interview with Orson Welles was very helpful in constructing the scene of Hemingway's fight with him.

I am, as so often when I'm writing, incredibly grateful for the *New York Times* online archives, which I turn to again and again for precise details about historical events. For this novel, I turned to "Hemingway Slaps Eastman in Face" from August 14, 1937, for the scene in Max Perkins's office. The Hemingway dispatches from Spain in the archives were a godsend, including the April 25, 1937, Raven piece titled "War Is Vividly Reflected in Madrid," which Gellhorn suggests in a 1950 letter to David Gurewitsch (included in *Selected Letters*) drove her, finally, to fall in love with Hemingway.

Other sources I relied on include *Eleanor Roosevelt, Vol. 2: The Defining Years (1933–1938)* by Blanche Wiesen Cook; *Ernest Hemingway on Writing*, edited by Larry W. Phillips; *Hemingway's Boat* by Paul Hendrickson; *Hemingway and Fitzgerald* by Matthew Bruccoli; *Hemingway in Cuba* by Hilary Hemingway and Carlene Brennen; *The Hemingway Women* by Bernice Kert; "The 'Survivor': Martha Gellhorn and Ernest Hemingway" from Lesley McDowell's *Between the Sheets*; *An Unfinished Woman* by Lillian Hellman; and *Dorothy Parker: What Fresh Hell Is This?* by Marion Meade. Two pdfs I found online, L. Hartmann's Spanish Civil War thesis and H. L. Salmon's thesis, "Martha Gellhorn and Ernest Hemingway: A literary relationship," were also helpful.

I am blessed to have Marly Rusoff as my literary champion, and thankful she put this manuscript in the kind and capable hands of Danielle Marshall. Thanks also to Dawn Stewart for her help with speaking engagements, and everyone at Lake Union who chipped in here.

So many friends and neighbors held my hand in so many ways in the course of this one, including my Wednesday Sisters neighborhood book group, and Amy and Borge, Eric and Elaine, Debbie and Curtis, Dave and Camilla, John and Sherry, Brenda, Darby, Sheri, Liza, and Ellie, but none more than Jennifer Belt DuChene, whose friendship is one of the very best bits of my life.

I'm thankful for the continued support of the entire extended Waite-Clayton gang (including the Levy wing), especially my parents, Don and Anna Waite, and my sons, Chris and Nick Clayton; I am in this case extra grateful to Chris, whose own reading opened my eyes to the good of Ernest Hemingway.

And last but never least, Mac Clayton is amazing, unceasingly and in every respect.

ABOUT THE AUTHOR

Photo © 2015 Adrienne Defendi

Meg Waite Clayton is the *New York Times* bestselling author of five previous novels, including *The Race for Paris*, which received the David J. Langum, Sr. Prize in American Historical Fiction Honorary Mention; *The Wednesday Sisters*; and *The Language of Light*, which was a finalist for the Bellwether Prize. She's written for the *Los Angeles Times*, the *New York Times*, the *Washington Post*, the *San Francisco Chronicle*, *Forbes*, *Writer's Digest*, *Runner's World*, and public radio. A graduate of the University of Michigan and its law school, she lives in Palo Alto, California. She can be found online at www.megwaiteclayton.com, on Facebook at www.facebook.com/novelistmeg, and @megwclayton on Twitter.